PENGUIN TWENTIETH-CENTURY CLASSICS

THE MUSE'S TRAGEDY

Edith Wharton was born Edith Newbold Jones in New York in 1862. A member of an eminent New York family, she was educated privately in the United States and abroad. In 1885 she married Edward Robbins Wharton, who was twelve years her senior and from whom she was divorced in 1913. She spent long periods in Europe, where she gained her intimacy with numerous Continental languages and settings for her books. From 1910 until her death she made her home in France. During the war she was an unflinching worker; in France she ran a workroom for unemployed skilled women workers in her quarter; she fed French and Belgian refugees in her restaurants below cost price; she took entire charge of 600 Belgian children who had to leave their orphanage at the time of the German advance. In 1915 the French government gave her the cross of the Legion of Honour. She died in 1937.

Edith Wharton was a unique American novelist, distinguished by her literary powers and having at the same time great popular appeal. She started writing in 1897, but it was not until 1905 that she had an outstanding success with *The House of Mirth*. During her life she published more than forty volumes: novels, stories, verse, essays, travel books and memoirs. While the stark New England tragedy *Ethan Frome* (1911) is possibly her best-known work, it is the least typical of her art. This found full expression in her 'society' novels and particularly in Pulitzer Prize winner *The Age of Innocence* (1920), in which she analysed brilliantly the changing scene of fashionable American life and contrasted the manners of the New World with those of Old Europe.

EDITH WHARTON

THE MUSE'S TRAGEDY AND OTHER STORIES

EDITED WITH AN INTRODUCTION BY
CANDACE WAID

PENGUIN BOOKS

PENGUIN BOOKS

Published by the Penguin Group
Penguin Books Ltd, 27 Wrights Lane, London W8 5TZ, England
Penguin Books USA Inc., 375 Hudson Street, New York, New York 10014, USA
Penguin Books Australia Ltd, Ringwood, Victoria, Australia
Penguin Books Canada Ltd, 10 Alcorn Avenue, Toronto, Ontario, Canada M4V 3B2
Penguin Books (NZ) Ltd, 182–190 Wairau Road, Auckland 10, New Zealand

Penguin Books Ltd, Registered Offices: Harmondsworth, Middlesex, England

First published in the USA by Signet Classics, an imprint of New American Library,
a division of Penguin Books USA Inc., 1990
Published simultaneously in Canada
Published in Penguin Books 1992
3 5 7 9 10 8 6 4

Printed in England by Clays Ltd, St Ives plc

Contents

Introduction

Since the early years of the twentieth century, Edith Wharton has been recognized as one of the best American novelists. She won a Pulitzer Prize in 1921 for *The Age of Innocence*, and in 1924 she was the first woman and only the second novelist to receive the gold medal from the National Institute of Arts and Letters. Today she is primarily known for her novels, *The House of Mirth, Ethan Frome, Summer,* and *The Custom of the Country*. However, when *The House of Mirth* became Wharton's first best-seller in 1905, selling thirty thousand copies in the first three weeks it was published in book form, Wharton already had an international reputation as a short-story writer. Indeed, from 1891, when "Mrs. Manstey's View" appeared in *Scribner's*, to 1937, when her final ghost story was published in the year of her death, Edith Wharton was first and last a writer of stories.

Two years after the publication of *The House of Mirth*, in a letter to friend and fellow novelist Robert Grant, Wharton confessed, "I have always obscurely felt that I didn't know how to write a novel. I feel it more clearly after each attempt because it is in such sharp contrast to the sense of authority with which I take hold of a short story." Offering an astute assessment contrasting her relative skills as a writer of novels and a writer of stories, and suggesting her lifelong tendency to think about writing in terms of gender, Wharton describes what she calls her "weakest point": "I conceive my subjects like a man—that is, rather more architectonically & dramatically than most women—& then execute them like a woman; or rather, I sacrifice, to my desire for construction & breadth, the small incidental effects that women have always excelled in, the episodical characterisation, I mean." Wharton continues: "The worst of it is that this fault is congenital, & not the result of an ambition to do big things. As soon as I look at a subject from the novel-angle I see it in its relation to a larger whole, in all its remotest connotations; & I can't help trying to take them in, at the cost of the smaller realism that I arrive at, I think, better in my short stories."

Although the psychological, social, and ideological implications of Wharton's association of women and short stories are complex and require much analysis, it is true that when Wharton began her career as a writer the scene of American fiction was dominated by the female authors the less popular Hawthorne described as "the damned mob of scribbling women." She began writing for the literary magazines when domestic realism was at its height and writers such as Sarah Orne Jewett and Mary Wilkins Freeman (the rivals condemned by Wharton for their "rose-and-lavender pages") made their reputations as writers of stories for *The Atlantic, The Century, Harper's, Scribner's* and other literary magazines.

Despite her recognition of the short story as the province of women, however, Wharton criticized the local colorists of New England for a surface description that she saw as a betrayal of realism; and she saw in the short story the grounds for a deeper as well as a smaller realism. She looked to France and Russia for what seemed to her a more legitimate tradition of short fiction. Describing what the Russians added to the French invention of the *nouvelle*, Wharton explains in *The Writing of Fiction*: "In any really good subject, one has only to probe deep enough to come to tears; the Russians almost always dig to that depth. The result has been to give to the short story, as French and Russian art have combined to shape it, great closeness of texture with profundity of form. Instead of a loose web spread over the surface of life, they have made it, at its best, a shaft driven straight into the heart of experience."

The potential power of the short story is perhaps what attracted Wharton to the genre of the ghost story. (Almost a third of the eighty-six stories she published during her career might be characterized as ghost stories.) In the preface to *Ghosts*, Wharton's selection of her best supernatural tales, she describes a visceral genre in which the medium of communication, like the faculty used in the apprehension of ghosts, lies below the conscious intellect in "the warm darkness of the prenatal fluid." She insists that ghost stories need an active and intimate reader; the tale is meant to evoke, build upon, and feed upon the fears of the reader, who must have the immediacy of someone actually listening to a storyteller. Only through the reader's elaboration and amplification of the narrative through her or his own fears can the latent terror of the text be realized. "When I first began to read, and then to write ghost stories," Wharton explains, "I was conscious of a common medium between me and my readers, of their meeting me halfway among the primeval shadows, and filling in the gaps in my own narrative with sensations and divinations akin to my own."

Wharton's stories are successful, she claims, because they treat themes that frighten her; she emphasizes that the teller must be frightened in the telling of the story in order to bring out what she calls the "thermometrical" response: a "cold shiver" to the spine of the reader. In "Life and I," her unpublished autobiography, Wharton confesses that "till I was 27 or 8, I could not sleep in the room with a book containing a ghost story & that I have frequently had to burn books of this kind because it frightened me to know that they were downstairs in the library."* Obviously, not all of Wharton's stories were meant to have this kind of effect. Wharton's stories are comedies of manners more often than tales of the supernatural. They describe love, marriage, divorce, artists, and New York society, among other topics. In Wharton's hands, however, these subjects are often more frightening than ghosts—the most chilling moment might be the serving of tea, for example—and it could be argued that the short stories provide the most intimate record of Wharton's fears and desires as she negotiated the boundaries between art and life.

Born in 1862 into an elite New York family, Edith Wharton could claim a place among the New York Four Hun-

*Manuscript in Wharton collection; Beineke Library, Yale University.

dred, the society delimited by the number of people that could fit into Mrs. Vanderbilt's new ballroom. Whereas the fathers of Jane Austen, Charlotte and Emily Brontë, George Eliot, and Harriet Beecher Stowe were clergymen, Edith Wharton's father, George Frederic Jones, was a gentleman. Her mother indignantly insisted to New York shopkeepers who asked, "Which Mrs. Jones?" that she was "*the* Mrs. Jones." Wharton broke rank with even the men of her class when she identified herself as a professional—especially as a professional writer. She recalled growing up in a world where the practice of literature was held to be somewhere between manual labor and the occult arts.

The young Edith Jones never met an author, but her childhood revealed literary precosity. At the age of fifteen she secretly wrote a thirty-thousand-word novel entitled *Fast and Loose*, showing it only to a friend. True to its lurid title, the novel (written under the pseudonym of "Mr. Olivieri") was the story of an ill-fated romance. Most remarkable, however, were the reviews she wrote condemning her own work, mock reviews which she attributed to various prominent American and English periodicals. The devastating review she attributed to the *Nation* read: "In short, in such a case it is false charity to reader and writer to mince matters. —The English of it is that every character is a failure, the plot a vacuum, the style a fiasco. Is not—the disgusted reader is forced to ask—is not Mr. Olivieri very, very like a sick—sentimental school-girl who has begun her work with a fierce and bloody resolve to make it as bad as Wilhelm Meister, Consuelo, and 'Goodbye Sweetheart' together and has ended with a blush, and a general erasure of all the naughty words which her modest vocabulary could furnish?"

The young Wharton also tried poetry, and when she was sixteen her mother had a book of these verses privately and anonymously printed in Newport; these pallid poems were brought to the attention of the elderly Longfellow, who in turn selected several for publication in *The Atlantic*. Wharton herself sent a poem to *The World*, accompanied by a lengthy letter claiming that the irregular meter was intentional. Just before her seventeenth birthday, her parents broke with tradition and introduced her into society a year early because they feared that their daughter had become too bookish. Indeed, in the years that followed, years that included her marriage in 1885 to the boyish and sporting Teddy Wharton, she appeared to sacrifice her aspirations to be an author and accept the role of the young society matron.

In her autobiography, *A Backward Glance*, Wharton recalled the 1899 publication of her first collection of stories, *The Greater Inclination*, as an event that "broke the chains that had held me so long in a kind of torpor. For nearly twelve years," she wrote, "I had tried to adjust myself to the life I had lead since my marriage; but now I was overmastered by the longing to meet people who shared my interests." Wharton had submitted three poems for publication in 1889 and she published her first story in *Scribner's* in 1891; but she produced only about a story a year (some of which were rejected) until the spring of 1898, when she produced over a half dozen new stories; these included "The Muse's Tragedy," "Souls Belated," and "The Pelican," three of the finest stories Wharton ever wrote.

In the title she chose for her first book of fiction, *The Greater Inclination*, Wharton may be said to have named the parting of the ways in her own life, her inclination to pursue a life of letters. The significance, the greatness, of this inclination, may be read in the nervous breakdown she experienced in the fall of 1898 before she had finished the collection. From October through January, she stayed without visitors in a hotel in Philadelphia, where she underwent a version of the S. Weir Mitchell rest cure that is scathingly described in Charlotte Perkins Gilman's story, "The Yellow Wallpaper." In Wharton's case, the months of social isolation released her from the taxing devotion to the trivial that dominated her life as a society woman, and she emerged in 1899 determined to be a writer.

Wharton's first collection of stories brought her international notice. Soon after *The Greater Inclination* was published, she had the experience of walking into a London bookstore and being offered her "own first born as the book of the day." It would be the fate of Wharton—until very recently—to be praised as a female Henry James. "Only a woman to the manner born in society," read a review in *Literature*, "a woman, too, whose literary favorites or literary masters may have been Thackery or James, since she partakes of the spirit of the one, and has followed the exquisite craftmanship of the other, could have written 'The Pelican' or 'Souls Belated.' " Another reviewer singled out "The Muse's Tragedy" as being "as good as Henry James' best, with the something more which we men grope after in vain when we try to describe women and which a women does naturally." However, as R.W.B. Lewis has observed, the "citation of Henry James was not yet vexatious to Edith Wharton, particularly since it was being made in her favor."*

Thirty-eight at the century's turn, and the co-author of a book called *The Decoration of Houses* as well as the author of a collection of stories, Edith Wharton would go on to write twenty-three works of longer fiction, almost equally divided between novels and novellas. She published several books of poetry, a treatise on Italian villas and their gardens, travel books (including a book explaining French culture to American soldiers serving in World War I and a book reporting from the war-torn French front), an autobiography, and a book of literary criticism. Throughout her forty-six-year career as a writer of fiction, she continued to write short stories, publishing eighty-six stories, most of which she compiled in eleven different collections from the breakthrough *Greater Inclination* to the appropriately posthumous *Ghosts*.

The stories republished in this volume are drawn from the years prior to World War I—Wharton's most prolific period as a writer of short stories. The war was a personal as well as historical dividing point between the settled past and what seemed to be a fluid and unknowable world of change. The year 1914 marks the midpoint in Wharton's career as a writer of fiction. Wharton would later speak of the Great War as a great abyss, an historical chasm which marked the

*Citations included in R.W.B. Lewis, *Edith Wharton A Biography* (New York: Harper & Row, 1975), pp. 88-89.

dividing point between a familiar and knowable world and the chaos of a "roaring and discontinuous universe." In the years before the war, encouraged in part by the great demand for magazine fiction, she wrote twice as many stories as she did after 1914. This period, which also saw the publication of *The House of Mirth, Ethan Frome, The Reef,* and *The Custom of the Country,* was not merely prolific; in these years she wrote many of her finest stories.

Most of the stories collected here appeared in five of Wharton's best collections, *The Greater Inclination, The Descent of Man, Tales of Men and Ghosts, Xingu,* and *Ghosts. Crucial Instances* and *The Hermit and the Wild Woman*, two of Wharton's weaker collections, provide one story each, "Copy" and "The Last Asset." Also included is the 1893 story, "The Fullness of Life," which was not reprinted or collected during Wharton's lifetime. From her first stories, which were singled out for their perceptiveness about women, to the sharply witty social satire of *The Descent of Man* and *Xingu*, to the ghost stories designed to send shivers down the reader's spine, these stories display Wharton's versatility and insight as a writer of fiction.

While this selection of stories covers a wide range of themes and touches on many of Wharton's interests, it also reveals patterns and preoccupations in her thinking. Her early fiction, like all of her work, is dominated by a concern with what Lewis has called "the marriage question." However, almost equally important is her concern with the experience of the artist. These stories, set at the crossroads of art and life, tell of honesty and betrayal, romantic delusion and integrity. Many of the best stories fall into both of these categories; and indeed, many of the ghost stories also explore the differing pleas of love and art as well as the thresholds of the supernatural.

Stories such as "Souls Belated," "The Last Asset," "Autre Temps. . . ," and "The Other Two" are powerful because they juxtapose scenarios of marriage and divorce. "The Other Two," which is about a husband who learns too much as he observes his wife serving tea to her two former husbands, is acknowledged by critics as Wharton's masterpiece in the comedy of manners. No longer the individual woman he had imagined, his wife is revealed to be " 'as easy as an old shoe,' a shoe that too many feet had worn. Her elasticity was the result of tension in too many different directions. Alice Haskett—Alice Varick—Alice Waythorn—she had been each in turn, and had left hanging to each name a little of her privacy, a little of her personality, a little of the inmost self where the unknown god abides." Like "The Other Two," "Souls Belated," "The Last Asset," and "Autre Temps . . ." are stories about divorce and marriage but they might best be described as tragedies of mores. Set in worlds which provocatively offer illusions of freedom and change, these stories show characters subdued to the demands of convention, framed once again in the warp of an unbending social fabric.

Among Wharton's more unusual narratives in this line is "The Dilettante." Here we meet a man who, proud of having perfected the art of keeping emotional distance, has introduced his fiancée to the older woman he has been seeing for years. Early in his career the dilettante has learned that exchanging vows of love with a woman is "like the long walk back from a picnic, when one has to carry all the crockery one has finished using: it was the last time [he] ever allowed himself to be encumbered with the debris of a feast. He thus incidentally learned that the privilege of loving her is one of the least favors that a charming woman can accord; and in seeking to avoid the pitfalls of sentiment he had developed a science of evasion in which the woman of the moment became a mere implement of the game. He owed a great deal of delicate enjoyment to the cultivation of this art." It turns out that what is most damning about the dilettante's past life is not prior infidelities, but rather the evidence that "nothing has happened."

"The Mission of Jane" is another story about the loss of romantic illusions. A couple who adopt a baby become the parents of a domineering young woman who specializes in "moral calisthenics." Musing over what went wrong, the father recalls being allured "by the vision of severed hands meeting over a cradle, as the whole body of domestic fiction bears witness to their doing; and the fact that no such conjunction took place he could explain only on the ground that it was a borrowed cradle." In the end, husband and wife are brought together after being terrorized by their daughter. "His Father's Son" is another narrative that offers a twist on the story of relations between parents and children. Set at the moment of the son's decision to marry, "His Father's Son" is an ironic version of what Freud calls the "family romance." Here, the son thinks he has evidence that he was not spawned by the father, known as the inventor of a suspender buckle. As critics have noted, this story is particularly interesting as a fictional treatment of the false rumor about Wharton's illegitimacy, a rumor which also sprang from the effort to find a more auspicious parent to explain the inexplicably gifted daughter. However, like "The Mission of Jane," "His Father's Son" focuses on loneliness in marriage; and in the ironic conclusion, the question of mistaken identity turns on the father's adoption of a fictional persona through the writing of letters.

"The Fullness of Life" and "A Journey," two of Wharton's best stories from her early writing, offer woundingly direct critiques of marriage in stories that begin with the death of an important character. In "A Journey," a wife traveling on a train contemplates the decline of a once hopeful marriage that has been transformed by her husband's failing health. Discovering that he is dead and fearing that she will be forced off the train with the body at some unknown station she pretends that he is only sick and sleeping. "The Fullness of Life" begins with the death of the central female character, who escapes from her husband and his muddy boots by dying into an afterlife which might be best described as the kingdom of art.

Wharton appears to have understood the dangerously revelatory dimension of her own writing. She insisted on omitting "The Fullness of Life" from *The Greater Inclination* with a vehemence that suggests her fear of personal exposure. Writing to her publisher to explain her refusal to reprint both "The Fullness of Life" and "The Lamp of Psyche" in her first collection, she referred to "the old stories of which you speak so kindly," as "the excesses of youth. They were all written 'at the top of my voice,' & The Fullness of Life is one long shriek. —I may not write any better but at least I hope that I write in a lower key, & I fear that the voice of those early tales will drown all the others: it is for that reason that I prefer not to publish them."

Several of the stories included here focus on authors who have problems with their reading public. From the pretensions of the literary lunch club, the members of which claim to know the significance of "Xingu," to the distinguished philosopher of science in "The Descent of Man," who writes a spoof which the reading public takes seriously, writers must face the consequences of publication. In "The Legend," an author is rejected by the public even after his works have become a success. In "Expiation," a woman whose first novel, *Fast and Loose*, bears the title of Wharton's own first novel, bribes a bishop to condemn her work in order to increase sales. "The Eyes," which is arguably the best ghost story Wharton ever wrote, tells of a narcissistic man who is haunted after he lies to an aspiring but bad young writer by not telling him that he indulges in "lamentable twaddle."

"Copy" is a dialogue—virtually a short play—which tells the story of a successful woman novelist and her former lover, a famous poet, who meet after twenty years to struggle over the meaning and the ownership of their love letters. The woman novelist claims to have "died years ago." "What you see before you," she says, "is the figment of a reporter's brain—a monster manufactured out of newspaper paragraphs, with ink in its veins. A keen sense of copyright is my nearest approach to an emotion." "Copy" has strong ties to "The Pelican" and "The Muse's Tragedy," both of which pose the problem of the woman artist who is forced to choose between art and life.

In "The Pelican," Wharton creates an extraordinary comic figure who is not a writer but rather a performer of words. The story describes the lecturing career of Mrs. Amyot, who presents herself in the guise of a retiring woman who has been forced to face the public because of the debts left after the death of her alcoholic husband and the necessity of supporting "the baby." Over the course of thirty years, the lectures change while her autobiography remains the same.

Her appeal as a lecturer is founded on the formulaic retelling of an unchanging, sentimental story. From the outset, "Mrs. Amyot's art" is described as "simply an extension of coquetry: she flirted with her audience." Her style is based on this emotional appeal—"a personal accent" which is said to be "the moral equivalent of her dimple."

In contrast to the narrative excrescence of Mrs. Amyot, who appears "to be performing a trick analogous to that of the conjurer who pulls hundreds of yards of white paper out of his mouth," Mrs. Anerton of "The Muse's Tragedy" is mysteriously reticent. Mrs. Anerton has become a character in literary circles because the public has come to think of her as the Silvia of the *Sonnets to Silvia*, the woman who is thought to have inspired the great poet Vincent Rendle, whose letters she has prepared for publication. The outline of the story in its bare details recalls James' *The Aspern Papers*. Danzers, a scholar and poet whose work has been influenced by Vincent Rendle, has learned that Mrs. Anerton still exists. As he comes to know the mysterious correspondent of the late poet, he comes to feel that "in a certain sense Silvia had herself created the *Sonnets to Silvia*" and he learns the secret of the discreet asterisks that punctuate the poet's letters to his muse.

These stories reveal Wharton's anxiety that devoting herself to art like Mrs. Ambrose Dale in "Copy," Mrs. Anerton of "The Muse's Tragedy," or even the pathetic intellectual flirt, Mrs. Amyot in "The Pelican," may lead to a life of isolation and loneliness. The case against success is stated most boldly by Mrs. Dale as she argues: "Don't talk to me about living in the hearts of my readers! We both know what kind of domicile that is. Why, before long I shall become a classic! Bound in sets and kept on top of a bookshelf—brr, doesn't that sound freezing. I foresee the day when I shall be as lonely as an Etruscan museum!"

These depictions of women, however, can be read as autobiographical figures in deeper and more complex ways. Throughout her career Wharton was preoccupied with the place and indeed the possibility of the woman writer. From her first published novella, *The Touchstone*, to novels such as *The House of Mirth* and *The Custom of the Country*, Wharton was preoccupied with the relations between women and writing. What is remarkable about the early stories collected in this volume, however, is that they contain (along with *The Touchstone*) Wharton's most explicit depictions of women artists. Taken together, they help us to understand the more extended meditations on women and art that take place in her longer works of fiction, as well as the dilemmas that Wharton had to face in inventing herself as a writer at the beginning of the twentieth century. In a sense they provide a key for interpreting the characters and concerns in Wharton's later work.

Even the ghost stories can be read in this context. Wharton explores in these stories her frightened awareness of repressed stories about women and vulnerable men who become unquiet ghosts because of their inability to have a voice. Reflecting her fears about silence, inarticulateness, and strangulation, Wharton's ghost stories provide glimpses of an underworld that is present throughout her work and is associated with her consistent concern with the figure of Persephone. However, even Wharton's tales of the supernatural can move back into the realm of social criticism. In stories such as "Afterward," and the final story in this collection, "The Triumph of Night," Wharton suggests that modern social relations are an appropriate territory for terror. In these stories, Wharton introduces a form of what might be called "business gothic," in which the concealed forces of greed lead to unsettling realizations.

William Dean Howells explained the failure of the dramatization of *The House of Mirth* by telling Wharton: "What the American public always wants is a tragedy with a happy ending." In her short stories, Wharton excelled in creating comedies that had tragic endings. They are not as scandalous as they once were. After the publication of *Crucial Instances*, a reader wrote what Wharton called "surely one of the tersest and most vigorous letters ever penned by an amateur critic. 'Dear madam,' my unknown correspondent wrote, 'have you never known a respectable woman? If you have, in the name of decency write about her!' " However, in their social critiques and in their readings of characters—

especially the characters of women—Wharton's stories still can surprise the reader with their subtlety and wit. They tell us about Wharton the novelist, but as literary texts in themselves they demonstrate what Wharton meant when she referred to "the sense of authority with which I take hold of a short story."

—Candace Waid
Yale University

The Fullness of Life

For hours she had lain in a kind of gentle torpor, not unlike that sweet lassitude which masters one in the hush of a midsummer noon, when the heat seems to have silenced the very birds and insects, and, lying sunk in the tasseled meadow grasses, one looks up through a level roofing of maple leaves at the vast, shadowless, and unsuggestive blue. Now and then, at ever-lengthening intervals, a flash of pain darted through her, like the ripple of sheet lightning across such a midsummer sky; but it was too transitory to shake her stupor, that calm, delicious, bottomless stupor into which she felt herself sinking more and more deeply, without a disturbing impulse of resistance, an effort of reattachment to the vanishing edges of consciousness.

The resistance, the effort, had known their hour of violence; but now they were at an end. Through her mind, long harried by grotesque visions, fragmentary images of the life that she was leaving, tormenting lines of verse, obstinate presentments of pictures once beheld, indistinct impressions of rivers, towers, and cupolas, gathered in the length of journeys half forgotten—through her mind there now only moved a few primal sensations of colorless well-being; a vague satisfaction in the thought that she had swallowed her noxious last draught of medicine . . . and that she should never again hear the creaking of her husband's boots—those horrible boots—and that no one would come to bother her about the next day's dinner . . . or the butcher's book. . . .

At last even these dim sensations spent themselves in the

Scribner's magazine, XIV, December, 1893

thickening obscurity which enveloped her; a dusk now filled with pale geometric roses, circling softly, interminably before her, now darkened to a uniform blue-blackness, the hue of a summer night without stars. And into this darkness she felt herself sinking, sinking, with the gentle sense of security of one upheld from beneath. Like a tepid tide it rose around her, gliding ever higher and higher, folding in its velvety embrace her relaxed and tired body, now submerging her breast and shoulders, now creeping gradually, with soft inexorableness, over her throat to her chin, to her ears, to her mouth. . . . Ah, now it was rising too high; the impulse to struggle was renewed . . . her mouth was full . . . she was choking. . . . Help!

"It is all over," said the nurse, drawing down the eyelids with official composure.

The clock struck three. They remembered it afterward. Someone opened the window and let in a blast of that strange, neutral air which walks the earth between darkness and dawn; someone else led the husband into another room. He walked vaguely, like a blind man, on his creaking boots.

✣ II ✣

SHE stood, as it seemed, on a threshold, yet no tangible gateway was in front of her. Only a wide vista of light, mild yet penetrating, as the gathered glimmer of innumerable stars expanded gradually before her eyes, in blissful contrast to the cavernous darkness from which she had of late emerged.

She stepped forward, not frightened but hesitating, and as her eyes began to grow more familiar with the melting depths of light about her, she distinguished the outlines of a landscape, at first swimming in the opaline uncertainty of Shelley's vaporous creations, then gradually resolved into distincter shape—the vast unrolling of a sunlit plain, aerial forms of mountains, and presently the silver crescent of a river in the valley, and a blue stenciling of trees along its curve—something suggestive in its ineffable hue of an azure background of Leonardo's, strange, enchanting, mysterious, leading on the eye and the imagination into regions of fabulous delight. As she gazed, her heart beat with a soft and rapturous surprise; so exquisite a promise she read in the summons of that hyaline distance.

"And so death is not the end after all," in sheer gladness she heard herself exclaiming aloud. "I always knew that it couldn't be. I believed in Darwin, of course. I do still; but then Darwin himself said that he wasn't sure about the soul—at least, I think he did—and Wallace was a spiritualist; and then there was St. George Mivart—"

Her gaze lost itself in the ethereal remoteness of the mountains.

"How beautiful! How satisfying!" she murmured. "Perhaps now I shall really know what it is to live."

As she spoke she felt a sudden thickening of her heartbeats, and looking up she was aware that before her stood the Spirit of Life.

"Have you never really known what it is to live?" the Spirit of Life asked her.

"I have never known," she replied, "that fullness of life which we all feel ourselves capable of knowing; though my life has not been without scattered hints of it, like the scent of earth which comes to one sometimes far out at sea."

"And what do you call the fullness of life?" the Spirit asked again.

"Oh, I can't tell you, if you don't know," she said, almost reproachfully. "Many words are supposed to define it—love and sympathy are those in commonest use, but I am not even sure that they are the right ones, and so few people really know what they mean."

"You were married," said the Spirit, "yet you did not find the fullness of life in your marriage?"

"Oh, dear, no," she replied, with an indulgent scorn, "my marriage was a very incomplete affair."

"And yet you were fond of your husband?"

"You have hit upon the exact word; I was fond of him, yes, just as I was fond of my grandmother, and the house that I was born in, and my old nurse. Oh, I was fond of him, and we were counted a very happy couple. But I have sometimes thought that a woman's nature is like a great house full of rooms: there is the hall, through which everyone passes in going in and out; the drawing room, where one receives formal visits; the sitting room, where the members of the family come and go as they list; but beyond that, far beyond, are other rooms, the handles of whose doors perhaps are never turned; no one knows the way to them, no one knows whither they lead; and in the innermost room, the holy of holies, the soul sits alone and waits for a footstep that never comes."

"And your husband," asked the Spirit, after a pause, "never got beyond the family sitting room?"

"Never," she returned, impatiently; "and the worst of it was that he was quite content to remain there. He thought it perfectly beautiful, and sometimes, when he was admiring its commonplace furniture, insignificant as the chairs and tables of a hotel parlor, I felt like crying out to him: 'Fool, will you never guess that close at hand are rooms full of treasures and wonders, such as the eye of man hath not seen, rooms that no step has crossed, but that might be yours to live in, could you but find the handle of the door?' "

"Then," the Spirit continued, "those moments of which you lately spoke, which seemed to come to you like scattered hints of the fullness of life, were not shared with your husband?"

"Oh, no—never. He was different. His boots creaked, and he always slammed the door when he went out, and he never read anything but railway novels and the sporting advertisements in the papers—and—and, in short, we never understood each other in the least."

"To what influence, then, did you owe those exquisite sensations?"

"I can hardly tell. Sometimes to the perfume of a flower; sometimes to a verse of Dante or of Shakespeare; sometimes to a picture or a sunset, or to one of those calm days at sea, when one seems to be lying in the hollow of a blue pearl; sometimes, but rarely, to a word spoken by someone who chanced to give utterance, at the right moment, to what I felt but could not express."

"Someone whom you loved?" asked the Spirit.

"I never loved anyone, in that way," she said, rather sadly, "nor was I thinking of any one person when I spoke, but of two or three who, by touching for an instant upon a certain chord of my being, had called forth a single note of that strange melody which seemed sleeping in my soul. It has seldom happened, however, that I have owed such feelings to people; and no one ever gave me a moment of such happiness as it was my lot to feel one evening in the Church of Or San Michele, in Florence."

"Tell me about it," said the Spirit.

"It was near sunset on a rainy spring afternoon in Easter week. The clouds had vanished, dispersed by a sudden wind, and as we entered the church the fiery panes of the high windows shone out like lamps through the dusk. A priest was at the high altar, his white cope a livid spot in the incense-laden obscurity, the light of the candles flickering up and down like fireflies about his head; a few people knelt near by. We stole behind them and sat down on a bench close to the tabernacle of Orcagna.

"Strange to say, though Florence was not new to me, I had never been in the church before; and in that magical light I saw for the first time the inlaid steps, the fluted columns, the sculptured bas-reliefs and canopy of the marvelous shrine. The marble, worn and mellowed by the subtle hand of time, took on an unspeakable rosy hue, suggestive in some remote way of the honey-colored columns of the Parthenon, but more mystic, more complex, a color not born of the sun's inveterate kiss, but made up of cryptal twilight, and the flame of candles upon martyrs' tombs, and gleams of sunset through symbolic panes of chrysoprase and ruby; such a light as illumines the missals in the library of Siena, or burns like a hidden fire through the Madonna of Gian Bellini in the Church of the Redeemer, at Venice; the light of the Middle Ages, richer, more solemn, more significant than the limpid sunshine of Greece.

"The church was silent, but for the wail of the priest and the occasional scraping of a chair against the floor, and as I sat there, bathed in that light, absorbed in rapt contemplation of the marble miracle which rose before me, cunningly wrought as a casket of ivory and enriched with jewel-like incrustations and tarnished gleams of gold, I felt myself borne onward along a mighty current, whose source seemed to be in the very beginning of things, and whose tremendous waters gathered as they went all the mingled streams of human passion and endeavor. Life in all its varied manifestations of beauty and strangeness seemed weaving a rhythmical dance around me as I moved, and wherever the spirit of man had passed I knew that my foot had once been familiar.

"As I gazed, the medieval bosses of the tabernacle of Orcagna seemed to melt and flow into their primal forms, so that the folded lotus of the Nile and the Greek acanthus were braided with the runic knots and fish-tailed monsters of the North, and all the plastic terror and beauty born of man's hand from the Ganges to the Baltic quivered and mingled in Orcagna's apotheosis of Mary. And so the river bore me on, past the alien faces of antique civilizations and the familiar wonders of Greece, till I swam upon the fiercely rushing tide of the Middle Ages, with its swirling eddies of passion, its heaven-reflecting pools of poetry and art; I heard the rhythmic blow of the craftsmen's hammers in the goldsmiths' workshops and on the walls of churches, the party cries of armed factions in the narrow streets, the organ roll of Dante's verse, the crackle of the fagots around Arnold of Brescia, the twitter of the swallows to which St. Francis preached, the laughter of the ladies listening on the hillside to the quips of the Decameron, while plague-struck Florence howled beneath them—all this and much more I heard, joined in strange unison with voices earlier and more remote, fierce, passionate, or tender, yet subdued to such awful harmony that I thought of the song that the morning stars sang together and felt as though it were sounding in my ears. My heart beat to suffocation; the tears burned my lids; the joy, the mystery of it seemed too intolerable to be borne. I could not understand even then the words of the song; but I knew that if there had been someone at my side who could have heard it with me, we might have found the key to it together.

"I turned to my husband, who was sitting beside me in an attitude of patient dejection, gazing into the bottom of his hat; but at that moment he rose, and stretching his stiffened legs, said, mildly: 'Hadn't we better be going? There doesn't seem to be much to see here, and you know the table d'hôte dinner is at half-past six o'clock.' "

Her recital ended, there was an interval of silence; then the Spirit of Life said: "There is a compensation in store for such needs as you have expressed."

"Oh, then you *do* understand?" she exclaimed. "Tell me what compensation, I entreat you!"

"It is ordained," the Spirit answered, "that every soul which seeks in vain on earth for a kindred soul to whom it can lay bare its inmost being shall find that soul here and be united to it for eternity."

A glad cry broke from her lips. "Ah, shall I find him at last?" she cried, exultant.

"He is here," said the Spirit of Life.

She looked up and saw that a man stood near whose soul (for in that unwonted light she seemed to see his soul more clearly than his face) drew her toward him with an invincible force.

"Are you really he?" she murmured.

"I am he," he answered.

She laid her hand in his and drew him toward the parapet which overhung the valley.

"Shall we go down together," she asked him, "into that marvelous country; shall we see it together, as if with the self-same eyes, and tell each other in the same words all that we think and feel?"

"So," he replied, "have I hoped and dreamed."

"What?" she asked, with rising joy. "Then you, too, have looked for me?"

"All my life."

"How wonderful! And did you never, never find anyone in the other world who understood you?"

"Not wholly—not as you and I understand each other."

"Then you feel it, too? Oh, I am happy," she sighed.

They stood, hand in hand, looking down over the parapet upon the shimmering landscape which stretched forth beneath them into sapphirine space, and the Spirit of Life, who kept watch near the threshold, heard now and then a floating fragment of their talk blown backward like the stray swallows which the wind sometimes separates from their migratory tribe.

"Did you never feel at sunset—"

"Ah, yes; but I never heard anyone else say so. Did you?"

"Do you remember that line in the third canto of the *Inferno*?"

"Ah, that line—my favorite always. Is it possible—"

"You know the stooping 'Victory' in the frieze of the 'Nike Apteros'?"

"You mean the one who is tying her sandal? Then you have noticed, too, that all Botticelli and Mantegna are dormant in those flying folds of her drapery?"

"After a storm in autumn have you never seen—"

"Yes, it is curious how certain flowers suggest certain painters—the perfume of the carnation, Leonardo; that of the rose, Titian; the tube-rose, Crivelli—"

"I never supposed that anyone else had noticed it."

"Have you never thought—"

"Oh, yes, often and often; but I never dreamed that anyone else had."

"But surely you must have felt—"

"Oh, yes, yes; and you, too—"

"How beautiful! How strange—"

Their voices rose and fell, like the murmur of two fountains answering each other across a garden full of flowers. At length, with a certain tender impatience, he turned to her and said: "Love, why should we linger here? All eternity lies before us. Let us go down into that beautiful country together and make a home for ourselves on some blue hill above the shining river."

As he spoke, the hand she had forgotten in his was suddenly withdrawn, and he felt that a cloud was passing over the radiance of her soul.

"A home," she repeated, slowly, "a home for you and me to live in for all eternity?"

"Why not, love? Am I not the soul that yours has sought?"

"Y-yes—yes, I know—but, don't you see, home would not be like home to me, unless—"

"Unless?" he wonderingly repeated.

She did not answer, but she thought to herself, with an impulse of whimsical inconsistency. "Unless you slammed the door and wore creaking boots."

But he had recovered his hold upon her hand, and by imperceptible degrees was leading her toward the shining steps which descended to the valley.

"Come, O my soul's soul," he passionately implored, "why delay a moment? Surely you feel, as I do, that eternity itself is too short to hold such bliss as ours. It seems to me that I can see our home already. Have I not always seen it in my dreams? It is white, love, is it not, with polished columns, and a sculptured cornice against the blue? Groves of laurel and oleander and thickets of roses surround it; but from the terrace where we walk at sunset, the eye looks out over woodlands and cool meadows where, deep-bowered under ancient boughs, a stream goes delicately toward the river. Indoors our favorite pictures hang upon the walls and the rooms are lined with books. Think, dear, at last we shall have time to read them all. With which shall we begin? Come, help me to choose. Shall it be *Faust* or the *Vita Nuova, The Tempest* or *Les Caprices de Marianne*, or the thirty-first canto of the *Paradise*, or *Epipsychidion* or *Lycidas*? Tell me, dear, which one?"

As he spoke he saw the answer trembling joyously upon her lips; but it died in the ensuing silence, and she stood motionless, resisting the persuasion of his hand.

"What is it?" he entreated.

"Wait a moment," she said, with a strange hesitation in her voice. "Tell me first, are you quite sure of yourself? Is there no one on earth whom you sometimes remember?"

"Not since I have seen you," he replied; for, being a man, he had indeed forgotten.

Still she stood motionless, and he saw that the shadow deepened on her soul.

"Surely, love," he rebuked her, "it was not that which troubled you? For my part I have walked through Lethe. The past has melted like a cloud before the moon. I never lived until I saw you."

She made no answer to his pleadings, but at length, rousing herself with a visible effort, she turned away from him and moved toward the Spirit of Life, who still stood near the threshold.

"I want to ask you a question," she said, in a troubled voice.

"Ask," said the Spirit.

"A little while ago," she began, slowly, "you told me that every soul which has not found a kindred soul on earth is destined to find one here."

"And have you not found one?" asked the Spirit.

"Yes; but will it be so with my husband's soul also?"

"No," answered the Spirit of Life, "for your husband imagined that he had found his soul's mate on earth in you; and for such delusions eternity itself contains no cure."

She gave a little cry. Was it of disappointment or triumph?

"Then—then what will happen to him when he comes here?"

"That I cannot tell you. Some field of activity and happiness he will doubtless find, in due measure to his capacity for being active and happy."

She interrupted, almost angrily: "He will never be happy without me."

"Do not be too sure of that," said the Spirit.

She took no notice of this, and the Spirit continued: "He will not understand you here any better than he did on earth."

"No matter," she said; "I shall be the only sufferer, for he always thought that he understood me."

"His boots will creak just as much as ever—"

"No matter."

"And he will slam the door—"

"Very likely."

"And continue to read railway novels—"

She interposed, impatiently: "Many men do worse than that."

"But you said just now," said the Spirit, "that you did not love him."

"True," she answered, simply; "but don't you understand that I shouldn't feel at home without him? It is all very well for a week or two—but for eternity! After all, I never minded the creaking of his boots, except when my head ached, and I don't suppose it will ache *here*; and he was always so sorry when he had slammed the door, only he never *could* remember not to. Besides, no one else would know how to look after him, he is so helpless. His inkstand would never be filled, and he would always be out of stamps and visiting cards. He would never remember to have his umbrella re-covered, or to ask the price of anything before he bought it. Why, he wouldn't even know what novels to read. I always had to choose the kind he liked, with a murder or a forgery and a successful detective."

She turned abruptly to her kindred soul, who stood listening with a mien of wonder and dismay.

"Don't you see," she said, "that I can't possibly go with you?"

"But what do you intend to do?" asked the Spirit of Life.

"What do I intend to do?" she returned, indignantly. "Why, I mean to wait for my husband, of course. If he had come here first *he* would have waited for me for years and years; and it would break his heart not to find me here when he comes." She pointed with a contemptuous gesture to the magic vision of hill and vale sloping away to the translucent mountains. "He wouldn't give a fig for all that," she said, "if he didn't find me here."

"But consider," warned the Spirit, "that you are now choosing for eternity. It is a solemn moment."

"Choosing!" she said, with a half-sad smile. "Do you still keep up here that old fiction about choosing? I should have thought that *you* knew better than that. How can I help myself? He will expect to find me here when he comes, and he would never believe you if you told him that I had gone away with someone else—never, never."

"So be it," said the Spirit. "Here, as on earth, each one must decide for himself."

She turned to her kindred soul and looked at him gently, almost wistfully. "I am sorry," she said. "I should have liked to talk with you again; but you will understand, I know, and I dare say you will find someone else a great deal cleverer—"

And without pausing to hear his answer she waved him a swift farewell and turned back toward the threshold.

"Will my husband come soon?" she asked the Spirit of Life.

"That you are not destined to know," the Spirit replied.

"No matter," she said, cheerfully; "I have all eternity to wait in."

And still seated alone on the threshold, she listens for the creaking of his boots.

The Muse's Tragedy

DANYERS AFTERWARDS liked to fancy that he had recognized Mrs. Anerton at once; but that, of course, was absurd, since he had seen no portrait of her—she affected a strict anonymity, refusing even her photograph to the most privileged—and from Mrs. Memorall, whom he revered and cultivated as her friend, he had extracted but the one impressionist phrase: "Oh, well, she's like one of those old prints where the lines have the value of color."

He was almost certain, at all events, that he had been thinking of Mrs. Anerton as he sat over his breakfast in the empty hotel restaurant, and that, looking up on the approach of the lady who seated herself at the table near the window, he had said to himself, *"That might be she."*

Ever since his Harvard days—he was still young enough to think of them as immensely remote—Danyers had dreamed of Mrs. Anerton, the Silvia of Vincent Rendle's immortal sonnet cycle, the Mrs. A. of the *Life and Letters*. Her name was enshrined in some of the noblest English verse of the nineteenth century—and of all past or future centuries, as Danyers, from the standpoint of a maturer judgment, still believed. The first reading of certain poems—of the *Antinous*, the *Pia Tolomei*, the *Sonnets to Silvia*—had been epochs in Danyers' growth, and the verse seemed to gain in mellowness, in amplitude, in meaning as one brought to its interpretation more experience of life, a finer emotional sense. Where, in his boyhood, he had felt only the perfect, the almost austere beauty of form, the subtle interplay of vowel sounds, the rush and fullness of lyric emotion, he now thrilled to the close-packed significance of each line, the allusiveness of each word—his imagination lured hither and thither on fresh trails of thought, and perpetually spurred by the sense that, beyond what he had already discovered, more marvelous regions lay waiting to be explored. Danyers had written, at college, the prize essay on Rendle's poetry (it chanced to be the moment of the great man's death); he had fashioned the fugitive verse of his own Storm and Stress period on the forms which Rendle had first given to English meter, and when two years later the *Life and Letters* appeared, and the Silvia of the sonnets took substance as Mrs. A., he had included in his worship of Rendle the woman who had inspired not only such divine verse but such playful, tender, incomparable prose.

Danyers never forgot the day when Mrs. Memorall happened to mention that she knew Mrs. Anerton. He had known Mrs. Memorall for a year or more, and had somewhat contemptuously classified her as the kind of woman who runs cheap excursions to celebrities; when one afternoon she remarked, as she put a second lump of sugar in his tea:

"Is it right this time? You're almost as particular as Mary Anerton."

"Mary Anerton?"

"Yes, I never *can* remember how she likes her tea. Either it's lemon *with* sugar, or lemon without sugar, or cream without either, and whichever it is must be put into the cup before the tea is poured in; and if one hasn't remembered, one must begin all over again. I suppose it was Vincent Rendle's way of taking his tea and has become a sacred rite."

"Do you *know* Mrs. Anerton?" cried Danyers, disturbed by this careless familiarity with the habits of his divinity.

" 'And did I once see Shelley plain?' Mercy, yes! She and I were at school together—she's an American, you know. We were at a *pension* near Tours for nearly a year; then she went back to New York, and I didn't see her again till after her marriage. She and Anerton spent a winter in Rome while my husband was attached to our Legation there, and she used to be with us a great deal." Mrs. Memorall smiled reminiscently. "It was *the* winter."

"The winter they first met?"

"Precisely—but unluckily I left Rome just before the meeting took place. Wasn't it too bad? I might have been in the *Life and Letters*. You know he mentions that stupid Madame Vodki, at whose house he first saw her."

"And did you see much of her after that?"

"Not during Rendle's life. You know she has lived in Europe almost entirely, and though I used to see her off and on when I went abroad, she was always so engrossed, so preoccupied, that one felt one wasn't wanted. The fact is, she cared only about his friends—she separated herself gradually from all her own people. Now, of course, it's different; she's desperately lonely; she's taken to writing to me now and then; and last year, when she heard I was going abroad, she asked me to meet her in Venice, and I spent a week with her there."

"And Rendle?"

Mrs. Memorall smiled and shook her head. "Oh, I never was allowed a peep at *him*; none of her old friends met him, except by accident. Ill-natured people say that was the reason she kept him so long. If one happened in while he was there, he was hustled into Anerton's study, and the husband mounted guard till the inopportune visitor had departed. Anerton, you know, was really much more ridiculous about it than his wife. Mary was too clever to lose her head, or at least to show she'd lost it—but Anerton couldn't conceal his pride in the conquest. I've seen Mary shiver when he spoke of Rendle as *our poet*. Rendle always had to have a certain seat at the dinner table, away from the draft and not too near the fire, and a box of cigars that no one else was allowed to touch, and a writing table of his own in Mary's sitting room—and Anerton was always telling one of the great man's idiosyncrasies: how he never would cut the ends of his cigars, though Anerton himself had given him a gold cutter set with a star sapphire, and how untidy his writing table was, and how the housemaid had orders always to bring the wastepaper basket to her mistress before emptying it, lest some immortal verse should be thrown into the dustbin."

"The Anertons never separated, did they?"

"Separated? Bless you, no. He never would have left Rendle! And besides, he was very fond of his wife."

"And she?"

"Oh, she saw he was the kind of man who was fated to make himself ridiculous, and she never interfered with his natural tendencies."

From Mrs. Memorall, Danyers further learned that Mrs. Anerton, whose husband had died some years before her poet, now divided her life between Rome, where she had a small apartment, and England, where she occasionally went to stay with those of her friends who had been Rendle's. She had been engaged, for some time after his death, in editing some juvenilia which he had bequeathed to her care; but that task being accomplished, she had been left without definite occupation, and Mrs. Memorall, on the occasion of their last meeting, had found her listless and out of spirits.

"She misses him too much—her life is too empty. I told her so—I told her she ought to marry."

"Oh!"

"Why not, pray? She's a young woman still—what many people would call young," Mrs. Memorall interjected, with a parenthetic glance at the mirror. "Why not accept the inevitable and begin over again? All the King's horses and all the King's men won't bring Rendle to life—and besides, she didn't marry *him* when she had the chance."

Danyers winced slightly at this rude fingering of his idol. Was it possible that Mrs. Memorall did not see what an anticlimax such a marriage would have been? Fancy Rendle "making an honest woman" of Silvia; for so society would have viewed it! How such a reparation would have vulgarized their past—it would have been like "restoring" a masterpiece; and how exquisite must have been the perceptions of the woman who, in defiance of appearances, and perhaps of her own secret inclination, chose to go down to posterity as Silvia rather than as Mrs. Vincent Rendle!

Mrs. Memorall, from this day forth, acquired an interest in Danyers' eyes. She was like a volume of unindexed and discursive memoirs, through which he patiently plodded in the hope of finding embedded amid layers of dusty twaddle some precious allusion to the subject of his thought. When, some months later, he brought out his first slim volume, in which the remodeled college essay on Rendle figured among a dozen somewhat overstudied "appreciations," he offered a copy to Mrs. Memorall; who surprised him, the next time they met, with the announcement that she had sent the book to Mrs. Anerton.

Mrs. Anerton in due time wrote to thank her friend. Danyers was privileged to read the few lines in which, in terms that suggested the habit of "acknowledging" similar tributes, she spoke of the author's "feeling and insight," and was "so glad of the opportunity," etc. He went away disappointed, without clearly knowing what else he had expected.

The following spring, when he went abroad, Mrs. Memorall offered him letters to everybody, from the Archbishop of Canterbury to Louise Michel. She did not include Mrs. Anerton, however, and Danyers knew, from a previous conversation, that Silvia objected to people who "brought letters." He knew also that she traveled during the summer, and was unlikely to return to Rome before the term of his holiday should be reached, and the hope of meeting her was not included among his anticipations.

The lady whose entrance broke upon his solitary repast in the restaurant of the Hotel Villa d'Este had seated herself in such a way that her profile was detached against the window, and thus viewed, her domed forehead, small arched nose, and fastidious lip suggested a silhouette of Marie Antoinette. In the lady's dress and movements—in the very turn of her wrist as she poured out her coffee—Danyers thought he detected the same fastidiousness, the same air of tacitly excluding the obvious and unexceptional. Here was a woman who had been much bored and keenly interested. The waiter brought her a *Secolo*, and as she bent above it Danyers noticed that the hair rolled back from her forehead was turning gray; but her figure was straight and slender, and she had the invaluable gift of a girlish back.

The rush of Anglo-Saxon travel had not set toward the lakes, and with the exception of an Italian family or two, and a hump-backed youth with an *abbé*, Danyers and the lady had the marble halls of the Villa d'Este to themselves.

When he returned from his morning ramble among the hills he saw her sitting at one of the little tables at the edge of the lake. She was writing, and a heap of books and newspapers lay on the table at her side. That evening they met again in the garden. He had strolled out to smoke a last cigarette before dinner, and under the black vaulting of ilexes, near the steps leading down to the boat landing, he found her leaning on the parapet above the lake. At the sound of his approach she turned and looked at him. She had thrown a black lace scarf over her head, and in this somber setting her face seemed thin and unhappy. He remembered afterwards that her eyes, as they met his, expressed not so much sorrow as profound discontent.

To his surprise she stepped toward him with a detaining gesture.

"Mr. Lewis Danyers, I believe?"

He bowed.

"I am Mrs. Anerton. I saw your name on the visitors' list and wished to thank you for an essay on Mr. Rendle's poetry—or rather to tell you how much I appreciated it. The book was sent to me last winter by Mrs. Memorall."

She spoke in even melancholy tones, as though the habit of perfunctory utterance had robbed her voice of more spontaneous accents; but her smile was charming.

They sat down on a stone bench under the ilexes, and she told him how much pleasure his essay had given her. She thought it the best in the book—she was sure he had put more of himself into it than into any other; was she not right in conjecturing that he had been very deeply influenced by Mr. Rendle's poetry? *Pour comprendre il faut aimer*, and it seemed to her that, in some ways, he had penetrated the poet's inner meaning more completely than any other critic. There were certain problems, of course, that he had left untouched; certain aspects of that many-sided mind that he had perhaps failed to seize—

"But then you are young," she concluded gently, "and one could not wish you, as yet, the experience that a fuller understanding would imply."

❄ II ❄

SHE stayed a month at Villa d'Este, and Danyers was with her daily. She showed an unaffected pleasure in his society;

a pleasure so obviously founded on their common veneration of Rendle, that the young man could enjoy it without fear of fatuity. At first he was merely one more grain of frankincense on the altar of her insatiable divinity; but gradually a more personal note crept into their intercourse. If she still liked him only because he appreciated Rendle, she at least perceptibly distinguished him from the herd of Rendle's appreciators.

Her attitude toward the great man's memory struck Danyers as perfect. She neither proclaimed nor disavowed her identity. She was frankly Silvia to those who knew and cared; but there was no trace of the Egeria in her pose. She spoke often of Rendle's books, but seldom of himself; there was no posthumous conjugality, no use of the possessive tense, in her abounding reminiscences. Of the master's intellectual life, of his habits of thought and work, she never wearied of talking. She knew the history of each poem; by what scene or episode each image had been evoked; how many times the words in a certain line had been transposed; how long a certain adjective had been sought, and what had at last suggested it; she could even explain that one impenetrable line, the torment of critics, the joy of detractors, the last line of *The Old Odysseus*.

Danyers felt that in talking of these things she was no mere echo of Rendle's thought. If her identity had appeared to be merged in his it was because they thought alike, not because he had thought for her. Posterity is apt to regard the women whom poets have sung as chance pegs on which they hung their garlands; but Mrs. Anerton's mind was like some fertile garden wherein, inevitably, Rendle's imagination had rooted itself and flowered. Danyers began to see how many threads of his complex mental tissue the poet had owed to the blending of her temperament with his; in a certain sense Silvia had herself created the *Sonnets to Silvia*.

To be the custodian of Rendle's inner self, the door, as it were, to the sanctuary, had at first seemed to Danyers so comprehensive a privilege that he had the sense, as his friendship with Mrs. Anerton advanced, of forcing his way into a life already crowded. What room was there, among such towering memories, for so small an actuality as his?

Quite suddenly, after this, he discovered that Mrs. Memorall knew better: his fortunate friend was bored as well as lonely.

"You have had more than any other woman!" he had exclaimed to her one day: and her smile flashed a derisive light on his blunder. Fool that he was, not to have seen that she had not had enough! That she was young still—do years count?—tender, human, a woman; that the living have need of the living.

After that, when they climbed the alleys of the hanging park, resting in one of the little ruined temples, or watching, through a ripple of foliage, the remote blue flash of the lake, they did not always talk of Rendle or of literature. She encouraged Danyers to speak of himself; to confide his ambitions to her; she asked him the questions which are the wise woman's substitute for advice.

"You must write," she said, administering the most exquisite flattery that human lips could give.

Of course he meant to write—why not do something great in his turn? His best, at least; with the resolve, at the outset, that his best should be *the* best. Nothing less seemed possible with that mandate in his ears. How she had divined him; lifted and disentangled his groping ambitions; laid the awakening touch on his spirit with her creative *Let there be light!*

It was his last day with her, and he was feeling very hopeless and happy.

"You ought to write a book about *him*," she went on gently.

Danyers started; he was beginning to dislike Rendle's way of walking in unannounced.

"You ought to do it," she insisted. "A complete interpretation—a summing up of his style, his purpose, his theory of life and art. No one else could do it as well."

He sat looking at her perplexedly. Suddenly—dared he guess?

"I couldn't do it without you," he faltered.

"I could help you—I would help you, of course."

They sat silent, both looking at the lake.

It was agreed, when they parted, that he should rejoin her six weeks later in Venice. There they were to talk about the book.

❄ III ❄

Lago d'Iseo, August 14th.

WHEN I said good-bye to you yesterday I promised to come back to Venice in a week: I was to give you your answer then. I was not honest in saying that; I didn't mean to go back to Venice or to see you again. I was running away from you—and I mean to keep on running! If *you* won't, *I* must. Somebody must save you from marrying a disappointed woman of—well, you say years don't count, and why should they, after all, since you are not to marry me?

That is what I dare not go back to say. *You are not to marry me.* We have had our month together in Venice (such a good month, was it not?) and now you are to go home and write a book—any book but the one we—didn't talk of!—and I am to stay here, attitudinizing among my memories like a sort of female Tithonus. The dreariness of this enforced immortality!

But you shall know the truth. I care for you, or at least for your love, enough to owe you that.

You thought it was because Vincent Rendle had loved me that there was so little hope for you. I had had what I wanted to the full; wasn't that what you said? It is just when a man begins to think he understands a woman that he may be sure he doesn't! It is because Vincent Rendle *didn't love me* that there is no hope for you. I never had what I wanted, and never, never, never will I stoop to wanting anything else.

Do you begin to understand? It was all a sham then, you say? No, it was all real as far as it went. You are young—you haven't learned, as you will later, the thousand imperceptible signs by which one gropes one's way through the labyrinth of human nature; but didn't it strike you, sometimes, that I never told you any foolish little anecdotes about him? His trick, for instance, of twirling a paper knife round and round between his thumb and forefinger while he talked; his mania for saving the backs of notes; his greediness for wild strawberries, the little pungent Alpine ones; his childish delight in acrobats and jugglers; his way of always calling me *you—dear you*, every letter began—I never told you a word of all that, did I? Do you suppose I could have helped telling you, if he had loved me? These little things would have been mine, then, a part of my life—of our life—they would have slipped out in spite of me (it's only your unhappy woman who is always reticent and dignified). But there never was any "our life"; it was always "our lives" to the end. . . .

If you knew what a relief it is to tell someone at last, you would bear with me, you would let me hurt you! I shall never be quite so lonely again, now that someone knows.

Let me begin at the beginning. When I first met Vincent Rendle I was not twenty-five. That was twenty years ago. From that time until his death, five years ago, we were fast friends. He gave me fifteen years, perhaps the best fifteen years, of his life. The world, as you know, thinks that his greatest poems were written during those years; I am supposed to have "inspired" them, and in a sense I did. From the first, the intellectual sympathy between us was almost complete; my mind must have been to him (I fancy) like some perfectly tuned instrument on which he was never tired of playing. Someone told me of his once saying of me that I "always understood"; it is the only praise I ever heard of his giving me. I don't even know if he thought me pretty, though I hardly think my appearance could have been disagreeable to him, for he hated to be with ugly people. At all events he fell into the way of spending more and more of his time with me. He liked our house; our ways suited him. He was nervous, irritable; people bored him and yet he disliked solitude. He took sanctuary with us. When we traveled he went with us; in the winter he took rooms near us in Rome. In England or on the continent he was always with us for a good part of the year. In small ways I was able to help him in his work; he grew dependent on me. When we were apart he wrote to me continually—he liked to have me share in all he was doing or thinking; he was impatient for my criticism of every new book that interested him; I was a part of his intellectual life. The pity of it was that I wanted to be something more. I was a young woman and I was in love with him—not because he was Vincent Rendle, but just because he was himself!

People began to talk, of course—I was Vincent Rendle's Mrs. Anerton; when the *Sonnets to Silvia* appeared, it was whispered that I was Silvia. Wherever he went, I was invited; people made up to me in the hope of getting to know him; when I was in London my doorbell never stopped ringing. Elderly peeresses, aspiring hostesses, lovesick girls and struggling authors overwhelmed me with their assiduities. I hugged my success, for I knew what it meant—they thought that Rendle was in love with me! Do you know, at times, they almost made me think so too? Oh, there was no phase of folly I didn't go through. You can't imagine the excuses a woman will invent for a man's not telling her that he loves her—pitiable arguments that she would see through at a glance if any other woman used them! But all the while, deep down, I knew he had never cared. I should have known it if he had made love to me every day of his life. I could never guess whether he knew what people said about us—he listened so little to what people said; and cared still less, when he heard. He was always quite honest and straightforward with me; he treated me as one man treats another; and yet at times I felt he *must* see that with me it was different. If he did see, he made no sign. Perhaps he never noticed—I am sure he never meant to be cruel. He had never made love to me; it was no fault of his if I wanted more than he could give me. The *Sonnets to Silvia*, you say? But what are they? A cosmic philosophy, not a love poem; addressed to Woman, not to a woman!

But then, the letters? Ah, the letters! Well, I'll make a clean breast of it. You have noticed the breaks in the letters here and there, just as they seem to be on the point of growing a little—warmer? The critics, you may remember, praised the editor for his commendable delicacy and good taste (so rare in these days!) in omitting from the correspondence all personal allusions, all those *détails intimes* which should be kept sacred from the public gaze. They referred, of course, to the asterisks in the letters to Mrs. A. Those letters I myself prepared for publication; that is to say, I copied them out for the editor, and every now and then I put in a line of asterisks to make it appear that something had been left out. You understand? The asterisks were a sham—*there was nothing to leave out.*

No one but a woman could understand what I went through during those years—the moments of revolt, when I felt I must break away from it all, fling the truth in his face and never see him again; the inevitable reaction, when not to see him seemed the one unendurable thing, and I trembled lest a look or word of mine should disturb the poise of our friendship; the silly days when I hugged the delusion that he *must* love me, since everybody thought he did; the long periods of numbness, when I didn't seem to care whether he loved me or not. Between these wretched days came others when our intellectual accord was so perfect that I forgot everything else in the joy of feeling myself lifted up on the wings of his thought. Sometimes, then, the heavens seemed to be opened.

All this time he was so dear a friend! He had the genius of friendship, and he spent it all on me. Yes, you were right when you said that I have had more than any other woman. *Il faut de l'adresse pour aimer*, Pascal says; and I was so quiet, so cheerful, so frankly affectionate with him, that in all those years I am almost sure I never bored him. Could I have hoped as much if he had loved me?

You mustn't think of him, though, as having been tied to my skirts. He came and went as he pleased, and so did his fancies. There was a girl once (I am telling you everything), a lovely being who called his poetry "deep" and gave him *Lucile* on his birthday. He followed her to Switzerland one summer, and all the time that he was dangling after her (a little too conspicuously, I always thought, for a Great Man), he was writing to *me* about his theory of vowel combinations —or was it his experiments in English hexameter? The letters were dated from the very places where I knew they went and sat by waterfalls together and he thought out adjectives for her hair. He talked to me about it quite frankly afterwards. She was perfectly beautiful and it had been a pure delight to watch her; but she *would* talk, and her mind, he said, was "all elbows." And yet, the next year, when her marriage was announced, he went away alone, quite suddenly . . . and it was just afterwards that he published *Love's Viaticum*. Men are queer!

After my husband died—I am putting things crudely, you see—I had a return of hope. It was because he loved me, I argued, that he had never spoken; because he had always hoped some day to make me his wife; because he wanted to spare me the "reproach." Rubbish! I knew well enough, in my heart of hearts, that my one chance lay in the force of habit. He had grown used to me; he was no longer young; he dreaded new people and new ways; *il avait pris son pli.* Would it not be easier to marry me?

I don't believe he ever thought of it. He wrote me what people call "a beautiful letter"; he was kind, considerate, decently commiserating; then, after a few weeks, he slipped into his old way of coming in every afternoon, and our interminable talks began again just where they had left off. I heard later that people thought I had shown "such good taste" in not marrying him.

So we jogged on for five years longer. Perhaps they were the best years, for I had given up hoping. Then he died.

After his death—this is curious—there came to me a kind of mirage of love. All the books and articles written about him, all the reviews of the *Life*, were full of discreet allusions to Silvia. I became again the Mrs. Anerton of the glorious days. Sentimental girls and dear lads like you turned pink when somebody whispered, "That was Silvia you were talking to." Idiots begged for my autograph—publishers urged me to write my reminiscences of him—critics consulted me about the reading of doubtful lines. And I knew that, to all these people, I was the woman Vincent Rendle had loved.

After a while that fire went out too and I was left alone with my past. Alone—quite alone; for he had never really been with me. The intellectual union counted for nothing now. It had been soul to soul, but never hand in hand, and there were no little things to remember him by.

Then there set in a kind of Arctic winter. I crawled into myself as into a snow hut. I hated my solitude and yet dreaded anyone who disturbed it. That phase, of course, passed like the others. I took up life again, and began to read the papers and consider the cut of my gowns. But here was one question that I could not be rid of, that haunted me night and day. Why had he never loved me? Why had I been so much to him, and no more? Was I so ugly, so essentially unlovable, that though a man might cherish me as his mind's comrade, he could not care for me as a woman? I can't tell you how that question tortured me. It became an obsession.

My poor friend, do you begin to see? I had to find out what some other man thought of me. Don't be too hard on me! Listen first—consider. When I first met Vincent Rendle I was a young woman, who had married early and led the quietest kind of life; I had had no "experiences." From the hour of our first meeting to the day of his death I never looked at any other man, and never noticed whether any other man looked at me. When he died, five years ago, I knew the extent of my powers no more than a baby. Was it too late to find out? Should I never know *why*?

Forgive me—forgive me. You are so young; it will be an episode, a mere "document," to you so soon! And, besides, it wasn't as deliberate, as cold-blooded as these disjointed lines have made it appear. I didn't plan it, like a woman in a book. Life is so much more complex than any rendering of it can be. I liked you from the first—I was drawn to you (you must have seen that)—I wanted you to like me; it was not a mere psychological experiment. And yet in a sense it was that, too—I must be honest. I had to have an answer to that question; it was a ghost that had to be laid.

At first I was afraid—oh, so much afraid—that you cared for me only because I was Silvia, that you loved me because you thought Rendle had loved me. I began to think there was no escaping my destiny.

How happy I was when I discovered that you were growing jealous of my past; that you actually hated Rendle! My heart beat like a girl's when you told me you meant to follow me to Venice.

After our parting at Villa d'Este my old doubts reasserted themselves. What did I know of your feeling for me, after all? Were you capable of analyzing it yourself? Was it not likely to be two-thirds vanity and curiosity, and one-third literary sentimentality? You might easily fancy that you cared for Mary Anerton when you were really in love with

Silvia—the heart is such a hypocrite! Or you might be more calculating than I had supposed. Perhaps it was you who had been flattering *my* vanity in the hope (the pardonable hope!) of turning me, after a decent interval, into a pretty little essay with a margin.

When you arrived in Venice and we met again—do you remember the music on the lagoon, that evening, from my balcony?—I was so afraid you would begin to talk about the book—the book, you remember, was your ostensible reason for coming. You never spoke of it, and I soon saw your one fear was *I* might do so—might remind you of your object in being with me. Then I knew you cared for me! yes, at that moment really cared! We never mentioned the book once, did we, during that month in Venice?

I have read my letter over; and now I wish that I had said this to you instead of writing it. I could have felt my way then, watching your face and seeing if you understood. But, no, I could not go back to Venice; and I could not tell you (though I tried) while we were there together. I couldn't spoil that month—my one month. It was so good, for once in my life, to get away from literature.

You will be angry with me at first—but, alas! not for long. What I have done would have been cruel if I had been a younger woman; as it is, the experiment will hurt no one but myself. And it will hurt me horribly (as much as, in your first anger, you may perhaps wish), because it has shown me, for the first time, all that I have missed.

A Journey

As she lay in her berth, staring at the shadows overhead, the rush of the wheels was in her brain, driving her deeper and deeper into circles of wakeful lucidity. The sleeping car had sunk into its night silence. Through the wet window-pane she watched the sudden lights, the long stretches of hurrying blackness. Now and then she turned her head and looked through the opening in the hangings at her husband's curtain across the aisle. . . .

She wondered restlessly if he wanted anything and if she could hear him if he called. His voice had grown very weak within the last month and it irritated him when she did not hear. This irritability, this increasing childish petulance seemed to give expression to their imperceptible estrangement. Like two faces looking at one another through a sheet of glass they were close together, almost touching, but they could not hear or feel each other: the conductivity between them was broken. She, at least, had this sense of separation, and she fancied sometimes that she saw it reflected in the look with which he supplemented his failing word. Doubtless the fault was hers. She was too impenetrably healthy to be touched by the irrelevancies of disease. Her self-reproachful tenderness was tinged with the sense of his irrationality: she had a vague feeling that there was a purpose in his helpless tyrannies. The suddenness of the change had found her so unprepared. A year ago their pulses had beat to one robust measure; both had the same prodigal confidence in an exhaustless future. Now their energies no longer kept step: her still bounded ahead of life, pre-empting unclaimed regions of hope and activity, while his lagged behind, vainly struggling to overtake her.

When they married, she had such arrears of living to make up: her days had been as bare as the whitewashed schoolroom where she forced innutritious facts upon reluctant children. His coming had broken in on the slumber of circumstance, widening the present till it became the encloser of remotest chances. But imperceptibly the horizon narrowed. Life had a grudge against her: she was never to be allowed to spread her wings.

At first the doctors had said that six weeks of mild air would set him right; but when he came back this assurance was explained as having of course included a winter in a dry climate. They gave up their pretty house, storing the wedding presents and new furniture, and went to Colorado. She had hated it there from the first. Nobody knew her or cared about her; there was no one to wonder at the good match she had made, or to envy her the new dresses and the visiting cards which were still a surprise to her. And he kept growing worse. She felt herself beset with difficulties too evasive to be fought by so direct a temperament. She still loved him, of course; but he was gradually, undefinably ceasing to be himself. The man she had married had been strong, active, gently masterful: the male whose pleasure it is to clear a way through the material obstructions of life; but now it was she who was the protector, he who must be shielded from importunities and given his drops or his beef juice though the skies were falling. The routine of the sickroom bewildered her; this punctual administering of medicine seemed as idle as some uncomprehended religious mummery.

There were moments, indeed, when warm gushes of pity swept away her instinctive resentment of his condition, when she still found his old self in his eyes as they groped for each other through the dense medium of his weakness. But these moments had grown rare. Sometimes he frightened her: his sunken expressionless face seemed that of a stranger; his voice was weak and hoarse; his thin-lipped smile a mere muscular contraction. Her hand avoided his damp soft skin, which had lost the familiar roughness of health: she caught herself furtively watching him as she might have watched a strange animal. It frightened her to feel that this was the man she loved; there were hours when to tell him what she suffered seemed the one escape from her fears. But in general she judged herself more leniently, reflecting that she had perhaps been too long alone with him, and that she would feel differently when they were at home again, surrounded by her robust and buoyant family. How she had rejoiced when the doctors at last gave their consent to his going home! She knew, of course, what the decision meant; they both knew. It meant that he was to die; but they dressed the truth in hopeful euphemisms, and at times, in the joy of preparation, she really forgot the purpose of their journey, and slipped into an eager allusion to next year's plans.

At last the day of leaving came. She had a dreadful fear that they would never get away; that somehow at the last moment he would fail her; that the doctors held one of their accustomed treacheries in reserve; but nothing happened. They drove to the station, he was installed in a seat with a rug over his knees and a cushion at his back, and she hung out of the window waving unregretful farewells to the acquaintances she had really never liked till then.

The first twenty-four hours had passed off well. He revived a little and it amused him to look out of the window and to observe the humors of the car. The second day he began to grow weary and to chafe under the dispassionate stare of the freckled child with the lump of chewing gum. She had to explain to the child's mother that her husband was too ill to be disturbed: a statement received by that lady with a resentment visibly supported by the maternal sentiment of the whole car. . . .

That night he slept badly and the next morning his temperature frightened her: she was sure he was growing worse. The day passed slowly, punctuated by the small irritations of travel. Watching his tired face, she traced in its contractions every rattle and jolt of the train, till her own body vibrated with sympathetic fatigue. She felt the others observing him too, and hovered restlessly between him and the line of interrogative eyes. The freckled child hung about him like a fly; offers of candy and picture books failed to dislodge her: she twisted one leg around the other and watched him imperturbably. The porter, as he passed, lingered with vague proffers of help, probably inspired by philanthropic passengers swelling with the sense that "something ought to be done"; and one nervous man in a skull cap was audibly concerned as to the possible effect on his wife's health.

The hours dragged on in a dreary inoccupation. Towards dusk she sat down beside him and he laid his hand on hers. The touch startled her. He seemed to be calling her from far off. She looked at him helplessly and his smile went through her like a physical pang.

"Are you very tired?" she asked.

"No, not very."

"We'll be there soon now."

"Yes, very soon."

"This time tomorrow—"

He nodded and they sat silent. When she had put him to bed and crawled into her own berth she tried to cheer herself with the thought that in less than twenty-four hours they would be in New York. Her people would all be at the station to meet her—she pictured their round unanxious faces pressing through the crowd. She only hoped they would not tell him too loudly that he was looking splendidly and would be all right in no time: the subtler sympathies developed by long contact with suffering were making her aware of a certain coarseness of texture in the family sensibilities.

Suddenly she thought she heard him call. She parted the curtains and listened. No, it was only a man snoring at the other end of the car. His snores had a greasy sound, as though they passed through tallow. She lay down and tried to sleep. . . . Had she not heard him move? She started up trembling. . . . The silence frightened her more than any sound. He might not be able to make her hear—he might be calling her now. . . . What made her think of such things? It was merely the familiar tendency of an overtired mind to fasten itself on the most intolerable chance within the range of its forebodings. . . . Putting her head out, she listened: but she could not distinguish his breathing from that of the other pairs of lungs about her. She longed to get up and look at him, but she knew the impulse was a mere vent for her restlessness, and the fear of disturbing him restrained her. . . . The regular movement of his curtain reassured her, she knew not why; she remembered that he had wished her a cheerful good night; and the sheer inability to endure her fears a moment longer made her put them from her with an effort of her whole sound-tired body. She turned on her side and slept.

She sat up stiffly, staring out at the dawn. The train was rushing through a region of bare hillocks huddled against a lifeless sky. It looked like the first day of creation. The air of the car was close, and she pushed up her window to let in the keen wind. Then she looked at her watch: it was seven o'clock, and soon the people about her would be stirring. She slipped into her clothes, smoothed her disheveled hair and crept to the dressing room. When she had washed her face and adjusted her dress she felt more hopeful. It was always a struggle for her not to be cheerful in the morning. Her cheeks burned deliciously under the coarse towel and the wet hair about her temples broke into strong upward tendrils. Every inch of her was full of life and elasticity. And in ten hours they would be at home!

She stepped to her husband's berth: it was time for him to take his early glass of milk. The window shade was down, and in the dusk of the curtained enclosure she could just see that he lay sideways, with his face away from her. She leaned over him and drew up the shade. As she did so she touched one of his hands. It felt cold. . . .

She bent closer, laying her hand on his arm and calling him by name. He did not move. She spoke again more loudly; she grasped his shoulder and gently shook it. He lay motionless. She caught hold of his hand again: it slipped from her limply, like a dead thing. A dead thing?

Her breath caught. She must see his face. She leaned forward, and hurriedly, shrinkingly, with a sickening reluctance of the flesh, laid her hands on his shoulders and turned him over. His head fell back; his face looked small and smooth; he gazed at her with steady eyes.

She remained motionless for a long time, holding him

thus; and they looked at each other. Suddenly she shrank back: the longing to scream, to call out, to fly from him, had almost overpowered her. But a strong hand arrested her. Good God! If it were known that he was dead they would be put off the train at the next station—

In a terrifying flash of remembrance there arose before her a scene she had once witnessed in traveling, when a husband and wife, whose child had died in the train, had been thrust out at some chance station. She saw them standing on the platform with the child's body between them; she had never forgotten the dazed look with which they followed the receding train. And this was what would happen to her. Within the next hour she might find herself on the platform of some strange station, alone with her husband's body. . . . Anything but that! It was too horrible—She quivered like a creature at bay.

As she cowered there, she felt the train moving more slowly. It was coming then—they were approaching a station! She saw again the husband and wife standing on the lonely platform; and with a violent gesture she drew down the shade to hide her husband's face.

Feeling dizzy, she sank down on the edge of the berth, keeping away from his outstretched body, and pulling the curtains close, so that he and she were shut into a kind of sepulchral twilight. She tried to think. At all costs she must conceal the fact that he was dead. But how? Her mind refused to act: she could not plan, combine. She could think of no way but to sit there, clutching the curtains, all day long. . . .

She heard the porter making up her bed; people were beginning to move about the car; the dressing-room door was being opened and shut. She tried to rouse herself. At length with a supreme effort she rose to her feet, stepping into the aisle of the car and drawing the curtains tight behind her. She noticed that they still parted slightly with the motion of the car, and finding a pin in her dress she fastened them together. Now she was safe. She looked round and saw the porter. She fancied he was watching her.

"Ain't he awake yet?" he inquired.

"No," she faltered.

"I got his milk all ready when he wants it. You know you told me to have it for him by seven."

She nodded silently and crept into her seat.

At half-past eight the train reached Buffalo. By this time the other passengers were dressed and the berths had been folded back for the day. The porter, moving to and fro under his burden of sheets and pillows, glanced at her as he passed. At length he said: "Ain't he going to get up? You know we're ordered to make up the berths as early as we can."

She turned cold with fear. They were just entering the station.

"Oh, not yet," she stammered. "Not till he's had his milk. Won't you get it, please?"

"All right. Soon as we start again."

When the train moved on he reappeared with the milk. She took it from him and sat vaguely looking at it: her brain moved slowly from one idea to another, as though they were steppingstones set far apart across a whirling flood. At length she became aware that the porter still hovered expectantly.

"Will I give it to him?" he suggested.

"Oh, no," she cried, rising. "He—he's asleep yet, I think—"

She waited till the porter had passed on; then she unpinned the curtains and slipped behind them. In the semiobscurity her husband's face stared up at her like a marble mask with agate eyes. The eyes were dreadful. She put out her hand and drew down the lids. Then she remembered the glass of milk in her other hand: what was she to do with it? She thought of raising the window and throwing it out; but to do so she would have to lean across his body and bring her face close to his. She decided to drink the milk.

She returned to her seat with the empty glass and after a while the porter came back to get it.

"When'll I fold up his bed?" he asked.

"Oh, not now—not yet; he's ill—he's very ill. Can't you let him stay as he is? The doctor wants him to lie down as much as possible."

He scratched his head. "Well, if he's *really* sick—"

He took the empty glass and walked away, explaining to the passengers that the party behind the curtains was too sick to get up just yet.

She found herself the center of sympathetic eyes. A motherly woman with an intimate smile sat down beside her.

"I'm real sorry to hear your husband's sick. I've had a remarkable amount of sickness in my family and maybe I could assist you. Can I take a look at him?"

"Oh, no—no, please! He mustn't be disturbed."

The lady accepted the rebuff indulgently.

"Well, it's just as you say, of course, but you don't look to me as if you'd had much experience in sickness and I'd have been glad to assist you. What do you generally do when your husband's taken this way?"

"I—I let him sleep."

"Too much sleep ain't any too healthful either. Don't you give him any medicine?"

"Y—yes."

"Don't you wake him to take it?"

"Yes."

"When does he take the next dose?"

"Not for—two hours—"

The lady looked disappointed. "Well, if I was you I'd try giving it oftener. That's what I do with my folks."

After that many faces seemed to press upon her. The passengers were on their way to the dining car, and she was conscious that as they passed down the aisle they glanced curiously at the closed curtains. One lantern-jawed man with prominent eyes stood still and tried to shoot his projecting glance through the division between the folds. The freckled child, returning from breakfast, waylaid the passers with a buttery clutch, saying in a loud whisper, "He's sick"; and once the conductor came by, asking for tickets. She shrank into her corner and looked out of the window at the flying trees and houses, meaningless hieroglyphs of an endlessly unrolled papyrus.

Now and then the train stopped, and the newcomers on entering the car stared in turn at the closed curtains. More and more people seemed to pass—their faces began to blend fantastically with the images surging in her brain. . . .

Later in the day a fat man detached himself from the mist of faces. He had a creased stomach and soft pale lips. As he pressed himself into the seat facing her she noticed that he was dressed in black broadcloth, with a soiled white tie.

"Husband's pretty bad this morning, is he?"

"Yes."

"Dear, dear! Now that's terribly distressing, ain't it?" An apostolic smile revealed his gold-filled teeth. "Of course you know there's no sech thing as sickness. Ain't that a lovely thought? Death itself is but a deloosion of our grosser senses. On'y lay yourself open to the influx of the sperrit, submit yourself passively to the action of the divine force, and disease and dissolution will cease to exist for you. If you could indooce your husband to read this little pamphlet—"

The faces about her again grew indistinct. She had a vague recollection of hearing the motherly lady and the parent of the freckled child ardently disputing the relative advantages of trying several medicines at once, or of taking each in turn; the motherly lady maintaining that the competitive system saved time; the other objecting that you couldn't tell which remedy had effected the cure; their voices went on and on, like bell buoys droning through a fog. . . . The porter came up now and then with questions that she did not understand, but somehow she must have answered since he went away again without repeating them; every two hours the motherly lady reminded her that her husband ought to have his drops; people left the car and others replaced them. . . .

Her head was spinning and she tried to steady herself by clutching at her thoughts as they swept by, but they slipped away from her like bushes on the side of a sheer precipice down which she seemed to be falling. Suddenly her mind grew clear again and she found herself vividly picturing what would happen when the train reached New York. She shuddered as it occurred to her that he would be quite cold and that someone might perceive he had been dead since morning.

She thought hurriedly: "If they see I am not surprised they will suspect something. They will ask questions, and if I tell them the truth they won't believe me—no one would believe me! It will be terrible"—and she kept repeating to herself—"I must pretend I don't know. I must pretend I don't know. When they open the curtains I must go up to him quite naturally—and then I must scream!" She had an idea that the scream would be very hard to do.

Gradually new thoughts crowded upon her, vivid and urgent: she tried to separate and restrain them, but they beset her clamorously, like her school children at the end of a hot day, when she was too tired to silence them. Her head grew confused, and she felt a sick fear of forgetting her part, of betraying herself by some unguarded word or look.

"I must pretend I don't know," she went on murmuring. The words had lost their significance, but she repeated them mechanically, as though they had been a magic formula, until suddenly she heard herself saying: "I can't remember, I can't remember!"

Her voice sounded very loud, and she looked about her in terror; but no one seemed to notice that she had spoken.

As she glanced down the car her eye caught the curtains of her husband's berth, and she began to examine the monotonous arabesques woven through their heavy folds. The pattern was intricate and difficult to trace; she gazed fixedly at the curtains and as she did so the thick stuff grew transparent and through it she saw her husband's face—his dead face. She struggled to avert her look, but her eyes refused to move and her head seemed to be held in a vise. At last, with an effort that left her weak and shaking, she turned away; but it was of no use; close in front of her, small and smooth, was her husband's face. It seemed to be suspended in the air between her and the false braids of the woman who sat in front of her. With an uncontrollable gesture she stretched out her hand to push the face away, and suddenly she felt the touch of his smooth skin. She repressed a cry and half started from her seat. The woman with the false braids looked around, and feeling that she must justify her movement in some way she rose and lifted her traveling bag from the opposite seat. She unlocked the bag and looked into it; but the first object her hand met was a small flask of her husband's, thrust there at the last moment, in the haste of departure. She locked the bag and closed her eyes . . .

his face was there again, hanging between her eyeballs and lids like a waxen mask against a red curtain. . . .

She roused herself with a shiver. Had she fainted or slept? Hours seemed to have elapsed; but it was still broad day, and the people about her were sitting in the same attitudes as before.

A sudden sense of hunger made her aware that she had eaten nothing since morning. The thought of food filled her with disgust, but she dreaded a return of faintness, and remembering that she had some biscuits in her bag she took one out and ate it. The dry crumbs choked her, and she hastily swallowed a little brandy from her husband's flask. The burning sensation in her throat acted as a counterirritant, momentarily relieving the dull ache of her nerves. Then she felt a gently-stealing warmth, as though a soft air fanned her, and the swarming fears relaxed their clutch, receding through the stillness that enclosed her, a stillness soothing as the spacious quietude of a summer day. She slept.

Through her sleep she felt the impetuous rush of the train. It seemed to be life itself that was sweeping her on with headlong inexorable force—sweeping her into darkness and terror, and the awe of unknown days.—Now all at once everything was still—not a sound, not a pulsation. . . . She was dead in her turn, and lay beside him with smooth upstaring face. How quiet it was!—and yet she heard feet coming, the feet of the men who were to carry them away. . . . She could feel too—she felt a sudden prolonged vibration, a series of hard shocks, and then another plunge into darkness: the darkness of death this time—a black whirlwind on which they were both spinning like leaves, in wild uncoiling spirals, with millions and millions of the dead. . . .

She sprang up in terror. Her sleep must have lasted a long time, for the winter day had paled and the lights had been lit. The car was in confusion, and as she regained her self-possession she saw that the passengers were gathering up their wraps and bags. The woman with the false braids had brought from the dressing room a sickly ivy plant in a bottle, and the Christian Scientist was reversing his cuffs. The porter passed down the aisle with his impartial brush. An impersonal figure with a gold-banded cap asked for her husband's ticket. A voice shouted "Baiggage express!" and she heard the clicking of metal as the passengers handed over their checks.

Presently her window was blocked by an expanse of sooty wall, and the train passed into the Harlem tunnel. The journey was over; in a few minutes she would see her family pushing their joyous way through the throng at the station. Her heart dilated. The worst terror was past. . . .

"We'd better get him up now, hadn't we?" asked the porter, touching her arm.

He had her husband's hat in his hand and was meditatively revolving it under his brush.

She looked at the hat and tried to speak; but suddenly the car grew dark. She flung up her arms, struggling to catch at something, and fell face downward, striking her head against the dead man's berth.

The Pelican

SHE WAS very pretty when I first knew her, with the sweet straight nose and short upper lip of the cameo-brooch divinity, humanized by a dimple that flowered in her cheek whenever anything was said possessing the outward attributes of humor without its intrinsic quality. For the dear lady was providentially deficient in humor: the least hint of the real thing clouded her lovely eye like the hovering shadow of an algebraic problem.

I don't think nature had meant her to be "intellectual"; but what can a poor thing do, whose husband has died of drink when her baby is hardly six months old, and who finds her coral necklace and her grandfather's edition of the British Dramatists inadequate to the demands of the creditors?

Her mother, the celebrated Irene Astarte Pratt, had written a poem in blank verse on "The Fall of Man"; one of her aunts was dean of a girls' college; another had translated Euripides—with such a family, the poor child's fate was sealed in advance. The only way of paying her husband's debts and keeping the baby clothed was to be intellectual; and, after some hesitation as to the form her mental activity was to take, it was unanimously decided that she was to give lectures.

They began by being drawing-room lectures. The first time I saw her she was standing by the piano, against the flippant background of Dresden china and photographs, telling a roomful of women preoccupied with their spring

A late medieval fable describes the pelican (actually a symbol of Christ) as feeding her young with her own blood.

bonnets all she thought she knew about Greek art. The ladies assembled to hear her had given me to understand that she was "doing it for the baby," and this fact, together with the shortness of her upper lip and the bewildering co-operation of her dimple, disposed me to listen leniently to her dissertation. Happily, at that time Greek art was still, if I may use the phrase, easily handled: it was as simple as walking down a museum gallery lined with pleasant familiar Venuses and Apollos. All the later complications—the archaic and archaistic conundrums; the influences of Assyria and Asia Minor; the conflicting attributions and the wrangles of the erudite—still slumbered in the bosom of the future "scientific critic." Greek art in those days began with Phidias and ended with the Apollo Belvedere; and a child could travel from one to the other without danger of losing his way.

Mrs. Amyot had two fatal gifts: a capacious but inaccurate memory, and an extraordinary fluency of speech. There was nothing she did not remember—wrongly; but her halting facts were swathed in so many layers of rhetoric that their infirmities were imperceptible to her friendly critics. Besides, she had been taught Greek by the aunt who had translated Euripides; and the mere sound of the *aïs* and *oïs* that she now and then not unskillfully let slip (correcting herself, of course, with a start, and indulgently mistranslating the phrase), struck awe to the hearts of ladies whose only "accomplishment" was French—if you didn't speak too quickly.

I had then but a momentary glimpse of Mrs. Amyot, but a few months later I came upon her again in the New England university town where the celebrated Irene Astarte Pratt lived on the summit of a local Parnassus, with lesser muses and college professors respectfully grouped on the lower ledges of the sacred declivity. Mrs. Amyot, who, after her husband's death, had returned to the maternal roof (even during her father's lifetime the roof had been distinctively maternal); Mrs. Amyot, thanks to her upper lip, her dimple and her Greek, was already ensconced in a snug hollow of the Parnassian slope.

After the lecture was over it happened that I walked

home with Mrs. Amyot. From the incensed glances of two or three learned gentlemen who were hovering on the doorstep when we emerged, I inferred that Mrs. Amyot, at that period, did not often walk home alone; but I doubt whether any of my discomfited rivals, whatever his claims to favor, was ever treated to so ravishing a mixture of shyness and self-abandonment, of sham erudition and real teeth and hair, as it was my privilege to enjoy. Even at the opening of her public career Mrs. Amyot had a tender eye for strangers, as possible links with successive centers of culture to which in due course the torch of Greek art might be handed on.

She began by telling me that she had never been so frightened in her life. She knew, of course, how dreadfully learned I was, and when, just as she was going to begin, her hostess had whispered to her that I was in the room, she had felt ready to sink through the floor. Then (with a flying dimple) she had remembered Emerson's line—wasn't it Emerson's?—that beauty is its own excuse for *seeing*, and that had made her feel a little more confident, since she was sure that no one *saw* beauty more vividly than she—as a child she used to sit for hours gazing at an Etruscan vase on the bookcase in the library, while her sisters played with their dolls—and if *seeing* beauty was the only excuse one needed for talking about it, why, she was sure I would make allowances and not be *too* critical and sarcastic, especially if, as she thought probable, I had heard of her having lost her poor husband, and how she had to do it for the baby.

Being abundantly assured of my sympathy on these points, she went on to say that she had always wanted so much to consult me about her lectures. Of course, one subject wasn't enough (this view of the limitations of Greek art as a "subject" gave me a startling idea of the rate at which a successful lecturer might exhaust the universe); she must find others; she had not ventured on any as yet, but she had thought of Tennyson—didn't I *love* Tennyson? She *worshiped* him so that she was sure she could help others to understand him; or what did I think of a "course" on Raphael or Michelangelo—or on the heroines of Shakespeare? There were some fine steel engravings of Raphael's Madonnas and of the Sistine ceiling in her mother's library, and she had seen Miss Cushman in several Shakespearian roles, so that on these subjects also she felt qualified to speak with authority.

When we reached her mother's door she begged me to come in and talk the matter over; she wanted me to see the baby—she felt as though I should understand her better if I saw the baby—and the dimple flashed through a tear.

The fear of encountering the author of "The Fall of Man," combined with the opportune recollection of a dinner engagement, made me evade this appeal with the promise of returning on the morrow. On the morrow, I left too early to redeem my promise; and for several years afterwards I saw no more of Mrs. Amyot.

My calling at that time took me at irregular intervals from one to another of our larger cities, and as Mrs. Amyot was also peripatetic it was inevitable that sooner or later we should cross each other's path. It was therefore without surprise that, one snowy afternoon in Boston, I learned from the lady with whom I chanced to be lunching that, as soon as the meal was over, I was to be taken to hear Mrs. Amyot lecture.

"On Greek art?" I suggested.

"Oh, you've heard her then? No, this is one of the series called 'Homes and Haunts of the Poets.' Last week we had Wordsworth and the Lake Poets, today we are to have Goethe and Weimar. She is a wonderful creature—all the women of her family are geniuses. You know, of course, that her mother was Irene Astarte Pratt, who wrote a poem on 'The Fall of Man'; N. P. Willis called her the female Milton of America. One of Mrs. Amyot's aunts has translated Eurip—"

"And is she as pretty as ever?" I irrelevantly interposed.

My hostess looked shocked. "She is excessively modest and retiring. She says it is actual suffering for her to speak in public. You know she only does it for the baby."

Punctually at the hour appointed, we took our seats in a lecture hall full of strenuous females in ulsters. Mrs. Amyot was evidently a favorite with these austere sisters, for every corner was crowded, and as we entered a pale usher with an educated mispronunciation was setting forth to several dejected applicants the impossibility of supplying them with seats.

Our own were happily so near the front that when the curtains at the back of the platform parted, and Mrs. Amyot appeared, I was at once able to establish a comparison between the lady placidly dimpling to the applause of her public and the shrinking drawing-room orator of my earlier recollections.

Mrs. Amyot was as pretty as ever, and there was the same curious discrepancy between the freshness of her aspect and the staleness of her theme, but something was gone of the blushing unsteadiness with which she had fired her first random shots at Greek art. It was not that the shots were less uncertain, but that she now had an air of assuming that, for her purpose, the bull's-eye was everywhere, so that there was no need to be flustered in taking aim. This assurance had so facilitated the flow of her eloquence that she seemed to be performing a trick analogous to that of the conjurer who pulls hundreds of yards of white paper out of his mouth. From a large assortment of stock adjectives she chose, with unerring deftness and rapidity, the one that taste and discrimination would most surely have rejected, fitting out her subject with a whole wardrobe of slop-shop epithets irrelevant in cut and size. To the invaluable knack of not disturbing the association of ideas in her audience, she added the gift of what may be called a confidential manner—so that her fluent generalizations about Goethe and his place in literature (the lecture was, of course, manufactured out of Lewes's book) had the flavor of personal experience, of views sympathetically exchanged with her audience on the best way of knitting children's socks, or of putting up preserves for the winter. It was, I am sure, to this personal accent—the moral equivalent of her dimple—that Mrs. Amyot owed her prodigious, her irrational success. It was her art of transposing secondhand ideas into firsthand emotions that so endeared her to her feminine listeners.

To anyone not in search of "documents" Mrs. Amyot's success was hardly of a kind to make her more interesting, and my curiosity flagged with the growing conviction that the "suffering" entailed on her by public speaking was at most a retrospective pang. I was sure that she had reached the point of measuring and enjoying her effects, of deliberately manipulating her public; and there must indeed have been a certain exhilaration in attaining results so considerable by means involving so little conscious effort. Mrs. Amyot's art was simply an extension of coquetry: she flirted with her audience.

In this mood of enlightened skepticism I responded but languidly to my hostess' suggestion that I should go with her that evening to see Mrs. Amyot. The aunt who had translated Euripides was at home on Saturday evenings, and one met "thoughtful" people there, my hostess explained: it was one of the intellectual centers of Boston. My mood remained distinctly resentful of any connection between Mrs. Amyot and intellectuality, and I declined to go; but the next day I met Mrs. Amyot in the street.

She stopped me reproachfully. She had heard I was in Boston; why had I not come last night? She had been told that I was at her lecture, and it had frightened her—yes, really, almost as much as years ago in Hillbridge. She never *could* get over that stupid shyness, and the whole business was as distasteful to her as ever; but what could she do? There was the baby—he was a big boy now, and boys were *so* expensive! But did I really think she had improved the least little bit? And why wouldn't I come home with her now, and see the boy, and tell her frankly what I had thought of the lecture? She had plenty of flattery—people were *so* kind, and everyone knew that she did it for the baby—but what she felt the need of was criticism, severe, discriminating criticism like mine—oh, she knew that I was dreadfully discriminating!

I went home with her and saw the boy. In the early heat of her Tennyson worship Mrs. Amyot had christened him Lancelot, and he looked it. Perhaps, however, it was his black velvet dress and the exasperating length of his yellow curls, together with the fact of his having been taught to recite Browning to visitors, that raised to fever heat the itching of my palms in his Infant Samuel-like presence. I have since had reason to think that he would have preferred to be called Billy, and to hunt cats with the other boys in the block: his curls and his poetry were simply another outlet for Mrs. Amyot's irrepressible coquetry.

But if Lancelot was not genuine, his mother's love for him was. It justified everything—the lectures *were* for the baby, after all. I had not been ten minutes in the room before I was pledged to help Mrs. Amyot carry out her triumphant fraud. If she wanted to lecture on Plato she should—Plato must take his chance like the rest of us! There was no use, of course, in being "discriminating." I preserved sufficient reason to avoid that pitfall, but I suggested "subjects" and made lists of books for her with a fatuity that became more obvious as time attenuated the remembrance of her smile; I even remember thinking that some men might have cut the knot by marrying her, but I handed over Plato as a hostage and escaped by the afternoon train.

The next time I saw her was in New York, when she had become so fashionable that it was a part of the whole duty of woman to be seen at her lectures. The lady who suggested that of course I ought to go and hear Mrs. Amyot, was not very clear about anything except that she was perfectly lovely, and had had a horrid husband, and was doing it to support her boy. The subject of the discourse (I think it was on Ruskin) was clearly of minor importance, not only to my friend, but to the throng of well-dressed and absent-minded ladies who rustled in late, dropped their muffs, and pocketbooks, and undisguisedly lost themselves in the study of each other's apparel. They received Mrs. Amyot with warmth, but she evidently represented a social obligation like going to church, rather than any more personal interest; in fact, I suspect that every one of the ladies would have remained away, had they been sure that none of the others were coming.

Whether Mrs. Amyot was disheartened by the lack of sympathy between herself and her hearers, or whether the sport of arousing it had become a task, she certainly imparted her platitudes with less convincing warmth than of old. Her voice had the same confidential inflections, but it was like a voice reproduced by a gramophone: the real woman seemed far away. She had grown stouter without losing her dewy freshness, and her smart gown might have been taken to show either the potentialities of a settled income, or a politic concession to the taste of her hearers. As I listened I reproached myself for ever having suspected her of self-deception in saying that she took no pleasure in her work. I was sure now that she did it only for Lancelot, and judging from the size of her audience and the price of the tickets I concluded that Lancelot must be receiving a liberal education.

I was living in New York that winter, and in the rotation of dinners I found myself one evening at Mrs. Amyot's side. The dimple came out at my greeting as punctually as a cuckoo in a Swiss clock, and I detected the same automatic quality in the tone in which she made her usual pretty demand for advice. She was like a musical box charged with popular airs. They succeeded one another with breathless rapidity, but there was a moment after each when the cylinders scraped and whizzed.

Mrs. Amyot, as I found when I called on her, was living in a sunny flat, with a sitting room of flowers and a tea table that had the air of expecting visitors. She owned that she had been ridiculously successful. It was delightful, of course, on Lancelot's account. Lancelot had been sent to the best school in the country, and if things went well and people didn't tire of his silly mother he was to go to Harvard afterwards. During the next two or three years Mrs. Amyot kept her flat in New York, and radiated art and literature upon the suburbs. I saw her now and then, always stouter, better dressed, more successful and more automatic: she had become a lecturing machine.

I went abroad for a year or two and when I came back she had disappeared. I asked several people about her, but life had closed over her. She had been last heard of as lecturing—still lecturing—but no one seemed to know when or where.

It was in Boston that I found her at last, forlornly swaying to the oscillations of an overhead strap in a crowded trolley car. Her face had so changed that I lost myself in a startled reckoning of the time that had elapsed since our parting. She spoke to me shyly, as though aware of my hurried calculation, and conscious that in five years she ought not to have altered so much as to upset my notion of time. Then she seemed to set it down to her dress, for she nervously gathered her cloak over a gown that asked only to be concealed, and shrank into a seat behind the line of prehensile bipeds blocking the aisle of the car.

It was perhaps because she so obviously avoided me that I felt for the first time that I might be of use to her; and when she left the car I made no excuse for following her.

She said nothing of needing advice and did not ask me to walk home with her, concealing, as we talked, her transparent preoccupations under the guise of a sudden interest in all I had been doing since she had last seen me. Of what concerned her, I learned only that Lancelot was well and that for the present, she was not lecturing—she was tired and her doctor had ordered her to rest. On the doorstep of a shabby house she paused and held out her hand. She had been so glad to see me and perhaps if I were in Boston again—the tired dimple, as it were, bowed me out and closed the door on the conclusion of the phrase.

Two or three weeks later, at my club in New York, I found a letter from her. In it she owned that she was troubled, that of late she had been unsuccessful, and that, if I chanced to be coming back to Boston, and could spare her a little of that invaluable advice which—. A few days later the advice was at her disposal. She told me frankly what had happened. Her public had grown tired of her. She had seen it coming on for some time, and was shrewd enough in detecting the causes. She had more rivals than formerly—younger women, she admitted, with a smile that could still afford to be generous—and then her audiences had grown more critical and consequently more exacting. Lecturing—as she understood it—used to be simple enough. You chose your topic—Raphael, Shakespeare, Gothic Architecture, or some such big familiar "subject"—and read up about it for a week or so at the Athenaeum or the Astor Library, and then told your audience what you had read. Now, it appeared, that simple process was no longer adequate. People had tired of familiar "subjects"; it was the fashion to be interested in things that one hadn't always known about—natural selection, animal magnetism, sociology and comparative folklore; while, in literature, the demand had become equally difficult to meet, since Matthew Arnold had introduced the habit of studying the "influence" of one author on another. She had tried lecturing on influences, and had done very well as long as the public was satisfied with the tracing of such obvious influences as that of Turner on Ruskin, of Schiller on Goethe, of Shakespeare on English literature; but such investigations had soon lost all charm for her too-sophisticated audiences, who now demanded either that the influence or the influenced should be quite unknown, or that there should be no perceptible connection between the two. The zest of the performance lay in the measure of ingenuity with which the lecturer established a relation between two people who had probably never heard of each other, much less read each other's works. A pretty Miss Williams with red hair had, for instance, been lecturing with great success on the influence of the Rosicrucians upon the poetry of Keats, while somebody else had given a "course" on the influence of St. Thomas Aquinas upon Professor Huxley.

Mrs. Amyot, warmed by my participation in her distress, went on to say that the growing demand for evolution was what most troubled her. Her grandfather had been a pillar of the Presbyterian ministry, and the idea of her lecturing on Darwin or Herbert Spencer was deeply shocking to her mother and aunts. In one sense the family had staked its literary as well as its spiritual hopes on the literal inspiration of Genesis: what became of "The Fall of Man" in the light of modern exegesis?

The upshot of it was that she had ceased to lecture because she could no longer sell tickets enough to pay for the hire of a lecture hall; and as for the managers, they wouldn't look at her. She had tried her luck all through the Eastern States and as far south as Washington; but it was of no use, and unless she could get hold of some new subjects—or, better still, of some new audiences—she must simply go out of the business. That would mean the failure of all she had worked for, since Lancelot would have to leave Harvard. She paused, and wept some of the unbecoming tears that spring from real grief. Lancelot, it appeared, was to be a genius. He had passed his opening examinations brilliantly;

he had "literary gifts"; he had written beautiful poetry, much of which his mother had copied out, in reverentially slanting characters, in a velvet-bound volume which she drew from a locked drawer.

Lancelot's verse struck me as nothing more alarming than growing pains; but it was not to learn this that she had summoned me. What she wanted was to be assured that he was worth working for, an assurance which I managed to convey by the simple stratagem of remarking that the poems reminded me of Swinburne—and so they did, as well as of Browning, Tennyson, Rossetti, and all the other poets who supply young authors with original inspirations.

This point being established, it remained to be decided by what means his mother was, in the French phrase, to pay herself the luxury of a poet. It was clear that this indulgence could be bought only with counterfeit coin, and that the one way of helping Mrs. Amyot was to become a party to the circulation of such currency. My fetish of intellectual integrity went down like a ninepin before the appeal of a woman no longer young and distinctly foolish, but full of those dear contradictions and irrelevancies that will always make flesh and blood prevail against a syllogism. When I took leave of Mrs. Amyot I had promised her a dozen letters to Western universities and had half pledged myself to sketch out a lecture on the reconciliation of science and religion.

In the West she achieved a success which for a year or more embittered my perusal of the morning papers. The fascination that lures the murderer back to the scene of his crime drew my eye to every paragraph celebrating Mrs. Amyot's last brilliant lecture on the influence of something upon somebody; and her own letters—she overwhelmed me with them—spared me no detail of the entertainment given in her honor by the Palimpsest Club of Omaha or of her reception at the University of Leadville. The college professors were especially kind: she assured me that she had never before met with such discriminating sympathy. I winced at the adjective, which cast a sudden light on the vast machinery of fraud that I had set in motion. All over my native land, men of hitherto unblemished integrity were conniving with me in urging their friends to go and hear Mrs. Amyot lecture on the reconciliation of science and religion! My only hope was that, somewhere among the number of my accomplices, Mrs. Amyot might find one who would marry her in the defense of his convictions.

None, apparently, resorted to such heroic measures; for about two years later I was startled by the announcement that Mrs. Amyot was lecturing in Trenton, New Jersey, on modern theosophy in the light of the Vedas. The following week she was at Newark, discussing Schopenhauer in the light of recent psychology. The week after that I was on the deck of an ocean steamer, reconsidering my share in Mrs. Amyot's triumphs with the impartiality with which one views an episode that is being left behind at the rate of twenty knots an hour. After all, I had been helping a mother to educate her son.

The next ten years of my life were spent in Europe, and when I came home the recollection of Mrs. Amyot had become as inoffensive as one of those pathetic ghosts who are said to strive in vain to make themselves visible to the living. I did not even notice the fact that I no longer heard her spoken of; she had dropped like a dead leaf from the bough of memory.

A year or two after my return I was condemned to one of the worst punishments a worker can undergo—an enforced holiday. The doctors who pronounced the inhuman sentence decreed that it should be worked out in the South, and for a whole winter I carried my cough, my thermometer and my idleness from one fashionable orange grove to another. In the vast and melancholy sea of my disoccupation I clutched like a drowning man at any human driftwood within reach. I took a critical and depreciatory interest in the coughs, the thermometers and the idleness of my fellow sufferers; but to the healthy, the occupied, the transient I clung with undiscriminating enthusiasm.

In no other way can I explain, as I look back on it, the importance I attached to the leisurely confidences of a new arrival with a brown beard who, tilted back at my side on a hotel veranda hung with roses, imparted to me one afternoon the simple annals of his past. There was nothing in the tale to kindle the most inflammable imagination, and though the man had a pleasant frank face and a voice differing agreeably from the shrill inflections of our fellow lodgers, it is probable that under different conditions his discursive history of successful business ventures in a Western city would have affected me somewhat in the manner of a lullaby.

Even at the time I was not sure I liked his agreeable voice: it had a self-importance out of keeping with the humdrum nature of his story, as though a breeze engaged in shaking out a tablecloth should have fancied itself inflating a banner. But this criticism may have been a mere mark of my own fastidiousness, for the man seemed a simple fellow, satisfied with his middling fortunes, and already (he was not much past thirty) deep sunk in conjugal content.

He had just started on an anecdote connected with the cutting of his eldest boy's teeth, when a lady I knew, returning from her late drive, paused before us for a moment in the twilight, with the smile which is the feminine equivalent of beads to savages.

"Won't you take a ticket?" she said sweetly.

Of course I would take a ticket—but for what? I ventured to inquire.

"Oh, that's *so* good of you—for the lecture this evening. You needn't go, you know; we're none of us going; most of us have been through it already at Aiken and at Saint Augustine and at Palm Beach. I've given away my tickets to some new people who've just come from the North, and some of us are going to send our maids, just to fill up the room."

"And may I ask to whom you are going to pay this delicate attention?"

"Oh, I thought you knew—to poor Mrs. Amyot. She's been lecturing all over the South this winter; she's simply *haunted* me ever since I left New York—and we had six weeks of her at Bar Harbor last summer! One has to take tickets, you know, because she's a widow and does it for her son—to pay for his education. She's so plucky and nice about it, and talks about him in such a touching unaffected way, that everybody is sorry for her, and we all simply ruin ourselves in tickets. I do hope that boy's nearly educated!"

"Mrs. Amyot? Mrs. Amyot?" I repeated. "It she *still* educating her son?"

"Oh, do you know about her? Has she been at it long? There's some comfort in that, for I suppose when the boy's provided for the poor thing will be able to take a rest—and give us one!"

She laughed and held out her hand.

"Here's your ticket. Did you say *tickets*—two? Oh, thanks. Of course you needn't go."

"But I mean to go. Mrs. Amyot is an old friend of mine."

"Do you really? That's awfully good of you. Perhaps I'll go too if I can persuade Charlie and the others to come. And I wonder"—in a well-directed aside—"if your friend—?"

I telegraphed her under cover of the dusk that my friend was of too recent standing to be drawn into her charitable toils, and she masked her mistake under a rattle of friendly adjurations not to be late, and to be sure to keep a seat for her, as she had quite made up her mind to go even if Charlie and the others wouldn't.

The flutter of her skirts subsided in the distance, and my neighbor, who had half turned away to light a cigar, made no effort to reopen the conversation. At length, fearing he might have overheard the allusion to himself, I ventured to ask if he were going to the lecture that evening.

"Much obliged—I have a ticket," he said abruptly.

This struck me as in such bad taste that I made no answer; and it was he who spoke next.

"Did I understand you to say that you were an old friend of Mrs. Amyot's?"

"I think I may claim to be, if it is the same Mrs. Amyot I had the pleasure of knowing many years ago. My Mrs. Amyot used to lecture too—"

"To pay for her son's education?"

"I believe so."

"Well—see you later."

He got up and walked into the house.

In the hotel drawing room that evening there was but a meager sprinkling of guests, among whom I saw my brown-bearded friend sitting alone on a sofa, with his head against the wall. It could not have been curiosity to see Mrs. Amyot that had impelled him to attend the performance, for it would have been impossible for him, without changing his place, to command the improvised platform at the end of the room. When I looked at him he seemed lost in contemplation of the chandelier.

The lady from whom I had bought my tickets fluttered in late, unattended by Charlie and the others, and assuring me that she would *scream* if we had the lecture on Ibsen—she had heard it three times already that winter. A glance at the program reassured her: it informed us (in the lecturer's own slanting hand) that Mrs. Amyot was to lecture on the Cosmogony.

After a long pause, during which the small audience coughed and moved its chairs and showed signs of regretting that it had come, the door opened, and Mrs. Amyot stepped upon the platform. Ah, poor lady!

Someone said "Hush!" The coughing and chair shifting subsided, and she began.

It was like looking at one's self early in the morning in a cracked mirror. I had no idea I had grown so old. As for Lancelot, he must have a beard. A beard? The word struck me, and without knowing why I glanced across the room at my bearded friend on the sofa. Oddly enough he was looking at me, with a half-defiant, half-sullen expression; and as our glances crossed, and his fell, the conviction came to me that *he was Lancelot.*

I don't remember a word of the lecture; and yet there was enough of them to have filled a good-sized dictionary. The stream of Mrs. Amyot's eloquence had become a flood: one had the despairing sense that she had sprung a leak, and that until the plumber came there was nothing to be done about it.

The plumber came at length, in the shape of a clock striking ten; my companion, with a sigh of relief, drifted away in search of Charlie and the others; the audience scattered with the precipitation of people who had discharged a duty; and, without surprise, I found the brown-bearded stranger at my elbow.

We stood alone in the bare-floored room, under the flaring chandelier.

"I think you told me this afternoon that you were an old friend of Mrs. Amyot's?" he began awkwardly.

I assented.

"Will you come in and see her?"

"Now? I shall be very glad to, if—"

"She's ready; she's expecting you," he interposed.

He offered no further explanation, and I followed him in silence. He led me down the long corridor, and pushed open the door of a sitting room.

"Mother," he said, closing the door after we had entered, "here's the gentleman who says he used to know you."

Mrs. Amyot, who sat in an easy chair stirring a cup of bouillon, looked up with a start. She had evidently not seen me in the audience, and her son's description had failed to convey my identity. I saw a frightened look in her eyes; then, like a frost flower on a windowpane, the dimple expanded on her wrinkled cheek, and she held out her hand.

"I'm so glad," she said, "so glad!"

She turned to her son, who stood watching us. "You must have told Lancelot all about me—you've known me so long!"

"I haven't had time to talk to your son—since I knew he was your son," I explained.

Her brow cleared. "Then you haven't had time to say anything very dreadful?" she said with a laugh.

"It is he who has been saying dreadful things," I returned, trying to fall in with her tone.

I saw my mistake. "What things?" she faltered.

"Making me feel how old I am by telling me about his children."

"My grandchildren!" she exclaimed with a blush.

"Well, if you choose to put it so."

She laughed again, vaguely, and was silent. I hesitated a moment and then put out my hand.

"I see you are tired. I shouldn't have ventured to come in at this hour if your son—"

The son stepped between us. "Yes, I asked him to come," he said to his mother, in his clear self-assertive voice. "*I* haven't told him anything yet; but you've got to—now. That's what I brought him for."

His mother straightened herself, but I saw her eye waver.

"Lancelot—" she began.

"Mr. Amyot," I said, turning to the young man, "if your

mother will let me come back tomorrow, I shall be very glad—"

He struck his hand hard against the table on which he was leaning.

"No, sir! It won't take long, but it's got to be said now."

He moved nearer to his mother, and I saw his lip twitch under his beard. After all, he was younger and less sure of himself than I had fancied.

"See here, Mother," he went on, "there's something here that's got to be cleared up, and as you say this gentleman is an old friend of yours it had better be cleared up in his presence. Maybe he can help explain it—and if he can't, it's got to be explained to *him*."

Mrs. Amyot's lips moved, but she made no sound. She glanced at me helplessly and sat down. My early inclination to thrash Lancelot was beginning to reassert itself. I took up my hat and moved toward the door.

"Mrs. Amyot is under no obligation to explain anything whatever to me," I said curtly.

"Well! She's under an obligation to me, then—to explain something in your presence." He turned to her again. "Do you know what the people in this hotel are saying? Do you know what he thinks—what they all think? That you're doing this lecturing to support me—to pay for my education! They say you go round telling them so. That's what they buy the tickets for—they do it out of charity. Ask him if it isn't what they say—ask him if they weren't joking about it on the piazza before dinner. The others think I'm a little boy, but he's known you for years, and he must have known how old I was. *He* must have known it wasn't to pay for my education!"

He stood before her with his hands clenched, the veins beating in his temples. She had grown very pale, and her cheeks looked hollow. When she spoke her voice had an odd click in it.

"If—if these ladies and gentlemen have been coming to my lectures out of charity, I see nothing to be ashamed of in that—" she faltered.

"If they've been coming out of charity to *me*," he retorted, "don't you see you've been making me a party to a fraud? Isn't there any shame in that?" His forehead reddened. "Mother! Can't you see the shame of letting people think I was a deadbeat, who sponged on you for my keep? Let alone making us both the laughingstock of every place you go to!"

"I never did that, Lancelot!"

"Did what?"

"Made you a laughingstock—"

He stepped close to her and caught her wrist.

"Will you look me in the face and swear you never told people you were doing this lecturing business to support me?"

There was a long silence. He dropped her wrists and she lifted a limp handkerchief to her frightened eyes. "I did do it—to support you—to educate you—" she sobbed.

"We're not talking about what you did when I was a boy. Everybody who knows me knows I've been a grateful son. Have I ever taken a penny from you since I left college ten years ago?"

"I never said you had! How can you accuse your mother of such wickedness, Lancelot?"

"Have you never told anybody in this hotel—or anywhere else in the last ten years—that you were lecturing to support me? Answer me that!"

"How can you," she wept, "before a stranger?"

"Haven't you said such things about *me* to strangers?" he retorted.

"Lancelot!"

"Well—answer me, then. Say you haven't, Mother!" His voice broke unexpectedly and he took her hand with a gentler touch. "I'll believe anything you tell me," he said almost humbly.

She mistook his tone and raised her head with a rash clutch at dignity.

"I think you'd better ask this gentleman to excuse you first."

"No, by God, I won't!" he cried. "This gentleman says he knows all about you and I mean him to know all about me, too. I don't mean that he or anybody else under this roof shall go on thinking for another twenty-four hours that a cent of their money has ever gone into my pockets since I was old enough to shift for myself. And he shan't leave this room till you've made that clear to him."

He stepped back as he spoke and put his shoulders against the door.

"My dear young gentleman," I said politely, "I shall leave this room exactly when I see fit to do so—and that is now. I have already told you that Mrs. Amyot owes me no explanation of her conduct."

"But I owe you an explanation of mine—you and everyone who has bought a single one of her lecture tickets. Do you suppose a man who's been through what I went through while that woman was talking to you in the porch before dinner is going to hold his tongue, and not attempt to justify himself? No decent man is going to sit down under that sort of thing. It's enough to ruin his character. If you're my mother's friend, you owe it to me to hear what I've got to say."

He pulled out his handkerchief and wiped his forehead.

"Good God, Mother!" he burst out suddenly, "what did you do it for? Haven't you had everything you wanted ever since I was able to pay for it? Haven't I paid you back every cent you spent on me when I was in college? Have I ever gone back on you since I was big enough to work?" He turned to me with a laugh. "I thought she did it to amuse herself—and because there was such a demand for her lectures. *Such a demand!* That's what she always told me. When we asked her to come out and spend this winter with us in Minneapolis, she wrote back that she couldn't because she had engagements all through the South, and her manager wouldn't let her off. That's the reason why I came all the way on here to see her. We thought she was the most popular lecturer in the United States, my wife and I did! We were awfully proud of it too, I can tell you." He dropped into a chair, still laughing.

"How can you, Lancelot, how can you!" His mother, forgetful of my presence, was clinging to him with tentative caresses. "When you didn't need the money any longer I spent it all on the children—you know I did."

"Yes, on lace christening dresses and life-size rocking

horses with real manes! The kind of thing children can't do without."

"Oh, Lancelot, Lancelot—I loved them so! How can you believe such falsehoods about me?"

"What falsehoods about you?"

"That I ever told anybody such dreadful things?"

He put her back gently, keeping his eyes on hers. "Did you never tell anybody in this house that you were lecturing to support your son?"

Her hands dropped from his shoulders and she flashed round on me in sudden anger.

"I know what I think of people who call themselves friends and who come between a mother and her son!"

"Oh, Mother, Mother!" he groaned.

I went up to him and laid my hand on his shoulder.

"My dear man," I said "don't you see the uselessness of prolonging this?"

"Yes, I do," he answered abruptly; and before I could forestall his movement he rose and walked out of the room.

There was a long silence, measured by the lessening reverberations of his footsteps down the wooden floor of the corridor.

When they ceased I approached Mrs. Amyot, who had sunk into her chair. I held out my hand and she took it without a trace of resentment on her ravaged face.

"I sent his wife a sealskin jacket at Christmas!" she said, with the tears running down her cheeks.

Souls Belated

THEIR RAILWAY carriage had been full when the train left Bologna; but at the first station beyond Milan their only remaining companion—a courtly person who ate garlic out of a carpetbag—had left his crumb-strewn seat with a bow.

Lydia's eye regretfully followed the shiny broadcloth of his retreating back till it lost itself in the cloud of touts and cab drivers hanging about the station; then she glanced across at Gannett and caught the same regret in his look. They were both sorry to be alone.

"Par-ten-za!" shouted the guard. The train vibrated to a sudden slamming of doors; a waiter ran along the platform with a tray of fossilized sandwiches; a belated porter flung a bundle of shawls and band-boxes into a third-class carriage; the guard snapped out a brief *Partenza!* which indicated the purely ornamental nature of his first shout; and the train swung out of the station.

The direction of the road had changed, and a shaft of sunlight struck across the dusty red-velvet seats into Lydia's corner. Gannett did not notice it. He had returned to his *Revue de Paris*, and she had to rise and lower the shade of the farther window. Against the vast horizon of their leisure such incidents stood out sharply.

Having lowered the shade, Lydia sat down, leaving the length of the carriage between herself and Gannett. At length he missed her and looked up.

"I moved out of the sun," she hastily explained.

He looked at her curiously: the sun was beating on her through the shade.

"Very well," he said pleasantly; adding, "You don't mind?" as he drew a cigarette case from his pocket.

It was a refreshing touch, relieving the tension of her spirit with the suggestion that, after all, if he could *smoke—!* The relief was only momentary. Her experience of smokers was limited (her husband had disapproved of the use of tobacco) but she knew from hearsay that men sometimes smoked to get away from things; that a cigar might be the masculine equivalent of darkened windows and a headache. Gannett, after a puff or two, returned to his review.

It was just as she had foreseen; he feared to speak as much as she did. It was one of the misfortunes of their situation that they were never busy enough to necessitate, or even to justify, the postponement of unpleasant discussions. If they avoided a question it was obviously, unconcealably because the question was disagreeable. They had unlimited leisure and an accumulation of mental energy to devote to any subject that presented itself; new topics were in fact at a premium. Lydia sometimes had premonitions of a famine-stricken period when there would be nothing left to talk about, and she had already caught herself doling out piecemeal what, in the first prodigality of their confidences, she would have flung to him in a breath. Their silence therefore might simply mean that they had nothing to say; but it was another disadvantage of their position that it allowed infinite opportunity for the classification of minute differences. Lydia had learned to distinguish between real and factitious silences; and under Gannett's she now detected a hum of speech to which her own thoughts made breathless answer.

How could it be otherwise, with that thing between them? She glanced up at the rack overhead. The *thing* was there, in her dressing bag, symbolically suspended over her head and his. He was thinking of it now, just as she was; they had been thinking of it in unison ever since they had entered the train. While the carriage had held other travelers they had screened her from his thoughts; but now that he and she were alone she knew exactly what was passing through his mind; she could almost hear him asking himself what he should say to her.

* * *

The thing had come that morning, brought up to her in an innocent-looking envelope with the rest of their letters, as they were leaving the hotel at Bologna. As she tore it open, she and Gannett were laughing over some ineptitude of the local guidebook—they had been driven, of late, to make the most of such incidental humors of travel. Even when she had unfolded the document she took it for some unimportant business paper sent abroad for her signature, and her eye traveled inattentively over the curly *Whereases* of the preamble until a word arrested her: Divorce. There it stood, an impassable barrier, between her husband's name and hers.

She had been prepared for it, of course, as healthy people are said to be prepared for death, in the sense of knowing it must come without in the least expecting that it will. She had known from the first that Tillotson meant to divorce her—but what did it matter? Nothing mattered, in those first days of supreme deliverance, but the fact that she was free; and not so much (she had begun to be aware) that freedom had released her from Tillotson as that it had given her to Gannett. This discovery had not been agreeable to her self-esteem. She had preferred to think that Tillotson had himself embodied all her reasons for leaving him; and those he represented had seemed cogent enough to stand in no need of reinforcement. Yet she had not left him till she met Gannett. It was her love for Gannett that had made life with Tillotson so poor and incomplete a business. If she had never, from the first, regarded her marriage as a full canceling of her claims upon life, she had at least, for a number of years, accepted it as a provisional compensation,—she had made it "do." Existence in the commodious Tillotson mansion in Fifth Avenue—with Mrs. Tillotson senior commanding the approaches from the second-story front windows—had been reduced to a series of purely automatic acts. The moral atmosphere of the Tillotson interior was as carefully screened and curtained as the house itself: Mrs. Tillotson senior dreaded ideas as much as a draft in her back. Prudent people liked an even temperature; and to do anything unexpected was as foolish as going out in the rain. One of the chief advantages of being rich was that one need not be exposed to unforeseen contingencies: by the use of ordinary firmness and common sense one could make sure of doing exactly the same thing every day at the same hour. These doctrines, reverentially imbibed with his mother's milk, Tillotson (a model son who had never given his parents an hour's anxiety) complacently expounded to his wife, testifying to his sense of their importance by the regularity with which he wore galoshes on damp days, his punctuality at meals, and his elaborate precautions against burglars and contagious diseases. Lydia, coming from a smaller town, and entering New York life through the portals of the Tillotson mansion, had mechanically accepted this point of view as inseparable from having a front pew in church and a parterre box at the opera. All the people who came to the house revolved in the same small circle of prejudices. It was the kind of society in which, after dinner, the ladies compared the exorbitant charges of their children's teachers, and agreed that, even with the new duties on French clothes, it was cheaper in the end to get everything from Worth; while the husbands, over their cigars, lamented municipal corruption, and decided that the men to start a reform were those who had no private interests at stake.

To Lydia this view of life had become a matter of course, just as lumbering about in her mother-in-law's landau had come to seem the only possible means of locomotion, and listening every Sunday to a fashionable Presbyterian divine the inevitable atonement for having thought oneself bored on the other six days of the week. Before she met Gannett her life had seemed merely dull; his coming made it appear like one of those dismal Cruikshank prints in which the people are all ugly and all engaged in occupations that are either vulgar or stupid.

It was natural that Tillotson should be the chief sufferer from this readjustment of focus. Gannett's nearness had made her husband ridiculous, and a part of the ridicule had been reflected on herself. Her tolerance laid her open to a suspicion of obtuseness from which she must, at all costs, clear herself in Gannett's eyes.

She did not understand this until afterwards. At the time she fancied that she had merely reached the limits of endurance. In so large a charter of liberties as the mere act of leaving Tillotson seemed to confer, the small question of divorce or no divorce did not count. It was when she saw that she had left her husband only to be with Gannett that she perceived the significance of anything affecting their relations. Her husband, in casting her off, had virtually flung her at Gannett: it was thus that the world viewed it. The measure of alacrity with which Gannett would receive her would be the subject of curious speculation over afternoon tea tables and in club corners. She knew what would be said—she had heard it so often of others! The recollection bathed her in misery. The men would probably back Gannett to "do the decent thing"; but the ladies' eyebrows would emphasize the worthlessness of such enforced fidelity; and after all, they would be right. She had put herself in a position where Gannett "owed" her something; where, as a gentleman, he was bound to "stand the damage." The idea of accepting such compensation had never crossed her mind; the so-called rehabilitation of such a marriage had always seemed to her the only real disgrace. What she dreaded was the necessity of having to explain herself; of having to combat his arguments; of calculating, in spite of herself, the exact measure of insistence with which he pressed them. She knew not whether she most shrank from his insisting too much or too little. In such a case the nicest sense of proportion might be at fault; and how easily to fall into the error of taking her resistance for a test of his sincerity! Whichever way she turned, an ironical implication confronted her: she had the exasperated sense of having walked into the trap of some stupid practical joke.

Beneath all these preoccupations lurked the dread of what he was thinking. Sooner or later, of course, he would have to speak; but that, in the meantime, he should think, even for a moment, that there was any use in speaking, seemed to her simply unendurable. Her sensitiveness on this point was aggravated by another fear, as yet barely on the level of consciousness; the fear of unwillingly involving Gannett in the trammels of her dependence. To look upon him as the instrument of her liberation; to resist in herself the least tendency to a wifely taking possession of his future; had seemed to Lydia the one way of maintaining the dignity of their relation. Her view had not changed, but she was aware of a growing inability to keep her thoughts fixed on the essential point—the point of parting with Gannett. It was easy to face as long as she kept it sufficiently far off: but what was this act of mental postponement but a gradual encroachment on his future? What was needful was the courage to recognize the moment when, by some word or look, their voluntary fellowship should be transformed into a bondage the more wearing that it was based on none of those common obligations which make the most imperfect marriage in some sort a center of gravity.

When the porter, at the next station, threw the door open, Lydia drew back, making way for the hoped-for intruder; but none came, and the train took up its leisurely progress through the spring wheat fields and budding copses. She now began to hope that Gannett would speak before the next station. She watched him furtively, half-disposed to return to the seat opposite his, but there was an artificiality about his absorption that restrained her. She had never before seen him read with so conspicuous an air of warding off interruption. What could he be thinking of? Why should he be afraid to speak? Or was it her answer that he dreaded?

The train paused for the passing of an express, and he put down his book and leaned out of the window. Presently he turned to her with a smile.

"There's a jolly old villa out here," he said.

His easy tone relieved her, and she smiled back at him as she crossed over to his corner.

Beyond the embankment, through the opening in a mossy wall, she caught sight of the villa, with its broken balustrades, its stagnant fountains, and the stone satyr closing the perspective of a dusky grass walk.

"How should you like to live there?" he asked as the train moved on.

"There?"

"In some such place, I mean. One might do worse, don't you think so? There must be at least two centuries of solitude under those yew trees. Shouldn't you like it?"

"I—I don't know," she faltered. She knew now that he meant to speak.

He lit another cigarette. "We shall have to live somewhere, you know," he said as he bent above the match.

Lydia tried to speak carelessly. *"Je n'en vois pas la nécessité!* Why not live everywhere, as we have been doing?"

"But we can't travel forever, can we?"

"Oh, forever's a long word," she objected, picking up the review he had thrown aside.

"For the rest of our lives then," he said, moving nearer.

She made a slight gesture which caused his hand to slip from hers.

"Why should we make plans? I thought you agreed with me that it's pleasanter to drift."

He looked at her hesitatingly. "It's been pleasant, certainly; but I suppose I shall have to get at my work again some day. You know I haven't written a line since—all this time," he hastily amended.

She flamed with sympathy and self-reproach. "Oh, if you mean *that*—if you want to write—of course we must settle down. How stupid of me not to have thought of it sooner! Where shall we go? Where do you think you could work best? We oughtn't to lose any more time."

He hesitated again. "I had thought of a villa in these parts. It's quiet; we shouldn't be bothered. Should you like it?"

"Of course I should like it." She paused and looked away. "But I thought—I remember your telling me once that your best work had been done in a crowd—in big cities. Why should you shut yourself up in a desert?"

Gannett, for a moment, made no reply. At length he said, avoiding her eye as carefully as she avoided his: "It might be different now; I can't tell, of course, till I try. A writer ought not to be dependent on his *milieu*; it's a mistake to humor oneself in that way; and I thought that just at first you might prefer to be—"

She faced him. "To be what?"

"Well—quiet. I mean—"

"What do you mean by 'at first'?" she interrupted.

He paused again. "I mean after we are married."

She thrust up her chin and turned toward the window. "Thank you!" she tossed back at him.

"Lydia!" he exclaimed blankly; and she felt in every fiber of her averted person that he had made the inconceivable, the unpardonable mistake of anticipating her acquiescence.

The train rattled on and he groped for a third cigarette. Lydia remained silent.

"I haven't offended you?" he ventured at length, in the tone of a man who feels his way.

She shook her head with a sigh. "I thought you understood," she moaned. Their eyes met and she moved back to his side.

"Do you want to know how not to offend me? By taking it for granted, once for all, that you've said your say on the odious question and that I've said mine, and that we stand just where we did this morning before that—that hateful paper came to spoil everything between us!"

"To spoil everything between us? What on earth do you mean? Aren't you glad to be free?"

"I was free before."

"Not to marry me," he suggested.

"But I don't *want* to marry you!" she cried.

She saw that he turned pale. "I'm obtuse, I suppose," he said slowly. "I confess I don't see what you're driving at. Are you tired of the whole business? Or was I simply a—an excuse for getting away? Perhaps you didn't care to travel alone? Was that it? And now you want to chuck me?" His voice had grown harsh. "You owe me a straight answer, you know; don't be tenderhearted!"

Her eyes swam as she leaned to him. "Don't you see it's because I care—because I care so much? Oh, Ralph! Can't you see how it would humiliate me? Try to feel it as a woman would! Don't you see the misery of being made your wife in this way? If I'd known you as a girl—that would have been a real marriage! But now—this vulgar fraud upon society—and upon a society we despised and laughed at—this sneaking back into a position that we've voluntarily forfeited: don't you see what a cheap compromise it is? We neither of us believe in the abstract 'sacredness' of marriage; we both know that no ceremony is needed to consecrate our love for each other; what object can we have in marrying, except the secret fear of each that the other may escape, or the secret longing to work our way back gradually—oh, very gradually—into the esteem of the people whose conventional morality we have always ridiculed and hated? And the very fact that, after a decent interval, these same people would come and dine with us—the women who talk about the indissolubility of marriage, and who would let me die in a gutter today because I am 'leading a life of sin'—doesn't that disgust you more than their turning their backs on us now? I can stand being cut by them, but I couldn't stand their coming to call and asking what I meant to do about visiting that unfortunate Mrs. So-and-so!"

She paused, and Gannett maintained a perplexed silence.

"You judge things too theoretically," he said at length, slowly. "Life is made up of compromises."

"The life we ran away from—yes! If we had been willing to accept them"—she flushed—"we might have gone on meeting each other at Mrs. Tillotson's dinners."

He smiled slightly. "I didn't know that we ran away to found a new system of ethics. I supposed it was because we loved each other."

"Life is complex, of course; isn't it the very recognition of that fact that separates us from the people who see it *tout d'une pièce*? If *they* are right—if marriage is sacred in itself and the individual must always be sacrificed to the family—then there can be no real marriage between us, since our—our being together is a protest against the sacrifice of the individual to the family." She interrupted herself with a laugh. "You'll say now that I'm giving you a lecture on sociology! Of course one acts as one can—as one must, perhaps—pulled by all sorts of invisible threads; but at least one needn't pretend, for social advantages, to subscribe to a creed that ignores the complexity of human motives—that classifies people by arbitrary signs, and puts it in everybody's reach to be on Mrs. Tillotson's visiting list. It may be necessary that the world should be ruled by conventions—but if we believed in them, why did we break through them? And if we don't believe in them, is it honest to take advantage of the protection they afford?"

Gannett hesitated. "One may believe in them or not; but as long as they do rule the world it is only by taking advantage of their protection that one can find a *modus vivendi*."

"Do outlaws need a *modus vivendi*?"

He looked at her hopelessly. Nothing is more perplexing to man than the mental process of a woman who reasons her emotions.

She thought she had scored a point and followed it up passionately. "You do understand, don't you? You see how the very thought of the thing humiliates me! We are together today because we choose to be—don't let us look any farther than that!" She caught his hands. "*Promise* me you'll never speak of it again; promise me you'll never *think* of it even," she implored, with a tearful prodigality of italics.

Through what followed—his protests, his arguments, his final unconvinced submission to her wishes—she had a sense of his but half-discerning all that, for her, had made the moment so tumultuous. They had reached that memorable point in every heart history when, for the first time, the man seems obtuse and the woman irrational. It was the abundance of his intentions that consoled her, on reflection, for what they lacked in quality. After all, it would have been worse, incalculably worse, to have detected any overreadiness to understand her.

✤ II ✤

WHEN the train at nightfall brought them to their journey's end at the edge of one of the lakes, Lydia was glad that they were not, as usual, to pass from one solitude to another. Their wanderings during the year had indeed been like the flight of outlaws: through Sicily, Dalmatia, Transylvania and Southern Italy they had persisted in their tacit avoidance of their kind. Isolation, at first, had deepened the flavor of their happiness, as night intensifies the scent of certain flowers; but in the new phase on which they were entering, Lydia's chief wish was that they should be less abnormally exposed to the action of each other's thoughts.

She shrank, nevertheless, as the brightly-looming bulk of

the fashionable Anglo-American hotel on the water's brink began to radiate toward their advancing boat its vivid suggestion of social order, visitors' lists, Church services, and the bland inquisition of the *table d'hôte*. The mere fact that in a moment or two she must take her place on the hotel register as Mrs. Gannett seemed to weaken the springs of her resistance.

They had meant to stay for a night only, on their way to a lofty village among the glaciers of Monte Rosa; but after the first plunge into publicity, when they entered the dining room, Lydia felt the relief of being lost in a crowd, of ceasing for a moment to be the center of Gannett's scrutiny; and in his face she caught the reflection of her feeling. After dinner, when she went upstairs, he strolled into the smoking room, and an hour or two later, sitting in the darkness of her window, she heard his voice below and saw him walking up and down the terrace with a companion cigar at his side. When he came up he told her he had been talking to the hotel chaplain—a very good sort of fellow.

"Queer little microcosms, these hotels! Most of these people live here all summer and then migrate to Italy or the Riviera. The English are the only people who can lead that kind of life with dignity—those soft-voiced old ladies in Shetland shawls somehow carry the British Empire under their caps. *Civis Romanus sum*. It's a curious study—there might be some good things to work up here."

He stood before her with the vivid preoccupied stare of the novelist on the trail of a "subject." With a relief that was half painful she noticed that, for the first time since they had been together, he was hardly aware of her presence.

"Do you think you could write here?"

"Here? I don't know." His stare dropped. "After being out of things so long one's first impressions are bound to be tremendously vivid, you know. I see a dozen threads already that one might follow—"

He broke off with a touch of embarrassment.

"Then follow them. We'll stay," she said with sudden decision.

"Stay here?" He glanced at her in surprise, and then,

walking to the window, looked out upon the dusky slumber of the garden.

"Why not?" she said at length, in a tone of veiled irritation.

"The place is full of old cats in caps who gossip with the chaplain. Shall you like—I mean, it would be different if—"

She flamed up.

"Do you suppose I care? It's none of their business."

"Of course not; but you won't get them to think so."

"They may think what they please."

He looked at her doubtfully.

"It's for you to decide."

"We'll stay," she repeated.

Gannett, before they met, had made himself known as a successful writer of short stories and of a novel which had achieved the distinction of being widely discussed. The reviewers called him "promising," and Lydia now accused herself of having too long interfered with the fulfilment of his promise. There was a special irony in the fact, since his passionate assurances that only the stimulus of her companionship could bring out his latent faculty had almost given the dignity of a "vocation" to her course: there had been moments when she had felt unable to assume, before posterity, the responsibility of thwarting his career. And, after all, he had not written a line since they had been together: his first desire to write had come from renewed contact with the world! Was it all a mistake then? Must the most intelligent choice work more disastrously than the blundering combinations of chance? Or was there a still more humiliating answer to her perplexities? His sudden impulse of activity so exactly coincided with her own wish to withdraw, for a time, from the range of his observation, that she wondered if he too were not seeking sanctuary from intolerable problems.

"You must begin tomorrow!" she cried, hiding a tremor under the laugh with which she added, "I wonder if there's any ink in the inkstand?"

Whatever else they had at the Hotel Bellosguardo, they had, as Miss Pinsent said, "a certain tone." It was to Lady Susan Condit that they owed this inestimable benefit; an advantage ranking in Miss Pinsent's opinion above even the lawn tennis courts and the resident chaplain. It was the fact of Lady Susan's annual visit that made the hotel what it was. Miss Pinsent was certainly the last to underrate such a privilege: "It's so important, my dear, forming as we do a little family, that there should be someone to give *the tone*; and no one could do it better than Lady Susan—an earl's daughter and a person of such determination. Dear Mrs. Ainger now—who really *ought*, you know, when Lady Susan's away—absolutely refuses to assert herself." Miss Pinsent sniffed derisively. "A bishop's niece!—my dear, I saw her once actually give in to some South Americans—and before us all. She gave up her seat at table to oblige them—such a lack of dignity! Lady Susan spoke to her very plainly about it afterwards."

Miss Pinsent glanced across the lake and adjusted her auburn front.

"But of course I don't deny that the stand Lady Susan takes is not always easy to live up to—for the rest of us, I mean. Monsieur Grossart, our good proprietor, finds it trying at times, I know—he has said as much, privately, to Mrs. Ainger and me. After all, the poor man is not to blame for wanting to fill his hotel, is he? And Lady Susan is so difficult—so very difficult—about new people. One might almost say that she disapproves of them beforehand, on principle. And yet she's had warnings—she very nearly made a dreadful mistake once with the Duchess of Levens, who dyed her hair and—well, swore and smoked. One would have thought that might have been a lesson to Lady Susan." Miss Pinsent resumed her knitting with a sigh. "There are exceptions, of course. She took at once to you and Mr. Gannett—it was quite remarkable, really. Oh, I don't mean that either—of course not! It was perfectly natural—we *all* thought you so charming and interesting from the first day—we knew at once that Mr. Gannett was intellectual, by the magazines you took in; but you know what I mean. Lady Susan is so very—well, I won't say prejudiced, as Mrs. Ainger does—but so prepared *not* to like new people, that her taking to you in that way was a surprise to us all, I confess."

Miss Pinsent sent a significant glance down the long laurustinus alley from the other end of which two people—a lady and gentleman—were strolling toward them through the smiling neglect of the garden.

"In this case, of course, it's very different; that I'm willing to admit. Their looks are against them; but, as Mrs. Ainger says, one can't exactly tell them so."

"She's very handsome," Lydia ventured, with her eyes on the lady, who showed, under the dome of a vivid sunshade, the hourglass figure and superlative coloring of a Christmas chromo.

"That's the worst of it. She's too handsome."

"Well, after all, she can't help that."

"Other people manage to," said Miss Pinsent skeptically.

"But isn't it rather unfair of Lady Susan—considering that nothing is known about them?"

"But, my dear, that's the very thing that's against them. It's infinitely worse than any actual knowledge."

Lydia mentally agreed that, in the case of Mrs. Linton, it possibly might be.

"I wonder why they came here?" she mused.

"That's against them too. It's always a bad sign when loud people come to a quiet place. And they've brought van loads of boxes—her maid told Mrs. Ainger's that they meant to stop indefinitely."

"And Lady Susan actually turned her back on her in the salon?"

"My dear, she said it was for our sakes: that makes it so unanswerable! But poor Grossart *is* in a way! The Lintons have taken his most expensive suite, you know—the yellow damask drawing room above the portico—and they have champagne with every meal!"

They were silent as Mr. and Mrs. Linton sauntered by; the lady with tempestuous brows and challenging chin; the gentleman, a blond stripling, trailing after her, head downward, like a reluctant child dragged by his nurse.

"What does your husband think of them, my dear?" Miss Pinsent whispered as they passed out of earshot.

Lydia stooped to pick a violet in the border.

"He hasn't told me."

"Of your speaking to them, I mean. Would he approve of that? I know how very particular nice Americans are. I think your action might make a difference; it would certainly carry weight with Lady Susan."

"Dear Miss Pinsent, you flatter me!"

Lydia rose and gathered up her book and sunshade.

"Well, if you're asked for an opinion—if Lady Susan asks you for one—I think you ought to be prepared," Miss Pinsent admonished her as she moved away.

✣ III ✣

LADY SUSAN held her own. She ignored the Lintons, and her little family, as Miss Pinsent phrased it, followed suit. Even Mrs. Ainger agreed that it was obligatory. If Lady Susan owed it to the others not to speak to the Lintons, the others clearly owed it to Lady Susan to back her up. It was generally found expedient, at the Hotel Bellosguardo, to adopt this form of reasoning.

Whatever effect this combined action may have had upon the Lintons, it did not at least have that of driving them away. Monsieur Grossart, after a few days of suspense, had the satisfaction of seeing them settle down in his yellow damask *premier* with what looked like a permanent installation of palm trees and silk cushions, and a gratifying continuance in the consumption of champagne. Mrs. Linton trailed her Doucet draperies up and down the garden with the same challenging air, while her husband, smoking innumerable cigarettes, dragged himself dejectedly in her wake; but neither of them, after the first encounter with Lady Susan, made any attempt to extend their acquaintance. They simply ignored their ignorers. As Miss Pinsent resentfully observed, they behaved exactly as though the hotel were empty.

It was therefore a matter of surprise, as well as of displeasure, to Lydia, to find, on glancing up one day from her seat in the garden, that the shadow which had fallen across her book was that of the enigmatic Mrs. Linton.

"I want to speak to you," that lady said, in a rich hard voice that seemed the audible expression of her gown and her complexion.

Lydia started. She certainly did not want to speak to Mrs. Linton.

"Shall I sit down here?" the latter continued, fixing her intensely-shaded eyes on Lydia's face, "or are you afraid of being seen with me?"

"Afraid?" Lydia colored. "Sit down, please. What is it that you wish to say?"

Mrs. Linton, with a smile, drew up a garden chair and crossed one openwork ankle above the other.

"I want you to tell me what my husband said to your husband last night."

Lydia turned pale.

"My husband—to yours?" she faltered, staring at the other.

"Didn't you know they were closeted together for hours in the smoking room after you went upstairs? My man didn't get to bed until nearly two o'clock and when he did I couldn't get a word out of him. When he wants to be aggravating I'll back him against anybody living!" Her teeth and eyes flashed persuasively upon Lydia. "But you'll tell me what they were talking about, won't you? I know I can trust you—you look so awfully kind. And it's for his own good. He's such a precious donkey and I'm so afraid he's got into some beastly scrape or other. If he'd only trust his own old woman! But they're always writing to him and setting him against me. And I've got nobody to turn to." She laid her hand on Lydia's with a rattle of bracelets. "You'll help me, won't you?"

Lydia drew back from the smiling fierceness of her brows.

"I'm sorry—but I don't think I understand. My husband has said nothing to me of—of yours."

The great black crescents above Mrs. Linton's eyes met angrily.

"I say—is that true?" she demanded.

Lydia rose from her seat.

"Oh, look here, I didn't mean that, you know—you mustn't take one up so! Can't you see how rattled I am?"

Lydia saw that, in fact, her beautiful mouth was quivering beneath softened eyes.

"I'm beside myself!" the splendid creature wailed, dropping into her seat.

"I'm so sorry," Lydia repeated, forcing herself to speak kindly; "but how can I help you?"

Mrs. Linton raised her head sharply.

"By finding out—there's a darling!"

"Finding what out?"

"What Trevenna told him."

"Trevenna—?" Lydia echoed in bewilderment.

Mrs. Linton clapped her hand to her mouth.

"Oh, Lord—there, it's out! What a fool I am! But I supposed of course you knew; I supposed everybody knew." She dried her eyes and bridled. "Didn't you know that he's Lord Trevenna? I'm Mrs. Cope."

Lydia recognized the names. They had figured in a flamboyant elopement which had thrilled fashionable London some six months earlier.

"Now you see how it is—you understand, don't you?" Mrs. Cope continued on a note of appeal. "I knew you would—that's the reason I came to you. I suppose *he* felt the same thing about your husband; he's not spoken to another soul in the place." Her face grew anxious again. "He's awfully sensitive, generally—he feels our position, he says—as if it wasn't *my* place to feel that! But when he does get talking there's no knowing what he'll say. I know he's been brooding over something lately, and I *must* find out what it is—it's to his interest that I should. I always tell him that I think only of his interest; if he'd only trust me! But he's been so odd lately—I can't think what he's plotting. You will help me, dear?"

Lydia, who had remained standing, looked away uncomfortably.

"If you mean by finding out what Lord Trevenna has told my husband, I'm afraid it's impossible."

"Why impossible?"

"Because I infer that it was told in confidence."

Mrs. Cope stared incredulously.

"Well, what of that? Your husband looks such a dear—anyone can see he's awfully gone on you. What's to prevent your getting it out of him?"

Lydia flushed.

"I'm not a spy!" she exclaimed.

"A spy—a spy? How dare you?" Mrs. Cope flamed out. "Oh, I don't mean that either! Don't be angry with me—I'm so miserable." She essayed a softer note. "Do you call that spying—for one woman to help out another? I do need help so dreadfully! I'm at my wits' end with Trevenna, I am indeed. He's such a boy—a mere baby, you know; he's only two-and-twenty." She dropped her orbed lids. "He's younger than me—only fancy, a few months younger. I tell him he ought to listen to me as if I was his mother; oughtn't he now? But he won't, he won't! All his people are at him, you see—oh, I know *their* little game! Trying to get him away from me before I can get my divorce—that's what they're up to. At first he wouldn't listen to them; he used to toss their letters over to me to read; but now he reads them himself, and answers 'em too, I fancy; he's always shut up in his room, writing. If I only knew what his plan is I could stop him fast enough—he's such a simpleton. But he's dreadfully deep too—at times I can't make him out. But I know he's told your husband everything—I knew that last night the minute I laid eyes on him. And I *must* find out—you must help me—I've got no one else to turn to!"

She caught Lydia's fingers in a stormy pressure.

"Say you'll help me—you and your husband."

Lydia tried to free herself.

"What you ask is impossible; you must see that it is. No one could interfere in—in the way you ask."

Mrs. Cope's clutch tightened.

"You won't, then? You won't?"

"Certainly not. Let me go, please."

Mrs. Cope released her with a laugh.

"Oh, go by all means—pray don't let me detain you! Shall you go and tell Lady Susan Condit that there's a pair of us—or shall I save you the trouble of enlightening her?"

Lydia stood still in the middle of the path, seeing her antagonist through a mist of terror. Mrs. Cope was still laughing.

"Oh, I'm not spiteful by nature, my dear; but you're a little more than flesh and blood can stand! It's impossible, is it? Let you go, indeed! You're too good to be mixed up in my affairs, are you? Why, you little fool, the first day I laid eyes on you I saw that you and I were both in the same box—that's the reason I spoke to you."

She stepped nearer, her smile dilating on Lydia like a lamp through a fog.

"You can take your choice, you know; I always play fair. If you'll tell I'll promise not to. Now then, which is it to be?"

Lydia, involuntarily, had begun to move away from the pelting storm of words; but at this she turned and sat down again.

"You may go," she said simply. "I shall stay here."

✣ IV ✣

SHE stayed there for a long time, in the hypnotized contemplation, not of Mrs. Cope's present, but of her own past. Gannett, early that morning, had gone off on a long walk—he had fallen into the habit of taking these mountain tramps with various fellow lodgers; but even had he been within reach she could not have gone to him just then. She had to deal with herself first. She was surprised to find how, in the last months, she had lost the habit of introspection. Since their coming to the Hotel Bellosguardo she and Gannett had tacitly avoided themselves and each other.

She was aroused by the whistle of the three o'clock steamboat as it neared the landing just beyond the hotel gates. Three o'clock! Then Gannett would soon be back—he had told her to expect him before four. She rose hurriedly, her face averted from the inquisitorial façade of the hotel. She could not see him just yet; she could not go indoors. She slipped through one of the overgrown garden alleys and climbed a steep path to the hills.

It was dark when she opened their sitting-room door. Gannett was sitting on the window ledge smoking a cigarette. Cigarettes were now his chief resource: he had not written a line during the two months they had spent at the Hotel Bellosguardo. In that respect, it had turned out not to be the right *milieu* after all.

He started up at Lydia's entrance.

"Where have you been? I was getting anxious."

She sat down in a chair near the door.

"Up the mountain," she said wearily.

"Alone?"

"Yes."

Gannett threw away his cigarette: the sound of her voice made him want to see her face.

"Shall we have a little light?" he suggested.

She made no answer and he lifted the globe from the lamp and put a match to the wick. Then he looked at her.

"Anything wrong? You look done up."

She sat glancing vaguely about the little sitting room, dimly lit by the pallid-globed lamps, which left in twilight the outlines of the furniture, of his writing table heaped with books and papers, of the tea roses and jasmine drooping on the mantelpiece. How like home it had all grown—how like home!

"Lydia, what is wrong?" he repeated.

She moved away from him, feeling for her hatpins and turning to lay her hat and sunshade on the table.

Suddenly she said: "That woman has been talking to me."

Gannett stared.

"That woman? What woman?"

"Mrs. Linton—Mrs. Cope."

He gave a start of annoyance, still, as she perceived, not grasping the full import of her words.

"The deuce! She told you—?"

"She told me everything."

Gannett looked at her anxiously.

"What impudence! I'm so sorry that you should have been exposed to this, dear."

"Exposed!" Lydia laughed.

Gannett's brow clouded and they looked away from each other.

"Do you know *why* she told me? She had the best of reasons. The first time she laid eyes on me she saw that we were both in the same box."

"Lydia!"

"So it was natural, of course, that she should turn to me in a difficulty."

"What difficulty?"

"It seems she has reason to think that Lord Trevenna's people are trying to get him away from her before she gets her divorce—"

"Well?"

"And she fancied he had been consulting with you last night as to—as to the best way of escaping from her."

Gannett stood up with an angry forehead.

"Well—what concern of yours was all this dirty business? Why should she go to you?"

"Don't you see? It's so simple. I was to wheedle his secret out of you."

"To oblige that woman?"

"Yes; or, if I was unwilling to oblige her, then to protect myself."

"To protect yourself? Against whom?"

"Against her telling everyone in the hotel that she and I are in the same box."

"She threatened that?"

"She left me the choice of telling it myself or of doing it for me."

"The beast!"

There was a long silence. Lydia had seated herself on the sofa, beyond the radius of the lamp, and he leaned against the window. His next question surprised her.

"When did this happen? At what time, I mean?"

She looked at him vaguely.

"I don't know—after luncheon, I think. Yes, I remember; it must have been at about three o'clock."

He stepped into the middle of the room and as he approached the light she saw that his brow had cleared.

"Why do you ask?" she said.

"Because when I came in, at about half-past three, the mail was just being distributed, and Mrs. Cope was waiting as usual to pounce on her letters; you know she was always watching for the postman. She was standing so close to me that I couldn't help seeing a big official-looking envelope that was handed to her. She tore it open, gave one look at the inside, and rushed off upstairs like a whirlwind, with the director shouting after her that she had left all her other letters behind. I don't believe she ever thought of you again after that paper was put into her hand."

"Why?"

"Because she was too busy. I was sitting in the window, watching for you, when the five o'clock boat left, and who should go on board, bag and baggage, valet and maid, dressing bags and poodle, but Mrs. Cope and Trevenna. Just an hour and a half to pack up in! And you should have seen her when they started. She was radiant—shaking hands with everybody—waving her handkerchief from the deck—distributing bows and smiles like an empress. If ever a woman got what she wanted just in the nick of time that woman did. She'll be Lady Trevenna within a week, I'll wager."

"You think she has her divorce?"

"I'm sure of it. And she must have got it just after her talk with you."

Lydia was silent.

At length she said, with a kind of reluctance, "She was horribly angry when she left me. It wouldn't have taken long to tell Lady Susan Condit."

"Lady Susan Condit has not been told."

"How do you know?"

"Because when I went downstairs half an hour ago I met Lady Susan on the way—"

He stopped, half smiling.

"Well?"

"And she stopped to ask if I thought you would act as patroness to a charity concert she is getting up."

In spite of themselves they both broke into a laugh. Lydia's ended in sobs and she sank down with her face hidden. Gannett bent over her, seeking her hands.

"That vile woman—I ought to have warned you to keep away from her; I can't forgive myself! But he spoke to me in confidence; and I never dreamed—well, it's all over now."

Lydia lifted her head.

"Not for me. It's only just beginning."

"What do you mean?"

She put him gently aside and moved in her turn to the window. Then she went on, with her face turned toward the shimmering blackness of the lake, "You see of course that it might happen again at any moment."

"What?"

"This—this risk of being found out. And we could hardly count again on such a lucky combination of chances, could we?"

He sat down with a groan.

Still keeping her face toward the darkness, she said, "I want you to go and tell Lady Susan—and the others."

Gannett, who had moved towards her, paused a few feet off.

"Why do you wish me to do this?" he said at length, with less surprise in his voice than she had been prepared for.

"Because I've behaved basely, abominably, since we came here: letting these people believe we were married—lying with every breath I drew—"

"Yes, I've felt that too," Gannett exclaimed with sudden energy.

The words shook her like a tempest: all her thoughts seemed to fall about her in ruins.

"You—you've felt so?"

"Of course I have." He spoke with low-voiced vehemence. "Do you suppose I like playing the sneak any better than you do? It's damnable."

He had dropped on the arm of a chair, and they stared at each other like blind people who suddenly see.

"But you have liked it here," she faltered.

"Oh, I've liked it—I've liked it." He moved impatiently. "Haven't you?"

"Yes," she burst out; "that's the worst of it—that's what I can't bear. I fancied it was for your sake that I insisted on staying—because you thought you could write here; and perhaps just at first that really was the reason. But afterwards I wanted to stay myself—I loved it." She broke into a laugh. "Oh, do you see the full derision of it? These people—the very prototypes of the bores you took me away from, with the same fenced-in view of life, the same keep-off-the-grass morality, the same little cautious virtues and the same little frightened vices—well, I've clung to them, I've delighted in them, I've done my best to please them. I've toadied

Lady Susan, I've gossiped with Miss Pinsent, I've pretended to be shocked with Mrs. Ainger. Respectability! It was the one thing in life that I was sure I didn't care about, and it's grown so precious to me that I've stolen it because I couldn't get it in any other way."

She moved across the room and returned to his side with another laugh.

"I who used to fancy myself unconventional! I must have been born with a cardcase in my hand. You should have seen me with that poor woman in the garden. She came to me for help, poor creature, because she fancied that, having 'sinned,' as they call it, I might feel some pity for others who had been tempted in the same way. Not I! She didn't know me. Lady Susan would have been kinder, because Lady Susan wouldn't have been afraid. I hated the woman—my one thought was not to be seen with her—I could have killed her for guessing my secret. The one thing that mattered to me at that moment was my standing with Lady Susan!"

Gannett did not speak.

"And you—you've felt it too!" she broke out accusingly. "You've enjoyed being with these people as much as I have; you've let the chaplain talk to you by the hour about The Reign of Law and Professor Drummond. When they asked you to hand the plate in church I was watching you—*you wanted to accept.*"

She stepped close, laying her hand on his arm.

"Do you know, I begin to see what marriage is for. It's to keep people away from each other. Sometimes I think that two people who love each other can be saved from madness only by the things that come between them—children, duties, visits, bores, relations—the things that protect married people from each other. We've been too close together—that has been our sin. We've seen the nakedness of each other's souls."

She sank again on the sofa, hiding her face in her hands.

Gannett stood above her perplexedly: he felt as though she were being swept away by some implacable current while he stood helpless on its bank.

At length he said, "Lydia, don't think me a brute—but don't you see yourself that it won't do?"

"Yes, I see it won't do," she said without raising her head.

His face cleared.

"Then we'll go tomorrow."

"Go—where?"

"To Paris; to be married."

For a long time she made no answer; then she asked slowly, "Would they have us here if we were married?"

"Have us here?"

"I mean Lady Susan—and the others."

"Have us here? Of course they would."

"Not if they knew—at least, not unless they could pretend not to know."

He made an impatient gesture.

"We shouldn't come back here, of course; and other people needn't know—no one need know."

She sighed. "Then it's only another form of deception and a meaner one. Don't you see that?"

"I see that we're not accountable to any Lady Susans on earth!"

"Then why are you ashamed of what we are doing here?"

"Because I'm sick of pretending that you're my wife when you're not—when you won't be."

She looked at him sadly.

"If I were your wife you'd have to go on pretending. You'd have to pretend that I'd never been—anything else. And our friends would have to pretend that they believed what you pretended."

Gannett pulled off the sofa tassel and flung it away.

"You're impossible," he groaned.

"It's not I—it's our being together that's impossible. I only want you to see that marriage won't help it."

"What will help it then?"

She raised her head.

"My leaving you."

"Your leaving me?" He sat motionless, staring at the tassel which lay at the other end of the room. At length some impulse of retaliation for the pain she was inflicting made him say deliberately:

"And where would you go if you left me?"

"Oh!" she cried.

He was at her side in an instant.

"Lydia—Lydia—you know I didn't mean it; I couldn't mean it! But you've driven me out of my senses; I don't know what I'm saying. Can't you get out of this labyrinth of self-torture? It's destroying us both."

"That's why I must leave you."

"How easily you say it!" He drew her hands down and made her face him. "You're very scrupulous about yourself—and others. But have you thought of me? You have no right to leave me unless you've ceased to care—"

"It's because I care—"

"Then I have a right to be heard. If you love me you can't leave me."

Her eyes defied him.

"Why not?"

He dropped her hands and rose from her side.

"Can you?" he said sadly.

The hour was late and the lamp flickered and sank. She stood up with a shiver and turned toward the door of her room.

✣ V ✣

AT daylight a sound in Lydia's room woke Gannett from a troubled sleep. He sat up and listened. She was moving about softly, as though fearful of disturbing him. He heard her push back one of the creaking shutters; then there was a moment's silence, which seemed to indicate that she was waiting to see if the noise had roused him.

Presently she began to move again. She had spent a sleepless night, probably, and was dressing to go down to the garden for a breath of air. Gannett rose also; but some undefinable instinct made his movements as cautious as hers. He stole to his window and looked out through the slats of the shutter.

It had rained in the night and the dawn was gray and

lifeless. The cloud-muffled hills across the lake were reflected in its surface as in a tarnished mirror. In the garden, the birds were beginning to shake the drops from the motionless laurustinus boughs.

An immense pity for Lydia filled Gannett's soul. Her seeming intellectual independence had blinded him for a time to the feminine cast of her mind. He had never thought of her as a woman who wept and clung: there was a lucidity in her intuitions that made them appear to be the result of reasoning. Now he saw the cruelty he had committed in detaching her from the normal conditions of life; he felt, too, the insight with which she had hit upon the real cause of their suffering. Their life was "impossible," as she had said—and its worse penalty was that it had made any other life impossible for them. Even had his love lessened, he was bound to her now by a hundred ties of pity and self-reproach; and she, poor child, must turn back to him as Latude returned to his cell.

A new sound startled him: it was the stealthy closing of Lydia's door. He crept to his own and heard her footsteps passing down the corridor. Then he went back to the window and looked out.

A minute or two later he saw her go down the steps of the porch and enter the garden. From his post of observation her face was invisible, but something about her appearance struck him. She wore a long traveling cloak and under its folds he detected the outline of a bag or bundle. He drew a deep breath and stood watching her.

She walked quickly down the laurustinus alley toward the gate; there she paused a moment, glancing about the little shady square. The stone benches under the trees were empty, and she seemed to gather resolution from the solitude about her, for she crossed the square to the steamboat landing, and he saw her pause before the ticket office at the head of the wharf. Now she was buying her ticket. Gannett turned his head a moment to look at the clock: the boat was due in five minutes. He had time to jump into his clothes and overtake her—

He made no attempt to move; an obscure reluctance restrained him. If any thought emerged from the tumult of his sensations, it was that he must let her go if she wished it. He had spoken last night of his rights: what were they? At the last issue, he and she were two separate beings, not made one by the miracle of common forbearances, duties, abnegations, but bound together in a *noyade* of passion that left them resisting yet clinging as they went down.

After buying her ticket, Lydia had stood for a moment looking out across the lake; then he saw her seat herself on one of the benches near the landing. He and she, at that moment, were both listening for the same sound: the whistle of the boat as it rounded the nearest promontory. Gannett turned again to glance at the clock: the boat was due now.

Where would she go? What would her life be when she had left him? She had no near relations and few friends. There was money enough . . . but she asked so much of life, in ways so complex and immaterial. He thought of her as walking barefooted through a stony waste. No one would understand her—no one would pity her—and he, who did both, was powerless to come to her aid.

He saw that she had risen from the bench and walked toward the edge of the lake. She stood looking in the direction from which the steamboat was to come; then she turned to the ticket office, doubtless to ask the cause of the delay. After that she went back to the bench and sat down with bent head. What was she thinking of?

The whistle sounded; she started up, and Gannett involuntarily made a movement toward the door. But he turned back and continued to watch her. She stood motionless, her eyes on the trail of smoke that preceded the appearance of the boat. Then the little craft rounded the point, a dead white object on the leaden water: a minute later it was puffing and backing at the wharf.

The few passengers who were waiting—two or three peasants and a snuffy priest—were clustered near the ticket office. Lydia stood apart under the trees.

The boat lay alongside now; the gangplank was run out and the peasants went on board with their baskets of vegetables, followed by the priest. Still Lydia did not move. A bell began to ring querulously; there was a shriek of steam, and someone must have called to her that she would be late, for she started forward, as though in answer to a summons. She moved waveringly, and at the edge of the wharf she paused. Gannett saw a sailor beckon to her; the bell rang again and she stepped upon the gangplank.

Halfway down the short incline to the deck she stopped again; then she turned and ran back to the land. The gangplank was drawn in, the bell ceased to ring, and the boat backed out into the lake. Lydia, with slow steps, was walking toward the garden.

As she approached the hotel she looked up furtively and Gannett drew back into the room. He sat down beside a table; a Bradshaw lay at his elbow, and mechanically, without knowing what he did, he began looking out the trains to Paris.

Copy

A DIALOGUE

MRS. AMBROSE DALE—*forty, slender, still young—sits in her drawing room at the tea table. The winter twilight is falling, a lamp has been lit, there is a fire on the hearth, and the room is pleasantly dim and flower-scented. Books are scattered everywhere—mostly with autograph inscriptions "From the Author"—and a large portrait of* Mrs. Dale, *at her desk, with papers strewn about her, takes up one of the wall panels. Before* MRS. DALE *stands* HILDA, fair and twenty, her hands full of letters.

MRS. DALE. Ten more applications for autographs? Isn't it strange that people who'd blush to borrow twenty dollars don't scruple to beg for an autograph?

HILDA (*reproachfully*). Oh—

MRS. DALE. What's the difference, pray?

HILDA. Only that *your* last autograph sold for fifty—

MRS. DALE (*not displeased*). Ah?— I sent for you, Hilda, because I'm dining out tonight, and if there's nothing important to attend to among these letters you needn't sit up for me.

HILDA. You don't mean to work?

MRS. DALE. Perhaps; but I shan't need you. You'll see that my cigarettes and coffee machine are in place, and that I don't have to crawl about the floor in search of my pen wiper? That's all. Now about these letters—

HILDA (*impulsively*). Oh, Mrs. Dale—

MRS. DALE. Well?

HILDA. I'd rather sit up for you.

MRS. DALE. Child, I've nothing for you to do. I shall be blocking out the tenth chapter of *Winged Purposes* and it won't be ready for you till next week.

HILDA. It isn't that—but it's so beautiful to sit here, watching and listening, all alone in the night, and to feel that you're in there (*she points to the study door*) creating—. (*Impulsively.*) What do I care for sleep?

MRS. DALE (*indulgently*). Child—silly child!—Yes, I should have felt so at your age—it would have been an inspiration—

HILDA (*rapt*). It is!

MRS. DALE. But you must go to bed; I must have you fresh in the morning; for you're still at the age when one *is* fresh in the morning! (*She sighs.*) The letters? (*Abruptly.*) Do you take notes of what you feel, Hilda—here, all alone in the night, as you say?

HILDA (*shyly*). I have—

MRS. DALE (*smiling*). For the diary?

HILDA. (*Nods and blushes.*)

MRS. DALE (*caressingly*). Goose!—Well, to business. What is there?

HILDA. Nothing important, except a letter from Stroud & Fayerweather to say that the question of the royalty on *Pomegranate Seed* has been settled in your favor. The English publishers of *Immolation* write to consult you about a six-shilling edition; Olafson, the Copenhagen publisher, applies for permission to bring out a Danish translation of *The Idol's Feet*; and the editor of the *Semaphore* wants a new serial—I think that's all; except that *Woman's Sphere* and *The Droplight* ask for interviews—with photographs—

MRS. DALE. The same old story! I'm so tired of it all. (*To herself, in an undertone.*) But how should I feel if it all stopped? (*The servant brings in a card.*)

MRS. DALE (*reading it*). Is it possible? Paul Ventnor? (*To the servant.*) Show Mr. Ventnor up. (*To herself.*) Paul Ventnor!

HILDA (*breathless*). Oh, Mrs. Dale—*the* Mr. Ventnor?

MRS. DALE (*smiling*). I fancy there's only one.

HILDA. The great, great poet? (*Irresolute.*) No, I don't dare—

MRS. DALE (*with a tinge of impatience*). What?

HILDA (*fervently*). Ask you—if I might—oh, here in this corner, where he can't possibly notice me—stay just a moment? Just to see him come in? To see the meeting between you—the greatest novelist and the greatest poet of the age? Oh, it's too much to ask! It's an historic moment.

MRS. DALE. Why, I suppose it is. I hadn't thought of it in that light. Well (*smiling*), for the diary—

HILDA. Oh, thank you, *thank you!* I'll be off the very instant I've heard him speak.

MRS. DALE. The very instant, mind. (*She rises, looks at herself in the glass, smooths her hair, sits down again, and rattles the tea caddy.*) Isn't the room very warm? (*She looks over at her portrait.*) I've grown stouter since that was painted—. You'll make a fortune out of that diary, Hilda—

HILDA (*modestly*). Four publishers have applied to me already—

THE SERVANT (*announces*). Mr. Paul Ventnor.

(*Tall, nearly fifty, with an incipient stoutness buttoned into a masterly frock coat,* VENTNOR *drops his glass and advances vaguely, with a shortsighted stare.*)

VENTNOR. Mrs. Dale?

MRS. DALE. My dear friend! This is kind. (*She looks over her shoulder at Hilda, who vanishes through the door to the left.*) The papers announced your arrival, but I hardly hoped—

VENTNOR (*whose shortsighted stare is seen to conceal a deeper embarrassment*). You hadn't forgotten me, then?

MRS. DALE. Delicious! Do *you* forget that you're public property?

VENTNOR. Forgotten, I mean, that we were old friends?

MRS. DALE.Such old friends! May I remind you that it's nearly twenty years since we've met? Or do you find cold reminiscences indigestible?

VENTNOR. On the contrary, I've come to ask you for a dish of them—we'll warm them up together. You're my first visit.

MRS. DALE. How perfect of you! So few men visit their women friends in chronological order; or at least they generally do it the other way round, beginning with the present day and working back—if there's time—to prehistoric woman.

VENTNOR. But when prehistoric woman has become historic woman—?

MRS. DALE. Oh, it's the reflection of my glory that has guided you here, then?

VENTNOR. It's a spirit in my feet that has led me, at the first opportunity, to the most delightful spot I know.

MRS. DALE. Oh, the first opportunity—!

VENTNOR. I might have seen you very often before; but never just in the right way.

MRS. DALE. Is this the right way?

VENTNOR. It depends on you to make it so.

MRS. DALE. What a responsibility! What shall I do?

VENTNOR. Talk to me—make me think you're a little glad to see me; give me some tea and a cigarette; and say you're out to everyone else.

MRS. DALE. Is that all? (*She hands him a cup of tea.*) The cigarettes are at your elbow— And do you think I shouldn't have been glad to see you before?

VENTNOR. No; I think I should have been too glad to see *you.*

MRS. DALE. Dear me, what precautions! I hope you always wear galoshes when it looks like rain and never by any chance expose yourself to a draft. But I had an idea that poets courted the emotions—

VENTNOR. Do novelists?

MRS. DALE. If you ask *me*—on paper!

VENTNOR. Just so; that's safest. My best things about the sea have been written on shore. (*He looks at her thoughtfully.*) But it wouldn't have suited us in the old days, would it?

MRS. DALE (*sighing*). When we were real people!

VENTNOR. Real people?

MRS. DALE. Are *you*, now? I died years ago. What you see before you is a figment of the reporter's brain—a monster manufactured out of newspaper paragraphs, with ink in its veins. A keen sense of copyright is *my* nearest approach to an emotion.

VENTNOR (*sighing*). Ah, well, yes—as you say, we're public property.

MRS. DALE. If one shared equally with the public! But the last shred of my identity is gone.

VENTNOR. Most people would be glad to part with theirs on such terms. I have followed your work with immense interest. *Immolation* is a masterpiece. I read it last summer when it first came out.

MRS. DALE (*with a shade less warmth*). *Immolation* has been out three years.

VENTNOR. Oh, by Jove—no? Surely not—But one is so overwhelmed—one loses count. (*Reproachfully.*) Why have you never sent me your books?

MRS. DALE. For that very reason.

VENTNOR. (*deprecatingly*). You know I didn't mean it for you! And *my* first book—do you remember—was dedicated to you.

MRS. DALE. *Silver Trumpets*—

VENTNOR (*much interested*). Have you a copy still, by any chance? The first edition, I mean? Mine was stolen years ago. Do you think you could put your hand on it?

MRS. DALE (*taking a small shabby book from the table at her side*). It's here.

VENTNOR (*eagerly*). May I have it? Ah, thanks. This is *very* interesting. The last copy sold in London for £40, and they tell me the next will fetch twice as much. It's quite *introuvable*.

MRS. DALE. I know that. (*A pause. She takes the book from him, opens it, and reads, half to herself*—)

How much we two have seen together,
Of other eyes unwist,
Dear as in days of leafless weather
The willow's saffron mist,

Strange as the hour when Hesper swings
A-sea in beryl green,
While overhead on dalliant wings
The daylight hangs serene,

And thrilling as a meteor's fall
Through depths of lonely sky,
When each to each two watchers call:
I saw it!—So did I.

VENTNOR. Thin, thin—the troubadour tinkle. Odd how little promise there is in first volumes!

MRS. DALE (*with irresistible emphasis*). I thought there was a distinct promise in this!

VENTNOR (*seeing his mistake*). Ah—the one you would never let me fulfill? (*Sentimentally.*) How inexorable you were! You never dedicated a book to *me.*

MRS. DALE. I hadn't begun to write when we were—dedicating things to each other.

VENTNOR. Not for the public—but you wrote for me; and, wonderful as you are, you've never written anything since that I care for half as much as—

MRS. DALE (*interested*). Well?

VENTNOR. Your letters.

MRS. DALE (*in a changed voice*). My letters—do you remember them?

VENTNOR. When I don't, I reread them.

MRS. DALE (*incredulous*). You have them still?

VENTNOR (*unguardedly*). You haven't mine, then?

MRS. DALE (*playfully*). Oh, *you* were a celebrity already. Of course I kept them! (*Smiling.*) Think what they are worth now! I always keep them locked up in my safe over there. (*She indicates a cabinet.*)

VENTNOR (*after a pause*). I always carry yours with me.

MRS. DALE (*laughing*). You—

VENTNOR. Wherever I go. (*A longer pause. She looks at him fixedly.*) I have them with me now.

MRS. DALE (*agitated*). You—have them with you—now?

VENTNOR (*embarrassed*). Why not? One never knows—

MRS. DALE. Never knows—?

VENTNOR (*humorously*). Gad—when the bank examiner may come around. You forget I'm a married man.

MRS. DALE. Ah—yes.

VENTNOR (*sits down beside her*). I speak to you as I couldn't to anyone else—without deserving a kicking. You know how it all came about. (*A pause.*) You'll bear witness that it wasn't till you denied me all hope—

MRS. DALE (*a little breathless*). Yes, yes—

VENTNOR. Till you sent me from you—

MRS. DALE. It's so easy to be heroic when one is young!

One doesn't realize how long life is going to last afterward. (*Musing.*) Nor what weary work it is gathering up the fragments.

VENTNOR. But the time comes when one sends for the china-mender, and has the bits riveted together, and turns the cracked side to the wall—

MRS. DALE. And denies that the article was ever damaged?

VENTNOR. Eh? Well, the great thing, you see, is to keep one's self out of reach of the housemaid's brush. (*A pause.*) If you're married you can't—always. (*Smiling.*) Don't you hate to be taken down and dusted?

MRS. DALE (*with intention*). You forget how long ago my husband died. It's fifteen years since I've been an object of interest to anybody but the public.

VENTNOR (*smiling*). The only one of your admirers to whom you've ever given the least encouragement!

MRS. DALE. Say rather the most easily pleased!

VENTNOR. Or the only one you cared to please?

MRS. DALE. Ah, you *haven't* kept my letters!

VENTNOR (*gravely*). Is that a challenge? Look here, then! (*He draws a packet from his pocket and holds it out to her.*)

MRS. DALE (*taking the packet and looking at him earnestly*). Why have you brought me these?

VENTNOR. I didn't bring them; they came because I came—that's all. (*Tentatively.*) Are we unwelcome?

MRS. DALE (*who has undone the packet and does not appear to hear him*). The very first I ever wrote you—the day after we met at the concert. How on earth did you happen to keep it? (*She glances over it.*) How perfectly absurd! Well, it's not a compromising document.

VENTNOR. I'm afraid none of them are.

MRS. DALE (*quickly*). Is it to that they owe their immunity? Because one could leave them about like safety matches?—Ah, here's another I remember—I wrote that the day after we went skating together for the first time. (*She reads it slowly.*) How odd! How *very* odd!

VENTNOR. What?

MRS. DALE. Why, it's the most curious thing—I had a letter of this kind to do the other day, in the novel I'm at work on now—the letter of a woman who is just—just beginning—

VENTNOR. Yes—just beginning—?

MRS. DALE. And, do you know, I find the best phrase in it, the phrase I somehow regarded as the fruit of—well, of all my subsequent discoveries—is simply plagiarized, word for word, from this!

VENTNOR (*eagerly*). I told you so! You were all there!

MRS. DALE (*critically*). But the rest of it's poorly done—very poorly. (*Reads the letter over*). H'm—-I didn't know how to leave off. It takes me forever to get out of the door.

VENTNOR (*gayly*). Perhaps I was there to prevent you! (*After a pause.*) I wonder what I said in return?

MRS. DALE (*interested*). Shall we look? (*She rises.*) Shall we—really? I have them all here, you know. (*She goes toward the cabinet.*)

VENTNOR (*following her with repressed eagerness*). Oh—all!

MRS. DALE (*throws open the door of the cabinet, revealing a number of packets*). Don't you believe me now?

VENTNOR. Good heavens! How I must have repeated myself! But then you were so very deaf.

MRS. DALE (*takes out a packet and returns to her seat. Ventnor extends an impatient hand for the letters*). No—no; wait! I want to find your answer to the one I was just reading. (*After a pause.*) Here it is—yes, I thought so!

VENTNOR. What did you think?

MRS. DALE (*triumphantly*). I thought it was the one in which you quoted *Epipsychidion*—

VENTNOR. Mercy! Did I *quote* things? I don't wonder you were cruel.

MRS. DALE. Ah, and here's the other—the one I—the one I didn't answer—for a long time. Do you remember?

VENTNOR (*with emotion*). Do I remember? I wrote it the morning after we heard *Isolde*—

MRS. DALE (*disappointed*). No—no. *That* wasn't the one I didn't answer! Here—this is the one I mean.

VENTNOR (*takes it curiously*). Ah—h'm—this is very like unrolling a mummy—(*he glances at her*)—with a live grain of wheat in it, perhaps?—Oh, by Jove!

MRS. DALE. What?

VENTNOR. Why, this is the one I made a sonnet out of afterward! By Jove, I'd forgotten where that idea came from. You may know the lines perhaps? They're in the fourth volume of my *Complete Edition*—It's the thing beginning

Love came to me with unrelenting eyes—

one of my best, I rather fancy. Of course, here it's very crudely put—the values aren't brought out—ah! this touch is good though—very good. H'm, I dare say there might be other material. (*He glances toward the cabinet.*)

MRS. DALE (*dryly*). The live grain of wheat, as you said!

VENTNOR. Ah, well—my first harvest was sown on rocky ground—*now* I plant for the fowls of the air. (*Rising and walking toward the cabinet.*) When can I come and carry off all this rubbish?

MRS. DALE. Carry it off?

VENTNOR (*embarrassed*). My dear lady, surely between you and me explicitness is a burden. You must see that these letters of ours can't be left to take their chance like an ordinary correspondence—you said yourself we were public property.

MRS. DALE. To take their chance? Do you suppose that, in my keeping, your letters take any chances? (*Suddenly.*) Do mine—in yours?

VENTNOR (*still more embarrassed*). Helen—! (*He takes a turn through the room.*) You force me to remind you that you and I are differently situated—that in a moment of madness I sacrificed the only right you ever gave me—the right to love you better than any other woman in the world. (*A pause. She says nothing and he continues, with increasing difficulty—*) You asked me just now why I carried your letters about with me—kept them, literally, in my own hands. Well, suppose it's to be sure of their not falling into someone else's?

MRS. DALE. Oh!

VENTNOR (*throws himself into a chair*). For God's sake don't pity me!

MRS. DALE (*after a long pause*). Am I dull—or are you trying to say that you want to give me back my letters?

VENTNOR (*starting up*). I? Give you back—? God forbid! Your letters? Not for the world! The only thing I have left! But you can't dream that in *my* hands—

MRS. DALE (*suddenly*). You want yours, then?

VENTNOR (*repressing his eagerness*). My dear friend, if I'd ever dreamed that you'd kept them—?

MRS. DALE (*accusingly*). You *do* want them. (*A pause. He makes a deprecatory gesture.*) Why should they be less safe with me than mine with you? I never forfeited the right to keep them.

VENTNOR (*after another pause*). It's compensation enough, almost, to have you reproach me! (*He moves nearer to her, but she makes no response.*) You forget that I've forfeited *all* my rights—even that of letting you keep my letters.

MRS. DALE. You *do* want them! (*She rises, throws all the letters into the cabinet, locks the door and puts the key in her pocket.*) There's my answer.

VENTNOR. Helen—!

MRS. DALE. Ah, I paid dearly enough for the right to keep them, and I mean to! (*She turns to him passionately.*) Have you ever asked yourself how I paid for it? With what months and years of solitude, what indifference to flattery, what resistance to affection?—Oh, don't smile because I said affection, and not love. Affection's a warm cloak in cold weather; and I *have* been cold; and I shall keep on growing colder! Don't talk to me about living in the hearts of my readers! We both know what kind of a domicile that is. Why, before long I shall become a classic! Bound in sets and kept on the top bookshelf—brr, doesn't that sound freezing? I foresee the day when I shall be as lonely as an Etruscan museum! (*She breaks into a laugh.*) That's what I've paid for the right to keep your letters. (*She holds out her hand.*) And now give me mine.

VENTNOR. Yours?

MRS. DALE (*haughtily*). Yes; I claim them.

VENTNOR (*in the same tone*). On what ground?

MRS. DALE. Hear the man!—Because I wrote them, of course.

VENTNOR. But it seems to me that—under your inspiration, I admit—I also wrote mine.

MRS. DALE. Oh, I don't dispute their authenticity—it's yours I deny!

VENTNOR. Mine?

MRS. DALE. You voluntarily ceased to be the man who wrote me those letters—you've admitted as much. You traded paper for flesh and blood. I don't dispute your wisdom—only you must hold to your bargain! The letters are *all* mine.

VENTNOR (*groping between two tones*). Your arguments are as convincing as ever. (*He hazards a faint laugh.*) You're a marvelous dialectician—but, if we're going to settle the matter in the spirit of an arbitration treaty, why, there are accepted conventions in such cases. It's an odious way to put it, but since you won't help me, one of them is—

MRS. DALE. One of them is—?

VENTNOR. That it is usual—that technically, I mean, the letter—belongs to its writer—

MRS. DALE (*after a pause*). Such letters as *these*?

VENTNOR. Such letters especially—

MRS. DALE. But you couldn't have written them if I hadn't—been willing to read them. Surely there's more of myself in them than of you.

VENTNOR. Surely there's nothing in which a man puts more of himself than in his love letters!

MRS. DALE (*with emotion*). But a woman's love letters are like her child. They belong to her more than to anybody else—

VENTNOR. And a man's?

MRS. DALE (*with sudden violence*). Are all he risks!—There, take them. (*She flings the key of the cabinet at his feet and sinks into a chair.*)

VENTNOR (*starts as though to pick up the key; then approaches and bends over her*). Helen—oh, Helen!

MRS. DALE (*she yields her hands to him, murmuring:*) Paul! (*Suddenly she straightens herself and draws back illuminated.*) What a fool I am! I see it all now. You want them for your memoirs!

VENTNOR (*disconcerted*). Helen—

MRS. DALE (*agitated*). Come, come—the rule is to unmask when the signal's given! You want them for your memoirs.

VENTNOR (*with a forced laugh*). What makes you think so?

MRS. DALE (*triumphantly*). Because *I* want them for mine!

VENTNOR (*in a changed tone*). Ah—. (*He moves away from her and leans against the mantelpiece. She remains seated, with her eyes fixed on him.*)

MRS. DALE. I wonder I didn't see it sooner. Your reasons were lame enough.

VENTNOR (*ironically*). Yours were masterly. You're the more accomplished actor of the two. I was completely deceived.

MRS. DALE. Oh, I'm a novelist. I can keep up that sort of thing for five hundred pages!

VENTNOR. I congratulate you. (*A pause.*)

MRS. DALE (*moving to her seat behind the tea table*). I've never offered you any tea. (*She bends over the kettle.*) Why don't you take your letters?

VENTNOR. Because you've been clever enough to make it impossible for me. (*He picks up the key and hands it to her. Then abruptly*)—*Was* it all acting—just now?

MRS. DALE. By what right do you ask?

VENTNOR. By right of renouncing my claim to my letters. Keep them—and tell me.

MRS. DALE. I give you back your claim—and I refuse to tell you.

VENTNOR (*sadly*). Ah, Helen, if you deceived me, you deceived yourself also.

MRS. DALE. What does it matter, now that we're both undeceived? I played a losing game, that's all.

VENTNOR. Why losing—since all the letters are yours?

MRS. DALE. The letters? (*Slowly.*) I'd forgotten the letters—

VENTNOR (*exultant*). Ah, I knew you'd end by telling me the truth!

MRS. DALE. The truth? Where *is* the truth? (*Half to herself.*) I thought I was lying when I began—but the lies turned into truth as I uttered them! (*She looks at Ventnor.*) I *did* want your letters for my memoirs—I *did* think I'd kept them for that purpose—and I wanted to get mine back for the same reason—but now (*she puts out her hand and picks *up some of her letters, which are lying scattered on the table near her*)—how fresh they seem, and how they take me back to the time when we lived instead of writing about life!

VENTNOR (*smiling*). The time when we didn't prepare our impromptu effects beforehand and copyright our remarks about the weather!

MRS. DALE. Or keep our epigrams in cold storage and our adjectives under lock and key!

VENTNOR. When our emotions weren't worth ten cents a word, and a signature wasn't an autograph. Ah, Helen, after all, there's nothing like the exhilaration of spending one's capital!

MRS. DALE. Or wasting it, you mean. (*She points to the letters.*) Do you suppose we could have written a word of these if we'd known we were putting our dreams out at interest? (*She sits musing, with her eyes on the fire, and he watches her in silence.*) Paul, do you remember the deserted garden we sometimes used to walk in?

VENTNOR. The old garden with the high wall at the end of the village street? The garden with the ruined box borders and the broken-down arbor? Why, I remember every weed in the paths and every patch of moss on the walls!

MRS. DALE. Well—I went back there the other day. The village is immensely improved. There's a new hotel with gas fires, and a trolley in the main street; and the garden has been turned into a public park, where excursionists sit on cast-iron benches admiring the statue of an Abolitionist.

VENTNOR. An Abolitionist—how appropriate!

MRS. DALE. And the man who sold the garden has made a fortune that he doesn't know how to spend—

VENTNOR (*rising impulsively*). Helen, (*he approaches and lays his hands on her letters*), let's sacrifice our fortune and keep the excursionists out!

MRS. DALE (*with a responsive movement*). Paul, do you really mean it?

VENTNOR (*gayly*). Mean it? Why, I feel like a landed proprietor already! It's more than a garden—it's a park.

MRS. DALE. It's more than a park, it's a world—as long as we keep it to ourselves!

VENTNOR. Ah, yes—even the pyramids look small when

one sees a Cook's tourist on top of them! (*He takes the key from the table, unlocks the cabinet and brings out his letters, which he lays beside hers.*) Shall we burn the key to our garden?

MRS. DALE. Ah, then it will indeed be boundless! (*Watching him while he throws the letters into the fire.*)

VENTNOR (*turning back to her with a half-sad smile*). But not too big for us to find each other in?

MRS. DALE. Since we shall be the only people there! (*He takes both her hands and they look at each other a moment in silence. Then he goes out by the door to the right. As he reaches the door she takes a step toward him, impulsively; then turning back she leans against the chimneypiece, quietly watching the letters burn.*)

The Descent of Man

When Professor Linyard came back from his holiday in the Maine woods the air of rejuvenation he brought with him was due less to the influences of the climate than to the companionship he had enjoyed on his travels. To Mrs. Linyard's observant eye he had appeared to set out alone; but an invisible traveler had in fact accompanied him, and if his heart beat high it was simply at the pitch of his adventure: for the Professor had eloped with an idea.

No one who has not tried the experiment can divine its exhilaration. Professor Linyard would not have changed places with any hero of romance pledged to a flesh-and-blood abduction. The most fascinating female is apt to be encumbered with luggage and scruples: to take up a good deal of room in the present and overlap inconveniently into the future; whereas an idea can accommodate itself to a single molecule of the brain or expand to the circumference of the horizon. The Professor's companion had to the utmost this quality of adaptability. As the express train whirled him away from the somewhat inelastic circle of Mrs. Linyard's affections, his idea seemed to be sitting opposite him, and their eyes met every moment or two in a glance of joyous complicity; yet when a friend of the family presently joined him and began to talk about college matters, the idea slipped out of sight in a flash, and the Professor would have had no difficulty in proving that he was alone.

But if, from the outset, he found his idea the most agreeable of fellow travelers, it was only in the aromatic solitude of the woods that he tasted the full savor of his adventure. There, during the long cool August days, lying full length on the pine needles and gazing up into the sky, he would meet the eyes of his companion bending over him like a nearer heaven. And what eyes they were!—clear yet unfathomable, bubbling with inexhaustible laughter, yet drawing their freshness and sparkle from the central depths of thought! To a man who for twenty years had faced an eye reflecting the commonplace with perfect accuracy, these escapes into the inscrutable had always been peculiarly inviting; but hitherto the Professor's mental infidelities had been restricted by an unbroken and relentless domesticity. Now, for the first time since his marriage, chance had given him six weeks to himself, and he was coming home with his lungs full of liberty.

It must not be inferred that the Professor's domestic relations were defective: they were in fact so complete that it was almost impossible to get away from them. It is the happy husbands who are really in bondage; the little rift within the lute is often a passage to freedom. Marriage had given the Professor exactly what he had sought in it: a comfortable lining to life. The impossibility of rising to sentimental crises had made him scrupulously careful not to shirk the practical obligations of the bond. He took as it were a sociological view of his case, and modestly regarded himself as a brick in that foundation on which the state is supposed to rest. Perhaps if Mrs. Linyard had cared about entomology, or had taken sides in the war over the transmission of acquired characteristics, he might have had a less impersonal notion of marriage; but he was unconscious of any deficiency in their relation, and if consulted would probably have declared that he didn't want any woman bothering with his beetles. His real life had always lain in the universe of thought, in that enchanted region which, to those who have lingered there, comes to have so much more color and substance than the painted curtain hanging before it. The Professor's particular veil of Maia was a narrow strip of homespun woven in a monotonous pattern; but he had only to lift it to step into an empire.

This unseen universe was thronged with the most seductive shapes: the Professor moved Sultan-like through a seraglio of ideas. But of all the lovely apparitions that wove their spells about him, none had ever worn quite so persuasive an aspect as this latest favorite. For the others were mostly rather grave companions, serious-minded and elevating enough to have passed muster in a Ladies' Debating Club; but this new fancy of the Professor's was simply one embodied laugh. It was, in other words, the smile of relaxation at the end of a long day's toil: the flash of irony which the laborious mind projects, irresistibly, over labor conscientiously performed. The Professor had always been a hard worker. If he was an indulgent friend to his ideas he was also a stern taskmaster to them. For, in addition to their other duties, they had to support his family: to pay the butcher and baker, and provide for Jack's schooling and Millicent's dresses. The Professor's household was a modest one, yet it tasked his ideas to keep it up to his wife's standard. Mrs. Linyard was not an exacting wife, and she took enough pride in her husband's attainments to pay for her honors by turning Millicent's dresses and darning Jack's socks and going to the College receptions year after year in the same black silk with shiny seams. It consoled her to see an occasional mention of Professor Linyard's remarkable monograph on the Ethical Reactions of the Infusoria, or an allusion to his investigations into the Unconscious Cerebration of the Amoeba.

Still there were moments when the healthy indifference of Jack and Millicent reacted to the maternal sympathies; when Mrs. Linyard would have made her husband a railway director, if by this transformation she might have increased her boy's allowance and given her daughter a new hat, or a set of furs such as the other girls were wearing. Of such moments of rebellion the Professor himself was not wholly unconscious. He could not indeed understand why anyone should want a new hat; and as to an allowance, he had had much less money at college than Jack, and had yet managed to buy a microscope and collect a few "specimens"; while Jack was free from such expensive tastes! But the Professor did not let his want of sympathy interfere with the discharge of his paternal obligations. He worked hard to keep the wants of his family gratified, and it was precisely in the endeavor to attain this end that he at length broke down and had to cease from work altogether.

To cease from work was not to cease from thought of it; and in the unwonted pause from effort the Professor found himself taking a general survey of the field he had traveled. At last it was possible to lift his nose from the loom, to step a moment in front of the tapestry he had been weaving. From this first inspection of the pattern so long wrought over from behind, it was natural to glance a little farther and seek its reflection in the public eye. It was not indeed of his special task that he thought in this connection. He was but one of the great army of weavers at work among the threads of that cosmic woof; and what he sought was the general impression their labor had produced.

When Professor Linyard first plied his microscope, the audience of the man of science had been composed of a few fellow students, sympathetic or hostile as their habits of mind predetermined, but versed in the jargon of the profession and familiar with the point of departure. In the intervening quarter of a century, however, this little group had been swallowed up in a larger public. Everyone now read scientific books and expressed an opinion on them. The ladies and the clergy had taken them up first; now they had passed to the schoolroom and the kindergarten. Daily life was regulated on scientific principles; the daily papers had their "Scientific Jottings"; nurses passed examinations in hygienic science, and babies were fed and dandled according to the new psychology.

The very fact that scientific investigation still had, to some minds, the flavor of heterodoxy, gave it a perennial interest. The mob had broken down the walls of tradition to batten in the orchard of forbidden knowledge. The inaccessible goddess whom the Professor had served in his youth now offered her charms in the market place. And yet it was not the same goddess, after all, but a pseudo-science masquerading in the garb of the real divinity. This false goddess had her ritual and her literature. She had her sacred books, written by false priests and sold by millions to the faithful. In the most successful of these works, ancient dogma and modern discovery were depicted in a close embrace under the limelights of a hazy transcendentalism; and the tableau never failed of its effect. Some of the books designed on this popular model had lately fallen into the Professor's hands, and they filled him with mingled rage and hilarity. The rage soon died: he came to regard this mass of pseudo-literature as protecting the truth from desecration. But the hilarity remained, and flowed into the form of his idea. And the idea—the divine incomparable idea—was simply that he should avenge his goddess by satirizing her false interpreters. He would write a skit on the "popular" scientific book; he would so heap platitude on platitude, fallacy on fallacy, false analogy on false analogy, so use his superior knowledge to abound in the sense of the ignorant, that even the gross crowd would join in the laugh against its augurs. And the laugh should be something more than the distention of mental muscles; it should be the trumpet blast bringing down the walls of ignorance, or at least the little stone striking the giant between the eyes.

✥ II ✥

THE Professor, on presenting his card, had imagined that it would command prompt access to the publisher's sanctuary; but the young man who read his name was not moved to immediate action. It was clear that Professor Linyard of Hillbridge University was not a specific figure to the purveyors of popular literature. But the publisher was an old friend; and when the card had finally drifted to his office on the languid tide of routine he came forth at once to greet his visitor.

The warmth of his welcome convinced the Professor that he had been right in bringing his manuscript to Ned Harviss. He and Harviss had been at Hillbridge together, and the future publisher had been one of the wildest spirits in that band of college outlaws which yearly turns out so many inoffensive citizens and kind husbands and fathers. The Professor knew the taming qualities of life. He was aware that many of his most reckless comrades had been transformed into prudent capitalists or cowed wage earners; but he was almost sure that he could count on Harviss. So rare a sense of irony, so keen a perception of relative values, could hardly have been blunted even by twenty years' intercourse with the obvious.

The publisher's appearance was a little disconcerting. He looked as if he had been fattened on popular fiction; and his fat was full of optimistic creases. The Professor seemed to see him bowing into the office a long train of spotless heroines laden with the maiden tribute of the hundred-thousandth volume.

Nevertheless, his welcome was reassuring. He did not disown his early enormities, and capped his visitor's tentative allusions by such flagrant references to the past that the Professor produced his manuscript without a scruple.

"What—you don't mean to say you've been doing something in our line?"

The Professor smiled. "You publish scientific books sometimes, don't you?"

The publisher's optimistic creases relaxed a little. "H'm—it all depends—I'm afraid you're a little *too* scientific for us. We have a big sale for scientific breakfast foods, but nor for the concentrated essences. In your case, of course, I should be delighted to stretch a point; but in your own interest I ought to tell you that perhaps one of the educational houses would do you better."

The Professor leaned back, still smiling luxuriously.

"Well, look it over—I rather think you'll take it."

"Oh, we'll *take* it, as I say; but the terms might not—"

"No matter about the terms—"

The publisher threw his head back with a laugh. "I had no idea that science was so profitable; we find our popular novelists are the hardest hands at a bargain."

"Science is disinterested," the Professor corrected him. "And I have a fancy to have you publish this thing."

"That's immensely good of you, my dear fellow. Of course your name goes with a certain public—and I rather like the originality of our bringing out a work so out of our line. I dare say it may boom us both." His creases deepened at the thought, and he shone encouragingly on the Professor's leave-taking.

Within a fortnight, a line from Harviss recalled the Professor to town. He had been looking forward with immense zest to his second meeting; Harviss' college roar was in his tympanum, and he could already hear the protracted chuckle which would follow his friend's progress through the manuscript. He was proud of the adroitness with which he had kept his secret from Harviss, had maintained to the last the pretense of a serious work, in order to give the keener edge to his reader's enjoyment. Not since undergraduate days had the Professor tasted such a draught of pure fun as his anticipations now poured for him.

This time his card brought instant admission. He was bowed into the office like a successful novelist, and Harviss grasped him with both hands.

"Well—do you mean to take it?" he asked with a lingering coquetry.

"Take it? Take it, my dear fellow? It's in press already—you'll excuse my not waiting to consult you? There will be no difficulty about terms, I assure you, and we had barely time to catch the autumn market. My dear Linyard, why didn't you *tell* me?" His voice sank to a reproachful solemnity, and he pushed forward his own armchair.

The Professor dropped into it with a chuckle. "And miss the joy of letting you find out?"

"Well—it *was* a joy." Harviss held out a box of his best cigars. "I don't know when I've had a bigger sensation. It was so deucedly unexpected—and, my dear fellow, you've brought it so exactly to the right shop."

"I'm glad to hear you say so," said the Professor modestly.

Harviss laughed in rich appreciation. "I don't suppose you had a doubt of it; but of course I was quite unprepared. And it's so extraordinarily out of your line—"

The Professor took off his glasses and rubbed them with a slow smile.

"Would you have thought it so—at college?"

Harviss stared. "At college? Why, you were the most iconoclastic devil—"

There was a perceptible pause. The Professor restored his glasses and looked at his friend. "Well—?" he said simply.

"Well—?" echoed the other, still staring. "Ah—I see; you mean that that's what explains it. The swing of the pendulum, and so forth. Well, I admit it's not an uncommon phenomenon. I've conformed myself, for example, most of our crowd have, I believe; but somehow I hadn't expected it of you."

The close observer might have detected a faint sadness under the official congratulation of his tone; but the Professor was too amazed to have an ear for such fine shades.

"Expected it of me? Expected what of me?" he gasped. "What in heaven do you think this thing is?" And he struck his fist on the manuscript which lay between them.

Harviss had recovered his optimistic creases. He rested a benevolent eye on the document.

"Why, your apologia—your confession of faith, I should call it. You surely must have seen which way you were going? You can't have written it in your sleep?"

"Oh, no, I was wide awake enough," said the Professor faintly.

"Well, then, why are you staring at me as if I were *not*?" Harviss leaned forward to lay a reassuring hand on his visitor's worn coat sleeve. "Don't mistake me, my dear Linyard. Don't fancy there was the least unkindness in my allusion to your change of front. What is growth but the shifting of the standpoint? Why should a man be expected to look at life with the same eyes at twenty and—at our age? It never occurred to me that you could feel the least delicacy in admitting that you have come round a little—have fallen into line, so to speak."

But the Professor had sprung up as if to give his lungs more room to expand; and from them there issued a laugh which shook the editorial rafters.

"Oh, Lord, oh, Lord—is it really as good as that?"

Harviss had glanced instinctively toward the electric bell on his desk; he was evidently prepared for an emergency.

"My dear fellow—" he began in a soothing voice.

"Oh, let me have my laugh out, do," implored the Professor. "I'll—I'll quiet down in a minute; you needn't ring for the young man." He dropped into his chair again and grasped its arms to steady his shaking. "This is the best laugh I've had since college," he brought out between his paroxysms. And then, suddenly, he sat up with a groan. "But if it's as good as that it's a failure!" he exclaimed.

Harviss, stiffening a little, examined the tip of his cigar. "My dear Linyard," he said at length. "I don't understand a word you're saying."

The Professor succumbed to a fresh access, from the vortex of which he managed to fling out, "But that's the very core of the joke!"

Harviss looked at him resignedly. "What is?"

"Why, your not seeing—your not understanding—"

"Not understanding *what*?"

"Why, what the book is meant to be." His laughter subsided again and he sat gazing thoughtfully at the publisher. "Unless it means," he wound up, "that I've overshot the mark."

"If I am the mark, you certainly have," said Harviss, with a glance at the clock.

The Professor caught the glance and interpreted it. "The book is a skit," he said, rising.

The other stared. "A skit? It's not serious, you mean?"

"Not to me—but it seems you've taken it so."

"You never told me—" began the publisher in a ruffled tone.

"No, I never told you," said the Professor.

Harviss sat staring at the manuscript between them. "I don't pretend to be up on such recondite forms of humor," he said still stiffly. "Of course you address yourself to a very small class of readers."

"Oh, infinitely small," admitted the Professor, extending his hand toward the manuscript.

Harviss appeared to be pursuing his own train of thought. "That is," he continued, "if you insist on an ironical interpretation."

"If I insist on it—what do you mean?"

The publisher smiled faintly. "Well—isn't the book susceptible of another? If *I read it without seeing*—"

"Well?" murmured the other, fascinated.

"—Why shouldn't the rest of the world?" declared Harviss boldly. "I represent the Average Reader—that's my business, that's what I've been training myself to do for the last twenty years. It's a mission like another—the thing is to do it thoroughly; not to cheat and compromise. I know fellows who are publishers in business hours and dilettantes the rest of the time. Well, they never succeed: convictions are just as necessary in business as in religion. But that's not the point—I was going to say that if you'll let me handle this book as a genuine thing I'll guarantee to make it go."

The Professor stood motionless, his hand still on the manuscript.

"A genuine thing?" he echoed.

"A serious piece of work—the expression of your convictions. I tell you there's nothing the public likes as much as convictions—they'll always follow a man who believes in his own ideas. And this book is just on the line on popular interest. You've got hold of a big thing. It's full of hope and enthusiasm: it's written in the religious key. There are passages in it that would do splendidly in a Birthday Book—things that popular preachers would quote in their sermons. If you'd wanted to catch a big public you couldn't have gone about it in a better way. The thing's perfect for my purpose—I wouldn't let you alter a word of it. It will sell like a popular novel if you'll let me handle it in the right way."

✣ III ✣

WHEN the Professor left Harviss' office the manuscript remained behind. He thought he had been taken by the huge irony of the situation—by the enlarged, circumference of the joke. In its original form, as Harviss had said, the book would have addressed itself to a very limited circle: now it would include the world. The elect would understand; the crowd would not; and his work would thus serve a double purpose. And, after all, nothing was changed in the situation; not a word of the book was to be altered. The change was merely in the publisher's point of view, and in the "tip" he was to give the reviewers. The professor had only to hold his tongue and look serious.

These arguments found a strong reinforcement in the large premium which expressed Harviss' sense of his opportunity. As a satire the book would have brought its author nothing; in fact, its cost would have come out of his own pocket, since, as Harviss assured him, no publisher would have risked taking it. But as a profession of faith, as the recantation of an eminent biologist, whose leanings had hitherto been supposed to be toward a cold determinism, it would bring in a steady income to author and publisher. The offer found the Professor in a moment of financial perplexity. His illness, his unwonted holiday, the necessity of postponing a course of well-paid lectures, had combined to diminish his resources; and when Harviss offered him an advance of a thousand dollars the esoteric savor of the joke became irresistible. It was still as a joke that he persisted in regarding the transaction; and though he had pledged himself not to betray the real intent of the book, he held *in petto* the notion of some day being able to take the public into his confidence. As for the initiated, they would know at once: and however long a face he pulled his colleagues would see the tongue in his cheek. Meanwhile it fortunately happened that, even if the book should achieve the kind of triumph prophesied by Harviss, it would not appreciably injure its author's professional standing. Professor Linyard was known chiefly as a microscopist. On the structure and habits of a certain class of coleoptera he was the most distinguished living authority; but none save his intimate friends knew what generalizations on the destiny of man he had drawn from these special studies. He might have published a treatise on the Filioque without shaking the confidence of those on whose approval his reputation rested; and moreover he was sustained by the thought that one glance at his book would let them into its secret. In fact, so sure was he of this that he wondered the astute Harviss had cared to risk such speedy exposure. But Harviss had probably reflected that even in this reverberating age the opinions of the laboratory do not easily reach the street; and the Professor, at any rate, was not bound to offer advice on this point.

The determining cause of his consent was the fact that the book was already in press. The Professor knew little about the workings of the press, but the phrase gave him a sense of finality, of having been caught himself in the toils of that mysterious engine. If he had had time to think the matter over his scruples might have dragged him back; but his conscience was eased by the futility of resistance.

✣ IV ✣

MRS. LINYARD did not often read the papers; and there was therefore a special significance in her approaching her husband one evening after dinner with a copy of the *New York Investigator* in her hand. Her expression lent solemnity to the act: Mrs. Linyard had a limited but distinctive set of expressions, and she now looked as she did when the President of the University came to dine.

"You didn't tell me of this, Samuel," she said in a slightly tremulous voice.

"Tell you of what?" returned the Professor, reddening to the margin of his baldness.

"That you had published a book—I might never have heard of it if Mrs. Pease hadn't brought me the paper."

Her husband rubbed his eyeglasses and groaned. "Oh, you would have heard of it," he said gloomily.

Mrs. Linyard stared. "Did you wish to keep it from me, Samuel?" And as he made no answer, she added with irresistible pride: "Perhaps you don't know what beautiful things have been said about it."

He took the paper with a reluctant hand. "Has Pease been saying beautiful things about it?"

"The Professor? Mrs. Pease didn't say he had mentioned it."

The author heaved a sigh of relief. His book, as Harviss had prophesied, had caught the autumn market: had caught and captured it. The publisher had conducted the campaign like an experienced strategist. He had completely surrounded the enemy. Every newspaper, every periodical, held in ambush an advertisement of *The Vital Thing*. Weeks in advance the great commander had begun to form his lines of attack. Allusions to the remarkable significance of the coming work had appeared first in the scientific and literary reviews, spreading thence to the supplements of the daily journals. Not a moment passed without a quickening touch to the public consciousness: seventy millions of people were forced to remember at least once a day that Professor Linyard's book was on the verge of appearing. Slips emblazoned with the question: *Have you read "The Vital Thing"?*

fell from the pages of popular novels and whitened the floors of crowded streetcars. The query, in large lettering, assaulted the traveler at the railway bookstall, confronted him on the walls of elevated stations, and seemed, in its ascending scale, about to supplant the interrogations as to sapolio and stove polish which animate our rural scenery.

On the day of publication the Professor had withdrawn to his laboratory. The shriek of the advertisements was in his ears and his one desire was to avoid all knowledge of the event they heralded. A reaction of self-consciousness had set in, and if Harviss' check had sufficed to buy up the first edition of *The Vital Thing* the Professor would gladly have devoted it to that purpose. But the sense of inevitableness gradually subdued him, and he received his wife's copy of the *Investigator* with a kind of impersonal curiosity. The review was a long one, full of extracts: he saw, as he glanced over the latter, how well they would look in a volume of "Selections." The reviewer began by thanking his author "for sounding with no uncertain voice that note of ringing optimism, of faith in man's destiny and the supremacy of good, which has too long been silenced by the whining chorus of a decadent nihilism. . . . It is well," the writer continued, "when such reminders come to us not from the moralist but from the man of science—when from the desiccating atmosphere of the laboratory there rises this glorious cry of faith and reconstruction."

The review was minute and exhaustive. Thanks no doubt to Harviss' diplomacy, it had been given to the *Investigator's* "best man," and the Professor was startled by the bold eye with which his emancipated fallacies confronted him. Under the reviewer's handling they made up admirably as truths, and their author began to understand Harviss' regret that they should be used for any less profitable purpose.

The *Investigator*, as Harviss phrased it, "set the pace," and the other journals followed, finding it easier to let their critical man-of-all-work play a variation of the first reviewer's theme than to secure an expert to "do" the book afresh. But it was evident that the Professor had captured his public, for all the resources of the profession could not, as Harviss gleefully pointed out, have carried the book so straight to the heart of the nation. There was something noble in the way in which Harviss belittled his own share in the achievement, and insisted on the inutility of shoving a book which had started with such headway on.

"All I ask you is to admit that I saw what would happen," he said with a touch of professional pride. "I knew you'd struck the right note—I knew they'd be quoting you from Maine to San Francisco. Good as fiction? It's better—it'll keep going longer."

"Will it?" said the Professor with a slight shudder. he was resigned to an ephemeral triumph, but the thought of the book's persistency frightened him.

"I should say so! Why, you fit in everywhere—science, theology, natural history—and then the all-for-the-best element which is so popular just now. Why, you come right in with the How-to-Relax series, and they sell way up in the millions. And then the book's so full of tenderness—there are such lovely things in it about flowers and children. I didn't know an old Dryasdust like you could have such a lot of sentiment in him. Why, I actually caught myself sniveling over that passage about the snowdrops piercing the frozen earth; and my wife was saying the other day that, since she's read *The Vital Thing*, she begins to think you must write the 'What-Cheer Column,' in the *Inglenook*." He threw back his head with a laugh which ended in the inspired cry: "And, by George, sir, when the thing begins to slow off we'll start somebody writing against it, and that will run us straight up into another hundred thousand."

And as earnest of this belief he drew the Professor a supplementary check.

✥ V ✥

MRS. LINYARD'S knock cut short the importunities of the lady who had been trying to persuade the Professor to be taken by flashlight at his study table for the Christmas number of the *Inglenook*. On this point the Professor had fancied himself impregnable; but the unwonted smile with which he welcomed his wife's intrusion showed that his defenses were weakening.

The lady from the *Inglenook* took the hint with professional promptness, but said brightly, as she snapped the elastic around her notebook: "I shan't let you forget me, Professor."

The groan with which he followed her retreat was interrupted by his wife's question: "Do they pay you for these interviews, Samuel?"

The Professor looked at her with sudden attention. "Not directly," he said, wondering at her expression.

She sank down with a sigh. "Indirectly, then?"

"What is the matter, my dear? I gave you Harviss' second check the other day—"

Her tears arrested him. "Don't be hard on the boy, Samuel! I really believe your success has turned his head."

"The boy—what boy? My success—? Explain yourself, Susan!"

"It's only that Jack has—has borrowed some money—which he can't repay. But you mustn't think him altogether to blame, Samuel. Since the success of your book he has been asked about so much—it's given the children quite a different position. Millicent says that wherever they go the first question asked is, 'Are you any relation to the author of *The Vital Thing?*' Of course we're all very proud of the book; but it entails obligations which you may not have thought of in writing it."

The Professor sat gazing at the letters and newspaper clippings on the study table which he had just successfully defended from the camera of the *Inglenook*. He took up an envelope bearing the name of a popular weekly paper.

"I don't know that the *Inglenook* would help much," he said, "but I suppose this might."

Mrs. Linyard's eyes glowed with maternal avidity.

"What is it, Samuel?"

"A series of 'Scientific Sermons' for the Round-the-Gas-Log column of *The Woman's World*. I believe that journal has a larger circulation than any other weekly, and they pay in proportion."

He had not even asked the extent of Jack's indebtedness. It had been so easy to relieve recent domestic difficulties by the timely production of Harviss' two checks that it now seemed natural to get Mrs. Linyard out of the room by promising further reinforcements. The Professor had indignantly rejected Harviss' suggestion that he should follow up his success by a second volume on the same lines. He had sworn not to lend more than a passive support to the fraud of *The Vital Thing*; but the temptation to free himself from Mrs. Linyard prevailed over his last scruples, and within an hour he was at work on the "Scientific Sermons."

The Professor was not an unkind man. He really enjoyed making his family happy; and it was his own business if his reward for so doing was that it kept them out of his way. But the success of *The Vital Thing* gave him more than this negative satisfaction. It enlarged his own existence and opened new doors into other lives. The Professor, during fifty virtuous years, had been cognizant of only two types of women; the fond and foolish, whom one married, and the earnest and intellectual, whom one did not. Of the two, he infinitely preferred the former, even for conversational purposes. But as a social instrument woman was unknown to him; and it was not till he was drawn into the world on the tide of his literary success that he discovered the deficiencies in his classification of the sex. Then he learned with astonishment of the existence of a third type: the woman who is fond without foolishness and intellectual without earnestness. Not that the Professor inspired, or sought to inspire, sentimental emotions; but he expanded in the warm atmosphere of personal interest which some of his new acquaintances contrived to create about him. It was delightful to talk of serious things in a setting of frivolity, and to be personal without being domestic.

Even in this new world, where all subjects were touched on lightly, and emphasis was the only indelicacy, the Professor found himself constrained to endure an occasional reference to his book. It was unpleasant at first; but gradually he slipped into the habit of hearing it talked of, and grew accustomed to telling pretty women just how "it had first come to him."

Meanwhile the success of the "Scientific Sermons" was facilitating his family relations. His photograph in the *Inglenook,* to which the lady of the notebook had succeeded in appending a vivid interview, carried his fame to circles inaccessible even to *The Vital Thing*; and the Professor found himself the man of the hour. He soon grew used to the functions of the office, and gave out hundred-dollar interviews on every subject, from labor strikes to Babism, with a frequency which reacted agreeably on the domestic exchequer. Presently his head began to figure in the advertising pages of the magazines. Admiring readers learned the name of the only breakfast food in use at his table, of the ink with which "The Vital Thing" had been written, the soap with which the author's hands were washed, and the tissue builder which fortified him for further effort. These confidences endeared the Professor to millions of readers, and his head passed in due course from the magazine and the newspaper to the biscuit tin and the chocolate box.

✤ VI ✤

THE Professor, all the while, was leading a double life. While the author of *The Vital Thing* reaped the fruits of popular approval, the distinguished microscopist continued his laboratory work unheeded save by the few who were engaged in the same line of investigations. His divided allegiance had not hitherto affected the quality of his work: it seemed to him that he returned to the laboratory with greater zest after an afternoon in a drawing room where readings from "The Vital Thing" had alternated with plantation melodies and tea. He had long ceased to concern himself with what his colleagues thought of his literary career. Of the few whom he frequented, none had referred to *The Vital Thing*; and he knew enough of their lives to guess that their silence might as fairly be attributed to indifference as to disapproval. They were intensely interested in the Professor's views on beetles but they really cared very little what he thought of the Almighty.

The Professor entirely shared their feelings, and one of his chief reasons for cultivating the success which accident had bestowed on him, was that it enabled him to command a greater range of appliances for his real work. He had known what it was to lack books and instruments; and *The*

Vital Thing was the magic wand which summoned them to his aid. For some time he had been feeling his way along the edge of a discovery: balancing himself with professional skill on a plank of hypothesis flung across an abyss of uncertainty. The conjecture was the result of years of patient gathering of facts: its corroboration would take months more of comparison and classification. But at the end of the vista victory loomed. The Professor felt within himself that assurance of ultimate justification which, to the man of science, makes a lifetime seem the mere comma between premise and deduction. But he had reached the point where his conjectures required formulation. It was only by giving them expression, by exposing them to the comment and criticism of his associates, that he could test their final value; and this inner assurance was confirmed by the only friend whose confidence he invited.

Professor Pease, the husband of the lady who had opened Mrs. Linyard's eyes to the triumph of *The Vital Thing,* was the repository of her husband's scientific experiences. What he thought of *The Vital Thing* had never been divulged; and he was capable of such vast exclusions that it was quite possible that pervasive work had not yet reached him. In any case, it was not likely to affect his judgment of the author's professional capacity.

"You want to put that all in a book, Linyard," was Professor Pease's conclusion, after listening to the summary of his friend's projected work. "I'm sure you've got hold of something big; but to see it clearly yourself you ought to outline it for others. Take my advice—chuck everything else and get to work tomorrow. It's time you wrote a book, anyhow."

It's time you wrote a book, anyhow! The words smote the Professor with mingled pain and ecstasy: he could have wept over their significance. But his friend's other phrase reminded him with a start of Harviss. "You have got hold of a big thing—" it had been the publisher's first comment on "The Vital Thing." But what a world of meaning lay between the two phrases! It was the world in which the powers who fought for the Professor were destined to wage their final battle; and for the moment he had no doubt of the outcome.

"By George, I'll do it, Pease!" he said, stretching his hand to his friend.

The next day he went to town to see Harviss. He wanted to ask for an advance on the new popular edition of *The Vital Thing*. He had determined to drop a course of supplementary lectures at the University and to give himself up for a year to his book. To do this additional funds were necessary; but thanks to *The Vital Thing* they would be forthcoming.

The publisher received him as cordially as usual; but the response to his demand was not as prompt as his previous experience had entitled him to expect.

"Of course we'll be glad to do what we can for you, Linyard; but the fact is we've decided to give up the idea of the new edition for the present."

"You've given up the new edition?"

"Why, yes—we've done pretty well by *The Vital Thing*, and we're inclined to think it's *your* turn to do something for it now."

The Professor looked at him blankly. "What can I do for it?" he asked—"what *more*" his accent added.

"Why, put a little new life in it by writing something else. The secret of perpetual motion hasn't yet been discovered, you know, and it's one of the laws of literature that books which start with a rush are apt to slow down sooner than the crawlers. We've kept *The Vital Thing* going for eighteen months—but, hang it, it ain't so vital any more. We simply couldn't see our way to a new edition. Oh, I don't say it's dead yet—but it's moribund, and you're the only man who can resuscitate it."

The Professor continued to stare. "I—what can I do about it?" he stammered.

"Do? Why, write another like it—go it one better; you know the trick. The public isn't tired of you by any means; but you want to make yourself heard again before anybody else cuts in. Write another book—write two, and we'll sell them in sets in a box: "The Vital Thing Series." That will take tremendously in the holidays. Try and let us have a new volume by October—I'll be glad to give you a big advance if you'll sign a contract on that."

The Professor sat silent: there was too cruel an irony in the coincidence.

Harviss looked up at him in surprise.

"Well, what's the matter with taking my advice—you're not going out of literature, are you?"

The Professor rose from his chair. "No—I'm going into it," he said simply.

"Going into it?"

"I'm going to write a real book—a serious one."

"Good Lord! Most people think *The Vital Thing* is serious."

"Yes—but I mean something different."

"In your old line—beetles and so forth?"

"Yes," said the Professor solemnly.

Harviss looked at him with equal gravity. "Well, I'm sorry for that," he said, "because it takes you out of our bailiwick. But I suppose you've made enough money out of *The Vital Thing* to permit yourself a little harmless amusement. When you want more cash come back to us—only don't put it off too long, or some other fellow will have stepped into your shoes. Popularity don't keep, you know; and the hotter the success the quicker the commodity perishes."

He leaned back, cheerful and sententious, delivering his axioms with conscious kindliness.

The Professor, who had risen and moved to the door, turned back with a wavering step.

"When did you say another volume would have to be ready?" he faltered.

"I said October—but call it a month later. You don't need any pushing nowadays."

"And—you'd have no objection to letting me have a little advance now? I need some new instruments for my real work."

Harviss extended a cordial hand. "My dear fellow, that's talking—I'll write the check while you wait; and I dare say we can start up the cheap edition of *The Vital Thing* at the same time, if you'll pledge yourself to give us the book by

November. How much?" he asked, poised above his check-book.

In the street, the Professor stood staring about him, uncertain and a little dazed.

"After all, it's only putting it off for six months," he said to himself; "and I can do better work when I get my new instruments."

He smiled and raised his hat to the passing victoria of a lady in whose copy of *The Vital Thing* he had recently written:

Labor est etiam ipsa voluptas.

The Mission of Jane

LETHBURY, SURVEYING his wife across the dinner table, found his transient glance arrested by an indefinable change in her appearance.

"How smart you look! Is that a new gown?" he asked.

Her answering look seemed to deprecate his charging her with the extravagance of wasting a new gown on him, and he now perceived that the change lay deeper than any accident of dress. At the same time, he noticed that she betrayed her consciousness of it by a delicate, almost frightened blush. It was one of the compensations of Mrs. Lethbury's protracted childishness that she still blushed as prettily as at eighteen. Her body had been privileged not to outstrip her mind, and the two, as it seemed to Lethbury, were destined to travel together through an eternity of girlishness.

"I don't know what you mean," she said.

Since she never did, he always wondered at her bringing this out as a fresh grievance against him; but his wonder was unresentful, and he said good-humoredly: "You sparkle so that I thought you had on your diamonds."

She sighed and blushed again.

"It must be," he continued, "that you've been to a dressmaker's opening. You're absolutely brimming with illicit enjoyment."

She stared again, this time at the adjective. His adjectives always embarrassed her; their unintelligibleness savored of impropriety.

"In short," he summed up, "you've been doing something that you're thoroughly ashamed of."

To his surprise she retorted: "I don't see why I should be ashamed of it!"

Lethbury leaned back with a smile of enjoyment. When there was nothing better going he always liked to listen to her explanations.

"Well—?" he said.

She was becoming breathless and ejaculatory. "Of course you'll laugh—you laugh at everything!"

"That rather blunts the point of my derision, doesn't it?" he interjected; but she pushed on without noticing:

"It's so easy to laugh at things."

"Ah," murmured Lethbury with relish, "that's Aunt Sophronia's, isn't it?"

Most of his wife's opinions were heirlooms, and he took a quaint pleasure in tracing their descent. She was proud of their age, and saw no reason for discarding them while they were still serviceable. Some, of course, were so fine that she kept them for state occasions, like her great-grandmother's Crown Derby; but from the lady known as Aunt Sophronia she had inherited a stout set of everyday prejudices that were practically as good as new; whereas her husband's, as she noticed, were always having to be replaced. In the early days she had fancied there might be a certain satisfaction in taxing him with the fact; but she had long since been silenced by the reply: "My dear, I'm not a rich man, but I never use an opinion twice if I can help it."

She was reduced, therefore, to dwelling on his moral deficiencies; and one of the most obvious of these was his refusal to take things seriously. On this occasion, however, some ulterior purpose kept her from taking up his taunt.

"I'm not in the least ashamed!" she repeated, with the air of shaking a banner to the wind; but the domestic atmosphere being calm, the banner drooped unheroically.

"That," said Lethbury judicially, "encourages me to infer that you ought to be, and that, consequently, you've been giving yourself the unusual pleasure of doing something I shouldn't approve of."

She met this with an almost solemn directness.

"No," she said. "You won't approve of it. I've allowed for that."

"Ah," he exclaimed, setting down his liqueur glass. "You've worked out the whole problem, eh?"

"I believe so."

"That's uncommonly interesting. And what is it?"

She looked at him quietly. "A baby."

If it was seldom given her to surprise him, she had attained the distinction for once.

"A baby?"

"Yes."

"A—human baby?"

"Of course!" she cried, with the virtuous resentment of the woman who has never allowed dogs in the house.

Lethbury's puzzled stare broke into a fresh smile. "A baby I shan't approve of? Well, in the abstract I don't think much of them, I admit. Is this an abstract baby?"

Again she frowned at the adjective; but she had reached a pitch of exaltation at which such obstacles could not deter her.

"It's the loveliest baby—" she murmured.

"Ah, then it's concrete. It exists. In this harsh world it draws its breath in pain—"

"It's the healthiest child I ever saw!" she indignantly corrected.

"You've seen it, then?"

Again the accusing blush suffused her. "Yes—I've seen it."

"And to whom does the paragon belong?"

And here indeed she confounded him. "To me—I hope," she declared.

He pushed his chair back with an articulate murmur. "To you—?"

"To *us*," she corrected.

"Good Lord!" he said. If there had been the least hint of hallucination in her transparent gaze—but no; it was as clear, as shallow, as easily fathomable as when he had first suffered the sharp surprise of striking bottom in it.

It occurred to him that perhaps she was trying to be funny: he knew that there is nothing more cryptic than the humor of the unhumorous.

"Is it a joke?" he faltered.

"Oh, I hope not. I want it so much to be a reality—"

He paused to smile at the limitations of a world in which jokes were not realities, and continued gently: "But since it is one already—"

"To us, I mean: to you and me. I want—" her voice wavered, and her eyes with it. "I have always wanted so dreadfully . . . it has been such a disappointment . . . not to . . ."

"I see," said Lethbury slowly.

But he had not seen before. It seemed curious now that he had never thought of her taking it in that way, had never surmised any hidden depths beneath her outspread obviousness. He felt as though he had touched a secret spring in her mind.

There was a moment's silence, moist and tremulous on her part, awkward and slightly irritated on his.

"You've been lonely, I suppose?" he began. It was odd, having suddenly to reckon with the stranger who gazed at him out of her trivial eyes.

"At times," she said.

"I'm sorry."

"It was not your fault. A man has so many occupations; and women who are clever—or very handsome—I suppose that's an occupation too. Sometimes I've felt that when dinner was ordered I had nothing to do till the next day."

"Oh," he groaned.

"It wasn't your fault," she insisted. "I never told you— but when I chose that rosebud paper for the front room upstairs, I always thought—"

"Well—?"

"It would be such a pretty paper—for a baby—to wake up in. That was years ago, of course; but it was rather an expensive paper . . . and it hasn't faded in the least . . ." she broke off incoherently.

"It hasn't faded?"

"No—and so I thought . . . as we don't use the room for anything . . . now that Aunt Sophronia is dead . . . I thought I might . . . you might . . . oh, Julian, if you could only have seen it just waking up in its crib!"

"Seen what—where? You haven't got a baby upstairs?"

"Oh, no—not *yet*," she said, with her rare laugh—the girlish bubbling of merriment that had seemed one of her chief graces in the early days. It occurred to him that he had not given her enough things to laugh about lately. But then she needed such very elementary things: she was as difficult to amuse as a savage. He concluded that he was not sufficiently simple.

"Alice," he said almost solemnly, "what *do* you mean?"

She hesitated a moment: he saw her gather her courage for a supreme effort. Then she said slowly, gravely, as though she were pronouncing a sacramental phrase:

"I'm so lonely without a little child—and I thought perhaps you'd let me adopt one. . . . It's at the hospital . . . its mother is dead . . . and I could . . . pet it, and dress it, and do things for it . . . and it's such a good baby . . . you can ask any of the nurses . . . it would never, *never* bother you by crying. . . ."

✣ II ✣

LETHBURY accompanied his wife to the hospital in a mood of chastened wonder. It did not occur to him to oppose her wish. He knew, of course, that he would have to bear the brunt of the situation: the jokes at the club, the inquiries, the explanations. He saw himself in the comic role of the adopted father and welcomed it as an expiation. For in his rapid reconstruction of the past he found himself cutting a shabbier figure than he cared to admit. He had always been intolerant of stupid people, and it was his punishment to be convicted of stupidity. As his mind traversed the years between his marriage and this unexpected assumption of paternity, he saw, in the light of an overheated imagination, many signs of unwonted crassness. It was not that he had ceased to think his wife stupid: she *was* stupid, limited, inflexible; but there was a pathos in the struggles of her swaddled mind, in its blind reachings toward the primal emotions. He had always thought she would have been happier with a child; but he had thought it mechanically, because it had so often been thought before, because it was in the nature of things to think it of every woman, because his wife was so eminently one of a species that she fitted into all the generalizations of the sex. But he had regarded this generalization as merely typical of the triumph of tradition over experience. Maternity was no doubt the supreme function of primitive woman, the one end to which her whole organism tended; but the law of increasing complexity had operated in both sexes, and he had not seriously supposed that, outside the world of Christmas fiction and anecdotic art, such truisms had any special hold on the feminine imagination. Now he saw that the arts in question were kept alive by the vitality of the sentiments they appealed to.

Lethbury was in fact going through a rapid process of readjustment. His marriage had been a failure, but he had preserved toward his wife the exact fidelity of act that is sometimes supposed to excuse any divagation of feeling; so that, for years, the tie between them had consisted mainly in his abstaining from making love to other women. The abstention had not always been easy, for the world is surprisingly well stocked with the kind of woman one ought to have married but did not; and Lethbury had not escaped the solicitation of such alternatives. His immunity had been purchased at the cost of taking refuge in the somewhat rarefied atmosphere of his perceptions; and his world being thus limited, he had given unusual care to its details, compensating himself for the narrowness of his horizon by the minute finish of his foreground. It was a world of fine shadings and the nicest proportions, where impulse seldom set a blundering foot, and the feast of reason was undisturbed by an intemperate flow of soul. To such a banquet his wife naturally remained uninvited. The diet would have disagreed with her, and she would probably have objected to the other guests. But Lethbury, miscalculating her needs, had hitherto supposed that he had made ample provision for them, and was consequently at liberty to enjoy his own fare without any reproach of mendicancy at his gates. Now he beheld her pressing a starved face against the windows of his life, and in his imaginative reaction he invested her with a pathos borrowed from the sense of his own shortcomings.

In the hospital the imaginative process continued with

increasing force. He looked at his wife with new eyes. Formerly she had been to him a mere bundle of negations, a labyrinth of dead walls and bolted doors. There was nothing behind the walls, and the doors led no whither: he had sounded and listened often enough to be sure of that. Now he felt like a traveler who, exploring some ancient ruin, comes on an inner cell, intact amid the general dilapidation, and painted with images which reveal the forgotten use of the building.

His wife stood by a white crib in one of the wards. In the crib lay a child, a year old, the nurse affirmed, but to Lethbury's eye a mere dateless fragment of humanity projected against a background of conjecture. Over this anonymous particle of life Mrs. Lethbury leaned, such ecstasy reflected in her face as strikes up, in Correggio's "Nightpiece," from the child's body to the mother's countenance. It was a light that irradiated and dazzled her. She looked up at an inquiry of Lethbury's, but as their glances met he perceived that she no longer saw him, that he had become as invisible to her as she had long been to him. He had to transfer his question to the nurse.

"What is the child's name?" he asked.

"We call her Jane," said the nurse.

✣ III ✣

LETHBURY, at first, had resisted the idea of a legal adoption; but when he found that his wife could not be brought to regard the child as hers till it had been made so by process of law, he promptly withdrew his objection. On one point only he remained inflexible; and that was the changing of the waif's name. Mrs. Lethbury, almost at once, had expressed a wish to rechristen it: she fluctuated between Muriel and Gladys, deferring the moment of decision like a lady wavering between two bonnets. But Lethbury was unyielding. In the general surrender of his prejudices this one alone held out.

"But Jane is so dreadful," Mrs. Lethbury protested.

"Well, we don't know that *she* won't be dreadful. She may grow up a Jane."

His wife exclaimed reproachfully. "The nurse says she's the loveliest—"

"Don't they always say that?" asked Lethbury patiently. He was prepared to be inexhaustibly patient now that he had reached a firm foothold of opposition.

"It's cruel to call her Jane," Mrs. Lethbury pleaded.

"It's ridiculous to call her Muriel."

"The nurse is *sure* she must be a lady's child."

Lethbury winced: he had tried, all along, to keep his mind off the question of antecedents.

"Well, let her prove it," he said, with a rising sense of exasperation. He wondered how he could ever have allowed himself to be drawn into such a ridiculous business; for the first time he felt the full irony of it. He had visions of coming home in the afternoon to a house smelling of linseed and paregoric, and of being greeted by a chronic howl as he went upstairs to dress for dinner. He had never been a club man, but he saw himself becoming one now.

The worst of his anticipations were unfulfilled. The baby was surprisingly well and surprisingly quiet. Such infantile remedies as she absorbed were not potent enough to be perceived beyond the nursery; and when Lethbury could be induced to enter that sanctuary, there was nothing to jar his nerves in the mild pink presence of his adopted daughter. Jars there were, indeed: they were probably inevitable in the disturbed routine of the household; but they occurred between Mrs. Lethbury and the nurses, and Jane contributed to them only a placid stare which might have served as a rebuke to the combatants.

In the reaction from his first impulse of atonement, Lethbury noted with sharpened perceptions the effect of the change of his wife's character. He saw already the error of supposing that it could work any transformation in her. It simply magnified her existing qualities. She was like a dried sponge put in water: she expanded, but she did not change her shape. From the standpoint of scientific observation it was curious to see how her stored instincts responded to the pseudo-maternal call. She overflowed with the petty maxims of the occasion. One felt in her the epitome, the consummation, of centuries of animal maternity, so that this little woman, who screamed at a mouse and was nervous about burglars, came to typify the cave mother rending her prey for her young.

It was less easy to regard philosophically the practical effects of her borrowed motherhood. Lethbury found with surprise that she was becoming assertive and definite. She no longer represented the negative side of his life; she showed, indeed, a tendency to inconvenient affirmations. She had gradually expanded her assumption of motherhood till it included his own share in the relation, and he suddenly found himself regarded as the father of Jane. This was a contingency he had not foreseen, and it took all his philosophy to accept it; but there were moments of compensation. For Mrs. Lethbury was undoubtedly happy for the first time in years; and the thought that he had tardily contributed to this end reconciled him to the irony of the means.

At first he was inclined to reproach himself for still viewing the situation from the outside, for remaining a spectator instead of a participant. He had been allured, for a moment, by the vision of severed hands meeting over a cradle, as the whole body of domestic fiction bears witness to their doing; and the fact that no such conjunction took place he could explain only on the ground that it was a borrowed cradle. He did not dislike the little girl. She still remained to him a hypothetical presence, a query rather than a fact; but her nearness was not unpleasant, and there were moments when her tentative utterances, her groping steps, seemed to loosen the dry accretions enveloping his inner self. But even at such moments—moments which he invited and caressed—she did not bring him nearer to his wife. He now perceived that he had made a certain place in his life for Mrs. Lethbury, and that she no longer fitted into it. It was too late to enlarge the space, and so she overflowed and encroached. Lethbury struggled against the sense of submergence. He let down barrier after barrier, yielding privacy after privacy; but his wife's personality continued to dilate. She was no longer herself alone: she was herself and Jane. Gradually, a monstrous fusion of identity, she became herself, himself and Jane; and instead of trying to adapt her to a spare crevice of his character, he found himself carelessly squeezed into the smallest compartment of the domestic economy.

✣ IV ✣

He continued to tell himself that he was satisfied if his wife was happy; and it was not till the child's tenth year that he felt a doubt of her happiness.

Jane had been a preternaturally good child. During the eight years of her adoption she had caused her foster parents no anxiety beyond those connected with the usual succession of youthful diseases. But her unknown progenitors had given her a robust constitution, and she passed unperturbed through measles, chicken pox and whooping cough. If there was any suffering it was endured vicariously by Mrs. Lethbury, whose temperature rose and fell with the patient's, and who could not hear Jane sneeze without visions of a marble angel weeping over a broken column. But though Jane's prompt recoveries continued to belie such premonitions, though her existence continued to move forward on an even keel of good health and good conduct, Mrs. Lethbury's satisfaction showed no corresponding advance. Lethbury, at first, was disposed to add her disappointment to the long list of feminine inconsistencies with which the sententious observer of life builds up his favorable induction; but circumstances presently led him to take a kindlier view of the case.

Hitherto his wife had regarded him as a negligible factor in Jane's evolution. Beyond providing for his adopted daughter, and effacing himself before her, he was not expected to contribute to her well-being. But as time passed he appeared to his wife in a new light. It was he who was to educate Jane. In matters of the intellect, Mrs. Lethbury was the first to declare her deficiencies—to proclaim them, even, with a certain virtuous superiority. She said she did not pretend to be clever, and there was no denying the truth of the assertion. Now, however, she seemed less ready, not to own her limitations, but to glory in them. Confronted with the problem of Jane's instruction she stood in awe of the child.

"I have always been stupid, you know," she said to Lethbury with a new humility, "and I'm afraid I shan't know what is best for Jane. I'm sure she has a wonderfully good mind, and I should reproach myself if I didn't give her every opportunity." She looked at him helplessly. "You must tell me what ought to be done."

Lethbury was not unwilling to oblige her. Somewhere in his mental lumber room there rusted a theory of education such as usually lingers among the impedimenta of the childless. He brought this out, refurbished it, and applied it to Jane. At first he thought his wife had not overrated the quality of the child's mind. Jane seemed extraordinarily intelligent. Her precocious definiteness of mind was encouraging to her inexperienced preceptor. She had no difficulty in fixing her attention, and he felt that very fact he imparted was being etched in metal. He helped his wife to engage the best teachers, and for a while continued to take an ex-official interest in his adopted daughter's studies. But gradually his interest waned. Jane's ideas did not increase with her acquisitions. Her young mind remained a mere receptacle for facts: a kind of cold storage from which anything which had been put there could be taken out at a moment's notice, intact but congealed. She developed, moreover, an inordinate pride in the capacity of her mental storehouse, and a tendency to pelt her public with its contents. She was overheard to jeer at her nurse for not knowing when the Saxon Heptarchy had fallen, and she alternately dazzled and depressed Mrs. Lethbury by the wealth of her chronological allusions. She showed no interest in the significance of the facts she amassed: she simply collected dates as another child might have collected stamps or marbles. To her foster mother she seemed a prodigy of wisdom; but Lethbury saw; with a secret movement of sympathy, how the aptitudes in which Mrs. Lethbury gloried were slowly estranging her from her child.

"She is getting too clever for me," his wife said to him, after one of Jane's historical flights, "but I am so glad that she will be a companion to you."

Lethbury groaned in spirit. He did not look forward to Jane's companionship. She was still a good little girl: but there was something automatic and formal in her goodness, as though it were a kind of moral calisthenics which she went through for the sake of showing her agility. An early consciousness of virtue had moreover constituted her the natural guardian and adviser of her elders. Before she was fifteen she had set about reforming the household. She took Mrs. Lethbury in hand first; then she extended her efforts to the servants, with consequences more disastrous to the domestic harmony; and lastly she applied herself to Lethbury. She proved to him by statistics that he smoked too much, and that it was injurious to the optic nerve to read in bed. She took him to task for not going to church more regularly, and pointed out to him the evils of desultory reading. She suggested that a regular course of study encourages mental concentration, and hinted that inconsecutiveness of thought is a sign of approaching age.

To her adopted mother her suggestions were equally pertinent. She instructed Mrs. Lethbury in an improved way of making beef stock, and called her attention to the unhygienic qualities of carpets. She poured out distracting facts about bacilli and vegetable mold, and demonstrated that curtains and picture frames are a hotbed of animal organisms. She learned by heart the nutritive ingredients of the principal articles of diet, and revolutionized the cuisine by an attempt to establish a scientific average between starch and phosphates. Four cooks left during this experiment, and Lethbury fell into the habit of dining at the club.

Once or twice, at the outset, he had tried to check Jane's ardor; but his efforts resulted only in hurting his wife's feelings. Jane remained impervious, and Mrs. Lethbury resented any attempt to protect her from her daughter. Lethbury saw that she was consoled for the sense of her own inferiority by the thought of what Jane's intellectual companionship must be to him; and he tried to keep up the illusion by enduring with what grace he might the blighting edification of Jane's discourse.

✣ V ✣

As Jane grew up he sometimes avenged himself by wondering if his wife was still sorry that they had not called her

Muriel. Jane was not ugly; she developed, indeed, a kind of categorical prettiness which might have been a projection of her mind. She had a creditable collection of features, but one had to take an inventory of them to find out that she was goodlooking. The fusing grace had been omitted.

Mrs. Lethbury took a touching pride in her daughter's first steps in the world. She expected Jane to take by her complexion those whom she did not capture by her learning. But Jane's rosy freshness did not work any perceptible ravages. Whether the young men guessed the axioms on her lips and detected the encyclopedia in her eyes, or whether they simply found no intrinsic interest in these features, certain it is, that, in spite of her mother's heroic efforts, and of incessant calls on Lethbury's purse, Jane, at the end of her first season, had dropped hopelessly out of the running. A few duller girls found her interesting, and one or two young men came to the house with the object of meeting other young women; but she was rapidly becoming one of the social supernumeraries who are asked out only because they are on people's lists.

The blow was bitter to Mrs. Lethbury; but she consoled herself with the idea that Jane had failed because she was too clever. Jane probably shared this conviction; at all events she betrayed no consciousness of failure. She had developed a pronounced taste for society, and went out, unweariedly and obstinately, winter after winter, while Mrs. Lethbury toiled in her wake, showering attentions on oblivious hostesses. To Lethbury there was something at once tragic and exasperating in the sight of their two figures, the one conciliatory, the other dogged, both pursuing with unabated zeal the elusive prize of popularity. He even began to feel a personal stake in the pursuit, not as it concerned Jane but as it affected his wife. He saw that the latter was the victim of Jane's disappointment: that Jane was not above the crude satisfaction of "taking it out" of her mother. Experience checked the impulse to come to his wife's defense; and when his resentment was at its height, Jane disarmed him by giving up the struggle.

Nothing was said to mark her capitulation; but Lethbury noticed that the visiting ceased and that the dressmaker's bills diminished. At the same time Mrs. Lethbury made it known that Jane had taken up charities; and before long Jane's conversation confirmed this announcement. At first Lethbury congratulated himself on the change; but Jane's domesticity soon began to weigh on him. During the day she was sometimes absent on errands of mercy; but in the evening she was always there. At first she and Mrs. Lethbury sat in the drawing room together, and Lethbury smoked in the library; but presently Jane formed the habit of joining him there, and he began to suspect that he was included among the objects of her philanthropy.

Mrs. Lethbury confirmed the suspicion. "Jane has grown very serious-minded lately," she said. "She imagines that she used to neglect you and she is trying to make up for it. Don't discourage her," she added innocently.

Such a plea delivered Lethbury helpless to his daughter's ministrations; and he found himself measuring the hours he spent with her by the amount of relief they must be affording her mother. There were even moments when he read a furtive gratitude in Mrs. Lethbury's eye.

But Lethbury was no hero, and he had nearly reached the limit of vicarious endurance when something wonderful happened. They never quite knew afterward how it had come about, or who first perceived it; but Mrs. Lethbury one day gave tremulous voice to their discovery.

"Of course," she said, "he comes here because of Elise." The young lady in question, a friend of Jane's, was possessed of attractions which had already been found to explain the presence of masculine visitors.

Lethbury risked a denial. "I don't think he does," he declared.

"But Elise is thought very pretty," Mrs. Lethbury insisted.

"I can't help that," said Lethbury doggedly.

He saw a faint light in his wife's eyes; but she remarked carelessly; "Mr. Budd would be a very good match for Elise."

Lethbury could hardly repress a chuckle: he was so exquisitely aware that she was trying to propitiate the gods.

For a few weeks neither said a word; then Mrs. Lethbury once more reverted to the subject.

"It is a month since Elise went abroad," she said.

"Is it?"

"And Mr. Budd seems to come here just as often—"

"Ah," said Lethbury with heroic indifference; and his wife hastily changed the subject.

Mr. Winstanley Budd was a young man who suffered from an excess of manner. Politeness gushed from him in the driest seasons. He was always performing feats of drawing-room chivalry, and the approach of the most unobtrusive female threw him into attitudes which endangered the furniture. His features, being of the cherubic order, did not lend themselves to this role; but there were moments when he appeared to dominate them, to force them into compliance with an aquiline ideal. The range of Mr. Budd's social benevolence made its object hard to distinguish. He spread his cloak so indiscriminately that one could not always interpret the gesture, and Jane's impassive manner had the effect of increasing his demonstrations: she threw him into paroxysms of politeness.

At first he filled the house with his amenities; but gradually it became apparent that his most dazzling effects were directed exclusively to Jane. Lethbury and his wife held their breath and looked away from each other. They pretended not to notice the frequency of Mr. Budd's visits, they struggled against an imprudent inclination to leave the young people too much alone. Their conclusions were the result of indirect observation, for neither of them dared to be caught watching Mr. Budd: they behaved like naturalists on the trail of a rare butterfly.

In his efforts not to notice Mr. Budd, Lethbury centered his attentions on Jane; and Jane, at this crucial moment, wrung from him a reluctant admiration. While her parents went about dissembling their emotions, she seemed to have none to conceal. She betrayed neither eagerness nor surprise; so complete was her unconcern that there were moments when Lethbury feared it was obtuseness, when he could hardly help whispering to her that now was the moment to lower the net.

Meanwhile the velocity of Mr. Budd's gyrations increased with the ardor of courtship; his politeness became incandescent, and Jane found herself the center of a pyrotechnical display culminating in the "set piece" of an offer of marriage.

Mrs. Lethbury imparted the news to her husband one evening after their daughter had gone to bed. The announcement was made and received with an air of detachment, as though both feared to be betrayed into unseemly exultation; but Lethbury, as his wife ended, could not repress the inquiry, "Have they decided on a day?"

Mrs. Lethbury's superior command of her features enabled her to look shocked. "What can you be thinking of? He only offered himself at five!"

"Of course—of course—" stammered Lethbury "—but nowadays people marry after such short engagements—"

"Engagement!" said his wife solemnly. "There is no engagement."

Lethbury dropped his cigar. "What on earth do you mean?"

"Jane is thinking it over."

"*Thinking it over?*"

"She has asked for a month before deciding."

Lethbury sank back with a gasp. Was it genius or was it madness? He felt incompetent to decide; and Mrs. Lethbury's next words showed that she shared his difficulty.

"Of course I don't want to hurry Jane—"

"Of course not," he acquiesced.

"But I point out to her that a young man of Mr. Budd's impulsive temperament might—might be easily discouraged—"

"Yes; and what did she say?"

"She said that if she was worth winning she was worth waiting for."

✣ VI ✣

THE period of Mr. Budd's probation could scarcely have cost him as much mental anguish as it caused his would-be parents-in-law.

Mrs. Lethbury, by various ruses, tried to shorten the ordeal, but Jane remained inexorable; and each morning Lethbury came down to breakfast with the certainty of finding a letter of withdrawal from her discouraged suitor.

When at length the decisive day came, and Mrs. Lethbury, at its close, stole into the library with an air of chastened joy, they stood for a moment without speaking; then Mrs. Lethbury paid a fitting tribute to the proprieties by faltering out: "It will be dreadful to have to give her up—"

Lethbury could not repress a warning gesture; but even as it escaped him he realized that his wife's grief was genuine.

"Of course, of course," he said, vainly sounding his own emotional shallows for an answering regret. And yet it was his wife who had suffered most from Jane!

He had fancied that these sufferings would be effaced by the milder atmosphere of their last weeks together; but felicity did not soften Jane. Not for a moment did she relax her dominion; she simply widened it to include a new subject. Mr. Budd found himself under orders with the others; and a new fear assailed Lethbury as he saw Jane assume prenuptial control of her betrothed. Lethbury had never felt any strong personal interest in Mr. Budd; but as Jane's prospective husband the young man excited his sympathy. To his surprise he found that Mrs. Lethbury shared the feeling.

"I'm afraid he may find Jane a little exacting," she said, after an evening dedicated to a stormy discussion of the wedding arrangements. "She really ought to make some concessions. If he *wants* to be married in a black frock coat instead of a dark gray one—" She paused and looked doubtfully at Lethbury.

"What can I do about it?" he said.

"You might explain to him—tell him that Jane's isn't always— "

Lethbury made an impatient gesture. "What are you afraid of? His finding her out or his not finding her out?"

Mrs. Lethbury flushed. "You put it so dreadfully!"

Her husband mused for a moment; then he said with an air of cheerful hypocrisy: "After all, Budd is old enough to take care of himself."

But the next day Mrs. Lethbury surprised him. Late in the afternoon she entered the library, so breathless and inarticulate that he scented a catastrophe.

"I've done it!" she cried.

"Done what?"

"Told him." She nodded toward the door. "He's just gone. Jane is out, and I had a chance to talk to him alone."

Lethbury pushed a chair forward and she sank into it.

"What did you tell him? That she is *not* always—"

Mrs. Lethbury lifted a tragic eye. "No; I told him that she always *is*—"

"Always *is*—?"

"Yes."

There was a pause. Lethbury made a call on his hoarded philosophy. He saw Jane suddenly reinstated in her evening seat by the library fire; but an answering chord in him thrilled at his wife's heroism.

"Well—what did he say?"

Mrs. Lethbury's agitation deepened. It was clear that the blow had fallen.

"He . . . he said . . . that we . . . had never understood Jane . . . or appreciated her . . ." The final syllables were lost in her handkerchief, and she left him marveling at the mechanism of woman.

After that, Lethbury faced the future with an undaunted eye. They had done their duty—at least his wife had done hers—and they were reaping the usual harvest of ingratitude with zest seldom accorded to such reaping. There was a marked change in Mr. Budd's manner, and his increasing coldness sent a genial glow through Lethbury's system. It was easy to bear with Jane in the light of Mr. Budd's disapproval.

There was a good deal to be borne in the last days, and the brunt of it fell on Mrs. Lethbury. Jane marked her transition to the married state by a seasonable but incongruous display of nerves. She became sentimental, hysterical and reluctant. She quarreled with her betrothed and threatened to return the ring. Mrs. Lethbury had to intervene, and Lethbury felt the hovering sword of destiny. But the blow was suspended. Mr. Budd's chivalry was proof against all his bride's caprices and his devotion throve on her cruelty. Lethbury feared that he was too faithful, too enduring, and longed to urged him to vary his tactics. Jane presently reappeared with the ring on her finger, and consented to try on the wedding dress; but her uncertainties, her reactions, were prolonged till the final day.

When it dawned, Lethbury was still in an ecstasy of apprehension. Feeling reasonably sure of the principal actors he had centered his fears on incidental possibilities. The clergyman might have a stroke, or the church might burn down, or there might be something wrong with the license. He did all that was humanly possible to avert such contingencies, but there remained that incalculable factor known as the hand of God. Lethbury seemed to feel it groping for him.

At the altar it almost had him by the nape. Mr. Budd was late; and for five immeasurable minutes Lethbury and Jane faced a churchful of conjecture. Then the bridegroom appeared, flushed but chivalrous, and explaining to his father-in-law under cover of the ritual that he had torn his glove and had to go back for another.

"You'll be losing the ring next," muttered Lethbury; but Mr. Budd produced this article punctually, and a moment or two later was bearing its wearer captive down the aisle.

At the wedding breakfast Lethbury caught his wife's eye fixed on him in mild disapproval, and understood that his hilarity was exceeding the bounds of fitness. He pulled himself together and tried to subdue his tone; but his jubilation bubbled over like a champagne glass perpetually refilled. The deeper his draughts the higher it rose.

It was at the brim when, in the wake of the dispersing guests, Jane came down in her traveling dress and fell on her mother's neck.

"I can't leave you!" she wailed, and Lethbury felt as suddenly sobered as a man under a shower. But if the bride was reluctant her captor was relentless. Never had Mr. Budd been more dominant, more aquiline. Lethbury's last fears were dissipated as the young man snatched Jane from her mother's bosom and bore her off to the brougham.

The brougham rolled away, the last milliner's girl forsook her post by the awning, the red carpet was folded up, and the house door closed. Lethbury stood alone in the hall with his wife. As he turned toward her, he noticed the look of tired heroism in her eyes, the deepened lines of her face. They reflected his own symptoms too accurately not to appeal to him. The nervous tension had been horrible. He went up to her, and an answering impulse made her lay a hand on his arm. He held it there a moment.

"Let us go off and have a jolly little dinner at a restaurant," he proposed.

There had been a time when such a suggestion would have surprised her to the verge of disapproval; but now she agreed to it at once.

"Oh, that would be so nice," she murmured with a great sigh of relief and assuagement.

Jane had fulfilled her mission after all: she had drawn them together at last.

The Other Two

WAYTHORN, on the drawing-room hearth, waited for his wife to come down to dinner.

It was their first night under his own roof, and he was surprised at his thrill of boyish agitation. He was not so old, to be sure—his glass gave him little more than the five-and-thirty years to which his wife confessed—but he had fancied himself already in the temperate zone; yet here he was listening for her step with a tender sense of all it symbolized, with some old trail of verse about the garlanded nuptial doorposts floating through his enjoyment of the pleasant room and the good dinner just beyond it.

They had been hastily recalled from their honeymoon by the illness of Lily Haskett, the child of Mrs. Waythorn's first marriage. The little girl, at Waythorn's desire, had been transferred to his house on the day of her mother's wedding, and the doctor, on their arrival, broke the news that she was ill with typhoid, but declared that all the symptoms were favorable. Lily could show twelve years of unblemished health, and the case promised to be a light one. The nurse spoke as reassuringly, and after a moment of alarm Mrs. Waythorn had adjusted herself to the situation. She was very fond of Lily—her affection for the child had perhaps been her decisive charm in Waythorn's eyes—but she had the perfectly balanced nerves which her little girl had inherited, and no woman ever wasted less tissue in unproductive worry. Waythorn was therefore quite prepared to see her come in presently, a little late because of a last look at Lily, but as serene and well-appointed as if her good-night kiss had been laid on the brow of health. Her composure was restful to him; it acted as ballast to his somewhat unstable sensibilities. As he pictured her bending over the child's bed he thought how soothing her presence must be in illness: her very step would prognosticate recovery.

His own life had been a gray one, from temperament rather than circumstance, and he had been drawn to her by the unperturbed gaiety which kept her fresh and elastic at an age when most women's activities are growing either slack or febrile. He knew what was said about her; for, popular as she was, there had always been a faint undercurrent of detraction. When she had appeared in New York, nine or ten years earlier, as the pretty Mrs. Haskett whom Gus Varick had unearthed somewhere—was it in Pittsburg or Utica—society, while promptly accepting her, had reserved the right to cast a doubt on its own indiscrimination. Inquiry, however, established her undoubted connection with a socially reigning family, and explained her recent divorce as the natural result of a runaway match at seventeen; and as nothing was known of Mr. Haskett it was easy to believe the worst of him.

Alice Haskett's remarriage with Gus Varick was a passport to the set whose recognition she coveted, and for a few years the Varicks were the most popular couple in town. Unfortunately the alliance was brief and stormy, and this time the husband had his champions. Still, even Varick's stanchest supporters admitted that he was not meant for matrimony, and Mrs. Varick's grievances were of a nature to bear the inspection of the New York courts. A New York divorce is in itself a diploma of virtue, and in the semiwidowhood of this second separation Mrs. Varick took on an air of sanctity, and was allowed to confide her wrongs to some of the most scrupulous ears in town. But when it was known that she was to marry Waythorn there was a momentary reaction. Her best friends would have preferred to see her remain in the role of the injured wife, which was as becoming to her as crepe to a rosy complexion. True, a decent time had elapsed, and it was not even suggested that Waythorn had supplanted his predecessor. People shook their heads over him, however, and one grudging friend, to whom he affirmed that he took the step with his eyes open, replied oracularly: "Yes—and with your ears shut."

Waythorn could afford to smile at these innuendoes. In the Wall Street phrase, he had "discounted" them. He knew that society has not yet adapted itself to the consequences of divorce, and that till the adaptation takes place every woman who uses the freedom the law accords her must be her own social justification. Waythorn had an amused confidence in his wife's ability to justify herself. His expectations were fulfilled, and before the wedding took place Alice Varick's group had rallied openly to her support. She took it all imperturbably: she had a way of surmounting obstacles without seeming to be aware of them, and Waythorn looked back with wonder at the trivialities over which he had worn his nerves thin. He had the sense of having found refuge in a richer, warmer nature than his own, and his satisfaction, at the moment, was humorously summed up in the thought that his wife, when she had done all she could for Lily, would not be ashamed to come down and enjoy a good dinner.

The anticipation of such enjoyment was not, however, the sentiment expressed by Mrs. Waythorn's charming face when she presently joined him. Though she had put on her most engaging tea gown she had neglected to assume the smile that went with it, and Waythorn thought he had never seen her look so nearly worried.

"What is it?" he asked. "Is anything wrong with Lily?"

"No; I've just been in and she's still sleeping." Mrs. Waythorn hesitated. "But something tiresome has happened."

He had taken her two hands, and now perceived that he was crushing a paper between them.

"This letter?"

"Yes—Mr. Haskett has written—I mean his lawyer has written."

Waythorn felt himself flush uncomfortably. He dropped his wife's hands.

"What about?"

"About seeing Lily. You know the courts—"

"Yes, yes," he interrupted nervously.

Nothing was known about Haskett in New York. He was

vaguely supposed to have remained in the outer darkness from which his wife had been rescued, and Waythorn was one of the few who were aware that he had given up his business in Utica and followed her to New York in order to be near his little girl. In the days of his wooing, Waythorn had often met Lily on the doorstep, rosy and smiling, on her way "to see papa."

"I am so sorry," Mrs. Waythorn murmured.

He roused himself. "What does he want?"

"He wants to see her. You know she goes to him once a week."

"Well—he doesn't expect her to go to him now, does he?"

"No—he has heard of her illness; but he expects to come here."

"Here?"

Mrs. Waythorn reddened under his gaze. They looked away from each other.

"I'm afraid he has the right . . . You'll see. . . ." She made a proffer of the letter.

Waythorn moved away with a gesture of refusal. He stood staring about the softly-lighted room, which a moment before had seemed so full of bridal intimacy.

"I'm so sorry," she repeated. "If Lily could have been moved—"

"That's out of the question," he returned impatiently.

"I suppose so."

Her lip was beginning to tremble, and he felt himself a brute.

"He must come, of course," he said. "When is—his day?"

"I'm afraid—tomorrow."

"Very well. Send a note in the morning."

The butler entered to announce dinner.

Waythorn turned to his wife. "Come—you must be tired. It's beastly, but try to forget about it," he said, drawing her hand through his arm.

"You're so good, dear. I'll try," she whispered back.

Her face cleared at once, and as she looked at him across the flowers, between the rosy candleshades, he saw her lips waver back into a smile.

"How pretty everything is!" she sighed luxuriously.

He turned to the butler. "The champagne at once, please. Mrs. Waythorn is tired."

In a moment or two their eyes met above the sparkling glasses. Her own were quite clear and untroubled: he saw that she had obeyed his injunction and forgotten.

✣ II ✣

WAYTHORN, the next morning, went downtown earlier than usual. Haskett was not likely to come till the afternoon, but the instinct of flight drove him forth. He meant to stay away all day—he had thoughts of dining at his club. As his door closed behind him he reflected that before he opened it again it would have admitted another man who had as much right to enter it as himself, and the thought filled him with a physical repugnance.

He caught the elevated at the employees' hour, and found himself crushed between two layers of pendulous humanity. At Eighth Street the man facing him wriggled out, and another took his place. Waythorn glanced up and saw that it was Gus Varick. The men were so close together that it was impossible to ignore the smile of recognition on Varick's handsome overblown face. And after all—why not? They had always been on good terms, and Varick had been divorced before Waythorn's attentions to his wife began. The two exchanged a word on the perennial grievance of the congested trains, and when a seat at their side was miraculously left empty the instinct of self-preservation made Waythorn slip into it after Varick.

The latter drew the stout man's breath of relief. "Lord—I was beginning to feel like a pressed flower." He leaned back, looking unconcernedly at Waythorn. "Sorry to hear that Sellers is knocked out again."

"Sellers?" echoed Waythorn, starting at his partner's name.

Varick looked surprised. "You didn't know he was laid up with the gout?"

"No. I've been away—I only got back last night." Waythorn felt himself reddening in anticipation of the other's smile.

"Ah—yes; to be sure. And Sellers' attack came on two days ago. I'm afraid he's pretty bad. Very awkward for me, as it happens, because he was just putting through a rather important thing for me."

"Ah?" Waythorn wondered vaguely since when Varick had been dealing in "important things." Hitherto he had dabbled only in the shallow pools of speculation, with which Waythorn's office did not usually concern itself.

It occurred to him that Varick might be talking at random, to relieve the strain of their propinquity. That strain was becoming momentarily more apparent to Waythorn, and when, at Cortlandt Street, he caught sight of an acquaintance and had a sudden vision of the picture he and Varick must present to an initiated eye, he jumped up with a muttered excuse.

"I hope you'll find Sellers better," said Varick civilly, and he stammered back: "If I can be of any use to you—" and let the departing crowd sweep him to the platform.

At his office he heard that Sellers was in fact ill with the gout, and would probably not be able to leave the house for some weeks.

"I'm sorry it should have happened so, Mr. Waythorn," the senior clerk said with affable significance. "Mr. Sellers was very much upset at the idea of giving you such a lot of extra work just now."

"Oh, that's no matter," said Waythorn hastily. He secretly welcomed the pressure of additional business, and was glad to think that, when the day's work was over, he would have to call at his partner's on the way home.

He was late for luncheon, and turned in at the nearest restaurant instead of going to his club. The place was full, and the waiter hurried him to the back of the room to capture the only vacant table. In the cloud of cigar smoke Waythorn did not at once distinguish his neighbors: but presently, looking about him, he saw Varick seated a few feet off. This time, luckily, they were too far apart for conversation, and Varick, who faced another way, had probably not even seen him; but there was an irony in their renewed nearness.

Varick was said to be fond of good living, and as Waythorn sat dispatching his hurried luncheon he looked across half enviously at the other's leisurely degustation of his meal. When Waythorn first saw him he had been helping himself with critical deliberation to a bit of Camembert at the ideal point of liquefaction, and now, the cheese removed, he was just pouring his *café double* from its little two-storied earthen pot. He poured slowly, his ruddy profile bent over the task, and one beringed white hand steadying the lid of the coffee-pot; then he stretched his other hand to the decanter of cognac at his elbow, filled a liqueur glass, took a tentative sip, and poured the brandy into his coffee cup.

Waythorn watched him in a kind of fascination. What was he thinking of—only of the flavor of the coffee and the liqueur? Had the morning's meeting left no more trace in his thoughts than on his face? Had his wife so completely passed out of his life that even this odd encounter with her present husband, within a week after her remarriage, was no more than an incident in his day? And as Waythorn mused, another idea struck him: had Haskett ever met Varick as Varick and he had just met? The recollection of Haskett perturbed him, and he rose and left the restaurant, taking a circuitous way out to escape the placid irony of Varick's nod.

It was after seven when Waythorn reached home. He thought the footman who opened the door looked at him oddly.

"How is Miss Lily?" he asked in haste.

"Doing very well, sir. A gentleman—"

"Tell Barlow to put off dinner for half an hour," Waythorn cut him off, hurrying upstairs.

He went straight to his room and dressed without seeing his wife. When he reached the drawing room she was there, fresh and radiant. Lily's day had been good; the doctor was not coming back that evening.

At dinner Waythorn told her of Sellers' illness and of the resulting complications. She listened sympathetically, adjuring him not to let himself be overworked, and asking vague feminine questions about the routine of the office. Then she gave him the chronicle of Lily's day; quoted the nurse and doctor, and told him who had called to inquire. He had never seen her more serene and unruffled. It struck him, with a curious pang, that she was very happy in being with him, so happy that she found a childish pleasure in rehearsing the trivial incidents of her day.

After dinner they went to the library, and the servant put the coffee and liqueurs on a low table before her and left the room. She looked singularly soft and girlish in her rosy-pale dress, against the dark leather of one of his bachelor armchairs. A day earlier the contrast would have charmed him.

He turned away now, choosing a cigar with affected deliberation.

"Did Haskett come?" he asked, with his back to her.

"Oh, yes—he came."

"You didn't see him, of course?"

She hesitated a moment. "I let the nurse see him."

That was all. There was nothing more to ask. He swung round toward her, applying a match to his cigar. Well, the thing was over for a week, at any rate. He would try not to think of it. She looked up at him, a trifle rosier than usual, with a smile in her eyes.

"Ready for your coffee, dear?"

He leaned against the mantelpiece, watching her as she lifted the coffeepot. The lamplight struck a gleam from her bracelets and tipped her soft hair with brightness. How light and slender she was, and how each gesture flowed into the next! She seemed a creature all compact of harmonies. As the thought of Haskett receded, Waythorn felt himself yielding again to the joy of possessorship. They were his, those white hands with their flitting motions, his the light haze of hair, the lips and eyes. . . .

She set down the coffeepot, and reaching for the decanter of cognac, measured off a liqueur glass and poured it into his cup.

Waythorn uttered a sudden exclamation.

"What is the matter?" she said, startled.

"Nothing: only—I don't take cognac in my coffee."

"Oh, how stupid of me," she cried.

Their eyes met, and she blushed a sudden agonized red.

✣ III ✣

TEN days later, Mr. Sellers, still housebound, asked Waythorn to call on his way downtown.

The senior partner, with his swaddled foot propped up by the fire, greeted his associate with an air of embarrassment.

"I'm sorry, my dear fellow; I've got to ask you to do an awkward thing for me."

Waythorn waited, and the other went on, after a pause apparently given to the arrangement of his phrases: "The fact is, when I was knocked out I had just gone into a rather complicated piece of business for—Gus Varick."

"Well?" said Waythorn, with an attempt to put him at his ease.

"Well—it's this way: Varick came to me the day before my attack. He had evidently had an inside tip from somebody, and had made about a hundred thousand. He came to me for advice, and I suggested his going in with Vanderlyn."

"Oh, the deuce!" Waythorn exclaimed. He saw in a flash what had happened. The investment was an alluring one, but required negotiation. He listened quietly while Sellers put the case before him, and, the statement ended, he said: "You think I ought to see Varick?"

"I'm afraid I can't as yet. The doctor is obdurate. And this thing can't wait. I hate to ask you, but no one else in the office knows the ins and outs of it."

Waythorn stood silent. He did not care a farthing for the success of Varick's venture, but the honor of the office was to be considered, and he could hardly refuse to oblige his partner.

"Very well," he said, "I'll do it."

That afternoon, apprised by telephone, Varick called at the office. Waythorn, waiting in his private room, wondered what the others thought of it. The newspapers, at the time of Mrs. Waythorn's marriage, had acquainted their readers with every detail of her previous matrimonial ventures, and

Waythorn could fancy the clerks smiling behind Varick's back as he was ushered in.

Varick bore himself admirably. He was easy without being undignified, and Waythorn was conscious of cutting a much less impressive figure. Varick had no experience of business, and the talk prolonged itself for nearly an hour while Waythorn set forth with scrupulous precision the details of the proposed transaction.

"I'm awfully obliged to you," Varick said as he rose. "The fact is I'm not used to having much money to look after, and I don't want to make an ass of myself—" He smiled, and Waythorn could not help noticing that there was something pleasant about his smile. "It feels uncommonly queer to have enough cash to pay one's bills. I'd have sold my soul for it a few years ago!"

Waythorn winced at the allusion. He had heard it rumored that a lack of funds had been one of the determining causes of the Varick separation, but it did not occur to him that Varick's words were intentional. It seemed more likely that the desire to keep clear of embarrassing topics had fatally drawn him into one. Waythorn did not wish to be outdone in civility.

"We'll do the best we can for you," he said. "I think this is a good thing you're in."

"Oh, I'm sure it's immense. It's awfully good of you—" Varick broke off, embarrassed. "I suppose the thing's settled now—but if—"

"If anything happens before Sellers is about, I'll see you again," said Waythorn quietly. He was glad, in the end, to appear the more self-possessed of the two.

The course of Lily's illness ran smooth, and as the days passed Waythorn grew used to the idea of Haskett's weekly visit. The first time the day came round, he stayed out late, and questioned his wife as to the visit on his return. She replied at once that Haskett had merely seen the nurse downstairs, as the doctor did not wish anyone in the child's sickroom till after the crisis.

The following week Waythorn was again conscious of the recurrence of the day, but had forgotten it by the time he came home to dinner. The crisis of the disease came a few days later, with a rapid decline of fever, and the little girl was pronounced out of danger. In the rejoicing which ensued the thought of Haskett passed out of Waythorn's mind, and one afternoon, letting himself into the house with a latchkey, he went straight to his library without noticing a shabby hat and umbrella in the hall.

In the library he found a small effaced-looking man with a thinnish gray beard sitting on the edge of a chair. The stranger might have been a piano tuner, or one of those mysteriously efficient persons who are summoned in emergencies to adjust some detail of the domestic machinery. He blinked at Waythorn through a pair of gold-rimmed spectacles and said mildly: "Mr. Waythorn, I presume? I am Lily's father."

Waythorn flushed. "Oh—" he stammered uncomfortably. He broke off, disliking to appear rude. Inwardly he was trying to adjust the actual Haskett to the image of him projected by his wife's reminiscences. Waythorn had been allowed to infer that Alice's first husband was a brute.

"I am sorry to intrude," said Haskett, with his over-the-counter politeness.

"Don't mention it," returned Waythorn, collecting himself. "I suppose the nurse has been told?"

"I presume so. I can wait," said Haskett. He had a resigned way of speaking, as though life had worn down his natural powers of resistance.

Waythorn stood on the threshold, nervously pulling off his gloves.

"I'm sorry you've been detained. I will send for the nurse," he said; and as he opened the door he added with an effort: "I'm glad we can give you a good report of Lily." He winced as the *we* slipped out, but Haskett seemed not to notice it.

"Thank you, Mr. Waythorn. It's been an anxious time for me."

"Ah, well, that's past. Soon she'll be able to go to you." Waythorn nodded and passed out.

In his own room he flung himself down with a groan. He

hated the womanish sensibility which made him suffer so acutely from the grotesque chances of life. He had known when he married that his wife's former husbands were both living, and that amid the multiplied contacts of modern existence there were a thousand chances to one that he would run against one or the other, yet he found himself as much disturbed by his brief encounter with Haskett as though the law had not obligingly removed all difficulties in the way of their meeting.

Waythorn sprang up and began to pace the room nervously. He had not suffered half as much from his two meetings with Varick. It was Haskett's presence in his own house that made the situation so intolerable. He stood still, hearing steps in the passage.

"This way, please," he heard the nurse say. Haskett was being taken upstairs, then: not a corner of the house but was open to him. Waythorn dropped into another chair, staring vaguely ahead of him. On his dressing table stood a photograph of Alice, taken when he had first known her. She was Alice Varick then—how fine and exquisite he had thought her! Those were Varick's pearls about her neck. At Waythorn's instance they had been returned before her marriage. Had Haskett ever given her any trinkets—and what had become of them, Waythorn wondered? He realized suddenly that he knew very little of Haskett's past or present situation; but from the man's appearance and manner of speech he could reconstruct with curious precision the surroundings of Alice's first marriage. And it startled him to think that she had, in the background of her life, a phase of existence so different from anything with which he had connected her. Varick, whatever his faults, was a gentleman, in the conventional, traditional sense of the term: the sense which at that moment seemed, oddly enough, to have most meaning to Waythorn. He and Varick had the same social habits, spoke the same language, understood the same allusions. But this other man . . . it was grotesquely uppermost in Waythorn's mind that Haskett had worn a made-up tie attached with an elastic. Why should that ridiculous detail symbolize the whole man? Waythorn was exasperated by his own paltriness, but the fact of the tie expanded, forced itself on him, became as it were the key to Alice's past. He could see her, as Mrs. Haskett, sitting in a "front parlor" furnished in plush, with a pianola, and copy of *Ben Hur* on the center table. He could see her going to the theater with Haskett—or perhaps even to a "Church Sociable"—she in a "picture hat" and Haskett in a black frock coat, a little creased, with the made-up tie on an elastic. On the way home they would stop and look at the illuminated shop windows, lingering over the photographs of New York actresses. On Sunday afternoons Haskett would take her for a walk, pushing Lily ahead of them in a white enameled perambulator, and Waythorn had a vision of the people they would stop and talk to. He could fancy how pretty Alice must have looked, in a dress adroitly constructed from the hints of a New York fashion paper, and how she must have looked down on the other women, chafing at her life, and secretly feeling that she belonged in a bigger place.

For the moment his foremost thought was one of wonder at the way in which she had shed the phase of existence which her marriage with Haskett implied. It was as if her whole aspect, every gesture, every inflection, every allusion, were a studied negation of that period of her life. If she had denied being married to Haskett she could hardly have stood more convicted of duplicity than in this obliteration of the self which had been his wife.

Waythorn started up, checking himself in the analysis of her motives. What right had he to create a fantastic effigy of her and then pass judgment on it? She had spoken vaguely of her first marriage as unhappy, had hinted, with becoming reticence, that Haskett had wrought havoc among her young illusions. . . . It was a pity for Waythorn's peace of mind that Haskett's very inoffensiveness shed a new light on the nature of those illusions. A man would rather think that his wife has been brutalized by her first husband than that the process has been reversed.

✣ IV ✣

"MR. WAYTHORN, I didn't like that French governess of Lily's."

Haskett, subdued and apologetic, stood before Waythorn in the library, revolving his shabby hat in his hand.

Waythorn, surprised in his armchair over the evening paper, stared back perplexedly at his visitor.

"You'll excuse my asking to see you," Haskett continued. "But this is my last visit, and I thought if I could have a word with you it would be a better way than writing to Mrs. Waythorn's lawyer."

Waythorn rose uneasily. He did not like the French governess either; but that was irrelevant.

"I am not so sure of that," he returned stiffly; "but since you wish it I will give your message to—my wife." He always hesitated over the possessive pronoun in addressing Haskett.

The latter sighed. "I don't know as that will help much. She didn't like it when I spoke to her."

Waythorn turned red. "When did you see her?" he asked.

"Not since the first day I came to see Lily—right after she was taken sick. I remarked to her then that I didn't like the governess."

Waythorn made no answer. He remembered distinctly that, after that first visit, he had asked his wife if she had seen Haskett. She had lied to him then, but she had respected his wishes since; and the incident cast a curious light on her character. He was sure she would not have seen Haskett that first day if she had divined that Waythorn would object, and the fact that she did not divine it was almost as disagreeable to the latter as the discovery that she had lied to him.

"I don't like the woman," Haskett was repeating with mild persistency. "She ain't straight. Mr. Waythorn—she'll teach the child to be underhand. I've noticed a change in Lily—she's too anxious to please—and she don't always tell the truth. She used to be the straightest child, Mr. Waythorn—" He broke off, his voice a little thick. "Not but what I want her to have a stylish education," he ended.

Waythorn was touched. "I'm sorry, Mr. Haskett; but frankly, I don't quite see what I can do."

Haskett hesitated. Then he laid his hat on the table, and advanced to the hearthrug, on which Waythorn was standing. There was nothing aggressive in his manner, but he had the solemnity of a timid man resolved on a decisive measure.

"There's just one thing you can do, Mr. Waythorn," he said. "You can remind Mrs. Waythorn that, by the decree of the courts, I am entitled to have a voice in Lily's bringing-up." He paused, and went on more deprecatingly: "I'm not the kind to talk about enforcing my rights, Mr. Waythorn. I don't know as I think a man is entitled to rights he hasn't known how to hold on to; but this business of the child is different. I've never let go there—and I never meant to."

The scene left Waythorn deeply shaken. Shamefacedly, in indirect ways, he had been finding out about Haskett; and all that he had learned was favorable. The little man, in order to be near his daughter, had sold out his share in a profitable business in Utica, and accepted a modest clerkship in a New York manufacturing house. He boarded in a shabby street and had few acquaintances. His passion for Lily filled his life. Waythorn felt that this exploration of Haskett was like groping about with a dark lantern in his wife's past; but he saw now that there were recesses his lantern had not explored. He had never inquired into the exact circumstances of his wife's first matrimonial rupture. On the surface all had been fair. It was she who had obtained the divorce, and the court had given her the child. But Waythorn knew how many ambiguities such a verdict might cover. The mere fact that Haskett retained a right over his daughter implied an unsuspected compromise. Waythorn was an idealist. He always refused to recognize unpleasant contingencies till he found himself confronted with them, and then he saw them followed by a spectral train of consequences. His next days were thus haunted, and he determined to try to lay the ghosts by conjuring them up in his wife's presence.

When he repeated Haskett's request a flame of anger

passed over her face; but she subdued it instantly and spoke with a slight quiver of outraged motherhood.

"It is very ungentlemanly of him," she said.

The word grated on Waythorn. "That is neither here nor there. It's a bare question of rights."

She murmured: "It's not as if he could ever be a help to Lily— "

Waythorn flushed. This was even less to his taste. "The question is," he repeated, "what authority has he over her?"

She looked downward, twisting herself a little in her seat. "I am willing to see him—I thought you objected," she faltered.

In a flash he understood that she knew the extent of Haskett's claims. Perhaps it was not the first time she had resisted them.

"My objecting has nothing to do with it," he said coldly; "if Haskett has a right to be consulted you must consult him."

She burst into tears, and he saw that she expected him to regard her as a victim.

Haskett did not abuse his rights. Waythorn had felt miserably sure that he would not. But the governess was dismissed, and from time to time the little man demanded an interview with Alice. After the first outburst she accepted the situation with her usual adaptability. Haskett had once reminded Waythorn of the piano tuner, and Mrs. Waythorn, after a month or two, appeared to class him with that domestic familiar. Waythorn could not but respect the father's tenacity. At first he had tried to cultivate the suspicion that Haskett might be "up" to something, that he had an object in securing a foothold in the house. But in his heart Waythorn was sure of Haskett's single-mindedness; he even guessed in the latter a mild contempt for such advantages as his relation with the Waythorns might offer. Haskett's sincerity of purpose made him invulnerable, and his successor had to accept him as a lien on the property.

Mr. Sellers was sent to Europe to recover from his gout, and Varick's affairs hung on Waythorn's hands. The negotiations were prolonged and complicated; they necessitated frequent conferences between the two men, and the interests of the firm forbade Waythorn's suggesting that his client should transfer his business to another office.

Varick appeared well in the transaction. In moments of relaxation his coarse streak appeared, and Waythorn dreaded his geniality; but in the office he was concise and clear-headed, with a flattering deference to Waythorn's judgement. Their business relations being so affably established, it would have been absurd for the two men to ignore each other in society. The first time they met in a drawing room, Varick took up their intercourse in the same easy key, and his hostess' grateful glance obliged Waythorn to respond to it. After that they ran across each other frequently, and one evening at a ball Waythorn, wandering through the remoter rooms, came upon Varick seated beside his wife. She colored a little, and faltered in what she was saying; but Varick nodded to Waythorn without rising, and the latter strolled on.

In the carriage, on the way home, he broke out nervously: "I didn't know you spoke to Varick."

Her voice trembled a little. "It's the first time—he happened to be standing near me; I didn't know what to do. It's so awkward, meeting everywhere—and he said you had been very kind about some business."

"That's different," said Waythorn.

She paused a moment. "I'll do just as you wish," she returned pliantly. "I thought it would be less awkward to speak to him when we meet."

Her pliancy was beginning to sicken him. Had she really no will of her own—no theory about her relation to these men? She had accepted Haskett—did she mean to accept Varick? It was "less awkward," as she had said, and her instinct was to evade difficulties or to circumvent them. With sudden vividness Waythorn saw how the instinct had developed. She was "as easy as an old shoe"—a shoe that too many feet had worn. Her elasticity was the result of tension in too many different directions. Alice Haskett—Alice Varick—Alice Waythorn—she had been each in turn, and had left hanging to each name a little of her privacy, a little of her personality, a little of the inmost self where the unknown god abides.

"Yes—it's better to speak to Varick," said Waythorn wearily.

✤ V ✤

THE winter wore on, and society took advantage of the Waythorns' acceptance of Varick. Harassed hostesses were grateful to them for bridging over a social difficulty, and Mrs. Waythorn was held up as a miracle of good taste. Some experimental spirits could not resist the diversion of throwing Varick and his former wife together, and there were those who thought he found a zest in the propinquity. But Mrs. Waythorn's conduct remained irreproachable. She neither avoided Varick nor sought him out. Even Waythorn could not but admit that she had discovered the solution of the newest social problem.

He had married her without giving much thought to that problem. He had fancied that a woman can shed her past like a man. But now he saw that Alice was bound to hers both by the circumstances which forced her into continued relation with it, and by the traces it had left on her nature. With grim irony Waythorn compared himself to a member of a syndicate. He held so many shares in his wife's personality and his predecessors were his partners in the business. If there had been any element of passion in the transaction he would have felt less deteriorated by it. The fact that Alice took her change of husbands like a change of weather reduced the situation to mediocrity. He could have forgiven her for blunders, for excesses; for resisting Haskett, for yielding to Varick; for anything but her acquiescence and her tact. She reminded him of a juggler tossing knives; but the knives were blunt and she knew they would never cut her.

And then, gradually, habit formed a protecting surface for his sensibilities. If he paid for each day's comfort with the small change of his illusions, he grew daily to value the comfort more and set less store upon the coin. He had drifted into a dulling propinquity with Haskett and Varick and he took refuge in the cheap revenge of satirizing the situation. He even began to reckon up the advantages which accrued from it, to ask himself if it were not better to own a third of a wife who knew how to make a man happy than a whole one who had lacked opportunity to acquire the art. For it *was* an art, and made up, like all others, of concessions, eliminations and embellishments; of lights judiciously thrown and shadows skillfully softened. His wife knew exactly how to manage the lights, and he knew exactly to what training she owed her skill. He even tried to trace the source of his obligations, to discriminate between the influences which had combined to produce his domestic happiness; he perceived that Haskett's commonness had made Alice worship good breeding, while Varick's liberal construction of the marriage bond had taught her to value the conjugal virtues; so that he was directly indebted to his predecessors for the devotion which made his life easy if not inspiring.

From this phase he passed into that of complete acceptance. He ceased to satirize himself because time dulled the irony of the situation and the joke lost its humor with its sting. Even the sight of Haskett's hat on the hall table had ceased to touch the springs of epigram. The hat was often seen there now, for it had been decided that it was better for Lily's father to visit her than for the little girl to go to his boardinghouse. Waythorn, having acquiesced in this arrangement, had been surprised to find how little difference it made. Haskett was never obtrusive, and the few visitors who met him on the stairs were unaware of his identity. Waythorn did not know how often he saw Alice, but with himself Haskett was seldom in contact.

One afternoon, however, he learned on entering that Lily's father was waiting to see him. In the library he found Haskett occupying a chair in his usual provisional way. Waythorn always felt grateful to him for not leaning back.

"I hope you'll excuse me, Mr. Waythorn," he said rising. "I wanted to see Mrs. Waythorn about Lily, and your man asked me to wait here till she came in."

"Of course," said Waythorn, remembering that a sudden leak had that morning given over the drawing room to the plumbers.

He opened his cigar case and held it out to his visitor, and Haskett's acceptance seemed to mark a fresh stage in their intercourse. The spring evening was chilly, and Waythorn invited his guest to draw up his chair to the fire. He meant to find an excuse to leave Haskett in a moment; but he was tired and cold, and after all the little man no longer jarred on him.

The two were enclosed in the intimacy of their blended cigar smoke when the door opened and Varick walked into the room. Waythorn rose abruptly. It was the first time that Varick had come to the house, and the surprise of seeing him, combined with the singular inopportuneness of his arrival, gave a new edge to Waythorn's blunted sensibilities. He stared at his visitor without speaking.

Varick seemed too preoccupied to notice his host's embarrassment.

"My dear fellow," he exclaimed in his most expansive tone, "I must apologize for tumbling in on you in this way, but I was too late to catch you downtown, and so I thought—"

He stopped short, catching sight of Haskett, and his sanguine color deepened to a flush which spread vividly under his scant blond hair. But in a moment he recovered himself and nodded slightly. Haskett returned the bow in silence, and Waythorn was still groping for speech when the footman came in carrying a tea table.

The intrusion offered a welcome vent to Waythorn's nerves. "What the deuce are you bringing this here for?" he said sharply.

"I beg your pardon, sir, but the plumbers are still in the drawing room, and Mrs. Waythorn said she would have tea in the library." The footman's perfectly respectful tone implied a reflection on Waythorn's reasonableness.

"Oh, very well," said the latter resignedly, and the footman proceeded to open the folding tea table and set out its complicated appointments. While this interminable process continued the three men stood motionless, watching it with a fascinated stare, till Waythorn, to break the silence, said to Varick, "Won't you have a cigar?"

He held out the case he had just tendered to Haskett, and Varick helped himself with a smile. Waythorn looked about for a match, and finding none, proffered a light from his own cigar. Haskett, in the background, held his ground mildly, examining his cigar tip now and then, and stepping forward at the right moment to knock its ashes into the fire.

The footman at last withdrew, and Varick immediately began: "If I could just say half a word to you about this business—"

"Certainly," stammered Waythorn; "in the dining room—"

But as he placed his hand on the door it opened from without, and his wife appeared on the threshold.

She came in fresh and smiling, in her street dress and hat, shedding a fragrance from the boa which she loosened in advancing.

"Shall we have tea in here, dear?" she began; and then she caught sight of Varick. Her smile deepened, veiling a slight tremor of surprise.

"Why, how do you do?" she said with a distinct note of pleasure.

As she shook hands with Varick she saw Haskett standing behind him. Her smile faded for a moment, but she recalled it quickly, with a scarcely perceptible side glance at Waythorn.

"How do you do, Mr. Haskett?" she said, and shook hands with him a shade less cordially.

The three men stood awkwardly before her, till Varick, always the most self-possessed, dashed into an explanatory phrase.

"We—I had to see Waythorn a moment on business," he stammered, brick-red from chin to nape.

Haskett stepped forward with his air of mild obstinacy. "I am sorry to intrude; but you appointed five o'clock—" he directed his resigned glance to the timepiece on the mantel.

She swept aside their embarrassment with a charming gesture of hospitality.

"I'm so sorry—I'm always late; but the afternoon was so lovely." She stood drawing off her gloves, propitiatory and graceful, diffusing about her a sense of ease and familiarity in which the situation lost its grotesqueness. "But before talking business," she added brightly, "I'm sure everyone wants a cup of tea."

She dropped into her low chair by the tea table, and the

two visitors, as if drawn by her smile, advanced to receive the cups she held out.

She glanced about for Waythorn, and he took the third cup with a laugh.

The Dilettante

It was on an impulse hardly needing the arguments he found himself advancing in its favor, that Thursdale, on his way to the club, turned as usual into Mrs. Vervain's street.

The "as usual" was his own qualification of the act; a convenient way of bridging the interval—in days and other sequences—that lay between this visit and the last. It was characteristic of him that he instinctively excluded his call two days earlier, with Ruth Gaynor, from the list of his visits to Mrs. Vervain: the special conditions attending it had made it no more like a visit to Mrs. Vervain than an engraved dinner invitation is like a personal letter. Yet it was to talk over his call with Miss Gaynor that he was now returning to the scene of that episode; and it was because Mrs. Vervain could be trusted to handle the talking over as skillfully as the interview itself that, at her corner, he had felt the dilettante's irresistible craving to take a last look at a work of art that was passing out of his possession.

On the whole, he knew no one better fitted to deal with the unexpected than Mrs. Vervain. She excelled in the rare art of taking things for granted, and Thursdale felt a pardonable pride in the thought that she owed her excellence to his training. Early in his career, Thursdale had made the mistake, at the outset of his acquaintance with a lady, of telling her that he loved her, and exacting the same avowal in return. The latter part of that episode had been like the long walk back from a picnic, when one has to carry all the crockery one has finished using: it was the last time Thursdale ever allowed himself to be encumbered with the debris of a feast. He thus incidentally learned that the privilege of loving her is one of the least favors that a charming woman can accord; and in seeking to avoid the pitfalls of sentiment he had developed a science of evasion in which the woman of the moment became a mere implement of the game. He owed a great deal of delicate enjoyment to the cultivation of this art. The perils from which it had been his refuge became naïvely harmless: was it possible that he who now took his easy way along the levels had once preferred to gasp on the raw heights of emotion? Youth is a high-colored season; but he had the satisfaction of feeling that he had entered earlier than most into that chiaroscuro of sensation where every half-tone has its value.

As a promoter of this pleasure no one he had known was comparable to Mrs. Vervain. He had taught a good many women not to betray their feelings, but he had never before had such fine material to work with. She had been surprisingly crude when he first knew her; capable of making the most awkward inferences, of plunging through thin ice, of recklessly undressing her emotions; but she had acquired, under the discipline of his reticences and evasions, a skill almost equal to his own, and perhaps more remarkable in that it involved keeping time with any tune he played and reading at sight some uncommonly difficult passages.

It had taken Thursdale seven years to form this fine talent; but the result justified the effort. At the crucial moment she had been perfect: her way of greeting Miss Gaynor had made him regret that he had announced his engagement by letter. It was an evasion that confessed a difficulty; a deviation implying an obstacle, where, by common consent, it was agreed to see none; it betrayed, in short, a lack of confidence in the completeness of his method. It had been his pride never to put himself in a position which had to be quitted, as it were, by the back door; but here, as he perceived, the main portals would have opened for him of their own accord. All this, and much more, he read in the finished naturalness with which Mrs. Vervain had met Miss Gaynor. He had never seen a better piece of work: there was no overeagerness, no suspicious warmth, above all (and this gave her art the grace of a natural quality) there were none of those damnable implications whereby a woman, in welcoming her friend's betrothed, may keep him on pins and needles while she laps the lady in complacency. So masterly a performance, indeed, hardly needed the offset of Miss Gaynor's doorstep words—"To be so kind to me, how she must have liked you!"—though he caught himself wishing it lay within the bounds of fitness to transmit them, as a final tribute, to the one woman he knew who was unfailingly certain to enjoy a good thing. It was perhaps the one drawback to his new situation that it might develop good things which it would be impossible to hand on to Margaret Vervain.

The fact that he had made the mistake of underrating his friend's powers, the consciousness that his writing must have betrayed his distrust of her efficiency, seemed an added reason for turning down her street instead of going on to the club. He would show her that he knew how to value her; he would ask her to achieve with him a feat infinitely rarer and more delicate than the one he had appeared to avoid. Incidentally, he would also dispose of the interval of time before dinner: ever since he had seen Miss Gaynor off, an hour earlier, on her return journey to Buffalo, he had been wondering how he should put in the rest of the afternoon. It was absurd, how he missed the girl. . . . Yes, that was it: the desire to talk about her was, after all, at the bottom of his impulse to call on Mrs. Vervain! It was absurd, if you like—but it was delightfully rejuvenating. He could recall the time when he had been afraid of being obvious: now he felt that his return to the primitive emotions might be as restorative as a holiday in the Canadian woods. And it was precisely by the girl's candor, her directness, her lack of complications, that he was taken. The sense that she might say something rash at any moment was positively exhilarating: if she had thrown her arms about him at the station he would not have given a thought to his crumpled dignity. It surprised Thursdale to find what freshness of heart he brought to the adventure; and though his sense of irony prevented his ascribing his intactness to any conscious purpose, he could but rejoice in the fact that his sentimental economies had left him such a large surplus to draw upon.

Mrs. Vervain was at home—as usual. When one visits the

cemetery one expects to find the angel on the tombstone, and it struck Thursdale as another proof of his friend's good taste that she had been in no undue haste to change her habits. The whole house appeared to count on his coming; the footman took his hat and overcoat as naturally as though there had been no lapse in his visits; and the drawing room at once enveloped him in that atmosphere of tacit intelligence which Mrs. Vervain imparted to her very furniture.

It was a surprise that, in this general harmony of circumstances, Mrs. Vervain should herself sound the first false note.

"You?" she exclaimed; and the book she held slipped from her hand.

It was crude, certainly; unless it were a touch of the finest art. The difficulty of classifying it disturbed Thursdale's balance.

"Why not?" he said, restoring the book. "Isn't it my hour?" And as she made no answer, he added gently, "Unless it's someone else's?"

She laid the book aside and sank back into her chair. "Mine, merely," she said.

"I hope that doesn't mean that you're unwilling to share it?"

"With you? By no means. You're welcome to my last crust."

He looked at her reproachfully. "Do you call this the last?"

She smiled as he dropped into the seat across the hearth. "It's a way of giving it more flavor!"

He returned the smile. "A visit to you doesn't need such condiments."

She took this with just the right measure of retrospective amusement.

"Ah, but I want to put into this one a very special taste," she confessed.

Her smile was so confident, so reassuring, that it lulled him into the imprudence of saying: "Why should you want it to be different from what was always so perfectly right?"

She hesitated. "Doesn't the fact that it's the last constitute a difference?"

"The last—my last visit to you?"

"Oh, metaphorically, I mean—there's a break in the continuity."

Decidedly, she was pressing too hard: unlearning his arts already!

"I don't recognize it," he said. "Unless you make me—" he added, with a note that slightly stirred her attitude of languid attention.

She turned to him with grave eyes. "You recognize no difference whatever?"

"None—except an added link in the chain."

"An added link?"

"In having one more thing to like you for—your letting Miss Gaynor see why I had already so many." He flattered himself that this turn had taken the least hint of fatuity from the phrase.

Mrs. Vervain sank into her former easy pose. "Was it that you came for?" she asked, almost gaily.

"If it is necessary to have a reason—that was one."

"To talk to me about Miss Gaynor?"

"To tell you how she talks about you."

"That will be very interesting—especially if you have seen her since her second visit to me."

"Her second visit?" Thursdale pushed his chair back with a start and moved to another. "She came to see you again?"

"This morning, yes—by appointment."

He continued to look at her blankly. "You sent for her?"

"I didn't have to—she wrote and asked me last night. But no doubt you have seen her since."

Thursdale sat silent. He was trying to separate his words from his thoughts, but they still clung together inextricably. "I saw her off just now at the station."

"And she didn't tell you that she had been here again?"

"There was hardly time, I suppose—there were people about—" he floundered.

"Ah, she'll write, then."

He regained his composure. "Of course she'll write: very often, I hope. You know I'm absurdly in love," he cried audaciously.

She tilted her head back, looking up at him as he leaned

against the chimney piece. He had leaned there so often that the attitude touched a pulse which set up a throbbing in her throat. "Oh, my poor Thursdale!" she murmured.

"I suppose it's rather ridiculous," he owned; and as she remained silent, he added, with a sudden break—"Or have you another reason for pitying me?"

Her answer was another question. "Have you been back to your rooms since you left her?"

"Since I left her at the station? I came straight here."

"Ah, yes—you *could*: there was no reason—" Her words passed into a silent musing.

Thursdale moved nervously nearer. "You said you had something to tell me?"

"Perhaps I had better let her do so. There may be a letter at your rooms."

"A letter? What do you mean? A letter from *her*? What has happened?"

His paleness shook her, and she raised a hand of reassurance. "Nothing has happened—perhaps that is just the worst of it. You always *hated*, you know," she added incoherently, "to have things happen: you never would let them."

"And now—"

"Well, that was what she came here for: I supposed you had guessed. To know if anything had happened."

"Had happened?" He gazed at her slowly. "Between you and me?" he said with a rush of light.

The words were so much cruder than any that had ever passed between them, that the color rose to her face; but she held his startled gaze.

"You know girls are not quite as unsophisticated as they used to be. Are you surprised that such an idea should occur to her?"

His own color answered hers: it was the only reply that came to him.

Mrs. Vervain went on smoothly: "I supposed it might have struck you that there were times when we presented that appearance."

He made an impatient gesture. "A man's past is his own!"

"Perhaps—it certainly never belongs to the woman who

has shared it. But one learns such truths only by experience; and Miss Gaynor is naturally inexperienced."

"Of course—but—supposing her act a natural one—" he floundered lamentably among his innuendoes "—I still don't see—how there was anything—"

"Anything to take hold of? There wasn't—"

"Well, then—?" escaped him, in undisguised satisfaction; but as she did not complete the sentence he went on with a faltering laugh: "She can hardly object to the existence of a mere friendship between us!"

"But she does," said Mrs. Vervain.

Thursdale stood perplexed. He had seen, on the previous day, no trace of jealousy or resentment in his betrothed: he could still hear the candid ring of the girl's praise of Mrs. Vervain. If she were such an abyss of insincerity as to dissemble distrust under such frankness, she must at least be more subtle than to bring her doubts to her rival for solution. The situation seemed one through which one could no longer move in a penumbra, and he let in a burst of light with the direct query: "Won't you explain what you mean?"

Mrs. Vervain sat silent, not provokingly, as though to prolong his distress, but as if, in the attenuated phraseology he had taught her, it was difficult to find words robust enough to meet his challenge. It was the first time he had ever asked her to explain anything; and she had lived so long in dread of offering elucidations which were not wanted, that she seemed unable to produce one on the spot.

At last she said slowly: "She came to find out if you were really free."

Thursdale colored again. "Free?" he stammered, with a sense of physical disgust at contact with such crassness.

"Yes—if I had quite done with you." She smiled in recovered security. "It seems she likes clear outlines; she has a passion for definitions."

"Yes—well?" he said, wincing at the echo of his own subtlety.

"Well—and when I told her that you had never belonged to me, she wanted me to define *my* status—to know exactly where I had stood all along."

Thursdale sat gazing at her intently; his hand was not yet on the clue. "And even when you had told her that—"

"Even when I had told her that I had had no status—that I had never stood anywhere, in any sense she meant," said Mrs. Vervain, slowly, "even then she wasn't satisfied, it seems."

He uttered an uneasy exclamation. "She didn't believe you, you mean?"

"I mean that she *did* believe me: too thoroughly."

"Well, then—in God's name, what did she want?"

"Something more—those were the words she used."

"Something more? Between—between you and me? Is it a conundrum?" He laughed awkwardly.

"Girls are not what they were in my day; they are no longer forbidden to contemplate the relation of the sexes."

"So it seems!" he commented. "But since, in this case, there wasn't any—" he broke off, catching the dawn of a revelation in her gaze.

"That's just it. The unpardonable offence has been—in our not offending."

He flung himself down despairingly. "I give up! What did you tell her?" he burst out with sudden crudeness.

"The exact truth. If I had only known," she broke off with a beseeching tenderness, "won't you believe that I would still have lied for you?"

"Lied for me? Why on earth should you have lied for either of us?"

"To save you—to hide you from her to the last! As I've hidden you from myself all these years!" She stood up with a sudden tragic import in her movement. "You believe me capable of that, don't you? If I had only guessed—but I have never known a girl like her; she had the truth out of me with a spring."

"The truth that you and I had never—"

"Had never—never in all these years! Oh, she knew why—she measured us both in a flash. She didn't suspect me of having haggled with you—her words pelted me like hail. 'He just took what he wanted—sifted and sorted you to suit his taste. Burnt out the gold and left a heap of cinders. And you let him—you let yourself be cut in bits'—she mixed her metaphors a little—'be cut in bits, and used or discarded, while all the while every drop of blood in you belonged to him! But he's Shylock—he's Shylock—and you have bled to death of the pound of flesh he has cut off you.' But she despises me the most, you know—far, far the most—" Mrs. Vervain ended.

The words fell strangely on the scented stillness of the room: they seemed out of harmony with its setting of afternoon intimacy, the kind of intimacy on which, at any moment, a visitor might intrude without perceptibly lowering the atmosphere. It was as though a grand opera singer had strained the acoustics of a private music room.

Thursdale stood up, facing his hostess. Half the room was between them, but they seemed to stare close at each other now that the veils of reticence and ambiguity had fallen.

His first words were characteristic: "She *does* despise me, then?" he exclaimed.

"She thinks the pound of flesh you took was a little too near the heart."

He was excessively pale. "Please tell me exactly what she said of me."

"She did not speak much of you: she is proud. But I gather that while she understands love or indifference, her eyes have never been opened to the many intermediate shades of feeling. At any rate, she expressed an unwillingness to be taken with reservations—she thinks you would have loved her better if you had loved someone else first. The point of view is original—she insists on a man with a past!"

"Oh, a past—if she's serious—I could rake up a past!" he said with a laugh.

"So I suggested: but she has her eyes on this particular portion of it. She insists on making it a test case. She wanted to know what you had done to me; and before I could guess her drift I blundered into telling her."

Thursdale drew a difficult breath. "I never supposed—your revenge is complete," he said slowly.

He heard a little gasp in her throat. "My revenge? When I sent for you to warn you—to save you from being surprised as *I* was surprised?"

"You're very good—but it's rather late to talk of saving me." He held out his hand in the mechanical gesture of leave-taking.

"How you must care!—for I never saw you so dull," was her answer. "Don't you see that it's not too late for me to help you?" And as he continued to stare, she brought out sublimely: "Take the rest—in imagination! Let it at least be of that much use to you. Tell her I lied to her—she's too ready to believe it! And so, after all, in a sense, I shan't have been wasted."

His stare hung on her, widening to a kind of wonder. She gave the look back brightly, unblushingly, as though the expedient were too simple to need oblique approaches. It was extraordinary how a few words had swept them from an atmosphere of the most complex dissimulations to this contact of naked souls.

It was not in Thursdale to expand with the pressure of fate; but something in him cracked with it, and the rift let in new light. He went up to his friend and took her hand.

"You would do it—you would do it!"

She looked at him, smiling, but her hand shook.

"Good-bye," he said, kissing it.

"Good-bye? You are going—?"

"To get my letter."

"Your letter? The letter won't matter, if you will only do what I ask."

He returned her gaze. "I might, I suppose, without being out of character. Only, don't you see that if your plan helped me it could only harm her?"

"Harm *her*?"

"To sacrifice you wouldn't make me different. I shall go on being what I have always been—sifting and sorting, as she calls it. Do you want my punishment to fall on *her*?"

She looked at him long and deeply. "Ah, if I had to choose between you—!"

"You would let her take her chance? But I can't, you see, I must take my punishment alone."

She drew her hand away, sighing. "Oh, there will be no punishment for either of you."

"For either of us? There will be the reading of her letter for me."

She shook her head with a slight laugh. "There will be no letter."

Thursdale faced about from the threshold with fresh life in his look. "No letter? You don't mean—"

"I mean that she's been with you since I saw her—she's seen you and heard your voice. If there *is* a letter, she has recalled it—from the first station, by telegraph."

He turned back to the door, forcing an answer to her smile. "But in the meanwhile I shall have read it," he said.

The door closed on him, and she hid her eyes from the dreadful emptiness of the room.

Expiation

"I CAN NEVER," said Mrs. Fetherel, "hear the bell ring without a shudder."

Her unruffled aspect—she was the kind of woman whose emotions never communicate themselves to her clothes—and the conventional background of the New York drawing room, with its pervading implication of an imminent tea tray and of an atmosphere in which the social functions have become purely reflex, lent to her declaration a relief not lost on her cousin Mrs. Clinch, who, from the other side of the fireplace, agreed, with a glance at the clock, that it *was* the hour for bores.

"Bores!" cried Mrs. Fetherel impatiently, "If I shuddered at *them,* I should have a chronic ague!"

She leaned forward and laid a sparkling finger on her cousin's shabby black knee. "I mean the newspaper clippings," she whispered.

Mrs. Clinch returned a glance of intelligence. "They've begun already?"

"Not yet; but they're sure to now, at any minute, my publisher tells me."

Mrs. Fetherel's look of apprehension sat oddly on her small features, which had an air of neat symmetry somehow suggestive of being set in order every morning by the housemaid. Someone (there were rumors that it was her cousin) had once said that Paula Fetherel would have been very pretty if she hadn't looked so like a moral axiom in a copybook hand.

Mrs. Clinch received her confidence with a smile. "Well," she said, "I suppose you were prepared for the consequences of authorship?"

Mrs. Fetherel blushed brightly. "It isn't their coming," she owned—"it's their coming *now*."

"Now?"

"The Bishop's in town."

Mrs. Clinch leaned back and shaped her lips to a whistle which deflected in a laugh. "Well!" she said.

"You see!" Mrs. Fetherel triumphed.

"Well—weren't you prepared for the Bishop?"

"Not now—at least, I hadn't thought of his seeing the clippings."

"And why should he see them?"

"Bella—*won't* you understand? It's John."

"John?"

"Who has taken the most unexpected tone—one might almost say out of perversity."

"Oh, perversity—" Mrs. Clinch murmured, observing her cousin between lids wrinkled by amusement. "What tone has John taken?"

Mrs. Fetherel threw out her answer with the desperate gesture of a woman who lays bare the traces of a marital fist. "The tone of being proud of my book."

The measure of Mrs. Clinch's enjoyment overflowed in laughter.

"Oh, you may laugh," Mrs Fetherel insisted, "but it's no joke to me. In the first place, John's liking the book is so—so—such a false note—it puts me in such a ridiculous position; and then it has set him watching for the reviews—who would ever have suspected John of knowing that books were *reviewed*? Why, he's actually found out about the clipping bureau, and whenever the postman rings I hear John rush out of the library to see if there are any yellow envelopes. Of course, when they *do* come he'll bring them into the drawing room and read them aloud to everybody who happens to be here—and the Bishop is sure to happen to be here!"

Mrs. Clinch repressed her amusement. "The picture you draw is a lurid one," she conceded, "but your modesty strikes me as abnormal, especially in an author. The chances are that some of the clippings will be rather pleasant reading. The critics are not all union men."

Mrs. Fetherel stared. "Union men?"

"Well, I mean they don't all belong to the well-known Society-for-the-Persecution-of-Rising-Authors. Some of them have even been known to defy its regulations and say a good word for a new writer."

"Oh, I dare say," said Mrs. Fetherel, with the laugh her cousin's epigram exacted. "But you don't quite see my point. I'm not at all nervous about the success of my book—my publisher tells me I have no need to be—but I *am* afraid of its being a *succès de scandale.*"

"Mercy!" said Mrs. Clinch, sitting up.

The butler and footman at this moment appeared with the tea tray and when they had withdrawn, Mrs. Fetherel, bending her brightly rippled head above the kettle, continued in a murmur of avowal, "The title, even, is a kind of challenge."

"*Fast and Loose,**" Mrs. Clinch mused. "Yes, it ought to take."

"I didn't choose it for that reason!" the author protested. "I should have preferred something quieter—less pronounced; but I was determined not to shirk the responsibility of what I had written. I want people to know beforehand exactly what kind of book they are buying."

"Well," said Mrs. Clinch, "that's a degree of conscientiousness that I've never met with before. So few books fulfill the promise of their titles that experienced readers never expect the fare to come up to the menu."

"*Fast and Loose* will be no disappointment on that score," her cousin significantly returned. "I've handled the subject without gloves. I've called a spade a spade."

"You simply make my mouth water! And to think I haven't been able to read it yet because every spare minute

* This is Edith Wharton's private joke. "Fast and Loose" was the title of a still unpublished fifteen-thousand word novella (her first completed work of fiction), which she wrote around 1877 or 1878. It is a theatrical and romantic story, which the author adorned, for her own amusement, with a series of mock reviews written in the style of the then current American periodicals. There are several extant manuscripts of the novella, which is being prepared for publication by Mrs. Violet Winner of the University of Virginia.

of my time has been given to correcting the proofs of 'How the Birds Keep Christmas'! There's an instance of the hardships of an author's life!"

Mrs. Fetherel's eye clouded. "Don't joke, Bella, please. I suppose to experienced authors there's always something absurd in the nervousness of a new writer, but in my case so much is at stake; I've put so much of myself into this book and I'm so afraid of being misunderstood . . . of being, as it were, in advance of my time . . . like poor Flaubert. . . . I *know* you'll think me ridiculous . . . and if only my own reputation were at stake, I should never give it a thought . . . but the idea of dragging John's name through the mire. . . ."

Mrs. Clinch, who had risen and gathered her cloak about her, stood surveying from her genial height her cousin's agitated countenance.

"Why did you use John's name, then?"

"That's another of my difficulties! I *had* to. There would have been no merit in publishing such a book under an assumed name; it would have been an act of moral cowardice. *Fast and Loose* is not an ordinary novel. A writer who dares to show up the hollowness of social conventions must have the courage of her convictions and be willing to accept the consequences of defying society. Can you imagine Ibsen or Tolstoi writing under a false name?" Mrs. Fetherel lifted a tragic eye to her cousin. "You don't know, Bella, how often I've envied you since I began to write. I used to wonder sometimes—you won't mind my saying so?—why, with all your cleverness, you hadn't taken up some more exciting subject than natural history; but I see now how wise you were. Whatever happens, you will never be denounced by the press!"

"Is that what you're afraid of?" asked Mrs. Clinch, as she grasped the bulging umbrella which rested against her chair. "My dear, if I had ever had the good luck to be denounced by the press, my brougham would be waiting at the door for me at this very moment, and I shouldn't have had to ruin this umbrella by using it in the rain. Why, you innocent, if I'd ever felt the slightest aptitude for showing up social conventions, do you suppose I should waste my time writing

'Nests Ajar' and 'How to Smell the Flowers'? There's a fairly steady demand for pseudo-science and colloquial ornithology, but it's nothing, simply nothing, to the ravenous call for attacks on social institutions—especially by those inside the institutions!"

There was often, to her cousin, a lack of taste in Mrs. Clinch's pleasantries, and on this occasion they seemed more than usually irrelevant.

"*Fast and Loose* was not written with the idea of a large sale."

Mrs. Clinch was unperturbed. "Perhaps that's just as well," she returned, with a philosophic shrug. "The surprise will be all the pleasanter, I mean. For of course it's going to sell tremendously; especially if you can get the press to denounce it."

"Bella, how *can* you? I sometimes think you say such things expressly to tease me; and yet I should think you of all women would understand my purpose in writing such a book. It has always seemed to me that the message I had to deliver was not for myself alone, but for all the other women in the world who have felt the hollowness of our social shams, the ignominy of bowing down to the idols of the market, but have lacked either the courage or the power to proclaim their independence; and I have fancied, Bella dear, that, however severely society might punish me for revealing its weaknesses, I could count on the sympathy of those who, like you"—Mrs. Fetherel's voice sank—"have passed through the deep waters."

Mrs. Clinch gave herself a kind of canine shake, as though to free her ample shoulders from any drop of the element she was supposed to have traversed.

"Oh, call them muddy rather than deep," she returned; "and you'll find, my dear, that women who've had any wading to do are rather shy of stirring up mud. It sticks—especially on white clothes."

Mrs. Fetherel lifted an undaunted brow. "I'm not afraid," she proclaimed; and at the same instant she dropped her teaspoon with a clatter and shrank back into her seat. "There's the bell," she exclaimed, "and I know it's the Bishop!"

It was in fact the Bishop of Ossining, who, impressively

announced by Mrs. Fetherel's butler, now made an entry that may best be described as not inadequate to the expectations the announcement raised. The Bishop always entered a room well; but, when unannounced, or preceded by a low church butler who gave him his surname, his appearance lacked the impressiveness conferred on it by the due specification of his diocesan dignity. The Bishop was very fond of his niece, Mrs. Fetherel, and one of the traits he most valued in her was the possession of a butler who knew how to announce a bishop.

Mrs. Clinch was also his niece; but, aside from the fact that she possessed no butler at all, she had laid herself open to her uncle's criticism by writing insignificant little books which had a way of going into five or ten editions, while the fruits of his own episcopal leisure—"The Wail of Jonah" (twenty) cantos in blank verse), and "Through a Glass Brightly"; or, "How to Raise Funds for a Memorial Window"— inexplicably languished on the back shelves of a publisher noted for his dexterity in pushing "devotional goods." Even this indiscretion the Bishop might, however, have condoned, had his niece thought fit to turn to him for support and advice at the painful juncture of her history when, in her own words, it became necessary for her to invite Mr. Clinch to look out for another situation. Mr. Clinch's misconduct was of the kind especially designed by Providence to test the fortitude of a Christian wife and mother, and the Bishop was absolutely distended with seasonable advice and edification; so that when Bella met his tentative exhortations with the curt remark that she preferred to do her own house cleaning unassisted, her uncle's grief at her ingratitude was not untempered with sympathy for Mr. Clinch.

It is not surprising, therefore, that the Bishop's warmest greetings were always reserved for Mrs. Fetherel; and on this occasion Mrs. Clinch thought she detected, in the salutation which fell to her share, a pronounced suggestion that her own presence was superfluous—a hint which she took with her usual imperturbable good humor.

✣ II ✣

LEFT alone with the bishop, Mrs. Fetherel sought the nearest refuge from conversation by offering him a cup of tea. The Bishop accepted with the preoccupied air of a man to whom, for the moment, tea is but a subordinate incident. Mrs. Fetherel's nervousness increased; and knowing that the surest way of distracting attention from one's own affairs is to affect an interest in those of one's companion, she hastily asked if her uncle had come to town on business.

"On business—yes—" said the Bishop in an impressive tone. "I had to see my publisher, who has been behaving rather unsatisfactorily in regard to my last book."

"Ah—your last book?" faltered Mrs. Fetherel, with a sickening sense of her inability to recall the name or nature of the work in question, and a mental vow never again to be caught in such ignorance of a colleague's productions.

" 'Through a Glass Brightly,' " the Bishop explained, with an emphasis which revealed his detection of her predicament. "You may remember that I sent you a copy last Christmas?"

"Of course I do!" Mrs. Fetherel brightened. "It was that delightful story of the poor consumptive girl who had no money, and two little brothers to support—"

"Sisters—idiot sisters—" the Bishop gloomily corrected.

"I mean sisters; and who managed to collect money enough to put up a beautiful memorial window to her—her grandfather, whom she had never seen—"

"But whose sermons had been her chief consolation and support during her long struggle with poverty and disease." The Bishop gave the satisfied sigh of the workman who reviews his completed task. "A touching subject, surely; and I believe I did it justice; at least so my friends assured me."

"Why, yes—I remember there was a splendid review of it in the *Reredos!*" cried Mrs. Fetherel, moved by the incipient instinct of reciprocity.

"Yes—by my dear friend Mrs. Gollinger, whose husband, the late Dean Gollinger, was under very particular obligations to me. Mrs. Gollinger is a woman of rare literary acumen, and her praise of my book was unqualified; but the public wants more highly seasoned fare, and the approval of a thoughtful churchwoman carries less weight than the sensational comments of an illiterate journalist." The Bishop bent a meditative eye on his spotless gaiters. "At the risk of horrifying you, my dear," he added, with a slight laugh, "I will confide to you that my best chance of a popular success would be to have my book denounced by the press."

"Denounced?" gasped Mrs. Fetherel. "On what ground?"

"On the ground of immorality." The Bishop evaded her startled gaze, "Such a thing is inconceivable to you, of course; but I am only repeating what my publisher tells me. If, for instance, a critic could be induced—I mean, if a critic were to be found, who called in question the morality of my heroine in sacrificing her own health and that of her idiot sisters in order to put up a memorial window to her grandfather, it would probably raise a general controversy in the newspapers, and I might count on a sale of ten or fifteen thousand within the next year. If he described her as morbid or decadent, it might even run to twenty thousand; but that is more than I permit myself to hope. In fact I should be satisfied with any general charge of immorality." The Bishop sighed again, "I need hardly tell you that I am actuated by no mere literary ambition. Those whose opinion I most value have assured me that the book is not without merit; but, though it does not become me to dispute their verdict, I can truly say that my vanity as an author is not at stake. I have, however, a special reason for wishing to increase the circulation of 'Through a Glass Brightly'; it was written for a purpose—a purpose I have greatly at heart—"

"I know," cried his niece sympathetically. "The chantry window—?"

"Is still empty, alas! and I had great hopes that, under Providence, my little book might be the means of filling it. All our wealthy parishioners have given lavishly to the cathedral, and it was for this reason that, in writing 'Through a Glass,' I addressed my appeal more especially to the less well-endowed, hoping by the example of my heroine to stimulate the collection of small sums throughout the entire diocese, and perhaps beyond it. I am sure," the Bishop feelingly concluded, "the book would have a widespread influence if people could only be induced to read it!"

His conclusion touched a fresh threat of association in Mrs. Fetherel's vibrating nerve centers. "I never thought of that!" she cried.

The Bishop looked at her inquiringly.

"That one's books may not be read at all! How dreadful!" she exclaimed.

He smiled faintly. "I had not forgotten that I was addressing an authoress," he said. "Indeed, I should not have dared to inflict my troubles on anyone not of the craft."

Mrs. Fetherel was quivering with the consciousness of her involuntary self-betrayal. "Oh, Uncle!" she murmured.

"In fact," the Bishop continued, with a gesture which seemed to brush away her scruples, "I came here partly to speak to you about your novel. 'Fast and Loose,' I think you call it?"

Mrs. Fetherel blushed assentingly.

"And is it out yet?" the Bishop continued.

"It came out about a week ago. But you haven't touched your tea and it must be quite cold. Let me give you another cup."

"My reason for asking," the Bishop went on, with the bland inexorableness with which, in his younger days, he had been known to continue a sermon after the senior warden had looked four times at his watch, "—my reason for asking is, that I hoped I might not be too late to induce you to change the title."

Mrs. Fetherel set down the cup she had filled. "The title?" she faltered.

The Bishop raised a reassuring hand. "Don't misunderstand me, dear child; don't for a moment imagine that I take it to be in any way indicative of the contents of the book. I know you too well for that. My first idea was that it had probably been forced on you by an unscrupulous publisher. I know too well to what ignoble compromises one may be driven in such cases!" He paused, as though to give her the opportunity of confirming this conjecture, but she preserved an apprehensive silence, and he went on, as though taking up the second point in his sermon: "Or, again, the name may have taken your fancy without your realizing all that it implies to minds more alive than yours to offensive innuendoes. It is—ahem—excessively suggestive, and I hope I am not too late to warn you of the false impression it is likely to produce on the very readers whose approbation you would most value. My friend Mrs. Gollinger, for instance—"

Mrs. Fetherel, as the publication of her novel testified, was in theory a woman of independent views; and if in practice she sometimes failed to live up to her standard, it was rather from an irresistible tendency to adapt herself to her environment than from any conscious lack of moral courage. The Bishop's exordium had excited in her that sense of opposition which such admonitions are apt to provoke; but as he went on she felt herself gradually enclosed in an atmosphere in which her theories vainly gasped for breath. The Bishop had the immense dialectical advantage of invalidating any conclusions at variance with his own by always assuming that his premises were among the necessary laws of thought. This method, combined with the habit of ignoring any classifications but his own, created an element in which the first condition of existence was the immediate adoption of his standpoint; so that his niece, as she listened, seemed to feel Mrs. Gollinger's Mechlin cap spreading its conventual shadow over her rebellious brow and the *Revue de Paris* at her elbow turning into a copy of the *Reredos*. She had meant to assure her uncle that she was quite aware of the significance of the title she had chosen, that it had been deliberately selected as indicating the subject of her novel, and that the book itself had been written in direct defiance of the class of readers for whose susceptibilities he was alarmed. The words were almost on her lips when the irresistible suggestion conveyed by the Bishop's tone and language deflected them into the apologetic murmur, "Oh, Uncle, you mustn't think—I never meant—" How much farther this current of reaction might have carried her the historian is unable to compute, for at this point the door opened and her husband entered the room.

"The first review of your book!" he cried, flourishing a yellow envelope. "My dear Bishop, how lucky you're here!"

Though the trials of married life have been classified and catalogued with exhaustive accuracy, there is one form of conjugal misery which has perhaps received inadequate attention; and that is the suffering of the versatile woman whose husband is not equally adapted to all her moods. Every woman feels for the sister who is compelled to wear a bonnet which does not "go" with her gown; but how much sympathy is given to her whose husband refuses to harmonize with the pose of the moment? Scant justice has, for instance, been done to the misunderstood wife whose husband persists in understanding her; to the submissive helpmate whose taskmaster shuns every opportunity of browbeating her, and to the generous and impulsive being whose bills are paid with philosophic calm. Mrs. Fetherel, as wives go, had been fairly exempt from trials of this nature, for her husband, if undistinguished by pronounced brutality or indifference, had at least the negative merit of being her intellectual inferior. Landscape gardeners, who are aware of the usefulness of a valley in emphasizing the height of a hill, can form an idea of the account to which an accomplished woman may turn such deficiences; and it need scarcely be said that Mrs. Fetherel had made the most of her opportunities. It was agreeably obvious to everyone, Fetherel included, that he was not the man to appreciate such a woman; but there are no limits to man's perversity, and he did his best to invalidate this advantage by admiring her without pretending to understand her. What she most suffered from was this fatuous approval; the maddening sense that, however she conducted herself, he would always admire her. Had he belonged to the class whose conversational supplies are drawn from the domestic circle, his wife's name would never have been off his lips; and to Mrs. Fetherel's sensitive perceptions his frequent silences were indicative of the fact that she was his one topic.

It was, in part, the attempt to escape this persistent approbation that had driven Mrs. Fetherel to authorship. She had fancied that even the most infatuated husband might be counted on to resent, at least negatively, an attack on the sanctity of the hearth; and her anticipations were heightened by a sense of the unpardonableness of her act. Mrs. Fetherel's relations with her husband were in fact complicated by an irrepressible tendency to be fond of him; and there was a certain pleasure in the prospect of a situation that justified the most explicit expiation.

These hopes Fetherel's attitude had already defeated. He read the book with enthusiasm, he pressed it on his friends, he sent a copy to his mother; and his very soul now hung on the verdict of the reviewers. It was perhaps this proof of his general inaptitude that made his wife doubly alive to his special defects; so that his inopportune entrance was aggravated by the very sound of his voice and the hopeless aberration of his smile. Nothing, to the observant, is more indicative of a man's character and circumstances than his way of entering a room. The Bishop of Ossining, for instance, brought with him not only an atmosphere of episcopal authority, but an implied opinion on the verbal inspiration of the Scriptures and on the attitude of the Church toward divorce; while the appearance of Mrs. Fetherel's husband produced an immediate impression of domestic felicity. His mere aspect implied that there was a well-filled nursery upstairs; that his wife, if she did not sew on his buttons, at least superintended the performance of that task; that they both went to church regularly, and that they dined with his mother every Sunday evening punctually at seven o'clock.

All this and more was expressed in the affectionate gesture with which he now raised the yellow envelope above Mrs. Fetherel's clutch; and knowing the uselessness of begging him not to be silly, she said, with a dry despair, "You're boring the Bishop horribly."

Fetherel turned a radiant eye on that dignitary. "She bores us all horribly, doesn't she, sir?" he exulted.

"Have you read it?" said his wife, uncontrollably.

"Read it? Of course not—it's just this minute come. I say, Bishop, you're not going—?"

"Not till I've heard this," said the Bishop, settling himself in his chair with an indulgent smile.

His niece glanced at him despairingly, "Don't let John's nonsense detain you," she entreated.

"Detain him? That's good," guffawed Fetherel. "It isn't as long as one of his sermons—won't take me five minutes to read. Here, listen to this, ladies and gentlemen: 'In this age of festering pessimism and decadent depravity, it is no surprise to the nauseated reviewer to open one more volume saturated with the fetid emanations of the sewer—' "

Fetherel, who was not in the habit of reading aloud, paused with a gasp, and the Bishop glanced sharply at his niece, who kept her gaze fixed on the teacup she had not yet succeeded in transferring to his hand.

" 'Of the sewer,' " her husband resumed; " 'but his wonder is proportionately great when he lights on a novel as sweetly inoffensive as Paula Fetherel's *Fast and Loose.* Mrs. Fetherel is, we believe, a new hand at fiction, and her work reveals frequent traces of inexperience; but these are more than atoned for by her pure fresh view of life and her altogether unfashionable regard for the reader's moral susceptibilities. Let no one be induced by its distinctly misleading title to forego the enjoyment of this pleasant picture of domestic life, which, in spite of a total lack of force in character drawing and of consecutiveness in incident, may be described as a distinctly pretty story."

✥ III ✥

It was several weeks later that Mrs. Clinch once more brought the plebeian aroma of heated tramcars and muddy street crossings into the violet-scented atmosphere of her cousin's drawing room.

"Well," she said, tossing a damp bundle of proof into the corner of a silk-cushioned bergère, "I've read it at last and I'm not so awfully shocked!"

Mrs. Fetherel, who sat near the fire with her head propped on a languid hand, looked up without speaking.

"Mercy, Paula," said her visitor, "you're ill."

Mrs. Fetherel shook her head. "I was never better," she said, mournfully.

"Then may I help myself to tea? Thanks."

Mrs. Clinch carefully removed her mended glove before taking a buttered tea cake; then she glanced again at her cousin.

"It's not what I said just now—?" she ventured.

"Just now?"

"About *Fast and Loose*? I came to talk it over."

Mrs. Fetherel sprang to her feet. "I never," she cried dramatically, "want to hear it mentioned again!"

"Paula!" exclaimed Mrs. Clinch, setting down her cup.

Mrs. Fetherel slowly turned on her an eye brimming with the incommunicable; then, dropping into her seat again, she added, with a tragic laugh: "There's nothing left to say."

"Nothing—?" faltered Mrs. Clinch, longing for another tea cake, but feeling the inappropriateness of the impulse in an atmosphere so charged with the portentous. "Do you mean that everything *has* been said?" She looked tentatively at her cousin. "Haven't they been nice?"

"They've been odious—odious—" Mrs. Fetherel burst out, with an ineffectual clutch at her handkerchief. "It's been perfectly intolerable!"

Mrs. Clinch, philosophically resigning herself to the propriety of taking no more tea, crossed over to her cousin and laid a sympathizing hand on that lady's agitated shoulder.

"It *is* a bore at first," she conceded; "but you'll be surprised to see how soon one gets used to it."

"I shall—never—get—used to it—" Mrs. Fetherel brokenly declared.

"Have they been so very nasty—all of them?"

"Every one of them!" the novelist sobbed.

"I'm so sorry, dear; it *does* hurt, I know—but hadn't you rather expected it?"

"Expected it?" cried Mrs. Fetherel, sitting up.

Mrs. Clinch felt her way warily. "I only mean, dear, that I fancied from what you said before the book came out that you rather expected—that you'd rather discounted—"

"Their recommending it to everybody as a perfectly harmless story?"

"Good gracious! Is *that* what they've done?"

Mrs. Fetherel speechlessly nodded.

"Every one of them?"

"Every one."

"Phew!" said Mrs. Clinch, with an incipient whistle.

"Why, you've just said it yourself!" her cousin suddenly reproached her.

"Said what?"

"That you weren't so *awfully* shocked—"

"I? Oh, well—you see, you'd keyed me up to such a pitch that it wasn't quite as bad as I expected—"

Mrs. Fetherel lifted a smile steeled for the worst. "Why not say at once," she suggested, "that it's a distinctly pretty story?"

"They haven't said *that*?"

"They've all said it."

"My poor Paula!"

"Even the Bishop—"

"The Bishop called it a pretty story?"

"He wrote me—I've his letter somewhere. The title rather scared him—he wanted me to change it; but when he'd read the book he wrote that it was all right and that he'd sent several copies to his friends."

"The old hypocrite!" cried Mrs. Clinch. "That was nothing but professional jealousy."

"Do you think so?" cried her cousin, brightening.

"Sure of it, my dear. His own books don't sell, and he knew the quickest way to kill yours was to distribute it through the diocese with his blessing."

"Then you don't really think it's a pretty story?"

"Dear me, no! Not nearly as bad as that—"

"You're so good, Bella—but the reviewers?"

"Oh, the reviewers," Mrs. Clinch jeered. She gazed meditatively at the cold remains of her tea cake. "Let me see," she said, suddenly; "do you happen to remember if the first review came out in an important paper?"

"Yes—the *Radiator*."

"That's it! I thought so. Then the others simply followed suit: they often do if a big paper sets the pace. Saves a lot of trouble. Now if you could only have got the *Radiator* to denounce you—"

"That's what the Bishop said!" cried Mrs. Fetherel.

"He did?"

"He said his only chance of selling 'Through a Glass Brightly' was to have it denounced on the ground of immorality."

"H'm," said Mrs. Clinch, "I thought he knew a trick or two." She turned an illuminated eye on her cousin. "You ought to get *him* to denounce *Fast and Loose*!" she cried.

Mrs. Fetherel looked at her suspiciously. "I suppose every book must stand or fall on its own merits," she said in an unconvinced tone.

"Bosh! That view is as extinct as the post chaise and the packet ship—it belongs to the time when people read books. Nobody does that now; the reviewer was the first to set the example, and the public was only too thankful to follow it. At first people read the reviews; now they read only the publishers' extracts from them. Even these are rapidly being replaced by paragraphs borrowed from the vocabulary of commerce. I often have to look twice before I am sure if I am reading a department store advertisement or the announcement of a new batch of literature. The publishers will soon be having their 'fall and spring openings' and their 'special importations for Horse Show Week.' But the Bishop is right, of course—nothing helps a book like a rousing attack on its morals; and as the publishers can't exactly proclaim the impropriety of their own wares, the task has to be left to the press or the pulpit."

"The pulpit?" Mrs. Fetherel mused.

"Why, yes. Look at those two novels in England last year."

Mrs. Fetherel shook her head hopelessly. "There is so much more interest in literature in England than here."

"Well, we've got to make the supply create the demand. The Bishop could run your novel up into the hundred thousands in no time."

"But if he can't make his own sell—"

"My dear, a man can't very well preach against his own writings!"

Mrs. Clinch rose and picked up her proofs.

"I'm awfully sorry for you, Paula dear," she concluded, "but I can't help being thankful that there's no demand for pessimism in the field of natural history. Fancy having to write 'The Fall of a Sparrow,' or 'How the Plants Misbehave'!"

✣ IV ✣

MRS. FETHEREL, driving up to the Grand Central Station one morning about five months later, caught sight of the distinguished novelist, Archer Hynes, hurrying into the waiting room ahead of her. Hynes, on his side, recognizing her brougham, turned back to greet her as the footman opened the carriage door.

"My dear colleague! Is it possible that we are traveling together?"

Mrs. Fetherel blushed with pleasure. Hynes had given her two columns of praise in the *Sunday Meteor,* and she had not yet learned to disguise her gratitude.

"I am going to Ossining," she said smilingly.

"So am I. Why, this is almost as good as an elopement."

"And it will end where elopements ought to—in church."

"In church? You're not going to Ossining to go to church?"

"Why not? There's a special ceremony in the cathedral—the chantry window is to be unveiled."

"The chantry window? How picturesque! What *is* a chantry? And why do you want to see it unveiled? Are you after copy—doing something in the Huysmans manner? 'La Cathédrale,' eh?"

"Oh, no," Mrs. Fetherel hesitated. "I'm going simply to please my uncle," she said, at last.

"Your uncle?"

"The Bishop, you know." She smiled.

"The Bishop—the Bishop of Ossining? Why, wasn't he the chap who made that ridiculous attack on your book? Is that prehistoric ass your uncle? Upon my soul, I think you're mighty forgiving to travel all the way to Ossining for one of his stained-glass sociables!"

Mrs. Fetherel's smiled flowed into a gentle laugh. "Oh, I've never allowed that to interfere with our friendship. My uncle felt dreadfully about having to speak publicly against my book—it was a great deal harder for him than for me—but he thought it his duty to do so. He has the very highest sense of duty."

"Well," said Hynes, with a shrug. "I don't know that he didn't do you a good turn. Look at that!"

They were standing near the bookstall and he pointed to a placard surmounting the counter and emblazoned with the conspicuous announcement: "*Fast and Loose.* New Edition with Author's Portrait. Hundred and Fiftieth Thousand."

Mrs. Fetherel frowned impatiently. "How absurd! They've no right to use my picture as a poster!"

"There's our train," said Hynes; and they began to push their way through the crowd surging toward one of the inner doors.

As they stood wedged between circumferent shoulders, Mrs. Fetherel became conscious of the fixed stare of a pretty girl who whispered eagerly to her companion. "Look, Myrtle! That's Paula Fetherel right behind us—I knew her in a minute!"

"Gracious—where?" cried the other girl, giving her head a twist which swept her Gainsborough plumes across Mrs. Fetherel's face.

The first speaker's words had carried beyond her companion's ear, and a lemon-colored woman in spectacles, who clutched a copy of the "Journal of Psychology" in one drab cotton-gloved hand, stretched her disengaged hand across the intervening barrier of humanity.

"Have I the privilege of addressing the distinguished author of *Fast and Loose*? If so, let me thank you in the name of the Woman's Psychological League of Peoria for your magnificent courage in raising the standard of revolt against—"

"You can tell us the rest in the car," said a fat man, pressing his good-humored bulk against the speaker's arm.

Mrs. Fetherel, blushing, embarrassed and happy, slipped into the space produced by this displacement, and a few moments later had taken her seat in the train.

She was a little late, and the other chairs were already filled by a company of elderly ladies and clergymen who seemed to belong to the same party, and were still busy exchanging greetings and settling themselves in their places.

One of the ladies, at Mrs. Fetherel's approach, uttered an exclamation of pleasure and advanced with outstretched hand. "My dear Mrs. Fetherel! I am so delighted to see you here. May I hope you are going to the unveiling of the chantry window? The dear Bishop so hoped that you would do so! But perhaps I ought to introduce myself. I am Mrs. Gollinger"—she lowered her voice expressively—"one of your uncle's oldest friends, one who has stood close to him through all this sad business, and who knows what he suffered when he felt obliged to sacrifice family affection to the call of duty."

Mrs. Fetherel, who had smiled and colored slightly at the beginning of this speech, received its close with a deprecating gesture.

"Oh, pray don't mention it," she murmured. "I quite understood how my uncle was placed—I bore him no ill will for feeling obliged to preach against my book."

"He understood that, and was so touched by it! He has often told me that it was the hardest task he was ever called upon to perform—and, do you know, he quite feels that this unexpected gift of the chantry window is in some way a return for his courage in preaching that sermon."

Mrs. Fetherel smiled faintly. "Does he feel that?"

"Yes; he really does. When the funds for the window were so mysteriously placed at his disposal, just as he had begun to despair of raising them, he assured me that he could not help connecting the fact with his denunciation of your book."

"Dear Uncle!" sighed Mrs. Fetherel. "Did he say that?"

"And now," continued Mrs. Gollinger, with cumulative rapture—"now that you are about to show, by appearing at the ceremony today, that there has been no break in your friendly relations, the dear Bishop's happiness will be complete. He was so longing to have you come to the unveiling!"

"He might have counted on me," said Mrs. Fetherel, still smiling.

"Ah, that is so beautifully forgiving of you!" cried Mrs. Gollinger enthusiastically. "But then, the Bishop has always assured me that your real nature was very different from that which—if you will pardon my saying so—seems to be revealed by your brilliant but—er—rather subversive book. 'If you only knew my niece, dear Mrs. Gollinger,' he always said, 'you would see that her novel was written in all innocence of heart'; and to tell you the truth, when I first read the book I didn't think it so very, *very* shocking. It wasn't till the dear Bishop had explained to me—but, dear me, I mustn't take up your time in this way when so many others are anxious to have a word with you."

Mrs. Fetherel glanced at her in surprise, and Mrs. Gollinger continued with a playful smile: "You forget that your face is familiar to thousands whom you have never seen. We all recognized you the moment you entered the train, and my friends here are so eager to make your acquaintance—even those"—her smile deepened—"who thought the dear Bishop not *quite unjustified* in his attack on your remarkable novel."

✥ V ✥

A RELIGIOUS light filled the chantry of Ossining Cathedral, filtering through the linen curtain which veiled the central window and mingling with the blaze of tapers on the richly adorned altar.

In this devout atmosphere, agreeably laden with the incense-like aroma of Easter lilies and forced lilacs, Mrs. Fetherel knelt with a sense of luxurious satisfaction. Beside her sat Archer Hynes, who had remembered that there was to be a church scene in his next novel and that his impressions of the devotional environment needed refreshing. Mrs. Fetherel was very happy. She was conscious that her entrance had sent a thrill through the female devotees who packed the chantry, and she had humor enough to enjoy the thought that, but for the good Bishop's denunciation of her book, the heads of his flock would not have been turned so eagerly in her direction. Moreover, as she entered she had caught sight of a society reporter, and she knew that her presence, and the fact that she was accompanied by Hynes, would be conspicuously proclaimed in the morning papers. All these evidences of the success of her handiwork might have turned a calmer head than Mrs. Fetherel's and though she had now learned to dissemble her gratification, it still filled her inwardly with a delightful glow.

The Bishop was somewhat late in appearing, and she employed the interval in meditating on the plot of her next novel, which was already partly sketched out, but for which she had been unable to find a satisfactory dénouement. By a not uncommon process of ratiocination, Mrs. Fetherel's success had convinced her of her vocation. She was sure now that it was her duty to lay bare the secret plague spots of society, and she was resolved that there should be no doubt as to the purpose of her new book. Experience had shown her that where she had fancied she was calling a spade a spade she had in fact been alluding in guarded terms to the drawing-room shovel. She was determined not to repeat the same mistake, and she flattered herself that her coming novel would not need an episcopal denunciation to insure its sale, however likely it was to receive this crowning evidence of success.

She had reached this point in her meditations when the choir burst into song and the ceremony of the unveiling began. The Bishop, almost always felicitous in his addresses to the fair sex, was never more so than when he was celebrating the triumph of one of his cherished purposes. There was a peculiar mixture of Christian humility and episcopal exultation in the manner with which he called attention to the Creator's promptness in responding to his demand for funds, and he had never been more happily inspired than in eulogizing the mysterious gift of the chantry window.

Though no hint of the donor's identity had been allowed to escape him, it was generally understood that the Bishop knew who had given the window, and the congregation awaited in a flutter of suspense the possible announcement of a name. None came, however, though the Bishop deliciously titillated the curiosity of his flock by circling ever closer about the interesting secret. He would not disguise from them, he said, that the heart which had divined his inmost wish had been a woman's—is it not to woman's intuitions that more than half the happiness of earth is owing? What man is obliged to learn by the laborious process of experience, woman's wondrous instinct tells her at a glance; and so it had been with this cherished scheme, this unhoped-for completion of their beautiful chantry. So much, at least, he was allowed to reveal; and indeed, had he not done so, the window itself would have spoken for him, since the first glance at its touching subject and exquisite design would show it to have originated in a woman's heart. This tribute to the sex was received with an audible sigh of contentment, and the Bishop, always stimulated by such evidence of his sway over his hearers, took up his theme with gathering eloquence.

Yes—a woman's heart had planned the gift, a woman's hand had executed it, and, might he add, without too far withdrawing the veil in which Christian beneficence ever loved to drape its acts—might he add that, under Providence, a book, a simple book, a mere tale, in fact, had had its share in the good work for which they were assembled to give thanks?

At this unexpected announcement, a ripple of excitement ran through the assemblage, and more than one head was abruptly turned in the direction of Mrs. Fetherel, who sat listening in an agony of wonder and confusion. It did not escape the observant novelist at her side that she drew down her veil to conceal an uncontrollable blush, and this evidence of dismay caused him to fix an attentive gaze on her, while from her seat across the aisle Mrs. Gollinger sent a smile of unctuous approval.

"A book—a simple book—" the Bishop's voice went on above this flutter of mingled emotions. "What is a book? Only a few pages and a little ink—and yet one of the mightiest instruments which Providence has devised for shaping the destinies of man . . . one of the most powerful influences for good or evil which the Creator has placed in the hands of his creatures. . . ."

The air seemed intolerably close to Mrs. Fetherel, and she drew out her scent bottle, and then thrust it hurriedly away, conscious that she was still the center of unenviable attention. And all the while the Bishop's voice droned on. . . .

"And of all forms of literature, fiction is doubtless that which has exercised the greatest sway, for good or ill, over the passions and imagination of the masses. Yes, my friends, I am the first to acknowledge it—no sermon, however eloquent, no theological treatise, however learned and convincing, has ever inflamed the heart and imagination like a novel—a simple novel. Incalculable is the power exercised over humanity by the great magicians of the pen—a power ever enlarging its boundaries and increasing its responsibilities as popular education multiplies the number of readers. . . . Yes, it is the novelist's hand which can pour balm on countless human sufferings, or inoculate mankind with the festering poison of a corrupt imagination. . . ."

Mrs. Fetherel had turned white, and her eyes were fixed with a blind stare of anger on the large-sleeved figure in the center of the chancel.

"And too often, alas, it is the poison and not the balm which the unscrupulous hand of genius proffers to its unsuspecting readers. But, my friends, why should I continue? None know better than an assemblage of Christian women, such as I am now addressing, the beneficent or baleful influences of modern fiction; and so, when I say that this beautiful chantry window of ours owes its existence in part to the romancer's pen"—the Bishop paused, and bending forward, seemed to seek a certain face among the countenances eagerly addressed to his—"when I say that this pen, which for personal reasons it does not become me to celebrate unduly—"

Mrs. Fetherel at this point half-rose, pushing back her chair, which scraped loudly over the marble floor; but Hynes involuntarily laid a warning hand on her arm, and she sank down with a confused murmur about the heat.

"When I confess that this pen, which for once at least has proved itself so much mightier than the sword, is that which was inspired to trace the simple narrative of 'Through a Glass Brightly' "—Mrs. Fetherel looked up with a gasp of mingled relief and anger—"when I tell you, my dear friends, that it was your Bishop's own work which first roused the mind of one of his flock to the crying need of a chantry window, I think you will admit that I am justified in celebrating the triumphs of the pen, even though it be the modest instrument which your own Bishop wields."

The Bishop paused impressively, and a faint gasp of surprise and disappointment was audible throughout the chantry. Something very different from this conclusion had been expected, and even Mrs. Gollinger's lips curled with a slightly ironic smile. But Archer Hynes's attention was chiefly reserved for Mrs. Fetherel, whose face had changed with astonishing rapidity from surprise to annoyance, from annoyance to relief, and then back again to something very like indignation.

The address concluded, the actual ceremony of the unveiling was about to take place, and the attention of the congregation soon reverted to the chancel, where the choir had grouped themselves beneath the veiled window, prepared to burst into a chant of praise as the Bishop drew back the hanging. The moment was an impressive one, and every eye was fixed on the curtain. Even Hynes's gaze strayed to it for a moment, but soon returned to his neighbor's face; and then he perceived that Mrs. Fetherel, alone of all the persons present, was not looking at the window. Her eyes were fixed in an indignant stare on the Bishop; a flush of anger burned becomingly under her veil, and her hands nervously crumpled the beautifully printed program of the ceremony.

Hynes broke into a smile of comprehension. He glanced at the Bishop, and back at the Bishop's niece; then, as the episcopal hand was solemnly raised to draw back the curtain, he bent and whispered in Mrs. Fetherel's ear:

"Why, you gave it yourself! You wonderful woman, of course you gave it yourself!"

Mrs. Fetherel raised her eyes to his with a start. Her blush deepened and her lips shaped a hasty "No"; but the denial was deflected into the indignant murmur—"It wasn't *his* silly book that did it, anyhow!"

The Lady's Maid's Bell

It was the autumn after I had the typhoid. I'd been three months in hospital, and when I came out I looked so weak and tottery that the two or three ladies I applied to were afraid to engage me. Most of my money was gone, and after I'd boarded for two months, hanging about the employment agencies, and answering any advertisement that looked any way respectable, I pretty nearly lost heart, for fretting hadn't made me fatter, and I didn't see why my luck should ever turn. It did though—or I thought so at the time. A Mrs. Railton, a friend of the lady that first brought me out to the States, met me one day and stopped to speak to me: she was one that had always a friendly way with her. She asked me what ailed me to look so white, and when I told her, "Why, Hartley," says she, "I believe I've got the very place for you. Come in tomorrow and we'll talk about it."

The next day, when I called, she told me the lady she'd in mind was a niece of hers, a Mrs. Brympton, a youngish lady, but something of an invalid, who lived all the year round at her country place on the Hudson, owing to not being able to stand the fatigue of town life.

"Now, Hartley," Mrs. Railton said, in that cheery way that always made me feel things must be going to take a turn for the better—"now understand me; it's not a cheerful place I'm sending you to. The house is big and gloomy; my niece is nervous, vaporish; her husband—well, he's generally away; and the two children are dead. A year ago I would as soon have thought of shutting a rosy active girl like you into a vault; but you're not particularly brisk yourself just now, are you? and a quiet place, with country air and wholesome food and early hours, ought to be the very thing for you. Don't mistake me," she added, for I suppose I looked a trifle downcast; "you may find it dull but you won't be unhappy. My niece is an angel. Her former maid, who died last spring, had been with her twenty years and worshiped the ground she walked on. She's a kind mistress to all, and where the mistress is kind, as you know, the servants are generally good-humored, so you'll probably get on well enough with the rest of the household. And you're the very woman I want for my niece; quiet, well-mannered, and educated above your station. You read aloud well, I think? That's a good thing; my niece likes to be read to. She wants a maid that can be something of a companion: her last was, and I can't say how she misses her. It's a lonely life. . . . Well, have you decided?"

"Why, ma'am," I said, "I'm not afraid of solitude."

"Well, then, go; my niece will take you on my recommendation. I'll telegraph her at once and you can take the afternoon train. She has no one to wait on her at present, and I don't want you to loose any time."

I was ready enough to start, yet something in me hung back; and to gain time I asked, "And the gentleman, ma'am?"

"The gentleman's almost always away, I tell you," said Mrs. Railton, quicklike—"and when he's there," says she suddenly, "you've only to keep out of his way."

I took the afternoon train and got to the station at about four o'clock. A groom in a dogcart was waiting, and we drove off at a smart pace. It was a dull October day, with rain hanging close overhead, and by the time we turned into Brympton Place woods the daylight was almost gone. The drive wound through the woods for a mile or two, and came out on a gravel court shut in with thickets of tall black-looking shrubs. There were no lights in the windows, and the house *did* look a bit gloomy.

I had asked no questions of the groom, for I never was one to get my notion of new masters from their other servants: I prefer to wait and see for myself. But I could tell by the look of everything that I had got into the right kind of house, and that things were done handsomely. A pleasant-faced cook met me at the back door and called the housemaid to show me up to my room. "You'll see madam later," she said. "Mrs. Brympton has a visitor."

I hadn't fancied Mrs. Brympton was a lady to have many visitors, and somehow the words cheered me. I followed the housemaid upstairs, and saw, through a door on the upper landing, that the main part of the house seemed well furnished, with dark paneling and a number of old portraits. Another flight of stairs led up up to the servants' wing. It was almost dark now, and the housemaid excused herself for not having brought a light. "But there's matches in your room," she said, "and if you go careful you'll be all right. Mind the step at the end of the passage. Your room is just beyond."

I looked ahead as she spoke, and halfway down the passage I saw a woman standing. She drew back into a doorway as we passed and the housemaid didn't appear to notice her. She was a thin woman with a white face, and a dark gown and apron. I took her for the housekeeper and thought it odd that she didn't speak, but just gave me a long look as she went by. My room opened into a square hall at the end of the passage. Facing my door was another which stood open: the housemaid exclaimed when she saw it:

"There—Mrs. Blinder's left that door open again!" said she, closing it.

"Is Mrs. Blinder the housekeeper?"

"There's no housekeeper: Mrs. Blinder's the cook."

"And is that her room?"

"Laws, no," said the housemaid, crosslike. "That's nobody's room. It's empty, I mean, and the door hadn't ought to be open. Mrs. Brympton wants it kept locked."

She opened my door and led me into a neat room, nicely furnished, with a picture or two on the walls; and having lit a candle she took leave, telling me that the servants' hall tea was at six, and that Mrs. Brympton would see me afterward.

I found them a pleasant-spoken set in the servants' hall, and by what they let fall I gathered that, as Mrs. Railton had said, Mrs. Brympton was the kindest of ladies; but I didn't take much notice of their talk, for I was watching to see the pale woman in the dark gown come in. She didn't show herself, however, and I wondered if she ate apart; but if she wasn't the housekeeper, why should she? Suddenly it struck me that she might be a trained nurse, and in that case her meals would of course be served in her room. If Mrs. Brympton was an invalid it was likely enough she had a nurse. The idea annoyed me, I own, for they're not always the easiest to get on with, and if I'd known I shouldn't have taken the place. But there I was and there was no use pulling a long face over it; and not being one to ask questions I waited to see what would turn up.

When tea was over the housemaid said to the footman: "Has Mr. Ranford gone?" and when he said yes, she told me to come up with her to Mrs. Brympton.

Mrs. Brympton was lying down in her bedroom. Her lounge stood near the fire and beside it was a shaded lamp. She was a delicate-looking lady, but when she smiled I felt there was nothing I wouldn't do for her. She spoke very pleasantly, in a low voice, asking me my name and age and so on, and if I had everything I wanted, and if I wasn't afraid of feeling lonely in the country.

"Not with you I wouldn't be, madam," I said, and the words surprised me when I'd spoken them, for I'm not an impulsive person; but it was just as if I'd thought aloud.

She seemed pleased at that, and said she hoped I'd continue in the same mind; then she gave me a few directions about her toilet, and said Agnes the housemaid would show me next morning where things were kept.

"I am tired tonight, and shall dine upstairs," she said. "Agnes will bring me my tray, so that you may have time to unpack and settle yourself; and later you may come and undress me."

"Very well, ma'am, I said. "You'll ring, I suppose?"

I thought she looked odd.

"No—Agnes will fetch you," says she quickly, and took up her book again.

Well—that was certainly strange: a lady's maid having to be fetched by the housemaid whenever her lady wanted her! I wondered if there were no bells in the house; but the next day I satisfied myself that there was one in every room, and a special one ringing from my mistress's room to mine; and after that it did strike me as queer that, whenever Mrs.

Brympton wanted anything, she rang for Agnes, who had to walk the whole length of the servants' wing to call me.

But that wasn't the only queer thing in the house. The very next day I found out that Mrs. Brympton had no nurse; and then I asked Agnes about the woman I had seen in the passage the afternoon before. Agnes said she had seen no one, and I saw that she thought I was dreaming. To be sure, it was dusk when we went down the passage, and she had excused herself for not bringing a light; but I had seen the woman plain enough to know her again if we should meet. I decided that she must have been a friend of the cook's, or of one of the other women servants; perhaps she had come down from town for a night's visit, and the servants wanted it kept secret. Some ladies are very stiff about having their servants' friends in the house overnight. At any rate, I made up my mind to ask no more questions.

In a day or two another odd thing happened. I was chatting one afternoon with Mrs. Blinder, who was a friendly-disposed woman, and had been longer in the house than the other servants, and she asked me if I was quite comfortable and had everything I needed. I said I had no fault to find with my place or with my mistress, but I thought it odd that in so large a house there was no sewing room for the lady's maid.

"Why," says she, "there *is* one: the room you're in is the old sewing room."

"Oh," said I; "and where did the other lady's maid sleep?"

At that she grew confused, and said hurriedly that the servants' rooms had all been changed about last year, and she didn't rightly remember.

That struck me as peculiar, but I went on as if I hadn't noticed: "Well, there's a vacant room opposite mine, and I mean to ask Mrs. Brympton if I mayn't use that as a sewing room."

To my astonishment, Mrs. Blinder went white, and gave my hand a kind of squeeze. "Don't do that, my dear," said she, trembling-like. "To tell you the truth, that was Emma Saxon's room, and my mistress has kept it closed ever since her death."

"And who was Emma Saxon?"

"Mrs. Brympton's former maid."

"The one that was with her so many years?" said I, remembering what Mrs. Railton had told me.

Mrs. Blinder nodded.

"What sort of woman was she?"

"No better walked the earth," said Mrs. Blinder. "My mistress loved her like a sister."

"But I mean—what did she look like?"

Mrs. Blinder got up and gave me a kind of angry stare. "I'm no great hand at describing," she said; "and I believe my pastry's rising." And she walked off into the kitchen and shut the door after her.

✤ II ✤

I HAD been near a week at Brympton before I saw my master. Word came that he was arriving one afternoon, and a change passed over the whole household. It was plain that nobody loved him below stairs. Mrs. Blinder took uncommon care with the dinner that night, but she snapped at the kitchenmaid in a way quite unusual with her; and Mr. Wace, the butler, a serious, slow-spoken man, went about his duties as if he'd been getting ready for a funeral. He was a great Bible reader, Mr. Wace was, and had a beautiful assortment of texts at his command; but that day he used such dreadful language, that I was about to leave the table, when he assured me it was all out of Isaiah; and I noticed that whenever the master came Mr. Wace took to the prophets.

About seven, Agnes called me to my mistress' room; and there I found Mr. Brympton. He was standing on the hearth; a big fair bull-necked man, with a red face and little bad-tempered blue eyes; the kind of a man a young simpleton might have thought handsome, and would have been like to pay dear for thinking it.

He swung about when I came in, and looked me over in a trice. I knew what the look meant, from having experienced it once or twice in my former places. Then he turned his back on me, and went on talking to his wife; and I knew what *that* meant, too. I was not the kind of morsel he was after. The typhoid had served me well enough in one way: it kept that kind of gentleman at arm's length.

"This is my new maid, Hartley," says Mrs. Brympton in her kind voice; and he nodded and went on with what he was saying.

In a minute or two he went off, and left my mistress to dress for dinner, and I noticed as I waited on her that she was white, and chill to the touch.

Mr. Brympton took himself off the next morning, and the whole house drew a long breath when he drove away. As for my mistress, she put on her hat and furs (for it was a fine winter morning) and went out for a walk in the gardens, coming back quite fresh and rosy, so that for a minute, before her color faded, I could guess what a pretty young lady she must have been, and not so long ago, either.

She had met Mr. Ranford in the grounds, and the two came back together, I remember, smiling and talking as they walked along the terrace under my window. That was the first time I saw Mr. Ranford, though I had often heard his name mentioned in the hall. He was a neighbor, it appeared, living a mile or two beyond Brympton, at the end of the village; and as he was in the habit of spending his winters in the country he was almost the only company mistress had at that season. He was a slight tall gentleman of about thirty, and I thought him rather melancholy looking till I saw his smile, which had a kind of surprise in it, like the first warm day in spring. He was a great reader, I heard, like my mistress, and the two were forever borrowing books of one another, and sometimes (Mr. Wace told me) he would read aloud to Mrs. Brympton by the hour, in the big dark library where she sat in the winter afternoons. The servants all liked him, and perhaps that's more of a compliment than the masters suspect. He had a friendly word for every one of us, and we were all glad to think that Mrs. Brympton had a pleasant companionable gentleman like that to keep her company when the master was away. Mr. Ranford seemed on excellent terms with Mr. Brympton too; though I couldn't but wonder that two gentlemen so unlike each other should be so friendly. But then I knew how the real quality can keep their feelings to themselves.

As for Mr. Brympton, he came and went, never staying more than a day or two, cursing the dullness and the solitude, grumbling at everything, and (as I soon found out) drinking a deal more than was good for him. After Mrs. Brympton left the table he would sit half the night over the old Brympton port and madeira, and once, as I was leaving my mistress's room rather later than usual, I met him coming up the stairs in such a state that I turned sick to think of what some ladies have to endure and hold their tongue about.

The servants said very little about their master; but from what they let drop I could see it had been an unhappy match from the beginning. Mr. Brympton was coarse, loud and pleasure-loving; my mistress quiet, retiring, and perhaps a trifle cold. Not that she was not always pleasant-spoken to him: I thought her wonderfully forbearing; but to a gentleman as free as Mr. Brympton I dare say she seemed a little offish.

Well, things went on quietly for several weeks. My mistress was kind, my duties were light, and I got on well with the other servants. In short, I had nothing to complain of; yet there was always a weight on me. I can't say why it was so, but I know it was not the loneliness that I felt. I soon got used to that; and being still languid from the fever, I was thankful for the quiet and the good country air. Nevertheless, I was never quite easy in my mind. My mistress, knowing I had been ill, insisted that I should take my walk regularly, and often invented errands for me: a yard of ribbon to be fetched from the village, a letter posted, or a book returned to Mr. Ranford. As soon as I was out of doors my spirits rose, and I looked forward to my walks through the bare moist-smelling woods; but the moment I caught sight of the house again my heart dropped down like a stone in a well. It was not a gloomy house exactly, yet I never entered it but a feeling of gloom came over me.

Mrs. Brympton seldom went out in winter; only on the finest days did she walk an hour at noon on the south terrace. Excepting Mr. Ranford, we had no visitors but the doctor, who drove over from town about once a week. He sent for me once or twice to give me sone trifling direction about my mistress, and though he never told me what her illness was, I thought, from a waxy look she had now and then of a morning, that it might be the heart that ailed her. The season was soft and unwholesome, and in January we had a long spell of rain. That was a sore trial to me, I own, for I couldn't go out, and sitting over my sewing all day, listening to the drip, drip of the eaves, I grew so nervous that the least sound made me jump. Somehow, the thought of that locked room across the passage began to weigh on me. Once or twice, in the long rainy nights, I fancied I heard noises there; but that was nonsense, of course, and the daylight drove such notions out of my head. Well, one morning Mrs. Brympton gave me quite a start of pleasure by telling me she wished me to go to town for some shopping. I hadn't known till then how low my spirits had fallen. I set off in high glee, and my first sight of the crowded streets and the cheerful-looking shops quite took me out of myself. Toward afternoon, however, the noise and confusion began to tire me, and I was actually looking forward to the quiet of Brympton, and thinking how I should enjoy the drive home through the dark woods, when I ran across an old acquaintance, a maid I had once been in service with. We had lost sight of each other for a number of years, and I had to stop and tell her what had happened to me in the interval. When I mentioned where I was living she rolled up her eyes and pulled a long face.

"What! The Mrs. Brympton that lives all the year at her place on the Hudson? My dear, you won't stay there three months."

"Oh, but I don't mind the country," says I, offended somehow at her tone. "Since the fever I'm glad to be quiet."

She shook her head. "It's not the country I'm thinking of. All I know is she's had four maids in the last six months, and the last one, who was a friend of mine, told me nobody could stay in the house."

"Did she say why?" I asked.

"No—she wouldn't give me her reason. But she says to me, 'Mrs. Ansey,' she says, 'if ever a young woman as you know of thinks of going there, you tell her it's not worthwhile to unpack her boxes.' "

"Is she young and handsome?" said I, thinking of Mr. Brympton.

"Not her! She's the kind that mothers engage when they've gay young gentlemen at college."

Well, though I knew the woman was an idle gossip, the words stuck in my head, and my heart sank lower than ever as I drove up to Brympton in the dusk. There *was* something about the house—I was sure of it now. . . .

When I went in to tea I heard that Mr. Brympton had arrived, and I saw at a glance that there had been a disturbance of some kind. Mrs. Blinder's hand shook so that she could hardly pour the tea, and Mr. Wace quoted the most dreadful texts full of brimstone. Nobody said a word to me then, but when I went up to my room Mrs. Blinder followed me.

"Oh, my dear," says she, taking my hand, "I'm so glad and thankful you've come back to us!"

That struck me, as you may imagine. "Why," said I, "did you think I was leaving for good?"

"No, no, to be sure," said she, a little confused, "but I can't a-bear to have madam left alone for a day even." She pressed my hand hard, and, "Oh, Miss Hartley," says she, "be good to your mistress, as you're a Christian woman." And with that she hurried away, and left me staring.

A moment later Agnes called me to Mrs. Brympton. Hearing Mr. Brympton's voice in her room, I went round by the dressing room, thinking I would lay out her dinner gown before going in. The dressing room is a large room with a window over the portico that looks toward the gardens. Mr. Brympton's apartments are beyond. When I went in, the door into the bedroom was ajar, and I heard Mr. Brympton saying angrily: "One would suppose he was the only person fit for you to talk to."

"I don't have many visitors in winter," Mrs. Brympton answered quietly.

"You have *me*!" he flung at her, sneeringly.

"You are here so seldom," said she.

"Well—whose fault is that? You make the place about as lively as the family vault."

With that I rattled the toilet things, to give my mistress warning, and she rose and called me in.

The two dined alone, as usual, and I knew by Mr. Wace's manner at supper that things must be going badly. He quoted the prophets something terrible, and worked on the kitchenmaid so that she declared she wouldn't go down alone to put the cold meat in the icebox. I felt nervous myself, and after I had put my mistress to bed I was half tempted to go down again and persuade Mrs. Blinder to sit up awhile over a game of cards. But I heard her door closing for the night and so I went on to my own room. The rain had begun again, and the drip, drip, drip seemed to be dropping into my brain. I lay awake listening to it, and turning over what my friend in town had said. What puzzled me was that it was always the maids who left. . . .

After a while I slept; but suddenly a loud noise wakened me. My bell had rung. I sat up, terrified by the unusual sound, which seemed to go on jangling through the darkness. My hands shook so that I couldn't find the matches. At length I struck a light and jumped out of bed. I began to think I must have been dreaming; but I looked at the bell against the wall, and there was the little hammer still quivering.

I was just beginning to huddle on my clothes when I heard another sound. This time it was the door of the locked room opposite mine softly opening and closing. I heard the sound distinctly, and it frightened me so that I stood stock still. Then I heard a footstep hurrying down the passage toward the main house. The floor being carpeted, the sound was very faint, but I was quite sure it was a woman's step. I turned cold with the thought of it, and for a minute or two I dursn't breathe or move. Then I came to my senses.

"Alice Hartley," says I to myself, "someone left that room just now and ran down the passage ahead of you. That idea isn't pleasant, but you may as well face it. Your mistress has rung for you, and to answer her bell you've got to go the way that other woman has gone."

Well—I did it. I never walked faster in my life, yet I thought I should never get to the end of the passage or reach Mrs. Brympton's room. On the way I heard nothing and saw nothing; all was dark and quiet as the grave. When

I reached my mistress' door the silence was so deep that I began to think I must be dreaming, and was half minded to turn back. Then a panic seized me, and I knocked.

There was no answer, and I knocked again, loudly. To my astonishment the door was opened by Mr. Brympton. He started back when he saw me, and in the light of my candle his face looked red and savage.

"You?" he said, in a queer voice. *"How many of you are there, in God's name?"*

At that I felt the ground give under me; but I said to myself that he had been drinking, and answered as steadily as I could: "May I go in, sir? Mrs. Brympton has rung for me."

"You may all go in, for what I care," says he, and, pushing by me, walked down the hall to his own bedroom. I looked after him as he went, and to my surprise I saw that he walked as straight as a sober man.

I found my mistress lying very weak and still, but she forced a smile when she saw me, and signed me to pour out some drops for her. After that she lay without speaking, her breath coming quick, and her eyes closed. Suddenly she groped out with her hand, and *"Emma,"* says she, faintly.

"It's Hartley, madam," I said. "Do you want anything?"

She opened her eyes wide and gave me a startled look.

"I was dreaming," she said. "You may go, now, Hartley, and thank you kindly. I'm quite well again, you see." And she turned her face away from me.

✣ III ✣

THERE WAS no more sleep for me that night, and I was thankful when daylight came.

Soon afterward, Agnes called me to Mrs. Brympton. I was afraid she was ill again, for she seldom sent for me before nine, but I found her sitting up in bed, pale and drawn-looking, but quite herself.

"Hartley," says she quickly, "will you put on your things at once and go down to the village for me? I want this prescription made up—" here she hesitated a minute and blushed "—and I should like you to be back again before Mr. Brympton is up."

"Certainly, madam," I said.

"And—stay a moment—" she called me back as if an idea had just struck her "—while you're waiting for the mixture, you'll have time to go on to Mr. Ranford's with this note."

It was a two mile walk to the village, and on my way I had time to turn things over in my mind. It struck me as peculiar that my mistress should wish the prescription made up without Mr. Brympton's knowledge; and, putting this together with the scene of the night before, and with much else that I had noticed and suspected, I began to wonder if the poor lady was weary of her life, and had come to the mad resolve of ending it. The idea took such hold on me that I reached the village on a run, and dropped breathless into a chair before the chemist's counter. The good man, who was just taking down his shutters, stared at me so hard that it brought me to myself.

"Mr. Limmel," I says, trying to speak indifferently, "will you run your eye over this, and tell me if it's quite right?"

He put on his spectacles and studied the prescription.

"Why, it's one of Dr. Walton's," says he. "What should be wrong with it?"

"Well—is it dangerous to take?"

"Dangerous—how do you mean?"

I could have shaken the man for his stupidity.

"I mean—if a person was to take too much of it—by mistake of course—" says I, my heart in my throat.

"Lord bless you, no. It's only lime water. You might feed it to a baby by the bottleful."

I gave a great sigh of relief and hurried on to Mr. Ranford's. But on the way another thought struck me. If there was nothing to conceal about my visit to the chemist's, was it my other errand that Mrs. Brympton wished me to keep private? Somehow, that thought frightened me worse than the other. Yet the two gentlemen seemed fast friends, and I would have staked my head on my mistress' goodness. I felt ashamed of my suspicions, and concluded that I was still disturbed by the strange events of the night. I left the note at Mr. Ranford's, and hurrying back to Brympton, slipped in by a side door without being seen, as I thought.

An hour later, however, as I was carrying in my mistress's breakfast, I was stopped in the hall by Mr. Brympton.

"What were you doing out so early?" he says, looking hard at me.

"Early—me, sir?" I said, in a tremble.

"Come, come," he says, an angry red spot coming out on his forehead, "didn't I see you scuttling home through the shrubbery an hour or more ago?"

I'm a truthful woman by nature, but at that a lie popped out ready-made. "No, sir, you didn't," said I and looked straight back at him.

He shrugged his shoulders and gave a sullen laugh. "I suppose you think I was drunk last night?" he asked suddenly.

"No, sir, I don't," I answered, this time truthfully enough.

He turned away with another shrug. "A pretty notion my servants have of me!" I heard him mutter as he walked off.

Not till I had settled down to my afternoon's sewing did I realize how the events of the night had shaken me. I couldn't pass that locked door without a shiver. I knew I had heard someone come out of it, and walk down the passage ahead of me. I thought of speaking to Mrs. Blinder or to Mr. Wace, the only two in the house who appeared to have an inkling of what was going on, but I had a feeling that if I questioned them they would deny everything, and that I might learn more by holding my tongue and keeping my eyes open. The idea of spending another night opposite the locked room sickened me, and once I was seized with the notion of packing my trunk and taking the first train to town; but it wasn't in me to throw over a kind mistress in that manner, and I tried to go on with my sewing as if nothing had happened. I hadn't worked ten minutes before the sewing machine broke down. It was one I had found in the house, a good machine but a trifle out of order: Mrs. Blinder said it had never been used since Emma Saxon's death. I stopped to see what was wrong, and as I was working at the machine a drawer which I had never been able to open slid forward and a photograph fell out. I picked it up and sat looking at it in a maze. It was a woman's likeness, and I knew I had seen the face somewhere—the eyes had an asking look that I had felt on me before. And suddenly I remembered the pale woman in the passage.

I stood up, cold all over, and ran out of the room. My

heart seemed to be thumping in the top of my head, and I felt as if I should never get away from the look in those eyes. I went straight to Mrs. Blinder. She was taking her afternoon nap, and sat up with a jump when I came in.

"Mrs. Blinder," said I, "who is that?" And I held out the photograph.

She rubbed her eyes and stared.

"Why, Emma Saxon," says she. "Where did you find it?"

I looked hard at her for a minute. "Mrs. Blinder," I said, "I've seen that face before."

Mrs. Blinder got up and walked over to the looking glass. "Dear me! I must have been asleep," she says. "My front is all over one ear. And now do run along, Miss Hartley, dear, for I hear the clock striking four, and I must go down this very minute and put on the Virginia ham for Mr. Brympton's dinner."

✣ IV ✣

To all appearances, things went on as usual for a week or two. The only difference was that Mr. Brympton stayed on, instead of going off as he usually did, and that Mr. Ranford never showed himself. I heard Mr. Brympton remark on this one afternoon when he was sitting in my mistress' room before dinner:

"Where's Ranford?" says he. "He hasn't been near the house for a week. Does he keep away because I'm here?"

Mrs. Brympton spoke so low that I couldn't catch her answer.

"Well," he went on, "two's company and three's trumpery; I'm sorry to be in Ranford's way, and I suppose I shall have to take myself off again in a day or two and give him a show." And he laughed at his own joke.

The very next day, as it happened, Mr. Ranford called. The footman said the three were very merry over their tea in the library, and Mr. Brympton strolled down to the gate with Mr. Ranford when he left.

I have said that things went on as usual; and so they did with the rest of the household; but as for myself, I had never been the same since the night my bell had rung. Night after night I used to lie awake, listening for it to ring again, and for the door of the locked room to open stealthily. But the bell never rang, and I heard no sound across the passage. At last the silence began to be more dreadful to me than the most mysterious sounds. I felt that *someone* was cowering there, behind the locked door, watching and listening as I watched and listened, and I could almost have cried out, "Whoever you are, come out and let me see you face to face, but don't lurk there and spy on me in the darkness!"

Feeling as I did, you may wonder I didn't give warning. Once I very nearly did so; but at the last moment something held me back. Whether it was compassion for my mistress, who had grown more and more dependent on me, or unwillingness to try to a new place, or some other feeling that I couldn't put a name to, I lingered on as if spellbound, though every night was dreadful to me, and the days but little better.

For one thing, I didn't like Mrs. Brympton's looks. She had never been the same since that night, no more than I had. I thought she would brighten up after Mr. Brympton left, but though she seemed easier in her mind, her spirits didn't revive, nor her strength either. She had grown attached to me, and seemed to like to have me about; and Agnes told me one day that, since Emma Saxon's death, I was the only maid her mistress had taken to. This gave me a warm feeling for the poor lady, though after all there was little I could do to help her.

After Mr. Brympton's departure, Mr. Ranford took to coming again, though less often then formerly. I met him once or twice in the grounds, or in the village, and I couldn't but think there was a change in him too; but I set it down to my disordered fancy.

The weeks passed, and Mr. Brympton had now been a month absent. We heard he was cruising with a friend in the West Indies, and Mr. Wace said that was a long way off, but though you had the wings of a dove and went to the uttermost parts of the earth, you couldn't get away from the Almighty. Agnes said that as long as he stayed away from Brympton the Almighty might have him and welcome; and this raised a laugh, though Mrs. Blinder tried to look shocked, and Mr. Wace said the bears would eat us.

We were all glad to hear that the West Indies were a long way off, and I remember that, in spite of Mr. Wace's solemn looks, we had a very merry dinner that day in the hall. I don't know if it was because of my being in better spirits, but I fancied Mrs. Brympton looked better too, and seemed more cheerful in her manner. She had been for a walk in the morning, and after luncheon she lay down in her room, and I read aloud to her. When she dismissed me I went to my own room feeling quite bright and happy, and for first time in weeks walked past the locked door without thinking of it. As I sat down to my work I looked out and saw a few snowflakes falling. The sight was pleasanter than the eternal rain, and I pictured to myself how pretty the bare gardens would look in their white mantle. It seemed to me as if the snow would cover up all the dreariness, indoors as well as out.

The fancy had hardly crossed my mind when I heard a step at my side. I looked up, thinking it was Agnes.

"Well, Agnes—" said I, and the words froze on my tongue; for there, in the door, stood *Emma Saxon*.

I don't know how long she stood there. I only know I couldn't stir or take my eyes from her. Afterward I was terribly frightened, but at the time it wasn't fear I felt, but something deeper and quieter. She looked at me long and hard, and her face was just one dumb prayer to me—but how in the world was I to help her? Suddenly she turned, and I heard her walk down the passage. This time I wasn't afraid to follow—I felt that I must know what she wanted. I sprang up and ran out. She was at the other end of the passage, and I expected her to take the turn toward my mistress' room; but instead of that she pushed open the door that led to the backstairs. I followed her down the stairs, and across the passageway to the back door. The kitchen and hall were empty at that hour, the servants being off duty, except for the footman, who was in the pantry. At the door she stood still a moment, with another look at me; then she turned the handle, and stepped out. For a minute I hesitated. Where was she leading me to? The door had closed softly after her, and I opened it and looked out, half-expecting to find that she had disappeared. But I saw her a few yards off hurrying across the courtyard to the path through the woods. Her figure looked black and lonely in the snow, and for a second my heart failed me and I thought of turning back. But all the while she was drawing me after her; and catching up an old shawl of Mrs. Blinder's I ran out into the open.

Emma Saxon was in the wood path now. She walked on steadily, and I followed at the same pace, till we passed out of the gates and reached the highroad. Then she struck across the open fields to the village. By this time the ground was white, and as she climbed the slope of a bare hill ahead of me I noticed that she left no footprints behind her. At sight of that my heart shriveled up within me, and my knees were water. Somehow, it was worse here than indoors. She made the whole countryside seem lonely as the grave, with none but us two in it, and no help in the wide world.

Once I tried to go back; but she turned and looked at me, and it was as if she had dragged me with ropes. After that I followed her like a dog. We came to the village and she led me through it, past the church and the blacksmith's shop, and down the lane to Mr. Ranford's. Mr. Ranford's house stands close to the road: a plain old-fashioned building, with a flagged path leading to the door between box borders. The lane was deserted, and as I turned into it I saw Emma Saxon pause under the old elm by the gate. And now another fear came over me. I saw that we had reached the end of our journey, and that it was my turn to act. All the way from Brympton I had been asking myself what she wanted of me, but I had followed in a trance, as it were, and not till I saw her stop at Mr. Ranford's gate did my brain begin to clear itself. I stood a little way off in the snow, my heart beating fit to strangle me, and my feet frozen to the ground; and she stood under the elm and watched me.

I knew well enough that she hadn't led me there for nothing. I felt there was something I ought to say or do—but how was I to guess what it was? I had never thought harm of my mistress and Mr. Ranford, but I was sure now that, from one cause or another, some dreadful thing hung over them. *She* knew what it was; she would tell me if she could; perhaps she would answer it I questioned her.

It turned me faint to think of speaking to her; but I plucked up heart and dragged myself across the few yards between us. As I did so, I heard the house door open and saw Mr. Ranford approaching. He looked handsome and cheerful, as my mistress had looked that morning, and at sight of him the blood began to flow again in my veins.

"Why, Hartley," said he, "what's the matter? I saw you coming down the lane just now, and came out to see if you had taken root in the snow." He stopped and stared at me. "What are you looking at?" he says.

I turned toward the elm as he spoke, and his eyes followed me; but there was no one there. The lane was empty as far as the eye could reach.

A sense of helplessness came over me. She was gone, and I had not been able to guess what she wanted. Her last look had pierced me to the marrow; and yet it had not told me! All at once, I felt more desolate than when she had stood there watching me. It seemed as if she had left me all alone to carry the weight of the secret I couldn't guess. The snow went round me in great circles, and the ground fell away from me. . . .

A drop of brandy and the warmth of Mr. Ranford's fire soon brought me to, and I insisted on being driven back at once to Brympton. It was nearly dark, and I was afraid my mistress might be wanting me. I explained to Mr. Ranford that I had been out for a walk and had been taken with a fit of giddiness as I passed his gate. This was true enough; yet I never felt more like a liar than when I said it.

When I dressed Mrs. Brympton for dinner she remarked on my pale looks and asked what ailed me. I told her I had a headache, and she said she would not require me again that evening, and advised me to go to bed.

It was a fact that I could scarcely keep on my feet; yet I had no fancy to spend a solitary evening in my room. I sat downstairs in the hall as long as I could hold my head up; but by nine I crept upstairs, too weary to care what happened if I could but get my head on a pillow. The rest of the household went to bed soon afterward; they kept early hours when the master was away, and before ten I heard Mrs. Blinder's door close, and Mr. Wace's soon after.

It was a very still night, earth and air all muffled in snow. Once in bed I felt easier, and lay quiet, listening to the strange noises that come out in a house after dark. Once I thought I heard a door open and close again below: it might have been the glass door that led to the gardens. I got up and peered out of the window; but it was in the dark of the moon, and nothing visible outside but the streaking of snow against the panes.

I went back to bed and must have dozed, for I jumped awake to the furious ringing of my bell. Before my head was clear I had sprung out of bed, and was dragging on my clothes. *It is going to happen now,* I heard myself saying; but what I meant I had no notion. My hands seemed to be covered with glue—I thought I should never get into my clothes. At last I opened my door and peered down the passage. As far as my candle flame carried, I could see nothing unusual ahead of me. I hurried on, breathless; but as I pushed open the baize door leading to the main hall my heart stood still, for there at the head of the stairs was Emma Saxon, peering dreadfully down into the darkness.

For a second I couldn't stir; but my hand slipped from the door, and as it swung shut the figure vanished. At the same instant there came another sound from below stairs—a stealthy mysterious sound, as of a latchkey turning in the house door. I ran to Mrs. Brympton's room and knocked.

There was no answer, and I knocked again. This time I heard someone moving in the room; the bolt slipped back and my mistress stood before me. To my surprise I saw that she had not undressed for the night. She gave me a startled look.

"What is this, Hartley?" she says in a whisper. "Are you ill? What are you doing here at this hour?"

"I am not ill, madam; but my bell rang."

At that she turned pale, and seemed about to fall.

"You are mistaken," she said harshly; "I didn't ring. You must have been dreaming." I had never heard her speak in such a tone. "Go back to bed," she said, closing the door on me.

But as she spoke I heard sounds again in the hall below: a man's step this time; and the truth leaped out on me.

"Madam," I said, pushing past her, "there is someone in the house—"

"Someone—?"

"Mr. Brympton, I think—I hear his step below—"

A dreadful look came over her, and without a word, she dropped flat at my feet. I fell on my knees and tried to lift her: by the way she breathed I saw it was no common faint. But as I raised her head there came quick steps on the stairs and across the hall: the door was flung open, and there stood Mr. Brympton, in his traveling clothes, the snow dripping from him. He drew back with a start as he saw me kneeling by my mistress.

"What the devil is this?" he shouted. He was less high-colored than usual, and the red spot came out on his forehead.

"Mrs. Brympton has fainted, sir," said I.

He laughed unsteadily and pushed by me. "It's a pity she didn't choose a more convenient moment. I'm sorry to disturb her, but—"

I raised myself up aghast at the man's action.

"Sir," said I, "are you mad? What are you doing?"

"Going to meet a friend," said he, and seemed to make for the dressing room.

At that my heart turned over. I don't know what I thought or feared; but I sprang up and caught him by the sleeve.

"Sir, sir," said I, "for pity's sake look at your wife!"

He shook me off furiously.

"It seems that's done for me," says he, and caught hold of the dressing room door.

At that moment I heard a slight noise inside. Slight as it was, he heard it too, and tore the door open; but as he did so he dropped back. On the threshold stood Emma Saxon. All was dark behind her, but I saw her plainly, and so did he. He threw up his hands as if to hide his face from her; and when I looked again she was gone.

He stood motionless, as if the strength had run out of him; and in the stillness my mistress suddenly raised herself, and opening her eyes fixed a look on him. Then she fell back, and I saw the death flutter pass over her face. . . .

We buried her on the third day, in a driving snowstorm. There were few people in the church, for it was bad weather to come from town, and I've a notion my mistress was one that hadn't many near friends. Mr. Ranford was among the last to come, just before they carried her up the aisle. He was in black, of course, being such a friend of the family, and I never saw a gentleman so pale. As he passed me, I noticed that he leaned a trifle on a stick he carried; and I fancy Mr. Brympton noticed it too, for the red spot came out sharp on his forehead, and all through the service he kept staring across the church at Mr. Ranford, instead of following the prayers as a mourner should.

When it was over and we went out to the graveyard, Mr. Ranford had disappeared, and as soon as my poor mistress's body was underground, Mr. Brympton jumped into the carriage nearest the gate and drove off without a word to any of us. I heard him call out, "To the station," and we servants went back alone to the house.

The Last Asset

"THE DEVIL!" Paul Garnett exclaimed as he reread his note; and the dry old gentleman who was at the moment his only neighbor in the modest restaurant they both frequented, remarked with a smile: "You don't seem particularly disturbed at meeting him."

Garnett returned the smile. "I don't know why I apostrophized him, for he's not in the least present—except inasmuch as he may prove to be at the bottom of anything unexpected."

The old gentleman who, like Garnett, was an American, and spoke in the thin rarefied voice which seems best fitted to emit sententious truths, twisted his lean neck round to cackle out: "Ah, it's generally a woman who's at the bottom of the unexpected. Not," he added, leaning forward with deliberation to select a toothpick, "that that precludes the devil's being there too."

Garnett uttered the requisite laugh, and his neighbor, pushing back his plate, called out with a perfectly unbending American intonation: "Gassong! L'addition, silver play."

His repast, as usual, had been a simple one, and he left only thirty centimes in the plate on which his account was presented; but the waiter, to whom he was evidently a familiar presence, received the tribute with Latin amenity, and hovered helpfully about the table while the old gentleman cut and lighted his cigar.

"Yes," the latter proceeded, revolving the cigar meditatively between his thin lips, "they're generally both in the same hole, like the owl and the prairie dog in the natural history books of my youth. I believe it was all a mistake about the owl and the prairie dog, but it isn't about the unexpected. The fact is, the unexpected *is* the devil—the sooner you find that out, the happier you'll be." He leaned back, tilting his bald head against the blotched mirror behind him, and rambling on with gentle garrulity while Garnett attacked his omelet.

"Get your life down to routine—eliminate surprises. Arrange things so that, when you get up in the morning, you'll know exactly what's going to happen to you during the day—and the next day and the next. I don't say it's funny—it ain't. But it's better than being hit on the head by a brickbat. That's why I always take my meals at this restaurant. I know just how much onion they put in things—if I went to the next place I shouldn't. And I always take the same streets to come here—I've been doing it for ten years now. I know at which crossing to look out—I know what I'm going to see in the shop windows. It saves a lot of wear and tear to know what's coming. For a good many years I never *did* know, from one minute to another, and now I like to think that everything's cut and dried, and nothing unexpected can jump out at me like a tramp from a ditch."

He paused calmly to knock the ashes from his cigar and Garnett said with a smile: "Doesn't such a plan of life cut off nearly all the possibilities?"

The old gentleman made a contemptuous motion. "Possibilities of what? Of being multifariously miserable? There are lots of ways of being miserable, but there's only one way of being comfortable, and that is to stop running round after happiness. If you make up your mind not to be happy there's no reason why you shouldn't have a fairly good time."

"That was Schopenhauer's idea, I believe," the young man said, pouring his wine with the smile of youthful incredulity.

"I guess he hadn't the monopoly," responded his friend. "Lots of people have found out the secret—the trouble is that so few live up to it."

He rose from his seat, pushing the table forward, and standing passive while the waiter advanced with his shabby overcoat and umbrella. Then he nodded to Garnett, lifted his hat to the broad-bosomed lady behind the desk, and passed out into the street.

Garnett looked after him with a musing smile. The two had exchanged views on life for two years without so much as knowing each other's names. Garnett was a newspaper correspondent whose work kept him mainly in London, but on his periodic visits to Paris he lodged in a dingy hotel of the Latin quarter, the chief merit of which was its nearness to the cheap and excellent restaurant where the two Americans had made acquaintaince. But Garnett's assiduity in frequenting the place arose, in the end, less from the excellence of the food than from the enjoyment of his old friend's conversation. Amid the flashy sophistications of the Parisian life to which Garnett's trade introduced him, the American sage's conversation had the crisp and homely flavor of a native dish—one of the domestic compounds for which the exiled palate is supposed to yearn. It was a mark of the old man's impersonality that, in spite of the interest he inspired, Garnett had never got beyond idly wondering who he might be, where he lived, and what his occupations were. He was presumably a bachelor—a man of family ties, however relaxed, though he might have been as often absent from home, would not have been as regularly present in the same place—and there was about him a boundless desultoriness which renewed Garnett's conviction that there is no one on earth as idle as an American who is not busy. From certain allusions it was plain that he had lived many years in Paris, yet he had not taken the trouble to adapt his tongue to the local inflections, but spoke French with the accent of one who has formed his notion of the language from a phrase book.

The city itself seemed to have made as little impression on him as its speech. He appeared to have no artistic or intellectual curiosities, to remain untouched by the complex appeal of Paris, while preserving, perhaps the more strikingly from his very detachment, that odd American astuteness which seems the fruit of innocence rather than of experience. His nationality revealed itself again in a mild interest in the political problems of his adopted country, though they appeared to preoccupy him only as illustrating the boundless perversity of mankind. The exhibition of human folly never ceased to divert him, and though his examples of it seemed mainly drawn from the columns of one exiguous daily paper, he found there matter for endless variations on his favorite theme. If this monotony of topic did not weary the younger man, it was because he fancied he could detect under it the tragic note of the fixed idea—of some great moral upheaval which had flung his friend stripped and starving on the desert island of the little restaurant where they met. He hardly knew wherein he read this revelation—whether in the shabbiness of the sage's dress, the impersonal courtesy of his manner, or the shade of apprehension which lurked, indescribably, in his guileless yet suspicious eye. There were moments when Garnett could only define him by saying that he looked like a man who had seen a ghost.

✣ II ✣

AN apparition almost as startling had come to Garnett himself in the shape of the mauve note handed to him by his *concierge* as he was leaving the hotel for luncheon.

Not that, on the face of it, a missive announcing Mrs. Sam Newell's arrival at Ritz's, and her need of his presence there that day at five, carried any mark of the portentous. It was not her being at Ritz's that surprised him. The fact that she was chronically hard up, and had once or twice lately been so harshly confronted with the consequences as to accept—indeed solicit—a loan of five pounds from him: this circumstance, as Garnett knew, would never be allowed to affect the general tenor of her existence. If one came to Paris, where could one go but to Ritz's? Did he see her in some grubby hole across the river? Or in a family *pension* near the Place de l'Etoile? There was no affectation in her tendency to gravitate toward what was costliest and most conspicuous. In doing so she obeyed one of the profoundest instincts of her nature, and it was another instinct which taught her to gratify the first at any cost, even to that of dipping into the pocket of an impecunious journalist. It was a part of her strength—and of her charm, too—that she did such things naturally, openly, without any of the grimaces of dissimulation or compunction.

Her recourse to Garnett had of course marked a specially low ebb in her fortunes. Save in moments of exceptional dearth she had richer sources of supply; and he was nearly sure that by running over the "society column" of the Paris *Herald* he should find an explanation, not perhaps of her presence at Ritz's, but of her means of subsistence there. What perplexed him was not the financial but the social aspect of the case. When Mrs. Newell had left London in July she had told him that, between Cowes and Scotland, she and Hermy were provided for till the middle of October: after that, as she put it, they would have to look about. Why, then, when she had in her hand the opportunity of living for three months at the expense of the British aristocracy, did she rush off to Paris at heaven knew whose expense in the beginning of September? She was not a woman to act incoherently; if she made mistakes they were not of that kind. Garnett felt sure she would never willingly relax her hold on her distinguished friends—was it possible that it was they who had somewhat violently let go of her?

As Garnett reviewed the situation he began to see that this possibility had for some time been latent in it. He had felt that something might happen at any moment—and was not this the something he had obscurely foreseen? Mrs. Newell really moved too fast: her position was as perilous as that of an invading army without a base of supplies. She used up everything too quickly—friends, credit, influence, forbearance. It was so easy for her to acquire all these—what a pity she had never learned to keep them! He himself, for instance—the most insignificant of her acquisitions—was beginning to feel like a squeezed sponge at the mere thought of her; and it was this sense of exhaustion, of the inability to provide more, either materially or morally, which had provoked his exclamation on opening her note. From the first days of their acquaintance her prodigality had amazed him, but he had believed it to be surpassed by the infinity of her resources. If she exhausted old supplies she always had new ones to replace them. When one set of people began to find her impossible, another was always beginning to find her indispensable. Yes—but there were limits—there were only so many sets of people, at least in her classification, and when she came to an end of them, what then? Was this flight to Paris a sign that she had come to an end—was she going to try Paris because London had failed her? The time of year precluded such a conjecture. Mrs. Newell's Paris was nonexistent in September. The town was a desert of gaping trippers—he could as soon think of her seeking social restoration at Margate.

For a moment it occurred to him that she might have come over to renew her wardrobe; but he knew her dates too well to dwell long on this. It was in April and December that she visited the dressmakers: before December, he had heard her explain, one got nothing but "the American fashions." Mrs. Newell's scorn of all things American was somewhat illogically coupled with the determination to use her own Americanism to the utmost as a means of social advance. She had found out long ago that, on certain lines, it paid in London to be American, and she had manufactured for herself a personality independent of geographical or social demarcations, and presenting that remarkable blend of plantation dialect, Bowery slang and hyperbolic statement, which expresses the British idea of an unadulterated Americanism. Mrs. Newell, for all her talents, was not by nature either humorous or hyperbolic, and there were times when it would doubtless have been a relief to her to be as stolid as some of the persons whose dullness it was her fate to enliven. It was perhaps the need of relaxing which had drawn her into her odd intimacy with Garnett, with whom she did not have to be either scrupulously English or artificially American, since the impression she made on him was of no more consequence than that which she produced on her footman. Garnett was aware that he owed his success to his insignificance, but the fact affected him only as adding one more element to his knowledge of Mrs. Newell's character. He was as ready to sacrifice his personal vanity in such a cause as he had been, at the outset of their acquaintance, to sacrifice his professional pride to the opportunity of knowing her.

When he had accepted the position of "London correspondent" (with an occasional side glance at Paris) to the New York *Searchlight,* he had not understood that his work was to include the obligation of "interviewing"; indeed, had the possibility presented itself in advance, he would have met it by packing his valise and returning to the drudgery of his assistant editorship in New York. But when, after three months in Europe, he received a letter from his chief, suggesting that he should enliven the Sunday *Searchlight* by a series of "Talks with Smart Americans in London" (beginning say, with Mrs. Sam Newell), the change of focus already enabled him to view the proposal without passion. For his life on the edge of the great world caldron of art, politics and pleasure—of that high-spiced brew which is nowhere else so subtly and variously compounded—had bred in him an eagerness to taste of the heady mixture. He knew he should never have the full spoon at his lips, but he recalled the peasant girl in one of Browning's plays, who boasts of having eaten polenta cut with a knife which has carved an ortolan. Might not Mrs. Newell, who had so successfully cut a way into the dense and succulent mass of English society, serve as the knife to season his polenta?

He had expected, as the result of the interview, to which she promptly, almost eagerly, agreed, no more than the glimpse of brightly-lit vistas which a waiting messenger may catch through open doors; but instead he had found himself drawn at once into the inner sanctuary, not of London society, but of Mrs. Newell's relation to it. She had been candidly charmed by the idea of the interview: it struck him that she was conscious of the need of being freshened up. Her appearance was brilliantly fresh, with the inveterate freshness of the toilet table; her paint was as impenetrable as armor. But her personality was a little tarnished: she was in want of social renovation. She had been doing and saying the same things for too long a time. London, Cowes, Homburg, Scotland, Monte Carlo—that had been the round since Hermy was a baby. Hermy was her daughter, Miss Hermione Newell, who was called in presently to be shown off to the interviewer and add a paragraph to the celebration of her mother's charms.

Miss Newell's appearance was so full of an unassisted

freshness that for a moment Garnett made the mistake of fancying that she could fill a paragraph of her own. But he soon found that her vague personality was merely tributary to her parent's; that her youth and grace were, in some mysterious way, her mother's rather than her own. She smiled obediently on Garnett, but could contribute little beyond her smile, and the general sweetness of her presence, to the picture of Mrs. Newell's existence that it was the young man's business to draw. And presently he found that she had left the room without his noticing it.

He learned in time that this unnoticeableness was the most conspicuous thing about her. Burning at best with a mild light, she became invisible in the glare of her mother's personality. It was in fact only as a product of her environment that poor Hermione struck the imagination. With the smartest woman in London as her guide and example she had never developed a taste for dress, and with opportunities for enlightenment from which Garnett's fancy recoiled she remained simple, unsuspicious and tender, with an inclination to good works and afternoon church, a taste for the society of dull girls, and a clinging fidelity to old governesses and retired nursemaids. Mrs. Newell, whose boast it was that she looked facts in the face, frankly owned that she had not been able to make anything of Hermione. "If she has a role I haven't discovered it," she confessed to Garnett. "I've tried everything, but she doesn't fit in anywhere."

Mrs. Newell spoke as if her daughter were a piece of furniture acquired without due reflection, and for which no suitable place could be found. She got, of course, what she could out of Hermione, who wrote her notes, ran her errands, saw tiresome people for her, and occupied an intermediate office between that of lady's maid and secretary; but such small returns on her investment were not what Mrs. Newell had counted on. What was the use of producing and educating a handsome daughter if she did not, in some more positive way, contribute to her parent's advancement?

✣ III ✣

"It's about Hermy," Mrs. Newell said, rising from the heap of embroidered cushions which formed the background of her afternoon repose.

Her sitting room at Ritz's was full of warmth and fragrance. Long-stemmed roses filled the vases on the chimney piece, in which a fire sparkled with that effect of luxury which fires produce when the weather is not cold enough to justify them. On the writing table, among notes and cards, and signed photographs of celebrities, Mrs. Newell's gold inkstand, her jeweled pen holder, her heavily monogrammed dispatch box, gave back from their expensive surfaces the glint of the flame, which sought out and magnified the orient of the pearls among the lady's laces and found a mirror in the pink polish of her fingertips. It was just such a scene as a little September fire, lit for show and not for warmth, would delight to dwell on and pick out in all its opulent details; and even Garnett, inured to Mrs. Newell's capacity for extracting manna from the desert, reflected that she must have found new fields to glean.

"It's about Hermy," she repeated, making room for him at her side. "I had to see you at once. We came over yesterday from London."

Garnett, seating himself, continued his leisurely survey of the room. In the blaze of Mrs. Newell's refulgence Hermione, as usual, faded out of sight, and he hardly noticed her mother's allusion.

"I've never seen you more resplendent," he remarked.

She received the tribute with complacency. "The rooms are not bad, are they? We came over with the Woolsey Hubbards (you've heard of them, of course?—they're from Detroit), and really they do things very decently. Their motor met us at Boulogne, and the courier always wires ahead to have the rooms filled with flowers. This salon is really a part of their suite. I simply couldn't have afforded it myself."

She delivered these facts in a high decisive voice, which had a note like the clink of her many bracelets and the rattle of her ringed hands against the enameled cigarette case that she held out to Garnett after helping herself from its contents.

"You are always meeting such charming people," said the young man with mild irony; and, reverting to her first remark, he bethought himself to add: "I hope Miss Hermione is not ill?"

"Ill? She was never ill in her life," exclaimed Mrs. Newell, as though her daughter had been accused of an indelicacy.

"It was only that you said you had come over on her account."

"So I have. Hermione is to be married."

Mrs. Newell brought out the words impressively, drawing back to observe their effect on her visitor. It was such that he received them with a long silent stare, which finally passed into a cry of wonder. "Married? For heaven's sake, to whom?"

Mrs. Newell continued to regard him with a smile so serene and victorious that he saw she took his somewhat unseemly astonishment as a merited tribute to her genius. Presently she extended a glittering hand and took a sheet of notepaper from the blotter.

"You can have that put in tomorrow's *Herald*," she said.

Garnett, receiving the paper, read in Hermione's own finished hand: "A marriage has been arranged, and will shortly take place, between the Comte Louis du Trayas, son of the Marquis du Trayas de la Baume, and Miss Hermione Newell, daughter of Samuel C. Newell, Esq., of Elmira, N. Y. Comte Louis du Trayas belongs to one of the oldest and most distinguished families in France, and is equally well connected in England, being the nephew of Lord Saint Priscoe and a cousin of the Countess of Morningfield, whom he frequently visits at Adham and Portlow."

The perusal of this document filled Garnett with such deepening wonder that he could not, for the moment, even do justice to the strangeness of its being written out for publication in the bride's own hand. Hermione a bride! Hermione a future countess! Hermione on the brink of a marriage which would give her not only a great "situation" in the Parisian world but a footing in some of the best houses in England! Regardless of its unflattering implications, Garnett prolonged his stare of amazement till Mrs. Newell somewhat sharply exclaimed—"Well, didn't I always tell you she'd marry a Frenchman?"

Garnett, in spite of himself, smiled at this revised version of his hostess's frequent assertion that Hermione was too goody-goody to take in England, but that with her little dowdy air she might very well "go off" in the Faubourg if only a *dot* could be raked up—and the recollection flashed a new light on the versatility of Mrs. Newell's genius.

"But how did you do it—?" was on the tip of his tongue; and he had barely time to give the query the more conventional turn of: "How did it happen?"

"Oh, we were up at Glaish with the Edmund Fitzarthurs. Lady Edmund is a sort of cousin of the Morningfields', who have a shooting lodge near Glaish—a place called Portlow—and young Trayas was there with them. Lady Edmund, who is a dear, drove Hermy over to Portlow, and the thing was done in no time. He simply fell over head and ears in love with her. You know Hermy is really very handsome in her peculiar way. I don't think you've ever appreciated her," Mrs. Newell summed up with a note of reproach.

"I've appreciated her, I assure you; but one somehow didn't think of her marrying—so soon."

"Soon? She's three and twenty; but you've no imagination," said Mrs. Newell; and Garnett inwardly admitted that he had not enough to soar to the heights of her invention. For the marriage, of course, was her invention, a superlative stroke of business in which he was sure the principal parties had all been passive agents in which everyone, from the bankrupt and disreputable Fitzarthurs to the rich and immaculate Morningfields, had by some mysterious sleight of hand been made to fit into Mrs. Newell's designs. But it was not enough for Garnett to marvel at her work—he wanted to understand it, to take it apart, to find out how the trick had been done. It was true that Mrs. Newell had always said Hermy might go off in the Faubourg if she had a *dot*—but even Mrs. Newell's juggling could hardly conjure up a *dot*: such feats as she was able to perform in this line were usually made to serve her own urgent necessities. And besides, who was likely to take sufficient interest in Hermione to supply her with the means of marrying a French nobleman? The flowers ordered in advance by the Woolsey Hubbards' courier made Garnett wonder if that accomplished functionary had also wired over to have Miss Newell's settlements drawn up. But of all the comments hovering on his lips the only one he could decently formulate was the remark that he supposed Mrs. Newell and her daughter had come over to see the young man's family and make the final arrangements.

"Oh, they're made—everything's settled," said Mrs. Newell, looking him squarely in the eye. "You're wondering, of course, about the *dot*—Frenchmen never go off their heads to the extent of forgetting *that*; or at least their parents don't allow them to."

Garnett murmured a vague assent, and she went on without the least appearance of resenting his curiosity: "It all came about so fortunately. Only fancy, just the week they met I got a little legacy from an aunt in Elmira—a good soul I hadn't seen or heard of for years. I suppose I ought to have put on mourning for her, by the way, but it would have eaten up a good bit of the legacy, and I really needed it all for poor Hermy. Oh, it's not a fortune, you understand—but the young man is madly in love, and has always had his own way, so after a lot of correspondence it's been arranged. They saw Hermy this morning, and they're enchanted."

"And the marriage takes place very soon?"

"Yes, in a few weeks, here. His mother is an invalid and couldn't have gone to England. Besides, the French don't travel. And as Hermy has become a Catholic—"

"Already?"

Mrs. Newell stared. "It doesn't take long. And it suits Hermy exactly—she can go to church so much oftener. So I thought," Mrs. Newell concluded with dignity, "that a wedding at Saint Philippe du Roule would be the most suitable thing at this season."

"Dear me," said Garnett, "I am left breathless—I can't catch up with you. I suppose even the day is fixed, though Miss Hermione doesn't mention it," and he indicated the official announcement in his hand.

Mrs. Newell laughed. "Hermy had to write that herself, poor dear, because my scrawl's too hideous—but I dictated it. No, the day's not fixed—that's why I sent for you." There was a splendid directness about Mrs. Newell. It would never have occurred to her to pretend to Garnett that she had summoned him for the pleasure of his company.

"You've sent for me—to fix the day?" he inquired humorously.

"To remove the last obstacle to its being fixed."

"I? What kind of an obstacle could I have the least effect on?"

Mrs. Newell met his banter with a look which quelled it. "I want you to find her father."

"Her father? Miss Hermione's—?"

"My husband, of course. I suppose you know he's living."

Garnett blushed at his own clumsiness. "I—yes—that is, I really knew nothing—" he stammered, feeling that each word added to it. If Hermione was unnoticeable, Mr. Newell had always been invisible. The young man had never so much as given him a thought, and it was awkward to come on him so suddenly at a turn of the talk.

"Well, he is—living here in Paris," said Mrs. Newell, with a note of asperity which seemed to imply that her friend might have taken the trouble to post himself on this point.

"In Paris? But in that case isn't it quite simple—?"

"To find him? I dare say it won't be difficult, though he's rather mysterious. But the point is that I can't go to him—and that if I write to him he won't answer."

"Ah," said Garnett thoughtfully.

"And so you've got to find him for me, and tell him."

"Tell him what?"

"That he must come to the wedding—that we must show ourselves together at church and afterward in the sacristy."

She delivered the behest in her sharp imperative key, the tone of the born commander. But for once Garnett ventured to question her orders.

"And supposing he won't come?"

"He must if he cares for his daughter's happiness. She can't be married without him."

"Can't be married?"

"The French are like that—especially the old families. I was given to understand at once that my husband must appear—if only to establish the fact that we're not divorced."

"Ah—you're *not*, then?" escaped from Garnett.

"Mercy no! Divorce is stupid. They don't like it in Europe. And in this case it would have been the end of Hermy's marriage. They wouldn't think of letting their son marry the child of divorced parents."

"How fortunate, then—"

"Yes; but I always think of such things beforehand. And of course I've told them that my husband will be present."

"You think he will consent?"

"No; not at first; but you must make him. You must tell him how sweet Hermione is—and you must see Louis, and be able to describe their happiness. You must dine here tonight—he's coming. We're all dining with the Hubbards, and they expect you. They've given Hermy some very good diamonds—though I should have preferred a check, as she'll be horribly poor. But I think Kate Hubbard means to do something about the trousseau—Hermy is at Paquin's with her now. You've no idea how delightful all our friends have been. Ah, here is one of them now," she broke off smiling, as the door opened to admit, without preliminary announcement, a gentleman so glossy and ancient, with such a fixed unnatural freshness of smile and eye, that he gave Garnett the effect of having been embalmed and then enameled. It needed not the exotic-looking ribbon in the visitor's buttonhole, nor Mr. Newell's introduction of him as her friend Baron Schenkelderff, to assure Garnett of his connection with a race as ancient as his appearance.

Baron Schenkelderff greeted his hostess with paternal playfulness, and the young man with an ease which might have been acquired on the Stock Exchange and in the dressing rooms of "leading ladies." He spoke a faultless colorless English, from which one felt he might pass with equal mastery to half a dozen other languages. He inquired patronizingly for the excellent Hubbards, asked his hostess if she did not mean to give him a drop of tea and a cigarette, remarked that he need not ask if Hermione was still closeted with the dressmaker, and, on the waiter's coming in answer to his ring, ordered the tea himself, and added a request for *fine champagne*. It was not the first time that Garnett had seen such minor liberties taken in Mrs. Newell's drawing room, but they had hitherto been taken by persons who had at least the superiority of knowing what they were permitting themselves, whereas the young man felt almost sure that Baron Schenkelderff's manner was the most distinguished he could achieve; and this deepened the disgust with which, as the minutes passed, he yielded to the conviction that the Baron was Mrs. Newell's "aunt."

✣ IV ✣

GARNETT had always foreseen that Mrs. Newell might someday ask him to do something he should greatly dislike. He had never gone so far as to conjecture what it might be, but had simply felt that if he allowed his acquaintance with her to pass from spectatorship to participation he must be prepared to find himself, at any moment, in a queer situation.

The moment had come; and he was relieved to find that he could meet it by refusing her request. He had not always been sure that she would leave him this alternative. She had a way of involving people in her complications without their being aware of it; and Garnett had pictured himself in holes so tight that there might not be room for a wriggle. Happily in this case he could still move freely. Nothing compelled him to act as an intermediary between Mrs. Newell and her husband, and it was preposterous to suppose that, even in a life of such perpetual upheaval as hers, there were no roots which struck deeper than her casual intimacy with himself. She had simply laid hands on him because he happened to be within reach, and he would put himself out of reach by leaving for London on the morrow.

Having thus inwardly asserted his independence, he felt free to let his fancy dwell on the strangeness of the situation. He had always supposed that Mrs. Newell, in her flight through life, must have thrown a good many victims to the wolves, and had assumed that Mr. Newell had been among the number. That he had been dropped overboard at an early stage in the lady's career seemed probable from the fact that neither his wife nor his daughter ever mentioned him. Mrs. Newell was incapable of reticence, and if her husband had still been an active element in her life he would certainly have figured in her conversation. Garnett, if he thought of the matter at all, had concluded that divorce must long since have eliminated Mr. Newell; but he now saw how he had underrated his friend's faculty for using up the waste material of life. She had always struck him as the most extravagant of women, yet it turned out that by a miracle of thrift she had for years kept a superfluous husband on the chance that he might someday be useful. The day had come, and Mr. Newell was to be called from his obscurity. Garnett wondered what had become of him in the interval, and in what shape he would respond to the evocation. The fact that his wife feared he might not respond to it at all seemed to show that his exile was voluntary, or had at least come to appear preferable to other alternatives; but if that were the case it was curious he should not have taken legal means to free himself. He could hardly have had his wife's motives for wishing to maintain the vague tie between them; but conjecture lost itself in trying to picture what his point of view was likely to be, and Garnett, on his way to the Hubbards' dinner that evening, could not help regretting that circumstances denied him the opportunity of meeting so enigmatic a person. The young man's knowledge of Mrs. Newell's methods made him feel that her husband might be an interesting study. This, however, did not affect his resolve to keep clear of the business. He entered the Hubbards' dining room with the firm intention of refusing to execute Mrs. Newell's commission, and if he changed his mind in the course of the evening it was not owing to that lady's persuasions.

Garnett's curiosity as to the Hubbards' share in Hermione's marriage was appeased before he had been five minutes at their table.

Mrs. Woolsey Hubbard was an expansive blonde, whose ample but disciplined outline seemed the result of a well-matched struggle between her cook and her corset maker. She talked a great deal of what was appropriate in dress and conduct, and seemed to regard Mrs. Newell as a final arbiter on both points. To do or to wear anything inappropriate would have been extremely mortifying to Mrs. Hubbard, and she was evidently resolved, at the price of eternal vigilance, to prove her familiarity with what she frequently referred to as "the right thing." Mr. Hubbard appeared to have no such preoccupations. Garnett, if called on to describe him, would have done so by saying that he was the American who always pays. The young man, in the course of his foreign wanderings, had come across many fellow citizens of Mr. Hubbard's type in the most diverse company and surroundings; and wherever they were to be found, they always had their hands in their pockets. Mr. Hubbard's standard of gentility was the extent of a man's capacity to "foot the bill"; and as no one but an occasional compatriot cared to dispute the privilege with him he seldom had reason to doubt his social superiority.

Garnett, nevertheless, did not believe that this lavish pair were, as Mrs. Newell would have phrased it, "putting up" Hermione's *dot*. They would go very far in diamonds but they would hang back from securities. Their readiness to pay was indefinably mingled with a dread of being expected to, and their prodigalities would take flight at the first hint of coercion. Mrs. Newell, who had had a good deal of experience in managing this type of millionaire, could be trusted not to arouse their susceptibilities, and Garnett was therefore certain that the chimerical legacy had been extracted from other pockets. There were none in view but those of Baron Schenkelderff, who, seated at Mrs. Hubbard's right, with a new order in his buttonhole, and a fresh glaze upon his features, enchanted that lady by his careless references to crowned heads and his condescending approval of the champagne. Garnett was more than ever certain that it was the Baron who was paying; and it was this conviction which made him suddenly resolve that, at any cost, Hermione's marriage must take place. He had felt no special interest in the marriage except as one more proof of Mrs. Newell's extraordinary capacity; but now it appealed to him from the girl's own standpoint. For he saw, with a touch of compunction, that in the mephitic air of her surroundings a love story of miraculous freshness had flowered. He had only to intercept the glances which the young couple exchanged to find himself transported to the candid region of romance. It was evident that Hermione adored and was adored; that the lovers believed in each other and in everyone about them, and that even the legacy of the defunct aunt had not been too great a strain on their faith in human nature.

His first glance at the Comte Louis du Trayas showed Garnett that, by some marvel of fitness, Hermione had happened on a kindred nature. If the young man's long mild features and shortsighted glance revealed no special force of character, they showed a benevolence and simplicity as incorruptible as her own, and declared that their possessor, whatever his failings, would never imperil the illusions she had so wondrously preserved. The fact that the girl took her good fortune naturally, and did not regard herself as suddenly snatched from the jaws of death, added poignancy to the situation; for if she missed this way of escape, and was thrown back on her former life, the day of discovery could not be long deferred. It made Garnett shiver to think of her growing old between her mother and Schenkelderff, or such successors of the Baron's as might probably attend on Mrs. Newell's waning fortunes; for it was clear to him that the Baron marked the first stage in his friend's decline. When Garnett took leave that evening he had promised Mrs. Newell that he would try to find her husband.

✤ V ✤

IF Mr. Newell read in the papers the announcement of his daughter's marriage it did not cause him to lift the veil of seclusion in which his wife represented him as shrouded.

A round of the American banks in Paris failed to give Garnett his address, and it was only in chance talk with one of the young secretaries of the Embassy that he was put on Mr. Newell's track. The secretary's father, it appeared, had known the Newells some twenty years earlier. He had had business relations with Mr. Newell, who was then a man of property, with factories or something of the kind, the narrator thought, somewhere in western New York. There had been at this period, for Mrs. Newell, a phase of large hospitality and showy carriages in Washington and at Narragansett. Then her husband had had reverses, had lost heavily in Wall Street, and had finally drifted abroad and disappeared from sight. The young man did not know at what point in his financial decline Mr. Newell had parted company with his wife and daughter; "though you may bet your hat," he philosophically concluded, "that the old girl hung on as long as there were any pickings." He did not himself know Mr. Newell's address, but opined that it might be extracted from a certain official of the Consulate, if Garnett could give a sufficiently good reason for the request; and here in fact Mrs. Newell's emissary learned that her husband was to be found in an obscure street of the Luxembourg quarter.

In order to be near the scene of action, Garnett went to breakfast at his usual haunt, determined to dispatch his business as early in the day as politeness allowed. The headwaiter welcomed him to a table near that of the transatlantic sage, who sat in his customary corner, his head tilted back against the blistered mirror at an angle suggesting that in a freer civilization his feet would have sought the same level. He greeted Garnett affably and the two exchanged their usual generalizations on life till the sage rose to go; whereupon it occurred to Garnett to accompany him. His friend took the offer in good part, merely remarking that he was going to the Luxembourg Gardens, where it was his invariable habit, on good days, to feed the sparrows with the remains of his breakfast roll; and Garnett replied that, as it happened, his own business lay in the same direction.

"Perhaps, by the way," he added, "you can tell me how to find the rue Panonceaux, where I must go presently. I thought I knew this quarter fairly well, but I have never heard of it."

His companion came to a halt on the narrow pavement, to the confusion of the dense and desultory traffic which flows through the old streets of the Latin quarter. He fixed his mild eye on Garnett and gave a twist to the cigar which lingered in the corner of his mouth.

"The rue Panonceaux? It *is* an out-of-the-way hole, but I can tell you how to find it," he answered.

He made no motion to do so, however, but continued to bend on the young man the full force of his interrogative gaze; then he added: "Would you mind telling me your object in going there?"

Garnett looked at him with surprise: a question so unblushingly personal was strangely out of keeping with his friend's usual attitude of detachment. Before he could reply, however, the other had continued: "Do you happen to be in search of Samuel C. Newell?"

"Why, yes, I am," said Garnett with a start of conjecture.

His companion uttered a sigh. "I supposed so," he said resignedly; "and in that case," he added, "we may as well have the matter out in the Luxembourg."

Garnett had halted before him with deepening astonishment. "But you don't mean to tell me—?" he stammered.

The little man made a motion of assent. "I am Samuel C. Newell," he said; "and if you have no objection, I prefer not to break through my habit of feeding the sparrows. We are five minutes late as it is."

He quickened his pace without awaiting a reply from Garnett, who walked beside him in unsubdued wonder till they reached the Luxembourg Gardens, where Mr. Newell, making for one of the less frequented alleys, seated himself on a bench and drew the fragment of a roll from his pocket. His coming was evidently expected, for a shower of little dusky bodies at once descended on him, and the gravel fluttered with battling beaks and wings as he distributed his dole.

It was not till the ground was white with crumbs, and the first frenzy of his pensioners appeased, that he turned to Garnett and said: "I presume, sir, that you come from my wife."

Garnett colored with embarrassment: the more simply the old man took his mission the more complicated it appeared to himself.

"From your wife—and from Miss Newell," he said at length. "You have perhaps heard that your daughter is to be married."

"Oh, yes—I read the *Herald* pretty faithfully," said Miss Newell's parent, shaking out another handful of crumbs.

Garnett cleared his throat. "Then you have no doubt thought it natural that, under the circumstances, they should wish to communicate with you."

The sage continued to fix his attention on the sparrows. "My wife," he remarked, "might have written to me."

"Mrs. Newell was afraid she might not hear from you in reply."

"In reply? Why should she? I suppose she merely wishes to announce the marriage. She knows I have no money left to buy wedding presents," said Mr. Newell astonishingly.

Garnett felt his color deepen: he had a vague sense of standing as the representative of something guilty and enormous, with which he had rashly identified himself.

"I don't think you understand," he said. "Mrs. Newell and your daughter have asked me to see you because they're anxious that you should consent to appear at the wedding."

Mr. Newell, at this, ceased to give his attention to the birds, and turned a compassionate gaze on Garnett.

"My dear sir—I don't know your name—" he remarked, "would you mind telling me how long you've been acquainted with Mrs. Newell?" And without waiting for an answer he added: "If you wait long enough she will ask you to do some very disagreeable things for her."

This echo of his own thoughts gave Garnett a twinge of discomfort, but he made shift to answer good-humoredly: "If you refer to my present errand, I must tell you that I don't find it disagreeable to do anything which may be of service to Miss Hermione."

Mr. Newell fumbled in his pocket, as though searching unavailingly for another morsel of bread; then he said: "From her point of view I shall not be the most important person at the ceremony."

Garnett smiled. "That is hardly a reason—" he began; but he was checked by the brevity of tone with which his companion replied: "I am not aware that I am called upon to give you my reasons."

"You are certainly not," the young man rejoined, "except in so far as you are willing to consider me as the messenger of your wife and daughter."

"Oh, I accept your credentials," said the other with his dry smile; "what I don't recognize is their right to send a message."

This reduced Garnett to silence, and after a moment's pause Mr. Newell drew his watch from his pocket.

"I am sorry to cut the conversation short, but my days are

mapped out with a certain regularity, and this is the hour for my nap." He rose as he spoke and held out his hand with a glint of melancholy humor in his small clear eyes.

"You dismiss me, then? I am to take back a refusal?" the young man exclaimed.

"My dear sir, those ladies have got on very well without me for a number of years: I imagine they can put through this wedding without my help."

"You're mistaken, then; if it were not for that I shouldn't have undertaken this errand."

Mr. Newell paused as he was turning away. "Not for what?" he inquired.

"The fact that, as it happens, the wedding can't be put through without your help."

Mr. Newell's thin lips formed a noiseless whistle. "They've got to have my consent, have they? Well, is he a good young man?"

"The bridegroom?" Garnett echoed in surprise. "I hear the best accounts of him—and Miss Newell is very much in love."

Her parent met this with an odd smile. "Well, then, I give my consent—it's all I've got left to give," he added philosophically.

Garnett hesitated. "But if you consent—if you approve—why do you refuse your daughter's request?"

Mr. Newell looked at him a moment. "Ask Mrs. Newell!" he said. And as Garnett was again silent, he turned away with a slight gesture of leave-taking.

But in an instant the young man was at his side. "I will not ask your reasons, sir," he said, "but I will give you mine for being here. Miss Newell cannot be married unless you are present at the ceremony. The young man's parents know that she has a father living, and they give their consent only on condition that he appears at her marriage. I believe it is customary in old French families—"

"Old French families be damned!" said Mr. Newell, "She had better marry an American." And he made a more decided motion to free himself from Garnett's importunities.

But his resistance only strengthened the young man's. The more unpleasant the latter's task became, the more unwilling he grew to see his efforts end in failure. During the three days which had been consumed in his quest it had become clear to him that the bridegroom's parents, having been surprised to a reluctant consent, were but too ready to withdraw it on the plea of Mr. Newell's nonappearance. Mrs. Newell, on the last edge of tension, had confided to Garnett that the Morningfields were "being nasty"; and he could picture the whole powerful clan, on both sides of the Channel, arrayed in a common resolve to exclude poor Hermione from their ranks. The very inequality of the contest stirred in his blood, and made him vow that in this case, at least, the sins of the parents should not be visited on the children. In his talk with the young secretary he had obtained certain glimpses of Baron Schenkelderff's past that fortified this resolve. The Baron, at one time a familiar figure in a much-observed London set, had been mixed up in an ugly money-lending business ending in suicide, which had excluded him from the society most accessible to his race. His alliance with Mrs. Newell was doubtless a desperate attempt at rehabilitation, a forlorn hope on both sides, but likely to be an enduring tie because it represented, to both partners, their last chance of escape from social extinction. That Hermione's marriage was a mere stake in their game did not in the least affect Garnett's view of its urgency. If on their part it was a sordid speculation, to her it had the freshness of the first wooing. If it made of her a mere pawn in their hands, it would put her, so Garnett hoped, beyond further risk of such base uses; and to achieve this had become a necessity to him.

The sense that, if he lost sight of Mr. Newell, the latter might not easily be found again, nerved Garnett to hold his ground in spite of the resistance he encountered; and he tried to put the full force of his plea into the tone with which he cried: "Ah, you don't know your daughter!"

✣ VI ✣

MRS. NEWELL, that afternoon, met him on the threshold of her sitting room with a "Well?" of pent-up anxiety.

In the room itself, Baron Schenkelderff sat with crossed

legs and head thrown back, in an attitude which he did not see fit to alter at the young man's approach.

Garnett hesitated; but it was not the summariness of the Baron's greeting which he resented.

"You've found him?" Mrs. Newell exclaimed.

"Yes; but—"

She followed his glance and answered it with a slight shrug. "I can't take you into my room, because there's a dressmaker there, and she won't go because she's waiting to be paid. Schenkelderff," she exclaimed, "you're not wanted; please go and look out of the window."

The Baron rose, and, lighting a cigarette, laughingly retired to the embrasure. Mrs. Newell flung herself down and signed to Garnett to take a seat at her side.

"Well—you've found him? You've talked with him?"

"Yes; I've talked with him—for an hour."

She made an impatient movement. "That's too long! Does he refuse?"

"He doesn't consent."

"Then you mean—?"

"He wants time to think it over."

"Time? There *is* no time—did you tell him so?"

"I told him so; but you must remember that he has plenty. He has taken twenty-four hours."

Mrs. Newell groaned. "Oh, that's too much. When he thinks things over he always refuses."

"Well, he would have refused at once if I had not agreed to the delay."

She rose nervously from her seat and pressed her hands to her forehead. "It's too hard, after all I've done! The trousseau is ordered—think how disgraceful! You must have managed him badly; I'll go and see him myself."

The Baron, at this, turned abruptly from his study of the Place Vendome.

"My dear creature, for heaven's sake don't spoil everything!" he exclaimed.

Mrs. Newell colored furiously. "What's the meaning of that brilliant speech?"

"I was merely putting myself in the place of a man on whom you have ceased to smile."

He picked up his hat and stick, nodded knowingly to Garnett, and walked toward the door with an air of creaking jauntiness.

But on the threshold Mrs. Newell waylaid him.

"Don't go—I must speak to you," she said, following him into the antechamber; and Garnett remembered the dressmaker who was not to be dislodged from her bedroom.

In a moment Mrs. Newell returned, with a small flat packet which she vainly sought to dissemble in an inaccessible pocket.

"He makes everything too odious!" she exclaimed; but whether she referred to her husband or the Baron it was left to Garnett to decide.

She sat silent, nervously twisting her cigarette case between her fingers, while her visitor rehearsed the details of his conversation with Mr. Newell. He did not indeed tell her the arguments he had used to shake her husband's resolve, since in his eloquent sketch of Hermione's situation there had perforce entered hints unflattering to her mother; but he gave the impression that his hearer had in the end been moved, and for that reason had consented to defer his refusal.

"Ah, it's not that—it's to prolong our misery!" Mrs. Newell exclaimed; and after a moment she added drearily: "He's been waiting for such an opportunity for years."

It seemed needless for Garnett to protract his visit, and he took leave with the promise to report at once the result of his final talk with Mr. Newell. But as he was passing through the antechamber a side door opened and Hermione stood before him. Her face was flushed and shaken out of its usual repose, and he saw at once that she had been waiting for him.

"Mr. Garnett!" she said in a whisper.

He paused, considering her with surprise: he had never supposed her capable of such emotion as her voice and eyes revealed.

"I want to speak to you; we are quite safe here. Mamma is with the dressmaker," she explained, closing the door behind her, while Garnett laid aside his hat and stick.

"I am at your service," he said.

"You have seen my father? Mamma told me that you were to see him today," the girl went on, standing close to him in order that she might not have to raise her voice.

"Yes; I've seen him," Garnett replied with increasing wonder. Hermione had never before mentioned her father to him, and it was by a slight stretch of veracity that he had included her name in her mother's plea to Mr. Newell. He had supposed her to be either unconscious of the transaction, or else too much engrossed in her own happiness to give it a thought; and he had forgiven her the last alternative in consideration of the abnormal character of her filial relations. But he now saw that he must readjust his view of her.

"You went to ask him to come to the wedding; I know about it," Hermione continued. "Of course it's the custom—people will think it odd if he does not come." She paused, and then asked: "Does he consent?"

"No; he has not yet consented."

"Ah, I thought so when I saw Mamma just now!"

"But he hasn't quite refused—he has promised to think it over."

"But he hated it—he hated the idea?"

Garnett hesitated. "It seemed to arouse painful associations."

"Ah, it would—it would!" she exclaimed.

He was astonished at the passion of her accent; astonished still more at the tone with which she went on, laying her hand on his arm: "Mr. Garnett, he must not be asked—he has been asked too often to do things that he hated!"

Garnett looked at the girl with a shock of awe. What abysses of knowledge did her purity hide?

"But, my dear Miss Hermoine—" he began.

"I know what you are going to say," she interrupted him. "It is necessary that he should be present at the marriage, or the du Trayas will break it off. They don't want it very much, at any rate," she added with a strange candor, "and they'll not be sorry, perhaps—for of course Louis would have to obey them."

"So I explained to your father," Garnett assured her.

"Yes—yes; I knew you would put it to him. But that

makes no difference. He must not be forced to come unwillingly."

"But if he sees the point—after all, no one can force him!"

"No; but if it's painful to him—if it reminds him too much. . . . Oh, Mr. Garnett, I was not a child when he left us. . . . I was old enough to see . . . to see how it must hurt him even now to be reminded. Peace was all he asked for, and I want him to be left in peace!"

Garnett paused in deep embarrassment. "My dear child, there is no need to remind you that your own future—"

She had a gesture that recalled her mother. "My future must take care of itself; he must not be made to see us!" she said imperatively. And as Garnet remained silent she went on: "I have always hoped he didn't hate me, but he would hate me now if he were forced to see me."

"Not if he could see you at this moment!"

She lifted her face with swimming eyes.

"Well, go to him, then; tell him what I've said to you!"

Garnett continued to stand before her, deeply struck. "It might be the best thing," he reflected inwardly; but he did not give utterance to the thought. He merely put out his hand, holding Hermione's in a long pressure.

"I will do whatever you wish," he replied.

"You understand that I'm in earnest?" she urged.

"I'm quite sure of it."

"Then I want you to repeat to him what I've said—I want him to be left undisturbed. I don't want him ever to hear of us again!"

The next day, at the appointed hour, Garnett resorted to the Luxembourg Gardens, which Mr. Newell had named as a meeting place in preference to his own lodgings. It was clear he did not wish to admit the young man any farther into his privacy than the occasion required, and the extreme shabbiness of his dress hinted that pride might be the cause of his reluctance.

Garnett found him feeding the sparrows, but he desisted at the young man's approach, and said at once: "You won't thank me for bringing you all this distance."

"If that means that you're going to send me away with a refusal, I have come to spare you the necessity," Garnett answered.

Mr. Newell turned on him a glance of undisguised wonder, in which a tinge of disappointment might almost have been detected.

"Ah—they've got no use for me, after all?" he said ironically.

Garnett, in reply, related without comment his conversation with Hermione, and the message with which she had charged him. He remembered her words exactly and repeated them without modification, heedless of what they implied or revealed.

Mr. Newell listened with an immovable face, occasionally casting a crumb to his flock. When Garnett ended he asked: "Does her mother know of this?"

"Assuredly not!" cried Garnett with a movement of disgust.

"You must pardon me; but Mrs. Newell is a very ingenious woman." Mr. Newell shook out his remaining crumbs and turned thoughtfully toward Garnett.

"You believe it's quite clear to Hermione that these people will use my refusal as a pretext for backing out of the marriage?"

"Perfectly clear—she told me so herself."

"Doesn't she consider the young man rather chicken-hearted?"

"No; he has already put up a big fight for her, and you know the French look at these things differently. He's only twenty-three, and his marrying against his parents' approval is in itself an act of heroism."

"Yes; I believe they look at it that way," Mr. Newell assented. He rose and picked up the half-smoked cigar which he had laid on the bench beside him.

"What do they wear at these French weddings, anyhow? A dress suit, isn't it?" he asked.

The question was such a surprise to Garnett that for the moment he could only stammer out—"You consent then? I may go and tell her?"

"You may tell my girl—yes." He gave a vague laugh and added: "One way or another, my wife always gets what she wants."

✣ VII ✣

MR. NEWELL'S consent brought with it no accompanying concessions. In the first flush of his success Garnett had pictured himself as bringing together the father and daughter, and hovering in an attitude of benediction over a family group in which Mrs. Newell did not very distinctly figure.

But Mr. Newell's conditions were inflexible. He would "see the thing through" for his daughter's' sake; but he stipulated that in the meantime there should be no meetings or further communications of any kind. He agreed to be ready when Garnett called for him, at the appointed hour on the wedding day; but until then he begged to be left alone. To this decision he adhered immovably, and when Garnett conveyed it to Hermione she accepted it with a deep look of understanding. As for Mrs. Newell she was too much engrossed in the nuptial preparations to give her husband another thought. She had gained her point, she had disarmed her foes, and in the first flush of success she had no time to remember by what means her victory had been won. Even Garnett's services received little recognition, unless he found them sufficiently compensated by the new look in Hermione's eyes.

The principal figures in Mrs. Newell's foreground were the Woolsey Hubbards and Baron Schenkelderff. With these she was in hourly consultation, and Mrs. Hubbard went about aureoled with the importance of her close connection with an "aristocratic marriage," and dazzled by the Baron's familiarity with the intricacies of the Almanach de Gotha. In his society and Mrs. Newell's, Mrs. Hubbard evidently felt that she had penetrated to the sacred precincts where "the right thing" flourished in its native soil. As for Hermione, her look of happiness had returned, but with an undertint of melancholy, visible perhaps only to Garnett, but to him always hauntingly present. Outwardly she sank back into her passive self, resigned to serve as the brilliant lay figure on which Mrs. Newell hung the trophies of conquest. Preparations for the wedding were zealously pressed. Mrs. Newell knew the danger of giving people time to think things over, and her fears about her husband being allayed, she began to dread a new attempt at evasion on the part of the bridegroom's family.

"The sooner it's over the sounder I shall sleep!" she declared to Garnett; and all the mitigations of art could not conceal the fact that she was desperately in need of that restorative. There were moments, indeed, when he was sorrier for her than for her husband or her daughter; so black and unfathomable appeared the abyss into which she must slip back if she lost her hold on this last spar of safety.

But she did not lose her hold; his own experience, as well as her husband's declaration, might have told him that she always got what she wanted. How much she had wanted this particular thing was shown by the way in which, on the last day, when all peril was over, she bloomed out in renovated splendor. It gave Garnett a shivering sense of the ugliness of the alternative which had confronted her.

The day came; the showy coupé provided by Mrs. Newell presented itself punctually at Garnett's door, and the young man entered it and drove to the rue Panonceaux. It was a little melancholy back street, with lean old houses sweating rust and damp, and glimpses of pit-like gardens, black and sunless, between walls bristling with iron spikes. On the narrow pavement a blind man pottered along led by a red-eyed poodle: a little farther on a disheveled woman sat grinding coffee on the threshold of a *buvette*. The bridal carriage stopped before one of the doorways, with a clatter of hoofs and harness which drew the neighborhood to its windows, and Garnett started to mount the ill-smelling stairs to the fourth floor, on which he learned from the *concierge* that Mr. Newell lodged. But halfway up he met the latter descending and they turned and went down together.

Hermione's parent wore his usual imperturbable look, and his eye seemed as full as ever of generalizations on human folly; but there was something oddly shrunken and submerged in his appearance, as though he had grown smaller or his clothes larger. And on the last hypothesis Garnett paused—for it became evident to him that Mr. Newell had hired his dress suit.

Seated at the young man's side on the satin cushions, he remained silent while the carriage rolled smoothly and rapidly through the network of streets leading to the Boulevard Saint-Germain; only once he remarked, glancing at the elaborate fittings of the coupé: "Is this Mrs. Newell's carriage?"

"I believe so—yes," Garnett assented, with the guilty sense that in defining that lady's possessions it was impossible not to trespass on those of her friends.

Mr. Newell made no further comment, but presently requested his companion to rehearse to him once more the exact duties which were to devolve on him during the coming ceremony. Having mastered these he remained silent, fixing a dry speculative eye on the panorama of the brilliant streets, till the carriage drew up at the entrance of Saint Philippe du Roule.

With the same air of composure he followed his guide through the mob of spectators, and up the crimson velvet steps, at the head of which, but for a word from Garnett, a formidable Suisse, glittering with cocked hat and mace, would have checked the advance of the small crumpled figure so oddly out of keeping with the magnificence of the bridal party. The French fashion prescribing that the family *cortège* shall follow the bride to the altar, the vestibule of the church was thronged with the participators in the coming procession; but if Mr. Newell felt any nervousness at his sudden projection into this unfamiliar group, nothing in his look or manner betrayed it. He stood beside Garnett till a white-favored carriage, dashing up to the church with superlative glitter of highly groomed horseflesh and silver-plated harness, deposited the snowy apparition of the bride, supported by her mother; then, as Hermione entered the vestibule, he went forward quietly to meet her.

The girl, wrapped in the haze of her bridal veil, and a little confused, perhaps, by the anticipation of the meeting, paused a moment, as if in doubt, before the small oddly-clad figure which blocked her path—a horrible moment to Garnett, who felt a pang of misery at this satire on the infallibility of the filial instinct. He longed to make some sign, to break in some way the pause of uncertainty; but before he could move he saw Mrs. Newell give her daughter a sharp push, he saw a blush of compunction flood Hermione's face, and the girl, throwing back her veil, bent her tall head and flung her arms about her father.

Mr. Newell emerged unshaken from the embrace: it seemed to have no effect beyond giving an odder twist to his tie. He stood beside his daughter till the church doors were thrown open; then, at a sign from the verger, he gave her his arm, and the strange couple with the long train of fashion and finery behind them, started on their march to the altar.

Garnett had already slipped into the church and secured a post of vantage which gave him a side view over the assemblage. The building was thronged—Mrs. Newell had attained her ambition and given Hermione a smart wedding. Garnett's eye traveled curiously from one group to another—from the numerous representatives of the bridegroom's family, all stamped with the same air of somewhat dowdy distinction, the air of having had their thinking done for them for so long that they could no longer perform the act individually, and the heterogeneous company of Mrs. Newell's friends, who presented, on the opposite side of the nave, every variety of individual conviction in dress and conduct. Of the two groups that latter was decidedly the more interesting to Garnett, who observed that it comprised not only such recent acquisitions as the Woolsey Hubbards and the Baron, but also sundry more important figures which of late had faded to the verge of Mrs. Newell's horizon. Hermione's marriage had drawn them back, had once more made her mother a social entity, had in short already accomplished the object for which it had been planned and executed.

And as he looked about him Garnett saw that all the other actors in the show faded into insignificance beside the dominant figure of Mrs. Newell, became mere marionettes pulled hither and thither by the hidden wires of her intention. One and all they were there to serve her ends and accomplish her purpose: Schenkelderff and the Hubbards to pay for the show, the bride and bridegroom to seal and symbolize her social rehabilitation, Garnett himself as the humble instrument adjusting the different parts of the complicated machinery, and her husband, finally, as the last stake in her game, the last asset on which she could draw to rebuild her fallen fortunes. At the thought Garnett was filled with a deep disgust for what the scene signified, and for his own share in it. He had been her tool and dupe like the others; if he imagined that he was serving Hermione, it was for her mother's ends that he had worked. What right had he to sentimentalize a marriage founded on such base connivances, and how could he have imagined that in so doing he was acting a disinterested part?

While these thoughts were passing through his mind the ceremony had already begun, and the principal personages in the drama were ranged before him in the row of crimson velvet chairs which fills the foreground of a Catholic marriage. Through the glow of lights and the perfumed haze about the altar, Garnett's eyes rested on the central figures of the group, and gradually the others disappeared from his view and his mind. After all, neither Mrs. Newell's schemes nor his own share in them could ever unsanctify Hermione's marriage. It was one more testimony to life's indefatigable renewals, to nature's secret of drawing fragrance from corruption; and as his eyes turned from the girl's illuminated presence to the resigned and stoical figure sunk in the adjoining chair, it occurred to him that he had perhaps worked better than he knew in placing them, if only for a moment, side by side.

His Father's Son

AFTER HIS WIFE'S DEATH Mason Grew took the momentous step of selling out his business and moving from Wingfield, Connecticut, to Brooklyn.

For years he had secretly nursed the hope of such a change, but had never dared to suggest it to Mrs. Grew, a woman of immutable habits. Mr. Grew himself was attached to Wingfield, where he had grown up, prospered, and become what the local press described as "prominent." He was attached to his brick house with sandstone trimmings and a cast-iron area railing neatly sanded to match; to the similar row of houses across the street, with trolley wires forming a kind of aerial pathway between, and to the vista closed by the sandstone steeple of the church which he and his wife had always attended, and where their only child had been baptised.

It was hard to snap all these threads of association, yet still harder, now that he was alone, to live so far from his boy. Ronald Grew was practicing law in New York, and there was no more chance of his returning to live at Wingfield than of a river's flowing inland from the sea. Therefore to be near him his father must move; and it was characteristic of Mr. Grew, and of the situation generally, that the translation, when it took place, was to Brooklyn, and not to New York.

"Why you bury yourself in that hole I can't think," had been Ronald's comment; and Mr. Grew simply replied that rents were lower in Brooklyn, and that he had heard of a house there that would suit him. In reality he had said to himself—being the only recipient of his own confidences—

that if he went to New York he might be on the boy's mind; whereas, if he lived in Brooklyn, Ronald would always have a good excuse for not popping over to see him every other day. The sociological isolation of Brooklyn, combined with its geographical nearness, presented in fact the precise conditions that Mr. Grew sought. He wanted to be near enough to New York to go there often, to feel under his feet the same pavement that Ronald trod, to sit now and then in the same theaters, and find on his breakfast table the journals which, with increasing frequency, inserted Ronald's name in the sacred bounds of the society column. It had always been a trial to Mr. Grew to have to wait twenty-four hours to read that "among those present was Mr. Ronald Grew." Now he had it with his coffee, and left it on the breakfast table to the perusal of a hired girl cosmopolitan enough to do it justice. In such ways Brooklyn attested the advantages of its nearness to New York, while remaining, as regards Ronald's duty to his father, as remote and inaccessible as Wingfield.

It was not that Ronald shirked his filial obligations, but rather because of his heavy sense of them, that Mr. Grew so persistently sought to minimize and lighten them. It was he who insisted, to Ronald, on the immense difficulty of getting from New York to Brooklyn.

"Any way you look at it, it makes a big hole in the day; and there's not much use in the ragged rim left. You say you're dining out next Sunday? Then I forbid you to come over here to lunch. Do you understand me, sir? You disobey at the risk of your father's malediction! Where did you say you were dining? With the Waltham Bankshires again? Why, that's the second time in three weeks, ain't it? Big blow-out, I suppose? Gold plate and orchids—opera singers in afterward? Well, you'd be in a nice box if there was a fog on the river, and you got hung up halfway over. That'd be a handsome return for the attention Mrs. Bankshire has shown you—singling out a whipper-snapper like you twice in three weeks! (What's the daughter's name—Daisy?) No, *sir*—don't you come fooling round here next Sunday, or I'll set the dogs on you. And you wouldn't find me in anyhow, come to think of it. I'm lunching out myself, as it happens—yes, sir, *lunching out.* Is there anything especially comic in my lunching out? I don't often do it, you say? Well, that's no reason why I never should. Who with? Why, with—with old Dr. Bleaker: Dr. Eliphalet Bleaker. No, you wouldn't know about him—he's only an old friend of your mother's and mine."

Gradually Ronald's insistence became less difficult to overcome. With his customary sweetness and tact (as Mr. Grew put it) he began to "take the hint," to give in to "the old gentleman's" growing desire for solitude.

"I'm set in my ways, Ronny, that's about the size of it; I like to go tick-ticking along like a clock. I always did. And when you come bouncing in I never feel sure there's enough for dinner—or that I haven't sent Maria out for the evening. And I don't want the neighbors to see me opening my own door to my son. That's the kind of cringing snob I am. Don't give me away, will you? I want 'em to think I keep four or five powdered flunkeys in the hall day and night—same as the lobby of one of those Fifth Avenue hotels. And if you pop over when you're not expected, how am I going to keep up the bluff?"

Ronald yielded after the proper amount of resistance—his intuitive sense, in every social transaction, of the proper amount of force to be expended, was one of the qualities his father most admired in him. Mr. Grew's perceptions in this line were probably more acute than his son suspected. The souls of short thick-set men, with chubby features, mutton chop whiskers, and pale eyes peering between folds of fat like almond kernels in half-split shells—souls thus encased do not reveal themselves to the casual scrutiny as delicate emotional instruments. But in spite of the disguise in which he walked Mr. Grew vibrated exquisitely in response to every imaginative appeal; and his son Ronald was always stimulating and feeding his imagination.

Ronald in fact constituted Mr. Grew's one escape from the element of mediocrity which had always hemmed him in. To a man so enamored of beauty, and so little qualified to add to its sum total, it was a wonderful privilege to have bestowed on the world such a being. Ronald's resemblance to Mr. Grew's early conception of what he himself would have liked to look might have put new life into the discredited theory of prenatal influences. At any rate, if the young man owed his beauty, his distinction and his winning manner to the dreams of one of his parents, it was certainly to those of Mr. Grew, who, while outwardly devoting his life to the manufacture and dissemination of Grew's Secure Suspender Buckle, moved in an enchanted inward world peopled with all the figures of romance. In this company Mr.Grew cut as brilliant a figure as any of its noble phantoms; and to see his vision of himself projected on the outer world in the shape of a brilliant popular conquering son, seemed, in retrospect, to give to it a belated reality. There were even moments when, forgetting his face, Mr. Grew said to himself that if he'd had "half a chance" he might have done as well as Ronald; but this only fortified his resolve that Ronald should do infinitely better.

Ronald's ability to do well almost equaled his gift of looking well. Mr. Grew constantly affirmed to himself that the boy was "not a genius"; but, barring this slight deficiency, he had almost every gift that a parent could wish. Even at Harvard he had managed to be several desirable things at once—writing poetry in the college magazine, playing delightfully "by ear," acquitting himself creditably of his studies, and yet holding his own in the sporting set that formed, as it were, the gateway of the temple of Society. Mr. Grew's idealism did not preclude the frank desire that his son should pass through the gateway; but the wish was not prompted by material considerations. It was Mr. Grew's notion that, in the rough and hurrying current of a new civilization, the little pools of leisure and enjoyment must nurture delicate growths, material graces as well as moral refinements, likely to be uprooted and swept away by the rush of the main torrent. He based his theory on the fact that he had liked the few "society" people he had met—had found their manners simpler, their voices more agreeable, their views more consonant with his own, than those of the leading citizens of Wingfield. But then he had met very few.

Ronald's sympathies needed no urging in the same direction. He took naturally, dauntlessly, to all the high and exceptional things about which his father's imagination had so long ineffectually hovered—from the start he *was* what Mr. Grew had dreamed of being. And so precise, so detailed, was Mr. Grew's vision of his own imaginary career, that as Ronald grew up, and began to travel in a widening orbit, his father had an almost uncanny sense of the extent to which that career was enacting itself before him. At Harvard, Ronald had done exactly what the hypothetical Mason Grew would have done, had not his actual self, at the same age, been working his way up in old Slagden's button factory—the institution which was later to acquire fame, and even notoriety, as the birthplace of Grew's Secure Suspender Buckle. Afterward, at a period when the actual Grew had passed from the factory to the bookkeeper's desk, his invisible double had been reading law at Columbia—precisely again what Ronald did! But it was when the young man left the paths laid out for him by the parental hand, and cast himself boldly on the world, that his adventures began to bear the most astonishing resemblance to those of the unrealized Mason Grew. It was in New York that the scene of this hypothetical being's first exploits had always been laid; and it was in New York that Ronald was to achieve his first triumph. There was nothing small or timid about Mr. Grew's imagination; it had never stopped at anything between Wingfield and the metropolis. And the real Ronald had the same cosmic vision as his parent. He brushed aside with a contemptuous laugh his mother's entreaty that he should stay at Wingfield and continue the dynasty of the Grew Suspender Buckle. Mr. Grew knew that in reality Ronald winced at the Buckle, loathed it, blushed for his connection with it. Yet it was the Buckle that had seen him through Groton, Harvard and the Law School, and had permitted him to enter the office of a distinguished corporation lawyer, instead of being enslaved to some sordid business with quick returns. The Buckle had been Ronald's fairy godmother—yet his father did not blame him for abhorring and disowning it. Mr. Grew himself often bitterly regretted having attached his own name to the instrument of his material success, though, at the time, his doing so had been the natural expression of his romanticism. When he invented the Buckle, and took out his patent, he and his wife both felt that to bestow their name on it was like naming a battleship or a peak of the Andes.

Mrs. Grew had never learned to know better; but Mr. Grew had discovered his error before Ronald was out of school. He read it first in a black eye of his boy's. Ronald's symmetry had been marred by the insolent fist of a fourth former whom he had chastised for alluding to his father as "Old Buckles"; and when Mr. Grew heard the epithet he understood in a flash that the Buckle was a thing to blush for. It was too late then to dissociate his name from it, or to efface from the hoardings of the entire continent the picture of two gentlemen, one contorting himself in the abject effort to repair a broken brace, while the careless ease of the other's attitude proclaimed his trust in the Secure Suspender Buckle. These records were indelible, but Ronald could at least be spared all direct connection with them; and that day Mr. Grew decided that the boy should not return to Wingfield.

"You'll see," he had said to Mrs. Grew, "he'll take right hold in New York. Ronald's got my knack for taking hold," he added, throwing out his chest.

"But the way you took hold was in business," objected Mrs. Grew, who was large and literal.

Mr. Grew's chest collapsed, and he became suddenly conscious of his comic face in its rim of sandy whisker. "That's not the only way," he said, with a touch of wistfulness which escaped his wife's analysis.

"Well, of course you could have written beautifully," she rejoined with admiring eyes.

"*Written*? Me!" Mr. Grew became sardonic.

"Why, those letters—weren't *they* beautiful, I'd like to know?"

The couple exchanged a glance, innocently allusive and amused on the wife's part, and charged with a sudden tragic significance on the husband's.

"Well, I've got to be going along to the office now," he merely said, dragging himself out of his chair.

This had happened while Ronald was still at school; and now Mrs. Grew slept in the Wingfield cemetery, under a lifesize theological virtue of her own choosing, and Mr.

Grew's prognostications as to Ronald's ability to "take right hold" in New York were being more and more brilliantly fulfilled.

✣ II ✣

RONALD obeyed his father's injunction not to come to luncheon on the day of the Bankshires' dinner; but in the middle of the following week Mr. Grew was surprised by a telegram from his son.

"Want to see you important matter. Expect me tomorrow afternoon."

Mr. Grew received the telegram after breakfast. To peruse it he had lifted his eye from a paragraph of morning paper describing a fancy dress dinner which the Hamilton Gliddens' had given the night before for the housewarming of their new Fifth Avenue palace.

"Among the couples who afterward danced in the Poets' Quadrille were Miss Daisy Bankshire, looking more than usually lovely as Laura, and Mr. Ronald Grew as the young Petrarch."

Petrarch and Laura! Well—if *anything* meant anything, Mr. Grew supposed he knew what that meant. For weeks past he had noticed how constantly the names of the young people were coupled in the society notes he so insatiably devoured. Even the soulless reporter was getting into the habit of uniting them in his lists. And this Laura and Petrarch business was almost an announcement. . . .

Mr. Grew dropped the telegram, wiped his eyeglasses, and reread the paragraph. "Miss Daisy Bankshire . . . more than usually lovely . . ." Yes; she *was* lovely. He had often seen her photograph in the papers—seen her represented in every attitude of the mundane game: fondling her prize bulldog, taking a fence on her thoroughbred, dancing a *gavotte*, all patches and plumes, or fingering a guitar, all tulle and lilies; and once he had caught a glimpse of her at the theater. Hearing that Ronald was going to a fashionable first night with the Bankshires, Mr. Grew had for once overcome his repugnance to following his son's movements, and had secured for himself, under the shadow of the balcony, a stall whence he could observe the Bankshire box without fear of detection. Ronald had never known of his father's presence; and for three blessed hours Mr. Grew had watched his boy's handsome dark head bent above the fair hair and averted shoulder that were all he could catch of Miss Bankshire's beauties.

He recalled the vision now; and with it came, as usual, its ghostly double: the vision of his young self bending above such a shoulder and such shining hair. Needless to say that the real Mason Grew had never found himself in so enviable a situation. The late Mrs. Grew had no more resembled Miss Daisy Bankshire than he had looked like the happy victorious Ronald. And the mystery was that from their dull faces, their dull endearments, the miracle of Ronald should have sprung. It was almost—fantastically—as if the boy had been a changeling, child of a Latmian night, whom the divine companion of Mr. Grew's early reveries had secretly laid in the cradle of the Wingfield bedroom while Mr. and Mrs. Grew slept the sleep of conjugal indifference.

The young Mason Grew had not at first accepted this astral episode as the complete canceling of his claims on romance. He too had grasped at the high-hung glory; and, with his tendency to reach too far when he reached at all, had singled out the prettiest girl in Wingfield. When he recalled his stammered confession of love his face still tingled under her cool bright stare. His audacity had struck her dumb; and when she recovered her voice it was to fling a taunt at him.

"Don't be too discouraged, you know—have you ever thought of trying Addie Wicks?"

All Wingfield would have understood the gibe: Addie Wicks was the dullest girl in town. And a year later he had married Addie Wicks. . . .

He looked up from the perusal of Ronald's telegram with this memory in his mind. Now at last his dream was coming true! His boy would taste of the joys that had mocked his thwarted youth and his dull middle-age. And it was fitting that they should be realized in Ronald's destiny. Ronald was made to take happiness boldly by the hand and lead it home like a bride. He had the carriage, the confidence, the high faith in his fortune, that compel the wilful stars. And, thanks to the Buckle, he would also have the background of material elegance that became his conquering person. Since Mr. Grew had retired from business his investments had prospered, and he had been saving up his income for just such a purpose. His own wants were few: he had brought the Wingfield furniture to Brooklyn, and his sitting room was a replica of that in which the long years of his married life had been spent. Even the florid carpet on which Ronald's first footsteps had been taken was carefully matched when it became too threadbare. And on the marble center table, with its beaded cover and bunch of dyed pampas grass, lay the illustrated Longfellow and the copy of Ingersoll's lectures which represented literature to Mr. Grew when he had led home his bride. In the light of Ronald's romance, Mr. Grew found himself reliving, with mingled pain and tenderness, all the poor prosaic incidents of his own personal history. Curiously enough, with this new splendor on them they began to emit a faint ray of their own. His wife's armchair, in its usual place by the fire, recalled her placid unperceiving presence, seated opposite to him during the long drowsy years; and he felt her kindness, her equanimity, where formerly he had only ached at her obtuseness. And from the chair he glanced up at the discolored photograph on the wall above, with a withered laurel wreath suspended on a corner of the frame. The photograph represented a young man with a poetic necktie and untrammeled hair, leaning against a Gothic chair back, a roll of music in his hand; and beneath was scrawled a bar of Chopin, with the words: *"Adieu, Adèle."*

The portrait was that of the great pianist, Fortuné Dolbrowski; and its presence on the wall of Mr. Grew's sitting room commemorated the only exquisite hour of his life save that of Ronald's birth. It was some time before the latter event, a few months only after Mr. Grew's marriage, that he had taken his wife to New York to hear the great Dolbrowski. Their evening had been magically beautiful, and even Addie, roused from her usual inexpressiveness, had waked into a momentary semblance of life. "I never—I never—" she gasped out when they had regained their hotel bedroom, and sat staring back entranced at the evening's vision. Her large face was pink and tremulous, and she sat with her hands on knees, forgetting to roll up her bonnet strings and prepare her curl papers.

"I'd like to *write* him just how I felt—I wish I knew how!" she burst out in a final effervescence of emotion.

Her husband lifted his head and looked at her.

"Would you? I feel that way too," he said with a sheepish laugh. And they continued to stare at each other through a transfiguring mist of sound.

The scene rose before Mr. Grew as he gazed up at the pianist's photograph. "Well, I owe her that anyhow—poor Addie!" he said, with a smile at the inconsequences of fate. With Ronald's telegram in his hand he was in a mood to count his mercies.

✣ III ✣

"A CLEAR twenty-five thousand a year: that's what you can tell 'em with my compliments," said Mr. Grew, glancing complacently across the center table at his boy.

It struck him that Ronald's gift for looking his part in life had never so completely expressed itself. Other young men, at such a moment, would have been red, damp, tight about the collar; but Ronald's cheek was a shade paler, and the contrast made his dark eyes more expressive.

"A clear twenty-five thousand; yes, sir—that's what I always meant you to have."

Mr. Grew leaned carelessly back, his hands thrust in his pockets, as though to divert attention from the agitation of his features. He had often pictured himself rolling out that phrase to Ronald, and now that it was on his lips he could not control their tremor.

Ronald listened in silence, lifting a hand to his slight mustache, as though he, too, wished to hide some involuntary betrayal of emotion. At first Mr. Grew took his silence for an expression of gratified surprise; but as it prolonged itself it became less easy to interpret.

"I—see here, my boy; did you expect more? Isn't it

enough?" Mr. Grew cleared his throat. "Do *they* expect more?" he asked nervously. He was hardly able to face the pain of inflicting a disappointment on Ronald at the very moment when he had counted on putting the final touch to his bliss.

Ronald moved uneasily in his chair and his eyes wandered upward to the laurel-wreathed photograph of the pianist.

"*Is* it the money, Ronald? Speak out, my boy. We'll see, we'll look round—I'll manage somehow."

"No, no," the young man interrupted, abruptly raising his hand as though to check his father.

Mr. Grew recovered his cheerfulness. "Well, what's the trouble then, if *she's* willing?"

Ronald shifted his position again and finally rose from his seat and wandered across the room.

"Father," he said, coming back, "there's something I've got to tell you. I can't take your money."

Mr. Grew sat speechless a moment, staring blankly at his son; then he emitted a laugh. "My money? What are you talking about? What's this about my money? Why, it ain't *mine*, Ronny; it's all yours—every cent of it!"

The young man met his tender look with a gesture of tragic refusal.

"No, no, it's not mine—not even in the sense you mean. Not in any sense. Can't you understand my feeling so?"

"Feeling so? I don't know how you're feeling. I don't know what you're talking about. Are you too proud to touch any money you haven't earned? Is that what you're trying to tell me?"

"No. It's not that. You must know—"

Mr. Grew flushed to the rim of his bristling whiskers. "Know? Know *what*? Can't you speak out?"

Ronald hesitated, and the two faced each other for a long strained moment, during which Mr. Grew's congested countenance grew gradually pale again.

"What's the meaning of this? Is it because you've done something . . . something you're ashamed of . . . ashamed to tell me?" he gasped; and walking around the table he laid his hand gently on his son's shoulder. "There's nothing you can't tell me, my boy."

"It's not that. Why do you make it so hard for me?" Ronald broke out with passion. "You must have known this was sure to happen sooner or later."

"Happen? What was sure to hap—?" Mr. Grew's question wavered on his lip and passed into a tremulous laugh. "Is it something *I've* done that you don't approve of? Is it—is it *the Buckle* you're ashamed of, Ronald Grew?"

Ronald laughed too, impatiently. "The Buckle? No, I'm not ashamed of the Buckle; not any more than you are," he returned with a flush. "But I'm ashamed of all I owe to it—all I owe to you—when—when—" He broke off and took a few distracted steps across the room. "You might make this easier for me," he protested, turning back to his father.

"Make what easier? I know less and less what you're driving at," Mr. Grew groaned.

Ronald's walk had once more brought him beneath the photograph on the wall. He lifted his head for a moment and looked at it; then he looked again at Mr. Grew.

"Do you suppose I haven't always known?"

"Known—?"

"Even before you gave me those letters at the time of my mother's death—even before that, I suspected. I don't know how it began . . . perhaps from little things you let drop . . . you and she . . . and resemblances that I couldn't help seeing . . . in myself. . . . How on earth could you suppose I *shouldn't guess*? I always thought you gave me the letters as a way of telling me—"

Mr. Grew rose slowly from his chair. "The letters? Do you mean Dolbrowski's letters?"

Ronald nodded with white lips. "You must remember giving them to me the day after the funeral."

Mr. Grew nodded back. "Of course. I wanted you to have everything your mother valued."

"Well—how could I help knowing after that?"

"Knowing *what*?" Mr. Grew stood staring helplessly at his son. Suddenly his look caught at a clue that seemed to confront it with a deeper difficulty. "You thought—you thought those letters . . . Dolbrowski's letters . . . you thought they meant. . . ."

"Oh, it wasn't only the letters. There were so many other signs. My love of music—my—all my feelings about life . . . and art . . . and when you gave me the letters I thought you must mean me to know."

Mr. Grew had grown quiet. His lips were firm, and his small eyes looked out steadily from their creased lids.

"To know that you were Fortuné Dolbrowski son?"

Ronald made a mute sign of assent.

"I see. And what did you intend to do?"

"I meant to wait till I could earn my living, and then repay you . . . as far as I can ever repay you . . . for what you'd spent on me. . . . But now that there's a chance of my marrying . . . and that your generosity overwhelms me . . . I'm obliged to speak."

"I see," said Mr. Grew again. He let himself down into his chair, looking steadily and not unkindly at the young man. "Sit down too, Ronald. Let's talk."

Ronald made a protesting movement. "Is anything to be gained by it? You can't change me—change what I feel. The reading of those letters transformed my whole life—I was a boy till then: they made a man of me. From that moment I understood myself." He paused, and then looked up at Mr. Grew's face. "Don't imagine that I don't appreciate your kindness—your extraordinary generosity. But I can't go through life in disguise. And I want you to know that I have not won Daisy under false pretenses—"

Mr. Grew started up with the first expletive Ronald had ever heard on his lips.

"You damned young fool, you, you haven't *told* her—?"

Ronald raised his head with pride. "Oh, you don't know her, sir! She thinks no worse of me for knowing my secret. She is above and beyond all such conventional prejudices. She's *proud* of my parentage—" he straightened his slim young shoulders—"as I'm proud of it . . . yes, sir, proud of it. . . ."

Mr. Grew sank back into his seat with a dry laugh. "Well, you ought to be. You come of good stock. And you're your father's son, every inch of you!" He laughed again, as though the humor of the situation grew on him with its closer contemplation.

"Yes, I've always felt that," Ronald murmured, gravely.

"Your father's son, and no mistake." Mr. Grew leaned forward. "You're the son of as big a fool as yourself. And here he sits, Ronald Grew!"

The young man's color deepened to crimson; but his reply was checked by Mr. Grew's decisive gesture. "Here he sits, with all your young nonsense still alive in him. Don't you begin to see the likeness? If you don't I'll tell you the story of those letters."

Ronald stared. "What do you mean? Don't they tell their own story?"

"I supposed they did when I gave them to you; but you've given it a twist that needs straightening out." Mr. Grew squared his elbows on the table, and looked at the young man across the gift books and dyed pampas grass. "I wrote all the letters that Dolbrowski answered."

Ronald gave back his look in frowning perplexity. "*You* wrote them? I understand. His letters are all addressed to my mother."

"Yes. And he thought he was corresponding with her."

"But my mother—what did she think?"

Mr. Grew hesitated, puckering his thick lids. "Well, I guess she kinder thought it was a joke. Your mother didn't think about things much."

Ronald continued to bend a puzzled frown on the question. "I don't understand," he reiterated.

Mr. Grew cleared his throat with a nervous laugh. "Well, I don't know as you ever will—*quite*. But this is the way it came about. I had a toughish time of it when I was young. Oh, I don't mean so much the fight I had to put up to make my way—there was always plenty of fight in me. But inside of myself it was kinder lonesome. And the outside didn't attract callers." He laughed again, with an apologetic gesture toward his broad blinking face. "When I went round with the other young fellows I was always the forlorn hope—the one that had to eat the drumsticks and dance with the leftovers. As sure as there was a blighter at a picnic I had to swing her, and feed her, and drive her home. And all the time I was mad after all the things you've got—poetry and music and all the joy-forever business. So there were the pair of us—my face and my imagination—chained together, and fighting, and hating each other like poison.

"Then your mother came along and took pity on me. It sets up a gawky fellow to find a girl who ain't ashamed to be seen walking with him Sundays. And I was grateful to your mother, and we got along first-rate. Only I couldn't say things to her—and she couldn't answer. Well—one day, a few months after we were married, Dolbrowski came to New York, and the whole place went wild about him. I'd never heard any good music, but I'd always had an inkling of what it must be like, though I couldn't tell you to this day how I knew. Well, your mother read about him in the papers too, and she thought it'd be the swagger thing to go to New York and hear him play—so we went. . . . I'll never forget that evening. Your mother wasn't easily stirred up—she never seemed to need to let off steam. But that night she seemed to understand the way I felt. And when we got back to the hotel she said to me: 'I'd like to tell him how I feel. I'd like to sit right down and write to him.'

" 'Would you?' I said. 'So would I.'

"There was paper and pens there before us, and I pulled a sheet toward me, and began to write. 'Is this what you'd like to say to him?' I asked her when the letter was done. And she got pink and said: 'I don't understand it, but it's lovely.' And she copied it out and signed her name to it, and sent it."

Mr. Grew paused, and Ronald sat silent, with lowered eyes.

"That's how it began; and that's where I thought it would end. But it didn't, because Dolbrowski answered. His first letter was dated January 10, 1872. I guess you'll find I'm correct. Well, I went back to hear him again, and I wrote him after the performance, and he answered again. And after that we kept it up for six months. Your mother always copied the letters and signed them. She seemed to think it was a kinder joke, and she was proud of his answering my letters. But she never went back to New York to hear him, though I saved up enough to give her the treat again. She was too lazy, and she let me go without her. I heard him three times in New York; and in the spring he came to

Wingfield and played once at the Academy. Your mother was sick and couldn't go; so I went alone. After the performance I meant to get one of the directors to take me in to see him; but when the time came, I just went back home and wrote to him instead. And the month after, before he went back to Europe, he sent your mother a last little note, and that picture hanging up there. . . ."

Mr. Grew paused again, and both men lifted their eyes to the photograph.

"Is that all?" Ronald slowly asked.

"That's all—every bit of it," said Mr. Grew.

"And my mother—my mother never even spoke to Dolbrowski?"

"Never. She never even saw him but that once in New York at his concert."

The blood crept again to Ronald's face. "Are you sure of that, sir?" he asked in a trembling voice.

"Sure as I am that I'm sitting here. Why, she was too lazy to look at his letters after the first novelty wore off. She copied the answers just to humor me—but she always said she couldn't understand what we wrote."

"But how could you go on with such a correspondence? It's incredible!"

Mr. Grew looked at his son thoughtfully. "I suppose it is, to you. You've only had to put out your hand and get the things I was starving for—music, and good talk, and ideas. Those letters gave me all that. You've read them, and you know that Dolbrowski was not only a great musician but a great man. There was nothing beautiful he didn't see, nothing fine he didn't feel. For six months I breathed his air, and I've lived on it ever since. Do you begin to understand a little now?"

"Yes—a little. But why write in my mother's name? Why make it appear like a sentimental correspondence?"

Mr. Grew reddened to his bald temples. "Why, I tell you it began that way, as a kinder joke. And when I saw that the first letter pleased and interested him, I was afraid to tell him—*I couldn't* tell him. Do you suppose he'd gone on writing if he'd ever seen me, Ronny?"

Ronald suddenly looked at him with new eyes. "But he

must have thought your letters very beautiful—to go on as he did," he broke out.

"Well—I did my best," said Mr. Grew modestly.

Ronald pursued his idea. "Where *are* all your letters, I wonder? Weren't they returned to you at his death?"

Mr. Grew laughed. "Lord, no. I guess he had trunks and trunks full of better ones. I guess Queens and Empresses wrote to him."

"I should have liked to see your letters," the young man insisted.

"Well, they weren't bad," said Mr. Grew drily. "But I'll tell you one thing, Ronny," he added. Ronald raised his head with a quick glance, and Mr.Grew continued: "I'll tell you where the best of those letters is—it's in *you*. If it hadn't been for that one look at life I couldn't have made you what you are. Oh, I know you've done a good deal of your own making—but I've been there behind you all the time. And you'll never know the work I've spared you and the time I've saved you. Fortuné Dolbrowski helped me do that. I never saw things little again after I'd looked at 'em with him. And I tried to give you the big view from the start. . . . So that's what became of my letters."

Mr. Grew paused, and for a long time Ronald sat motionless, his elbows on the table, his face dropped on his hands.

Suddenly Mr. Grew's touch fell on his shoulder.

"Look at here, Ronald Grew—do you want me to tell you how you're feeling at this minute? Just a mite let down, after all, at the idea that you ain't the romantic figure you'd got to think yourself. . . . Well, that's natural enough, too; but I'll tell you what it proves. It proves you're my son right enough, if any more proof was needed. For it's just the kind of fool nonsense I used to feel at your age—and if there's anybody here to laugh at it's myself, and not you. And you can laugh at me just as much as you like. . . ."

The Legend

ARTHUR BERNALD could never afterward recall just when the first conjecture flashed on him: oddly enough, there was no record of it in the agitated jottings of his diary. But, as it seemed to him in retrospect, he had always felt that the queer man at the Wades' must be John Pellerin, if only for the negative reason that he couldn't imaginably be anyone else. It was impossible, in the confused pattern of the century's intellectual life, to fit the stranger in anywhere, save in the big gap which, some five and twenty years earlier, had been left by Pellerin's disappearance; and conversely, such a man as the Wades' visitor couldn't have lived for sixty years without filling, somewhere in space, a nearly equivalent void.

At all events, it was certainly not to Doctor Wade or to his mother that Bernald owed the hint: the good unconscious Wades, one of whose chief charms in the young man's eyes was that they remained so robustly untainted by Pellerinism, in spite of the fact that Doctor Wade's younger brother, Howland, was among its most impudently flourishing high priests.

The incident had begun by Bernald's running across Doctor Robert Wade one hot summer night at the University Club, and by Wade's saying, in the tone of unprofessional laxity which the shadowy stillness of the place invited: "I got hold of a queer fish at St. Martin's the other day—case of heat prostration picked up in Central Park. When we'd patched him up I found he had nowhere to go, and not a dollar in his pocket, and I sent him down to our place at Portchester to rebuild."

The opening roused his hearer's attention. Bob Wade had an instinctive sense of values that Bernald had learned to trust.

"What sort of chap? Young or old?"

"Oh, every age—full of years, and yet with a lot left. He called himself sixty on the books."

"Sixty's a good age for some kinds of living. And age is purely subjective. How has he used his sixty years?"

"Well—part of them in educating himself, apparently. He's a scholar—humanities, languages, and so forth."

"Oh—decayed gentleman," Bernald murmured, disappointed.

"Decayed? Not much!" cried the doctor with his accustomed literalness. "I only mentioned that side of Winterman—his name's Winterman—because it was the side my mother noticed first. I suppose women generally do. But it's only a part—a small part. The man's the big thing."

"Really big?"

"Well—there again. . . . When I took him down to the country, looking rather like a tramp from a 'Shelter,' with an untrimmed beard, and a suit of reach-me-downs he'd slept round the Park in for a week, I felt sure my mother'd carry the silver up to her room, and send for the gardener's dog to sleep in the hall. But she didn't."

"I see. 'Women and children love him.' Oh, Wade!" Bernald groaned.

"Not a bit of it! You're out again. We don't love him, either of us. But we *feel* him—the air's charged with him. You'll see."

And Bernald agreed that he *would* see, the following Sunday. Wade's inarticulate attempts to characterize the stranger had struck his friend. The human revelation had for Bernald a poignant and ever-renewed interest, which his trade, as the dramatic critic of a daily paper, had hitherto failed to diminish. And he knew that Bob Wade, simple and undefiled by literature—Bernald's specific affliction—had a free and personal way of judging men, and the diviner's knack of reaching their hidden springs. During the days that followed, the young doctor gave Bernald further details about John Winterman: details not of fact—for in that respect the stranger's reticence was baffling—but of impression. It appeared that Winterman, while lying insensible in the Park, had been robbed of the few dollars he possessed; and on leaving the hospital still weak and half-blind, he had quite simply and unprotestingly accepted the Wades' offer to give him shelter till such time as he should be strong enough to work.

"But what's his work?" Bernald interjected. "Hasn't he at least told you that?"

"Well, writing. Some kind of writing." Doctor Bob always became vague when he approached the confines of literature. "He means to take it up again as soon as his eyes get right."

Bernald groaned again. "Oh, Lord—that finishes him; and *me*! He's looking for a publisher, of course—he wants a 'favorable notice.' I won't come!"

"He hasn't written a line for twenty years."

"A line of *what*? What kind of literature can one keep corked up for twenty years?"

Wade surprised him. "The real kind, I should say. But I don't know Winterman's line," the doctor added. "He speaks of the things he used to write as merely as 'stuff that wouldn't sell.' He has a wonderful confidential way of *not* telling one things. But he says he'll have to do something for his living as soon as his eyes are patched up, and that writing is the only trade he knows. The queer thing is that he seems pretty sure of selling *now*. He even talked of buying the bungalow off us, with an acre or two about it."

"The bungalow? What's that?"

"The studio down by the shore that we built for Howland when he thought he meant to paint." (Howland Wade, as Bernald knew, had experienced various "calls.") "Since he's taken to writing nobody's been near the place. I offered it to Winterman, and he camps there—cooks his meals, does his own housekeeping, and never comes up to the house except in the evenings, when he joins us on the verandah, in the dark, and smokes while my mother knits."

"A discreet visitor, eh?"

"More than he need be. My mother actually wanted him to stay on in the house—in her pink chintz room. Think of it! But he says houses smother him. I take it he's lived for years in the open."

"In the open where?"

"I can't make out, except that it was somewhere in the east. 'East of everything—beyond the day spring. In places not on the map.' That's the way he put it; and when I said: 'You've been an explorer, then?' he smiled in his beard, and answered: 'Yes; that's it—an explorer.' Yet he doesn't strike me as a man of action: hasn't the hands or the eyes."

"What sort of hands and eyes has he?"

Wade reflected. His range of observation was not large, but within its limits, it was exact and could give an account of itself.

"He's worked a lot with his hands, but that's not what they were made for. I should say they were extraordinarily delicate conductors of sensation. And his eye—his eye too. He hasn't used it to dominate people: he didn't care to. He simply looks through 'em all like windows. Makes them feel like the fellows who think they're made of glass. The mitigating circumstance is that he seems to see such a glorious landscape through me." Wade grinned at the thought of serving such a purpose.

"I see. I'll come on Sunday and be looked through!" Bernald cried.

✣ II ✣

BERNALD came on two successive Sundays; and the second time he lingered till the Tuesday.

"Here he comes!" Wade had said, the first evening, as the two young men, with Wade's mother, sat on the verandah, with the Virginia creeper drawing, between the arches, its black arabesques against a moon-lined sky.

Bernald heard a step on the gravel, and saw the red flit of a cigar through the shrubs. Then a loosely-moving figure obscured the patch of sky between the creepers, and the spark became the center of a dim bearded face, in which Bernald, through the darkness, discerned only a broad white gleam of forehead.

It was the young man's subsequent impression that

Winterman had not spoken much that first evening; at any rate, Bernald himself remembered chiefly what the Wades had said. And this was the more curious because he had come for the purpose of studying their visitor, and because there was nothing to distract his attention in Wade's slow phrases or his mother's artless comments. He reflected afterward that there must have been a mysteriously fertilizing quality in the stranger's silence: it had brooded over their talk like a rain cloud over a dry country.

Mrs. Wade, apparently fearing that her son might have given Bernald an exaggerated notion of their visitor's importance, had hastened to qualify it before the latter appeared.

"He's not what you or Howland would call intellectual—" (Bernald winced at the coupling of the names) "—not in the least *literary*; though he told Bob he used to write. I don't think, though, it could have been what Howland would call writing." Mrs. Wade always named her younger son with a reverential drop of the voice. She viewed literature much as she did Providence, as an inscrutable mystery; and she spoke of Howland as a dedicated being, set apart to perform secret rites within the veil of the sanctuary.

"I shouldn't say he had a quick mind," she continued, reverting to Winterman. "Sometimes he hardly seems to follow what we're saying. But he's got such sound ideas—when he does speak he's never silly. And clever people sometimes *are*, don't you think so?" Bernald sighed an unqualified assent. "And he's so capable. The other day something went wrong with the kitchen range, just as I was expecting some friends of Bob's for dinner; and do you know, when Mr. Winterman heard we were in trouble, he came and took a look, and knew at once what to do? I told him it was a dreadful pity he wasn't married!"

Close on midnight, when the session on the verandah ended, and the two young men were strolling down to the bungalow at Winterman's side, Bernald's mind reverted to the image of the fertilizing cloud. There was something brooding, pregnant, in the silent presence beside him: he had, in place of any circumscribing personal impression, a large hovering sense of manifold latent meanings. And he felt a thrill of relief when, halfway down the lawn, Doctor Bob was checked by a voice that called him back to the telephone.

"Now I'll be with him alone!" thought Bernald, with a throb like a lover's.

Under the low rafters of the bungalow Winterman had to grope for the lamp on his desk, and as its light struck up into his face Bernald's sense of the rareness of the opportunity increased. He couldn't have said why, for the face, with its bossed forehead, its shabby greyish beard and blunt Socratic nose, made no direct appeal to the eye. It seemed rather like a stage on which remarkable things might be enacted, like some shaggy moorland landscape dependent for form and expression on the clouds rolling over it, and the bursts of light between; and one of these flashed out in the smile with which Winterman, as if in answer to his companion's thought, said simply, as he turned to fill his pipe: "Now we'll talk."

So he'd known all along that they hadn't yet—and had guessed that, with Bernald, one might!

The young man's sudden glow of pleasure left him for a moment unable to meet the challenge; and in that moment he felt the sweep of something winged and summoning. His spirit rose to it with a rush, but just as he felt himself poised between the ascending pinions, the door opened and Bob Wade reappeared.

"Too bad! I'm sorry! It was from Howland, to say he can't come tomorrow after all." The doctor panted out his news with honest grief.

"I tried my best to pull it off for you, Winterman; and my brother *wants* to come—he's keen to talk to you and see what he can do. But you see he's so tremendously in demand. He'll try for another Sunday later on."

Winterman gave an untroubled nod. "Oh, he'll find me here. I shall work my time out slowly." He waved his hand toward the scattered sheets on the kitchen table which formed his desk.

"Not slowly enough to suit us," Wade answered hospitably. "Only, if Howland could have come he might have given you a tip or two—put you on the right track—shown you how to get in touch with the public."

Winterman, his hands in his pockets, lounged against the bare pine walls, twisting his pipe under his beard. "Does your brother enjoy the privilege of that contact?" he questioned gravely.

Wade stared a little. "Oh, of course Howland's not what you'd call a *popular* writer; he despises that kind of thing. But whatever he says goes with—well, with the chaps who count; and everyone tells me he's written *the* book on Pellerin. You must read it when you get back your eyes." He paused, as if to let the name sink in, but Winterman drew at his pipe with a blank face. "You must have heard of Pellerin, I suppose?" the doctor continued. "I've never read a word of him myself: he's too big a proposition for *me*. But one can't escape the talk about him. I have him crammed down my throat even in the hospital. The interns read him at the clinics. He tumbles out of the nurses' pockets. The patients keep him under their pillows. Oh, with most of them, of course, it's just a craze, like the last new game or puzzle: they don't understand him in the least. Howland says that even now, twenty-five years after his death, and with his books in everybody's hands, there are not twenty people who really understand Pellerin; and Howland ought to know, if anybody does. He's—what's their great word?—*interpreted* him. You must get Howland to put you through a course of Pellerin."

And as the young men, having taken leave of Winterman, retraced their way across the lawn, Wade continued to develop the theme of his brother's accomplishments.

"I wish I *could* get Howland to take an interest in Winterman: this is the third Sunday he's chucked us. Of course he does get bored with people consulting him about their writings—but I believe if he could only talk to Winterman he'd see something in him, as we do. And it would be such a godsend to the poor devil to have someone to advise him about his work. I'm going to make a desperate effort to get Howland here next Sunday."

* * *

It was then that Bernald vowed to himself that he would return the next Sunday at all costs. He hardly knew whether he was prompted by the impulse to shield Winterman from Howland Wade's ineptitude, or by the desire to see the latter abandon himself to the full shamelessness of its display; but of one fact he was assured—and that was of the existence in Winterman of some quality which would provoke Howland to the amplest exercise of his fatuity. "How he'll draw him—how he'll draw him!" Bernald chuckled, with a security the more unaccountable that his one glimpse of Winterman had shown the latter only as a passive subject for observation; and he felt himself avenged in advance for the injury of Howland Wade's existence.

✣ III ✣

THAT this hope was to be frustrated Bernald learned from Howland Wade's own lips, the day before the two young men were to have met at Portchester.

"I can't really, my dear fellow," the Interpreter lisped, passing a polished hand over the faded smoothness of his face. "Oh, an authentic engagement, I assure you: otherwise, to oblige old Bob I'd submit cheerfully to looking over his foundling's literature. But I'm pledged this week to the Pellerin Society of Kenosha: I had a hand in founding it, and for two years now they've been patiently waiting for a word from me—the *Fiat Lux*, so to speak. You see it's a ministry, Bernald—I assure you, I look upon my calling quite religiously."

As Bernald listened, his disappointment gradually changed to relief. Howland, on trial, always turned out to be too insufferable, and the pleasure of watching his antics was invariably lost in the impulse to put a sanguinary end to them.

"If he'd only kept his beastly pink hands off Pellerin," Bernald sighed, thinking for the hundredth time of the thick manuscript condemned to perpetual incarceration in his own desk by the publication of Howland's "definitive" work on the great man. One couldn't, *after* Howland Wade, expose one's self to the derision of writing about Pellerin: the eagerness with which Wade's book had been devoured proved, not that the public had enough appetite for another, but simply that, for a stomach so undiscriminating, anything better than Wade had given it would be too good. And Bernald, in the confidence that his own work was open to this objection, had stoically locked it up. Yet if he had resigned himself to the fact that Wade's book existed, and was already passing into the immortality of perpetual republication, he could not, after repeated trials, adjust himself to the author's talk about Pellerin. When Wade wrote of the great dead he was egregious, but in conversation he was familiar and fond. It might have been supposed that one of the beauties of Pellerin's hidden life and mysterious taking off would have been to guard him from the fingering of anecdote; but biographers like Howland Wade are born to rise above such obstacles. He might be vague or inaccurate in dealing with the few recorded events of his subject's life; but when he left fact for conjecture no one had a firmer footing. Whole chapters in his volume were constructed in the conditional mood and made up of hypothetical detail; and in talk, by the very law of the process, hypothesis became affirmation, and he was ready to tell you confidentially the exact circumstances of Pellerin's death, and of the "distressing incident" leading up to it. Bernald himself not only questioned the form under which this incident was shaping itself before posterity, but the very fact of its occurrence: he had never been able to discover any break in the dense cloud enveloping Pellerin's end. He had gone away— that was all that any of them knew: he who had so little, at any time, been with them or of them; and his going had so slightly stirred the public consciousness that the news of his death, laconically imparted from afar, had dropped unheeded into the universal scrap-basket, to be long afterward fished out, with all its details missing, when some inquiring spirit first became aware, by chance encounter with a volume in a London bookstall, not only that such a man as John Pellerin had died, but that he had ever lived, or written.

It need hardly be noted that Howland Wade had not been the pioneer in question: his had been the safer part of swelling the chorus when it rose, and gradually drowning the other voices by his own. He had pitched his note so screamingly, and held it so long, that he was now the accepted authority on Pellerin, not only in the land which had given birth to his genius but in the Europe which had first acclaimed it: and it was the central point of pain in Bernald's sense of the situation that a man who had so yearned for silence should have his grave piped over by such a voice as Wade's.

Bernald's talk with the Interpreter had revived this ache to the momentary exclusion of other sensations; and he was still sore with it when, the next afternoon, he arrived at Portchester for his second Sunday with the Wades.

At the station he had the surprise of seeing Winterman's face on the platform, and of hearing from him that Doctor Bob had been called away to assist at an operation in a distant town.

"Mrs. Wade wanted to put you off, but I believe the message came too late; so she sent me down to break the news to you," said Winterman, holding out his hand.

Perhaps because they were the first conventional words that Bernald had heard him speak, the young man was struck by the quality his intonation gave them.

"She wanted to send a carriage," Winterman added, "but I told her we'd walk back through the woods." He looked at Bernald with a kindliness that flushed the young man with pleasure.

"Are you strong enough? It's not too far?"

"Oh, no. I'm pulling myself together. Getting back to work is the slowest part of the business: not on account of my eyes—I can use them now, though not for reading; but some of the links between things are missing. It's a kind of broken spectrum . . . here, that boy will look after your bag."

The walk through the woods remained in Bernald's memory as an enchanted hour. He used the word literally, as descriptive of the way in which Winterman's contact changed the face of things, or perhaps restored them to their deeper meanings. And the scene they traversed—one of those little untended woods that still, in America, fringe the tawdry skirts of civilization—acquired, as a background to Winterman, the hush of a spot aware of transcendent visitings. Did he talk, or did he make Bernald talk? The young man never knew. He recalled only a sense of lightness and liberation, as if the hard walls of individuality had melted, and he were merged in the poet's deeper interfusion, yet without losing the least sharp edge of self. This general impression resolved itself afterward into the sense of Winterman's wide elemental range. His thought encircled things like the horizon at sea. He didn't, as it happened, touch on lofty themes—Bernald was gleefully aware that, to Howland Wade, their talk would hardly have been Talk at all—but Winterman's mind, applied to lowly topics, was like a lens that brought out microscopic delicacies and differences.

The lack of Sunday trains kept Doctor Bob for two days on the scene of his surgical duties, and during those two days Bernald seized every moment of communion with his friend's guest. Winterman, as Wade had said, was reticent concerning his personal affairs, or rather concerning the practical and material questions to which the term is generally applied. But it was evident that, in Winterman's case, the usual classification must be reversed, and that the discussion of ideas carried one much further into his intimacy than familiarity with the incidents of his life.

"That's exactly what Howland Wade and his tribe have never understood about Pellerin: that it's much less important to know how, or even why, he disapp—"

Bernald pulled himself up with a jerk, and turned to look full at his companion. It was late on the Monday evening, and the two men, after an hour's chat on the verandah to the tune of Mrs. Wade's knitting needles, had bidden their hostess good night and strolled back to the bungalow together.

"Come and have a pipe before you turn in," Winterman had said; and they had sat on together till midnight, with the door of the bungalow open on the heaving moonlit bay, and summer insects bumping against the chimney of the lamp. Winterman had just bent down to refill his pipe from the jar on the table, and Bernald, jerking about to catch him in the circle of lamplight, sat speechless, staring at a face that seemed suddenly to have substituted itself for Winterman's face, or rather to have taken on its features.

"No, they never saw that Pellerin's ideas *were* Pellerin. . . ." He continued to stare at Winterman. "Just as this man's ideas are—why, *are* Pellerin!"

The thought uttered itself in a kind of inner shout, and Bernald started upright with the violent impact of his conclusion. Again and again in the last forty-eight hours he had exclaimed to himself: "This is as good as Pellerin." Why hadn't he said till now: "This *is* Pellerin"? . . . Surprising as the answer was, he had no choice but to take it. He hadn't said so simply because Winterman was *better than Pellerin*— that there was so much more of him, so to speak. Yes; but—it came to Bernald in a flash—wouldn't there by this time have been any amount more of Pellerin? . . . The young man felt actually dizzy with the thought. That was it—there was the solution of the problem! This man was Pellerin, and more than Pellerin! It was so fantastic and yet so unanswerable that he burst into a sudden laugh.

Winterman, at the same moment, brought his palm down with a crash on the pile of manuscript covering the desk.

"What's the matter?" Bernald cried.

"My match wasn't out. In another minute the destruction of the library of Alexandria would have been a trifle compared to what you'd have seen." Winterman, with his large deep laugh, shook out the smoldering sheets. "And I should have been a pensioner on Doctor Bob the Lord knows how much longer!"

Bernald looked at him intently. "You've really got going again? The thing's actually getting into shape?"

"This particular thing *is* in shape. I drove at it hard all last week, thinking our friend's brother would be down on Sunday, and might look it over."

Bernald had to repress the tendency to another wild laugh. "Howland—you meant to show *Howland* what you've done?"

Winterman, looming against the moonlight, slowly turned a dusky shaggy head toward him.

"Isn't it a good thing to do?"

Bernald wavered, torn between loyalty to his friends and the grotesqueness of answering in the affirmative. After all, it was none of his business to furnish Winterman with an estimate of Howland Wade.

"Well, you see, you've never told me what your line *is*," he answered, temporizing.

"No, because nobody's ever told *me*. It's exactly what I want to find out," said the other genially.

"And you expect Wade—?"

"Why, I gathered from our good Doctor that it's his trade. Doesn't he explain—interpret?"

"In his own domain—which is Pellerinism."

Winterman gazed out musingly upon the moon-touched dusk of waters. "And what *is* Pellerinism?" he asked.

Bernald sprang to his feet with a cry. "Ah, I don't know—but you're Pellerin!"

They stood for a minute facing each other, among the uncertain swaying shadows of the room, with the sea breathing through it as something immense and inarticulate breathed through young Bernald's thoughts; then Winterman threw up his arms with a humorous gesture.

"Don't shoot!" he said.

✣ IV ✣

DAWN found them there, and the sun laid its beams on the rough floor of the bungalow, before either of the men was conscious of the passage of time. Bernald, vaguely trying to define his own state in retrospect, could only phrase it: "I floated . . . floated. . . ."

The gist of fact at the core of the extraordinary experience was simply that John Pellerin, twenty-five years earlier, had voluntarily disappeared, causing the rumor of his death to be reported to an inattentive world; and that now he had come back to see what the world had made of him.

"You'll hardly believe it of me; I hardly believe it of myself; but I went away in a rage of disappointment, of wounded pride—no, vanity! I don't know which cut deepest—the sneers or the silence—but between them, there wasn't an inch of me that wasn't raw. I had just the one thing in me: the message, the cry, the revelation. But nobody saw and nobody listened. Nobody wanted what I had to give. I was like a poor devil of a tramp looking for shelter on a bitter night, in a town with every door bolted and all the windows dark. And suddenly I felt that the easiest thing would be to lie down and go to sleep in the snow. Perhaps I'd a vague notion that if they found me there at daylight, frozen stiff, the pathetic spectacle might produce a reaction, a feeling of remorse. . . . So I took care to be found! Well, a good many thousand people die every day on the face of the globe; and I soon discovered that I was simply one of the thousands; and when I made that discovery I really died—and stayed dead a year or two. . . . When I came to life again I was off on the underside of the world, in regions unaware of what we know as 'the public.' Have you any notion how it shifts the point of view to wake under new constellations? I advise any man who's been in love with a woman under Cassiopeia to go and think about her under the Southern Cross. . . . It's the only way to tell the pivotal truths from the others. . . . I didn't believe in my theory any less—there was my triumph and my vindication! It held out, resisted, measured itself with the stars. But I didn't care a snap of my finger whether anybody else believed in it, or even knew it had been formulated. It escaped out of my books—my poor stillborn books—like Psyche from the chrysalis, and soared away into the blue, and lived there. I knew then how it frees an idea to be ignored; how apprehension circumscribes and deforms it. . . . Once I'd learned that, it was easy enough to turn to and shift for myself. I was sure now that my idea would live: the good ones are self-supporting. And meanwhile *I* had to learn to be so; and I tried my hand at a number of things . . . adventurous, menial, commercial. . . . It's not a bad thing for a man to have to live his life—and we nearly all manage to dodge it. Our first round with the Sphinx may strike something out of us—a book or a picture or a symphony; and we're amazed at our feat, and go on letting that first work breed others, as some animal forms reproduce each other without renewed fertilization. So there we are, committed to our first guess at the riddle; and our works look as like as successive impressions of the same plate, each with the lines a little fainter; whereas they ought to be—if we touch earth between times—as different from each other as those other creatures—jellyfish, aren't they, of a kind?—where successive generations produce new forms, and it takes a zoologist to see the hidden likeness. . . .

"Well, I proved my first guess, off there in the wilds, and it lived, and grew, and took care of itself. And I said, 'Someday it will make itself heard; but by that time my atoms will have waltzed into a new pattern.' Then, in Cashmere one day, I met a fellow in a caravan, with a dog-eared book in his pocket. He said he never stirred without it—wanted to know where I'd been, never to have heard of it. It was *my guess*—in its twentieth edition! . . . The globe spun round at that, and all of a sudden I was under the old stars. That's the way it happens when the ballast of vanity shifts! I'd lived a third of a life out there, unconscious of human opinion—because I supposed it was unconscious of *me*. But now—now! Oh, it was different. I wanted to know what they said. . . . Not exactly that, either: I wanted to know *what I'd made them say*. There's a difference. . . . And here I am," said John Pellerin, with a pull at his pipe.

So much Bernald retained of his companion's actual narrative; the rest was swept away under the tide of wonder that rose and submerged him as Pellerin—at some indefinitely later stage of their talk—picked up his manuscript and began to read. Bernald sat opposite, his elbows propped on the table, his eyes fixed on the swaying waters outside, from which the moon gradually faded, leaving them to make a denser blackness in the night. As Pellerin read, this density of blackness—which never for a moment seemed inert or unalive—was attenuated by imperceptible degrees, till a greyish pallor replaced it; then the pallor breathed and brightened, and suddenly dawn was on the sea.

Something of the same nature went on in the young man's mind while he watched and listened. He was conscious of a gradually withdrawing light, of an interval of obscurity full of the stir of invisible forces, and then of the victorious flush of day. And as the light rose, he saw how far he had traveled and what wonders the night had prepared. Pellerin had been right in saying that his first idea had survived, had borne the test of time; but he had given his hearer no hint of the extent to which it had been enlarged and modified, of the fresh implications it now unfolded. In a brief flash of retrospection Bernald saw the earlier books dwindle and fall into their place as mere precursors of this fuller revelation; then, with a leap of rage, he pictured Howland Wade's pink hands on the new treasure, and his prophetic feet upon the lecture platform.

✣ V ✣

"IT won't do—oh, he let him down as gently as possible, but it appears it simply won't do."

Doctor Bob imparted the ineluctable fact to Bernald while the two men, accidentally meeting at their club a few nights later, sat together over the dinner they had immediately agreed to share.

Bernald had left Portchester the morning after his strange discovery, and he and Bob Wade had not seen each other since. And now Bernald, moved by an irresistible instinct of postponement, had waited for his companion to bring up Winterman's name, and had even executed several conversational diversions in the hope of delaying its mention. For how could one talk of Winterman with the thought of Pellerin swelling one's breast?

"Yes; the very day Howland got back from Kenosha I brought the manuscript to town, and got him to read it. And yesterday evening I nailed him, and dragged an answer out of him."

"Then Howland hasn't seen Winterman yet?"

"No. He said: 'Before you let him loose on me I'll go over the stuff, and see if it's at all worth-while.' "

Bernald drew a freer breath. "And he found it wasn't?"

"Between ourselves, he found it was of no account at all. Queer, isn't it, when the *man* . . . but of course literature's another proposition. Howland says it's one of the cases where an idea might seem original and striking if one didn't happen to be able to trace its descent. And this is straight out of bosh—by Pellerin. . . . Yes: Pellerin. It seems that everything in the article that isn't pure nonsense is just Pellerinism. Howland thinks Winterman must have been tremendously struck by Pellerin's writings, and have lived too much out of the world to know that they've become the textbooks of modern thought. Otherwise, of course, he'd have taken more trouble to disguise his plagiarisms."

"I see," Bernald mused. "Yet you say there *is* an original element?"

"Yes; but unluckily it's no good."

"It's not—conceivably—in any sense a development of Pellerin's idea: a logical step farther?"

"Logical? Howland says it's twaddle at white heat."

Bernald sat silent, divided between the satisfaction of seeing the Interpreter rush upon his fate, and the despair of knowing that the state of mind he represented was indestructible. Then both emotions were swept away on a wave of pure joy, as he reflected that now, at last, Howland Wade had given him back John Pellerin.

The possession was one he did not mean to part with lightly; and the dread of its being torn from him constrained him to extraordinary precautions.

"You've told Winterman, I suppose? How did he take it?"

"Why, unexpectedly, as he does most things. You can never tell which way he'll jump. I thought he'd take a high tone, or else laugh it off; but he did neither. He seemed awfully cast down. I wished myself well out of the job when I saw how cut up he was."

Bernald thrilled at the words. Pellerin had shared his own pang, then—the "old woe of the world" at the perpetuity of human dullness!

"But what did he say to the charge of plagiarism—if you made it?"

"Oh, I told him straight out what Howland said. I thought it fairer. And his answer to that was the rummest part of all."

"What was it?" Bernald questioned, with a tremor.

"He said: 'That's queer, for I've never read Pellerin.' "

Bernald drew a deep breath. "Well—and I suppose you believed him?"

"I believed him, because I know him. But the public won't—the critics won't. And if the plagiarism is a pure coincidence it's just as bad for him as if it were a straight steal—isn't it?"

Bernald sighed his acquiescence.

"It bothers me awfully," Wade continued, knitting his kindly brows, "because I could see what a blow it was to him. He's got to earn his living, and I don't suppose he knows how to do anything but write. At his age it's hard to start fresh. I put that to Howland—asked him if there wasn't a chance he might do better if he only had a little encouragement. I can't help feeling he's got the essential thing in him. But of course I'm no judge when it comes to books. And Howland says it would be cruel to give him any hope." Wade paused, turned his wineglass about under a meditative stare, and then leaned across the table toward Bernald. "Look here—do you know what I've proposed to Winterman? That he should come to town with me tomorrow and go in the evening to hear Howland lecture to the Uplift Club. They're to meet at Mrs. Beecher Bain's, and Howland is to repeat the lecture that he gave the other day before the Pellerin Society at Kenosha. It will give Winterman a chance to get some notion of what Pellerin *was*: he'll get it much straighter from Howland than if he tried to plough through Pellerin's books. And then afterward—as if accidentally—I thought I might bring him and Howland together. If Howland could only see him and hear him talk, there's no knowing what might come of it. He couldn't help feeling the man's force, as we do; and he might give him a pointer—tell him what line to take. Anyhow, it would please Winterman, and take the edge off his disappointment. I saw that as soon as I proposed it."

"Someone who's never heard of Pellerin?"

Mrs. Beecher Bain, large, smiling, diffuse, reached out through the incoming throng on her threshold to detain Bernald with the question as he was about to move past her in the wake of his companion.

"Oh, keep straight on, Mr. Winterman!" she interrupted herself to call after the latter. "Into the back drawing room, please! And remember, you're to sit next to me—in the corner on the left, close under the platform."

She renewed her interrogative clutch on Bernald's sleeve. "Most curious! Doctor Wade has been telling me all about your friend—how remarkable you all think him. And it's actually true that he's never heard of Pellerin? Of course as soon as Doctor Wade told me *that*, I said 'Bring him!' It will be so extraordinarily interesting to watch the first impression. Yes, do follow him, dear Mr. Bernald, and be sure that you and he secure the seats next to me. Of course Alice Fosdick insists on being with us. She was wild with excitement when I told her she was to meet someone who'd never heard of Pellerin!"

On the indulgent lips of Mrs. Beecher Bain conjecture speedily passed into affirmation; and as Bernald's companion, broad and shaggy in his visible new evening clothes, moved down the length of the crowded rooms, he was already to the ladies drawing aside their skirts to let him pass, the interesting Huron of the fable.

How far he was aware of the character ascribed to him it was impossible for Bernald to discover. He was as unconscious as a tree or a cloud, and his observer had never known anyone so alive to human contacts and yet so secure from them. But the scene was playing such a lively tune on Bernald's own sensibilities that for the moment he could not adjust himself to the probable effect it produced on his companion. The young man, of late, had made but rare appearances in the group of which Mrs. Beecher Bain was one of the most indefatigable hostesses, and the Uplift Club the chief medium of expression. To a critic, obliged by his trade to cultivate convictions, it was the essence of luxury to leave them at home in his hours of ease; and Bernald gave his preference to circles in which less finality of judgment prevailed, and it was consequently less embarrassing to be caught without an opinion.

But in his fresher days he had known the spell of the Uplift Club and the thrill of moving among the Emancipated; and he felt an odd sense of rejuvenation as he looked at the rows of faces packed about the enbowered platform from which Howland Wade was presently to hand down the eternal verities. Many of these countenances belonged to the old days, when the gospel of Pellerin was unknown, and it had required considerable intellectual courage to avow one's acceptance of the very doctrines he had since demolished. The latter moral revolution seemed to have been accepted as submissively as a change in hairdressing; and it even struck Bernald that, in the case of many of the assembled ladies, their convictions were rather newer than their clothes.

One of the most interesting examples of this readiness of adaptation was actually, in the person of Miss Alice Fosdick, brushing his elbow with exotic amulets, and enveloping him in Arabian odors, as she leaned forward to murmur her sympathetic sense of the situation. Miss Fosdick, who was one of the most advanced exponents of Pellerinism, had large eyes and a plaintive mouth, and Bernald had always fancied that she might have been pretty if she had not been perpetually explaining things.

"Yes, I know—Isabella Bain told me all about him. (He can't hear us, can he?) And I wonder if you realize how remarkably interesting it is that we should have such an opportunity *now*—I mean the opportunity to see the impression of Pellerinism on a perfectly fresh mind. (You must introduce him as soon as the lecture's over.) I explained that to Isabella as soon as she showed me Doctor Wade's note. Of course you see why, don't you?" Bernald made a faint motion of acquiescence, which she instantly swept aside. "At least I think I can *make you see why*. (If you're sure he can't hear?) Why, it's just this—Pellerinism is in danger of becoming a truism. Oh, it's an awful thing to say! But then I'm not afraid of saying awful things! I rather believe it's my mission. What I mean is, that we're getting into the way of taking Pellerin for granted—as we do the air we breathe. We don't sufficiently lead our *conscious life* in him—we're gradually letting him become subliminal." She swayed closer to the young man, and he saw that she was making a graceful attempt to throw her explanatory net over his companion, who, evading Mrs. Bain's hospitable signal, had cautiously wedged himself into a seat between Bernald and the wall.

"*Did* you hear what I was saying, Mr. Winterman? (Yes, I know who you are, of course!) Oh, well, I don't really mind if you did. I was talking about you—about you and Pellerin. I was explaining to Mr. Bernald that what we need at this very minute is a Pellerin revival; and we need someone like you—to whom his message comes as a wonderful new interpretation of life—to lead the revival, and rouse us out of our apathy. . . .

"You see," she went on winningly, "it's not only the big public that needs it (of course *their* Pellerin isn't ours!). It's we, his disciples, his interpreters, we who discovered him and gave him to the world—we, the Chosen People, the Custodians of the Sacred Books, as Howland calls us—it's *we* who are in perpetual danger of sinking back into the old stagnant ideals, and practicing the Seven Deadly Virtues; it's *we* who need to count our mercies, and realize anew what he's done for us, and what we ought to do for him! And it's for that reason that I urged Mr. Wade to speak here, in the very inner sanctuary of Pellerinism, exactly as he would speak to the uninitiated—to repeat, simply, his Kenosha lecture, 'What Pellerinism Means' and we ought all, I think, to listen to him with the hearts of little children—just as *you* will, Mr. Winterman—as if he were telling us new things, and we—"

"Alice, *dear—*" Mrs. Bain murmured with a warning gesture; and Howland Wade, emerging between the palms, took the center of the platform.

A pang of commiseration shot through Bernald as he saw him there, so innocent and so exposed. His plump pulpy body, which made his evening dress fall into intimate and wrapper-like folds, was like a wide surface spread to the shafts of irony; and the ripples of his voice seemed to enlarge the vulnerable area as he leaned forward, poised on confidential finger tips, to say persuasively: "Let me try to tell you what Pellerinism means."

Bernald moved restlessly in his seat. He had the sense of being a party to something not wholly honorable. He ought not to have come; he ought not to have let his companion come. Yet how could he have done otherwise? John Pellerin's secret was his own. As long as he chose to remain John Winterman it was no one's business to gainsay him; and Bernald's scruples were really justifiable only in respect of his own presence on the scene. But even in this respect he ceased to feel them as soon as Howland Wade began to speak.

✣ VI ✣

IT had been arranged that Pellerin, after the meeting of the Uplift Club, should join Bernald at his rooms and spend the night there, instead of returning to Portchester. The plan had been eagerly elaborated by the young man, but he had been unprepared for the alacrity with which his wonderful friend accepted it. He was beginning to see that it was a part of Pellerin's wonderfulness to fall in, quite simply and naturally, with any arrangements made for his convenience, or tending to promote the convenience of others. Bernald perceived that his docility in such matters was proportioned to the force of resistance which, for nearly half a lifetime, had kept him, with his back to the wall, fighting alone against the powers of darkness. In such a scale of values how little the small daily alternatives must weigh!

At the close of Howland Wade's discourse, Bernald, charged with his prodigious secret, had felt the need to escape for an instant from the liberated rush of talk. The interest of watching Pellerin was so perilously great that the watcher felt it might, at any moment, betray him. He lingered in the drawing room long enough to see his friend enclosed in a mounting tide, above which Mrs. Beecher Bain and Miss Fosdick actively waved their conversational tridents; then he took refuge, at the back of the house, in a small dim library where, in his younger days, he had discussed personal immortality and the problem of consciousness with beautiful girls whose names he could not remember.

In this retreat he surprised Mr. Beecher Bain, a quiet man with a mild brow, who was smoking a surreptitious cigar over the last number of the *Strand*. Mr. Bain, at Bernald's approach, dissembled the *Strand* under a copy of the *Hibbert Journal*, but tendered his cigar case with the remark that stocks were heavy again; and Bernald blissfully abandoned himself to this unexpected contact with reality.

On his return to the drawing rooms he found that the tide had set toward the supper table, and when it finally carried him thither it was to land him in the welcoming arms of Bob Wade.

"Hullo, old man! Where have you been all this time?

Winterman? Oh, *he's* talking to Howland: yes, I managed it finally. I believe Mrs. Bain has steered them into the library, so that they shan't be disturbed. I gave her an idea of the situation, and she was awfully kind. We'd better leave them alone, don't you think? I'm trying to get a croquette for Miss Fosdick."

Bernald's secret leapt in his bosom, and he devoted himself to the task of distributing sandwiches and champagne while his pulses danced to the tune of the cosmic laughter. The vision of Pellerin and his Interpreter, face to face at last, had a Titanic grandeur that dwarfed all other comedy. "And I shall hear of it presently; in an hour or two he'll be telling me about it. And that hour will be all mine—mine and his!" The dizziness of the thought made it difficult for Bernald to preserve the balance of the supper plates he was distributing. Life had for him at that moment the completeness which seems to defy disintegration.

The throng in the dining room was thickening, and Bernald's efforts as purveyor were interrupted by frequent appeals, from ladies who had reached repleteness, that he should sit down and tell them all about his interesting friend. Winterman's fame, trumpeted abroad by Miss Fosdick, had reached the four corners of the Uplift Club, and Bernald found himself fabricating *de toutes pièces* a Winterman legend which should in some degree respond to the Club's demand for the human document. When at length he had acquitted himself of this obligation, and was free to work his way back through the lessening groups into the drawing room, he was at last rewarded by a glimpse of his friend, who, still densely encompassed, towered in the center of the room in all his sovereign ugliness.

Their eyes met across the crowd; but Bernald gathered only perplexity from the encounter. What were Pellerin's eyes saying to him? What orders, what confidences, what indefinable apprehension did their long look impart? The young man was still trying to decipher their message when he felt a tap on the arm, and turned to meet the rueful gaze of Bob Wade, whose meaning lay clearly enough on the surface of his good blue stare.

"Well, it won't work—it won't work," the doctor groaned.

"What won't?"

"I mean with Howland. Winterman won't. Howland doesn't take to him. Says he's crude—frightfully crude. And you know Howland hates crudeness."

"Oh, I know," Bernald exulted. It was the word he had waited for—he saw it now! Once more he was lost in wonder at Howland's miraculous faculty for always, as the naturalists said, being true to type.

"So I'm afraid it's all up with his chance of writing. At least *I* can do no more," said Wade, discouraged.

Bernald pressed him for further details. "Does Winterman seem to mind much? Did you hear his version?"

"His version?"

"I mean what he said to Howland."

"Why, no. What the deuce was there for him to say?"

"What indeed? I think I'll take him home," said Bernald gaily.

He turned away to join the circle from which a few minutes before, Pellerin's eyes had vainly and enigmatically signaled to him; but the circle had dispersed, and Pellerin himself was not in sight.

Bernald, looking about him, saw that during his brief aside with Wade the party had passed into the final phase of dissolution. People still delayed, in diminishing groups, but the current had set toward the doors, and every moment or two it bore away a few more lingerers. Bernald, from his post, commanded the clearing perspective of the two drawing rooms, and a rapid survey of their length sufficed to assure him that Pellerin was not in either. Taking leave of Wade, the young man made his way back to the drawing room, where only a few hardened feasters remained, and then passed on to the library which had been the scene of the late momentous colloquy. But the library too was empty, and drifting back to the inner drawing room Bernald found Mrs. Beecher Bain domestically putting out the candles on the mantelpiece.

"Dear Mr. Bernald! Do sit down and have a little chat. What a wonderful privilege it has been! I don't know when I've had such an intense impression."

She made way for him, in a corner of the sofa to which

she had sunk; and he echoed her vaguely: "You *were* impressed, then?"

"I can't express to you how it affected me! As Alice said, it was a resurrection—it was as if John Pellerin were actually here in the room with us!"

Bernald turned on her with a half audible gasp. "You felt that, dear Mrs. Bain?"

"We all felt it—everyone of us: I don't wonder the Greeks—it *was* the Greeks?—regarded eloquence as a supernatural power. As Alice says, when one looked at Howland Wade one understood what they meant by the Afflatus."

Bernald rose and held out his hand. "Oh, I see—it was Howland who made you feel as if Pellerin were in the room? And he made Miss Fosdick feel so too?"

"Why, of course. But why are you rushing off?"

"Because I must hunt up my friend, who's not used to such late hours."

"Your friend?" Mrs. Bain had to collect her thoughts. "Oh, Mr. Winterman, you mean? But he's gone already."

"Gone?" Bernald exclaimed, with an odd twinge of foreboding. Remembering Pellerin's signal across the crowd, he reproached himself for not having answered it more promptly. There had been a summons in the look—and it was certainly strange that his friend should have left the house without him.

"Are you quite sure?" he asked, with a startled glance at the clock.

"Oh, perfectly. He went half an hour ago. But you needn't hurry away on his account, for Alice Fosdick carried him off with her. I saw them leave together."

"Carried him off? She took him home with her, you mean?"

"Yes. You know what strange hours she keeps. She told me she was going to give him a Welsh rabbit, and explain Pellerinism to him."

"Oh, if she's going to explain—" Bernald murmured. But his amazement at the news struggled with a confused impatience to reach his rooms in time to be there for his friend's arrival. There could be no stranger spectacle beneath the stars than that of John Pellerin carried off by Miss Fosdick, and listening, in the small hours, to her elucidation of his doctrines; but Bernald knew enough of his sex to be aware that such an experiment may appear less humorous to its subject than to the detached observer. Even the Uplift Club and its connotations might benefit by the attraction of the unknown; and it was conceivable that to a traveler from Mesopotamia Miss Fosdick might present elements of interest which she had lost for the frequenters of Fifth Avenue. There was, at any rate, no denying that the affair had become unexpectedly complex, and that its further development promised to be rich in comedy.

In the contemplation of these possibilities Bernald sat over his fire, listening for Pellerin's ring. He had arranged his modest quarters with the reverent care of a celebrant awaiting the descent of his deity. He guessed Pellerin to be careless of visual detail, but sensitive to the happy blending of sensuous impressions: to the spell of lamplight on books, and of a deep chair placed where one could watch the fire. The chair was there, and Bernald, facing it across the hearth, already saw it filled by Pellerin's lounging figure. The autumn dawn came late, and even now they had before them the promise of some untroubled hours. Bernald, sitting there alone in the warm stillness of his room, and in the profounder hush of his expectancy, was conscious of gathering up all his sensibilities and perceptions into one exquisitely adjusted instrument of notation. Until now he had tasted Pellerin's society only in unpremeditated snatches and had always left him with a sense, on his own part, of waste and shortcoming. Now, in the lull of this dedicated hour, he felt that he should miss nothing, and forget nothing, of the initiation that awaited him. And catching sight of Pellerin's pipe, he rose and laid it carefully on a table by the armchair. . . .

"No. I've never had any news of him," Bernald heard himself repeating. He spoke in a low tone, and with the automatic utterance that alone made it possible to say the words.

They were addressed to Miss Fosdick, into whose neighborhood chance had thrown him at a dinner, a year or so later than their encounter at the Uplift Club. Hitherto he had successfully, and intentionally, avoided Miss Fosdick, not from any animosity toward that unconscious instrument of fate, but from an intense reluctance to pronounce the words which he knew he should have to speak if they met.

Now, as it turned out, his chief surprise was that she should wait so long to make him speak them. All through the dinner she had swept him along on a rapid current of talk which showed no tendency to linger or turn back upon the past. At first he ascribed her reserve to a sense of delicacy with which he reproached himself for not having credited her; then he saw that she had been carried so far beyond the point at which they had last faced each other, that she was finally borne back to it only by the merest hazard of associated ideas. For it appeared that the very next evening, at Mrs. Beecher Bain's, a Hindu Mahatma was to lecture to the Uplift Club on the Limits of the Subliminal; and it was owing to no less a person than Howland Wade that this exceptional privilege had been obtained.

"Of course Howland's known all over the world as the interpreter of Pellerinism, and the Aga Gautch, who had absolutely declined to speak anywhere in public, wrote to Isabella that he could not refuse anything that Mr. Wade asked. Did you know that Howland's lecture, 'What Pellerinism Means,' has been translated into twenty-two languages, and gone into a fifth edition in Icelandic? Why, that reminds me," Miss Fosdick broke off—"I've never heard what became of your queer friend—what was his name?—whom you and Bob Wade accused me of spiriting away the night that Howland gave that very lecture at Hatty Bain's. And I've never seen *you* since you rushed into the house the next morning, and dragged me out of bed to know what I'd done with him!"

With a sharp effort Bernald gathered himself together to have it out. "Well, what *did* you do with him?" he retorted.

She laughed her appreciation of his humor. "Just what I told you, of course. I said good-bye to him on Isabella's doorstep."

Bernald looked at her. "It's really true, then, that he didn't go home with you?"

She bantered back: "Have you suspected me, all this

time, of hiding his remains in the cellar?" And with a droop of her fine lids she added: "I wish he *had* come home with me, for he was rather interesting, and there were things about Pellerinism that I think I could have explained to him."

Bernald helped himself to a nectarine, and Miss Fosdick continued on a note of amused curiosity: "So you've really never had any news of him since that night?"

"No—I've never had any news of him."

"Not the least little message?"

"Not the least little message."

"Or a rumor or report of any kind?"

"Or a rumor or report of any kind."

Miss Fosdick's interest seemed to be revived by the undeniable strangeness of the case. "It's rather creepy, isn't it? What *could* have happened? You don't suppose he could have been waylaid and murdered?" she asked with brightening eyes.

Bernald shook his head serenely. "No. I'm sure he's safe—quite safe."

"But if you're sure, you must know something."

"No. I know nothing," he repeated.

She scanned him incredulously. "But what's your theory—for you must have a theory? What in the world can have become of him?"

Bernald returned her look and hesitated. "Do you happen to remember the last thing he said to you—the very last, on the doorstep, when he left you?"

"The last thing?" She poised her fork above the peach on her plate. "I don't think he said anything. Oh, yes—when I reminded him that he'd solemnly promised to come back with me and have a little talk he said he couldn't because he was going home."

"Well, then, I suppose," said Bernald, "he went home."

She glanced at him as if suspecting a trap. "Dear me, how flat! I always inclined to a mysterious murder. But of course you know more of him than you say."

She began to cut her peach, but paused above a lifted bit to ask, with a renewal of animation in her expressive eyes: "By the way, had you heard that Howland Wade has been gradually getting farther and father away from Pellerinism? It seems he's begun to feel that there's a Positivist element in it which is narrowing to anyone who has gone at all deeply into the Wisdom of the East. He was intensely interesting about it the other day, and of course I *do* see what he feels. . . . Oh, it's too long to tell you now; but if you could manage to come in to tea some afternoon soon—any day but Wednesday—I should so like to explain. . . ."

The Eyes

WE HAD BEEN PUT in the mood for ghosts, that evening, after an excellent dinner at our old friend Culwin's, by a tale of Fred Murchard's—the narrative of a strange personal visitation.

Seen through the haze of our cigars, and by the drowsy gleam of a coal fire, Culwin's library, with its oak walls and dark old bindings, made a good setting for such evocations; and ghostly experiences at first hand being, after Murchard's opening, the only kind acceptable to us, we proceeded to take stock of our group and tax each member for a contribution. There were eight of us, and seven contrived, in a manner more or less adequate, to fulfill the condition imposed. It surprised us all to find that we could muster such a show of supernatural impressions, for none of us, excepting Murchard himself and young Phil Frenham—whose story was the slightest of the lot—had the habit of sending our souls into the invisible. So that, on the whole, we had every reason to be proud of our seven "exhibits," and none of us would have dreamed of expecting an eighth from our host.

Our old friend, Mr. Andrew Culwin, who had sat back in his armchair, listening and blinking through the smoke circles with the cheerful tolerance of a wise old idol, was not the kind of man likely to be favored with such contacts, though he had imagination enough to enjoy, without envying, the superior privileges of his guests. By age and by education he belonged to the stout Positivist tradition, and his habit of thought had been formed in the days of the epic struggle between physics and metaphysics. But he had been, then and always, essentially a spectator, a humorous detached observer of the immense muddled variety show of life, slipping out of his seat now and then for a brief dip into the convivialities at the back of the house, but never, as far as one knew, showing the least desire to jump on the stage and do a "turn."

Among his contemporaries there lingered a vague tradition of his having, at a remote period, and in a romantic clime, been wounded in a duel; but this legend no more tallied with what we younger men knew of his character than my mother's assertion that he had once been "a charming little man with nice eyes" corresponded to any possible reconstitution of his physiognomy.

"He never can have looked like anything but a bundle of sticks," Murchard had once said of him. "Or a phosphorescent log, rather," some one else amended; and we recognized the happiness of this description of his small squat trunk, with the red blink of the eyes in a face like mottled bark. He had always been possessed of a leisure which he had nursed and protected, instead of squandering it in vain activities. His carefully guarded hours had been devoted to the cultivation of a fine intelligence and a few judiciously chosen habits; and none of the disturbances common to human experience seemed to have crossed his sky. Nevertheless, his dispassionate survey of the universe had not raised his opinion of that costly experiment, and his study of the human race seemed to have resulted in the conclusion that all men were superfluous, and women necessary only because someone had to do the cooking. On the importance of this point his convictions were absolute, and gastronomy was the only science which he revered as a dogma. It must be owned that his little dinners were a strong argument in favor of this view, besides being a reason—though not the main one—for the fidelity of his friends.

Mentally he exercised a hospitality less seductive but no less stimulating. His mind was like a forum, or some open meeting place for the exchange of ideas: somewhat cold and drafty, but light, spacious and orderly—a kind of academic grove from which all the leaves have fallen. In this privileged area a dozen of us were wont to stretch our muscles and expand our lungs; and, as if to prolong as much as possible the tradition of what we felt to be a vanishing institution, one or two neophytes were now and then added to our band.

Young Phil Frenham was the last, and the most interesting, of these recruits, and a good example of Murchard's somewhat morbid assertion that our old friend "liked 'em juicy." It was indeed a fact that Culwin, for all his dryness, specially tasted the lyric qualities in youth. As he was far too good an Epicurean to nip the flowers of soul which he gathered for his garden, his friendship was not a disintegrating influence: on the contrary, it forced the young idea to robuster bloom. And in Phil Frenham he had a good subject for experimentation. The boy was really intelligent, and the soundness of his nature was like the pure paste under a fine glaze. Culwin had fished him out of a fog of family dullness, and pulled him up to a peak in Darien; and the adventure hadn't hurt him a bit. Indeed, the skill with which Culwin had contrived to stimulate his curiosities without robbing them of their bloom of awe seemed to me a sufficient answer to Murchard's ogreish metaphor. There was nothing hectic in Frenham's efflorescence, and his old friend had not laid even a finger tip on the sacred stupidities. One wanted no better proof of that than the fact that Frenham still reverenced them in Culwin.

"There's a side of him you fellows don't see. *I* believe that story about the duel!" he declared; and it was of the very essence of this belief that it should impel him—just as our little party was dispersing—to turn back to our host with the joking demand: "And now you've got to tell us about *your* ghost!"

The outer door had closed on Murchard and the others; only Frenham and I remained; and the devoted servant who presided over Culwin's destinies, having brought a fresh supply of soda water, had been laconically ordered to bed.

Culwin's sociability was a night-blooming flower, and we knew that he expected the nucleus of his group to tighten around him after midnight. But Frenham's appeal seemed to disconcert him comically, and he rose from the chair in which he had just reseated himself after his farewells in the hall.

"*My* ghost? Do you suppose I'm fool enough to go to the expense of keeping one of my own, when there are so many charming ones in my friends' closets? Take another cigar," he said, revolving toward me with a laugh.

Frenham laughed too, pulling up his slender height before the chimney piece as he turned to face his short bristling friend.

"Oh," he said, "you'd never be content to share if you met one you really liked."

Culwin had dropped back into his armchair, his shock head embedded in the hollow of worn leather, his little eyes glimmering over a fresh cigar.

"Liked—*liked*? Good Lord!" he growled.

"Ah, you *have*, then!" Frenham pounced on him in the same instant, with a side glance of victory at me; but Culwin cowered gnomelike among his cushions, dissembling himself in a protective cloud of smoke.

"What's the use of denying it? You've seen everything, so of course you've seen a ghost!" his young friend persisted, talking intrepidly into the cloud. "Or, if you haven't seen one, it's only because you've seen two!"

The form of the challenge seemed to strike our host. He shot his head out of the mist with a queer tortoise-like motion he sometimes had, and blinked approvingly at Frenham.

"That's it," he flung at us on a shrill jerk of laughter; "it's only because I've seen two!"

The words were so unexpected that they dropped down and down into a deep silence, while we continued to stare at each other over Culwin's head, and Culwin stared at his ghosts. At length Frenham, without speaking, threw himself into the chair on the other side of the hearth, and leaned forward with his listening smile. . . .

✣ II ✣

"OH, of course they're not show ghosts—a collector wouldn't think anything of them. . . . Don't let me raise your hopes . . . their one merit is their numerical strength: the exceptional fact of their being *two*. But, as against this, I'm bound to admit that at any moment I could probably have exorcised them both by asking my doctor for a prescription, or my oculist for a pair of spectacles. Only, as I never could make up my mind whether to go to the doctor or the oculist—whether I was afflicted by an optical or a digestive delusion—I left them to pursue their interesting double life, though at times they made mine exceedingly uncomfortable. . . .

"Yes—uncomfortable; and you know how I hate to be uncomfortable! But it was part of my stupid pride, when the thing began, not to admit that I could be disturbed by the trifling matter of seeing two.

"And then I'd no reason, really, to suppose I was ill. As far as I knew I was simply bored—horribly bored. But it was part of my boredom—I remember—that I was feeling so uncommonly well, and didn't know how on earth to work off my surplus energy. I had come back from a long journey—down in South America and Mexico—and had settled down for the winter near New York with an old aunt who had known Washington Irving and corresponded with N. P. Willis. She lived, not far from Irvington, in a damp Gothic villa overhung by Norway spruces and looking exactly like a memorial emblem done in hair. Her personal appearance was in keeping with this image, and her own hair—of which there was little left—might have been sacrificed to the manufacture of the emblem.

"I had just reached the end of an agitated year, with considerable arrears to make up in money and emotion; and theoretically it seemed as though my aunt's mild hospitality would be as beneficial to my nerves as to my purse. But the deuce of it was that as soon as I felt myself safe and sheltered my energy began to revive; and how was I to work it off inside of a memorial emblem? I had, at that time, the illusion that sustained intellectual effort could engage a man's whole activity; and I decided to write a great book—I forget about what. My aunt, impressed by my plan, gave up to me her Gothic library, filled with classics bound in black cloth and daguerreotypes of faded celebrities; and I sat down at my desk to win myself a place among their number. And to facilitate my task she lent me a cousin to copy my manuscript.

"The cousin was a nice girl, and I had an idea that a nice girl was just what I needed to restore my faith in human nature, and principally in myself. She was neither beautiful nor intelligent—poor Alice Nowell!—but it interested me to see any woman content to be so uninteresting, and I wanted to find out the secret of her content. In doing this I handled it rather rashly, and put it out of joint—oh, just for a moment! There's no fatuity in telling you this, for the poor girl had never seen anyone but cousins. . . .

"Well, I was sorry for what I'd done, of course, and confoundedly bothered as to how I should put it straight. She was staying in the house, and one evening, after my aunt had gone to bed, she came down to the library to fetch a book she'd mislaid, like any artless heroine, on the shelves behind us. She was pink-nosed and flustered, and it suddenly occurred to me that her hair, though it was fairly thick and pretty, would look exactly like my aunt's when she grew older. I was glad I had noticed this, for it made it easier for me to decide to do what was right; and when I had found the book she hadn't lost I told her I was leaving for Europe that week.

"Europe was terribly far off in those days, and Alice knew at once what I meant. She didn't take it in the least as I'd expected—it would have been easier if she had. She held her book very tight, and turned away a moment to wind up the lamp on my desk—it had a ground-glass shade with vine leaves, and glass drops around the edge, I remember. Then she came back, held out her hand, and said: 'Good-bye.' And as she said it she looked straight at me and kissed me. I had never felt anything as fresh and shy and brave as her kiss. It was worse than any reproach, and it made me ashamed to deserve a reproach from her. I said to myself: 'I'll marry her, and when my aunt dies she'll leave us this house and I'll sit here at the desk and go on with my book; and Alice will sit over there with her embroidery and look at me as she's looking now. And life will go on like that for any number of years.' The prospect frightened me a little, but at the time it didn't frighten me as much as doing anything to hurt her; and ten minutes later she had my seal ring on her finger, and my promise that when I went abroad she should go with me.

"You'll wonder why I'm enlarging on this incident. It's because the evening on which it took place was the very evening on which I first saw the queer sight I've spoken of. Being at that time an ardent believer in a necessary sequence between cause and effect, I naturally tried to trace some kind of link between what had just happened to me in my aunt's library, and what was to happen a few hours later on the same night; and so the coincidence between the two events always remained in my mind.

"I went up to bed with rather a heavy heart, for I was bowed under the weight of the first good action I had ever consciously committed; and young as I was, I saw the gravity of my situation. Don't imagine from this that I had hitherto been an instrument of destruction. I had been merely a harmless young man, who had followed his bent and declined all collaboration with Providence. Now I had suddenly undertaken to promote the moral order of the world, and I felt a good deal like the trustful spectator who has given his gold watch to the conjurer, and doesn't know in what shape he'll get it back when the trick is over. . . . Still, a glow of self-righteousness tempered my fears, and I said to myself as I undressed that when I'd got used to being good it probably wouldn't make me as nervous as it did at the start. And by the time I was in bed, and had blown out my candle, I felt that I really *was* getting used to it, and that, as far as I'd got, it was not unlike sinking down into one of my aunt's very softest wool mattresses.

"I closed my eyes on this image, and when I opened them it must have been a good deal later, for my room had grown cold, and intensely still. I was waked by the queer feeling we all know—the feeling that there was something in the room that hadn't been there when I fell asleep. I sat up and strained my eyes into the darkness. The room was pitch black, and at first I saw nothing; but gradually a vague glimmer at the foot of the bed turned into two eyes staring back at me. I couldn't distinguish the features attached to them, but as I looked the eyes grew more and more distinct: they gave out a light of their own.

"The sensation of being thus gazed at was far from pleasant, and you might suppose that my first impulse would have been to jump out of bed and hurl myself on the invisible figure attached to the eyes. But it wasn't—my impulse was simply to lie still. . . . I can't say whether this was due to an immediate sense of the uncanny nature of the apparition—to the certainty that if I did jump out of bed I should hurl myself on nothing—or merely to the benumbing effect of the eyes themselves. They were the very worst eyes I've ever seen: a man's eyes—but what a man! My first thought was that he must be frightfully old. The orbits were sunk, and the thick red-lined lids hung over the eyeballs like blinds of which the cords are broken. One lid drooped a little lower than the other, with the effect of a crooked leer; and between these folds of flesh, with their scant bristle of lashes, the eyes themselves, small glassy disks with an agate-like rim, looked like sea pebbles in the grip of a starfish.

"But the age of the eyes was not the most unpleasant thing about them. What turned me sick was their expression of vicious security. I don't know how else to describe the fact that they seemed to belong to a man who had done a lot of harm in his life, but had always kept just inside the danger lines. They were not the eyes of a coward, but of someone much too clever to take risks; and my gorge rose at their look of base astuteness. Yet even that wasn't the worst; for as we continued to scan each other I saw in them a tinge of derision, and felt myself to be its object.

"At that I was seized by an impulse of rage that jerked me to my feet and pitched me straight at the unseen figure. But of course there wasn't any figure there, and my fists struck at emptiness. Ashamed and cold, I groped about for a match and lit the candles. The room looked just as usual—as I had known it would; and I crawled back to bed, and blew out the lights.

"As soon as the room was dark again the eyes reappeared; and I now applied myself to explaining them on scientific principles. At first I thought the illusion might have been caused by the glow of the last embers in the chimney; but the fireplace was on the other side of my bed, and so placed that the fire could not be reflected in my toilet glass, which was the only mirror in the room. Then it struck me that I might have been tricked by the reflection of the embers in some polished bit of wood or metal; and though I couldn't discover any object of the sort in my line of vision, I got up again, groped my way to the hearth, and covered what was left of the fire. But as soon as I was back in bed the eyes were back at its foot.

"They were an hallucination, then: that was plain. But the fact that they were not due to any external dupery didn't make them a bit pleasanter. For if they were a projection of my inner consciousness, what the deuce was the matter with that organ? I had gone deeply enough into the mystery of morbid pathological states to picture the conditions under which an exploring mind might lay itself open to such a midnight admonition; but I couldn't fit it to my present case. I had never felt more normal, mentally and physically; and the only unusual fact in my situation—that of having assured the happiness of an amiable girl—did not seem of a kind to summon unclean spirits about my pillow. But there were the eyes still looking at me.

"I shut mine, and tried to evoke a vision of Alice Nowell's. They were not remarkable eyes, but they were as wholesome as fresh water, and if she had had more imagination—or longer lashes—their expression might have been interesting. As it was, they did not prove very efficacious, and in a few moments I perceived that they had mysteriously changed into the eyes at the foot of the bed. It exasperated me more to feel these glaring at me through my shut lids than to see them, and I opened my eyes again and looked straight into their hateful stare. . . .

"And so it went on all night. I can't tell you what that night was like, nor how long it lasted. Have you ever lain in bed, hopelessly wide awake, and tried to keep your eyes shut, knowing that if you opened 'em you'd see something you dreaded and loathed? It sounds easy, but it's devilishly hard. Those eyes hung there and drew me. I had the *vertige de l'abime*, and their red lids were the edge of my abyss. . . . I had known nervous hours before: hours when I'd felt the wind of danger in my neck; but never this kind of strain. It wasn't that the eyes were awful; they hadn't the majesty of the powers of darkness. But they had—how shall I say?—a physical effect that was the equivalent of a bad smell: their look left a smear like a snail's. And I didn't see what business they had with me, anyhow—and I stared and stared, trying to find out.

"I don't know what effect they were trying to produce; but the effect they *did* produce was that of making me pack my portmanteau and bolt to town early the next morning. I left a note for my aunt, explaining that I was ill and had gone to see my doctor; and as a matter of fact I did feel uncommonly ill—the night seemed to have pumped all the blood out of me. But when I reached town I didn't go to the doctor's. I went to a friend's rooms, and threw myself on a bed, and slept for ten heavenly hours. When I woke it was the middle of the night and I turned cold at the thought of what might be waiting for me. I sat up, shaking, and stared into the darkness; but there wasn't a break in its blessed surface, and when I saw that the eyes were not there I dropped back into another long sleep.

"I had left no word for Alice when I fled, because I meant to go back the next morning. But the next morning I was too exhausted to stir. As the day went on the exhaustion increased, instead of wearing off like the fatigue left by an ordinary night of insomnia: the effect of the eyes seemed to be cumulative, and the thought of seeing them again grew intolerable. For two days I fought my dread; and on the third evening I pulled myself together and decided to go back the next morning. I felt a good deal happier as soon as I'd decided, for I knew that my abrupt disappearance, and the strangeness of my not writing, must have been very distressing to poor Alice. I went to bed with an easy mind, and fell asleep at once; but in the middle of the night I woke, and there were the eyes. . . .

"Well, I simply couldn't face them; and instead of going back to my aunt's I bundled a few things into a trunk and jumped aboard the first steamer for England. I was so dead tired when I got on board that I crawled straight into my berth, and slept most of the way over; and I can't tell you the bliss it was to wake from those long dreamless stretches and look fearlessly into the dark, *knowing* that I shouldn't see the eyes. . . .

"I stayed abroad for a year, and then I stayed for another; and during that time I never had a glimpse of them. That was enough reason for prolonging my stay if I'd been on a desert island. Another was, of course, that I had perfectly come to see, on the voyage over, the complete impossibility of my marrying Alice Nowell. The fact that I had been so slow in making this discovery annoyed me, and made me want to avoid explanations. The bliss of escaping at one stroke from the eyes, and from this other embarrassment, gave my freedom an extraordinary zest; and the longer I savored it the better I liked its taste.

"The eyes had burned such a hole in my consciousness that for a long time I went on puzzling over the nature of the apparition, and wondering if it would ever come back. But as time passed I lost this dread, and retained only the precision of the image. Then that faded in its turn.

"The second year found me settled in Rome, where I was planning, I believe, to write another great book—a definitive work on Etruscan influences in Italian art. At any rate, I'd found some pretext of the kind for taking a sunny apartment in the Piazza di Spagna and dabbling about in the Forum; and there, one morning, a charming youth came to me. As he stood there in the warm light, slender and smooth and hyacinthine, he might have stepped from a ruined altar—one to Antinous, say; but he'd come instead from New York, with a letter from (of all people) Alice Nowell. The letter—the first I'd had from her since our break—was simply a line introducing her young cousin, Gilbert Noyes, and appealing to me to befriend him. It appeared, poor lad, that he 'had talent,' and 'wanted to write'; and, an obdurate family having insisted that his calligraphy should take the form of double entry, Alice had intervened to win him six months' respite, during which he was to travel abroad on a meager pittance, and somehow prove his ability to increase it by his pen. The quaint conditions of the test struck me first: it seemed about as conclusive as a medieval 'ordeal.' Then I was touched by her having sent him to me. I had always wanted to do her some service, to justify myself in my own eyes rather than hers; and here was a beautiful occasion.

"I imagine it's safe to lay down the general principle that predestined geniuses don't, as a rule, appear before one in the spring sunshine of the Forum looking like one of its banished gods. At any rate, poor Noyes wasn't a predestined genius. But he *was* beautiful to see, and charming as a comrade. It was only when he began to talk literature that my heart failed me. I knew all the symptoms so well—the things he had 'in him,' and the things outside him that impinged! There's the real test, after all. It was always—punctually, inevitably, with the inexorableness of a mechanical law—it was *always* the wrong thing that struck him. I grew to find a certain fascination in deciding in advance exactly which wrong thing he'd select; and I acquired an astonishing skill at the game. . . .

"The worst of it was that his *bêtise* wasn't of the too obvious sort. Ladies who met him at picnics thought him intellectual; and even at dinners he passed for clever. I, who had him under the microscope, fancied now and then that he might develop some kind of a slim talent, something that he could make 'do' and be happy on; and wasn't that, after all, what I was concerned with? He was so charming—he continued to be so charming—that he called forth all my charity in support of this argument; and for the first few months I really believed there was a chance for him. . . .

"Those months were delightful. Noyes was constantly with me, and the more I saw of him the better I liked him. His stupidity was a natural grace—it was as beautiful, really, as his eyelashes. And he was so gay, so affectionate, and so happy with me, that telling him the truth would have been about as pleasant as slitting the throat of some gentle animal. At first I used to wonder what had put into that radiant head the detestable delusion that it held a brain. Then I began to see that it was simply protective mimicry—an instinctive ruse to get away from family life and an office desk. Not that Gilbert didn't—dear lad!—believe in himself. There wasn't a trace of hypocrisy in him. He was sure that his 'call' was irresistible, while to me it was the saving grace of his situation that it *wasn't*, and that a little money, a little leisure, a little pleasure would have turned him into an inoffensive idler. Unluckily, however, there was no hope of money, and with the alternative of the office desk before him he couldn't postpone his attempt at literature. The stuff he turned out was deplorable, and I see now that I knew it from the first. Still, the absurdity of deciding a man's whole future on a first trial seemed to justify me in withholding my verdict, and perhaps even in encouraging him a little, on the ground that the human plant generally needs warmth to flower.

"At any rate, I proceeded on that principle, and carried it to the point of getting his term of probation extended. When I left Rome he went with me, and we idled away a delicious summer between Capri and Venice. I said to myself: 'If he has anything in him, it will come out now,' and it *did*. He was never more enchanting and enchanted. There were moments of our pilgrimage when beauty born of murmuring sound seemed actually to pass into his face—but only to issue forth in a flood of the palest ink. . . .

"Well, the time came to turn off the tap; and I knew there was no hand but mine to do it. We were back in Rome, and I had taken him to stay with me, not wanting him to be alone in his *pension* when he had to face the necessity of renouncing his ambition. I hadn't, of course, relied solely on my own judgment in deciding to advise him to drop literature. I had sent his stuff to various people—editors and critics—and they had always sent it back with the same chilling lack of comment. Really there was nothing on earth to say.

"I confess I never felt more shabby than I did on the day when I decided to have it out with Gilbert. It was well enough to tell myself that it was my duty to knock the poor boy's hopes into splinters—but I'd like to know what act of gratuitous cruelty hasn't been justified on that plea? I've always shrunk from usurping the functions of Providence, and when I have to exercise them I decidedly prefer that it shouldn't be on an errand of destruction. Besides, in the last issue, who was I to decide, even after a year's trial, if poor Gilbert had it in him or not?

"The more I looked at the part I'd resolved to play, the less I liked it; and I liked it still less when Gilbert sat opposite me, with his head thrown back in the lamplight, just as Phil's is now. . . . I'd been going over his last manuscript, and he knew it, and he knew that his future hung on my verdict—we'd tacitly agreed to that. The manuscript lay between us, on my table—a novel, his first novel, if you please!—and he reached over and laid his hand on it, and looked up at me with all his life in the look.

"I stood up and cleared my throat, trying to keep my eyes away from his face and on the manuscript.

" 'The fact is, my dear Gilbert,' I began—

"I saw him turn pale, but he was up and facing me in an instant.

" 'Oh, look here, don't take on so, my dear fellow! I'm not so awfully cut up as all that!' His hands were on my shoulders, and he was laughing down on me from his full height, with a kind of mortally stricken gaiety that drove the knife into my side.

"He was too beautifully brave for me to keep up any humbug about my duty. And it came over me suddenly how I should hurt others in hurting him: myself first, since sending him home meant losing him; but more particularly poor Alice Nowell, to whom I had so longed to prove my good faith and my desire to serve her. It really seemed like failing her twice to fail Gilbert.

"But my intuition was like one of those lightning flashes that encircle the whole horizon, and in the same instant I saw what I might be letting myself in for if I didn't tell the truth. I said to myself: 'I shall have him for life'—and I'd never yet seen anyone, man or woman, whom I was quite sure of wanting on those terms. Well, this impulse of egotism decided me. I was ashamed of it, and to get away from it I took a leap that landed me straight in Gilbert's arms.

" 'The thing's all right, and you're all wrong!' I shouted up at him; and as he hugged me, and I laughed and shook in his clutch, I had for a minute the sense of self-complacency that is supposed to attend the footsteps of the just. Hang it all, making people happy *has* its charms.

"Gilbert, of course, was for celebrating his emancipation in some spectacular manner; but I sent him away alone to explode his emotions, and went to bed to sleep off mine. As I undressed I began to wonder what their aftertaste would be—so many of the finest don't keep! Still, I wasn't sorry, and I meant to empty the bottle, even if it *did* turn a trifle flat.

"After I got into bed I lay for a long time smiling at the memory of his eyes—his blissful eyes. . . . Then I fell asleep, and when I woke the room was deathly cold, and I sat up with a jerk—and there were *the other eyes*. . . .

"It was three years since I'd seen them, but I'd thought of them so often that I fancied they could never take me unawares again. Now, with their red sneer on me, I knew that I had never really believed they would come back, and that I was as defenseless as ever against them. . . . As before, it was the insane irrelevance of their coming that made it so horrible. What the deuce were they after, to leap out at me at such a time? I had lived more or less carelessly in the years since I'd seen them, though my worst indiscretions were not dark enough to invite the searchings of their infernal glare; but at this particular moment I was really in what might have been called a state of grace; and I can't tell you how the fact added to their horror. . . .

"But it's not enough to say they were as bad as before: they were worse. Worse by just so much as I'd learned of life in the interval; by all the damnable implications my wider experience read into them. I saw now what I hadn't seen before: that they were eyes which had grown hideous gradually, which had built up their baseness coral-wise, bit by bit, out of a series of small turpitudes slowly accumulated through the industrious years. Yes—it came to me that what made them so bad was that they'd grown bad so slowly. . . .

"There they hung in the darkness, their swollen lids dropped across the little watery bulbs rolling loose in the orbits, and the puff of flesh making a muddy shadow underneath—and as their stare moved with my movements, there came over me a sense of their tacit complicity, of a deep hidden understanding between us that was worse than the first shock of their strangeness. Not that I understood them; but that they made it so clear that someday I should. . . . Yes, that was the worst part of it, decidedly; and it was the feeling that became stronger each time they came back. . . . .

"For they got into the damnable habit of coming back. They reminded me of vampires with a taste for young flesh, they seemed so to gloat over the taste of a good conscience. Every night for a month they came to claim their morsel of mine: since I'd made Gilbert happy they simply wouldn't loosen their fangs. The coincidence almost made me hate him, poor lad, fortuitous as I felt it to be. I puzzled over it a good deal, but couldn't find any hint of an explanation except in the chance of his association with Alice Nowell. But then the eyes had let up on me the moment I had abandoned her, so they could hardly be the emissaries of a woman scorned, even if one could have pictured poor Alice charging such spirits to avenge her. That set me thinking, and I began to wonder if they would let up on me if I abandoned Gilbert. The temptation was insidious, and I had to stiffen myself against it; but really, dear boy! he was too charming to be sacrificed to such demons. And so, after all, I never found out what they wanted. . . ."

✤ III ✤

THE fire crumbled, sending up a flash which threw into relief the narrator's gnarled face under its grey-black stubble. Pressed into the hollow of the chair back, it stood out an instant like an intaglio of yellowish red-veined stone, with spots of enamel for the eyes; then the fire sank and it became once more a dim Rembrandtish blur.

Phil Frenham, sitting in a low chair on the opposite side of the hearth, one long arm propped on the table behind him, one hand supporting his thrown-back head, and his eyes fixed on his old friend's face, had not moved since the tale began. He continued to maintain his silent immobility after Culwin had ceased to speak, and it was I who, with a vague sense of disappointment at the sudden drop of the story, finally asked: "But how long did you keep on seeing them?"

Culwin, so sunk into his chair that he seemed like a heap of his own empty clothes, stirred a little, as if in surprise at my question. He appeared to have half-forgotten what he had been telling us.

"How long? Oh, off and on all that winter. It was infernal. I never got used to them. I grew really ill."

Frenham shifted his attitude, and as he did so his elbow struck against a small mirror in a bronze frame standing on the table behind him. He turned and changed its angle slightly; then he resumed his former attitude, his dark head thrown back on his lifted palm, his eyes intent on Culwin's face. Something in his silent gaze embarrassed me, and as if to divert attention from it I pressed on with another question:

"And you never tried sacrificing Noyes?"

"Oh, no. The fact is I didn't have to. He did it for me, poor boy!"

"Did it for you? How do you mean?"

"He wore me out—wore everybody out. He kept on pouring out his lamentable twaddle, and hawking it up and down the place till he became a thing of terror. I tried to wean him from writing—oh, ever so gently, you understand, by throwing him with agreeable people, giving him a chance to make himself felt, to come to a sense of what he *really* had to give. I'd foreseen this solution from the beginning—felt sure that, once the first ardor of authorship was quenched, he'd drop into his place as a charming parasitic thing, the kind of chronic Cherubino for whom, in old societies, there's always a seat at table, and a shelter behind the ladies' skirts. I saw him take his place as 'the poet': the poet who doesn't write. One knows the type in every drawing room. Living in that way doesn't cost much—I'd worked it all out in my mind, and felt sure that, with a little help, he could manage it for the next few years; and meanwhile he'd be sure to marry. I saw him married to a widow, rather older, with a good cook and a well-run house. And I actually had my eye on the widow. . . . Meanwhile I did everything to help the transition—lent him money to ease his conscience, introduced him to pretty women to make him forget his vows. But nothing would do him: he had but one idea in his beautiful obstinate head. He wanted the laurel and not the rose, and he kept on repeating Gautier's axiom, and battering and filing at his limp prose till he'd spread it out over Lord knows how many hundred pages. Now and then he would send a barrelful to a publisher, and of course it would always come back.

"At first it didn't matter—he thought he was 'misunderstood.' He took the attitudes of genius, and whenever an opus came home he wrote another to keep it company. Then he had a reaction of despair, and accused me of deceiving him, and Lord knows what. I got angry at that, and told him it was he who had deceived himself. He'd come to me determined to write, and I'd done my best to help him. That was the extent of my offence, and I'd done it for his cousin's sake, not his.

"That seemed to strike home, and he didn't answer for a minute. Then he said: 'My time's up and my money's up. What do you think I'd better do?'

" 'I think you'd better not be an ass,' I said.

" 'What do you mean by being an ass?' he asked.

"I took a letter from my desk and held it out to him.

" 'I mean refusing this offer of Mrs. Ellinger's: to be her secretary at a salary of five thousand dollars. There may be a lot more in it than that.'

"He flung out his hand with a violence that struck the letter from mine. 'Oh, I know well enough what's in it!' he said, red to the roots of his hair.

" 'And what's the answer, if you know?' I asked.

"He made none at the minute, but turned away slowly to the door. There, with his hand on the threshold, he stopped to say, almost under his breath: 'Then you really think my stuff's no good?'

"I was tired and exasperated, and I laughed. I don't defend my laugh—it was in wretched taste. But I must plead in extenuation that the boy was a fool, and that I'd done my best for him—I really had.

"He went out of the room, shutting the door quietly after him. That afternoon I left for Frascati, where I'd promised to spend the Sunday with some friends. I was glad to escape from Gilbert, and by the same token, as I learned that night, I had also escaped from the eyes. I dropped into the same lethargic sleep that had come to me before when I left off seeing them; and when I woke the next morning in my peaceful room above the ilexes, I felt the utter weariness and deep relief that always followed on that sleep. I put in two blessed nights at Frascati, and when I got back to my rooms in Rome I found that Gilbert had gone. . . . Oh, nothing tragic had happened—the episode never rose to *that.* He'd simply packed his manuscripts and left for America—for his family and the Wall Street desk. He left a decent enough note to tell me of his decision, and behaved altogether, in the circumstances, as little like a fool as it's possible for a fool to behave. . . ."

✣ IV ✣

CULWIN paused again, and Frenham still sat motionless, the dusky contour of his young head reflected in the mirror at his back.

"And what became of Noyes afterward?" I finally asked, still disquieted by a sense of incompleteness, by the need of some connecting thread between the parallel lines of the tale.

Culwin twitched his shoulders. "Oh, nothing became of him—because he became nothing. There could be no question of 'becoming' about it. He vegetated in an office, I believe, and finally got a clerkship in a consulate, and married drearily in China. I saw him once in Hong Kong, years afterward. He was fat and hadn't shaved. I was told he drank. He didn't recognize me."

"And the eyes?" I asked, after another pause which Frenham's continued silence made oppressive.

Culwin, stroking his chin, blinked at me meditatively through the shadows. "I never saw them after my last talk with Gilbert. Put two and two together if you can. For my part, I haven't found the link."

He rose, his hands in his pockets, and walked stiffly over to the table on which reviving drinks had been set out.

"You must be parched after this dry tale. Here, help yourself, my dear fellow. Here, Phil—" He turned back to the hearth.

Frenham made no response to his host's hospitable summons. He still sat in his low chair without moving, but as Culwin advanced toward him, their eyes met in a long look; after which the young man, turning suddenly, flung his arms across the table behind him, and dropped his face upon them.

Culwin, at the unexpected gesture, stopped short, a flush on his face.

"Phil—what the deuce? Why, have the eyes scared *you*? My dear boy—my dear fellow—I never had such a tribute to my literary ability, never!"

He broke into a chuckle at the thought, and halted on the hearthrug, his hands still in his pockets, gazing down at the youth's bowed head. Then, as Frenham still made no answer, he moved a step or two nearer.

"Cheer up, my dear Phil! It's years since I've seen them—apparently I've done nothing lately bad enough to call them out of chaos. Unless my present evocation of them has made *you* see them; which would be their worst stroke yet!"

His bantering appeal quivered off into an uneasy laugh, and he moved still nearer, bending over Frenham, and laying his gouty hands on the lad's shoulders.

"Phil, my dear boy, really—what's the matter? Why don't you answer? *Have* you seen the eyes?"

Frenham's face was still hidden, and from where I stood behind Culwin I saw the latter, as if under the rebuff of this unaccountable attitude, draw back slowly from his friend. As he did so, the light of the lamp on the table fell full on his congested face, and I caught its reflection in the mirror behind Frenham's head.

Culwin saw the reflection also. He paused, his face level with the mirror, as if scarcely recognizing the countenance in it as his own. But as he looked his expression gradually changed, and for an appreciable space of time he and the image in the glass confronted each other with a glare of slowly gathering hate. Then Culwin let go on Frenham's shoulders, and drew back a step. . . .

Frenham, his face still hidden, did not stir.

Afterward

"OH, THERE *is* one, of course, but you'll never know it."

The assertion, laughingly flung out six months earlier in a bright June garden, came back to Mary Boyne with a new perception of its significance as she stood, in the December dusk, waiting for the lamps to be brought into the library.

The words had been spoken by their friend Alida Stair, as they sat at tea on her lawn at Pangbourne, in reference to the very house of which the library in question was the central, the pivotal "feature." Mary Boyne and her husband, in quest of a country place in one of the southern or southwestern counties, had, on their arrival in England, carried their problem straight to Alida Stair, who had successfully solved it in her own case; but it was not until they had rejected, almost capriciously, several practical and judicious suggestions that she threw out: "Well, there's Lyng, in Dorsetshire. It belongs to Hugo's cousins, and you can get it for a song."

The reason she gave for its being obtainable on these terms—its remoteness from a station, its lack of electric light, hot water pipes, and other vulgar necessities—were exactly those pleading in its favor with two romantic Americans perversely in search of the economic drawbacks which were associated, in their tradition, with unusual architectural felicities.

"I should never believe I was living in an old house unless I was thoroughly uncomfortable," Ned Boyne, the more extravagant of the two, had jocosely insisted; "the least hint of convenience would make me think it had been bought out of an exhibition, with the pieces numbered, and set up again." And they had proceeded to enumerate, with humorous precision, their various doubts and demands, refusing to believe that the house their cousin recommended was *really* Tudor till they learned it had no heating system, or that the village church was literally in the grounds till she assured them of the deplorable uncertainty of the water supply.

"It's too uncomfortable to be true!" Edward Boyne had continued to exult as the avowal of each disadvantage was successively wrung from her; but he had cut short his rhapsody to ask, with a relapse to distrust: "And the ghost? You've been concealing from us the fact that there is no ghost!"

Mary, at the moment, had laughed with him, yet almost with her laugh, being possessed of several sets of independent perceptions, had been struck by a note of flatness in Alida's answering hilarity.

"Oh, Dorsetshire's full of ghosts, you know."

"Yes, yes; but that won't do. I don't want to have to drive ten miles to see somebody else's ghost. I want one of my own on the premises. *Is* there a ghost at Lyng?"

His rejoinder had made Alida laugh again, and it was then that she had flung back tantalizingly: "Oh, there *is* one, of course, but you'll never know it."

"Never know it?" Boyne pulled her up. "But what in the world constitutes a ghost except the fact of its being known for one?"

"I can't say. But that's the story."

"That there's a ghost, but that nobody knows it's a ghost?"

"Well—not till afterward, at any rate."

"Till afterward?"

"Not till long long afterward."

"But if it's once been identified as an unearthly visitant, why hasn't it *signalement* been handed down in the family? How has it managed to preserve its incognito?"

Alida could only shake her head. "Don't ask me. But it has."

"And then suddenly"—Mary spoke up as if from cavernous depths of divination—"suddenly, long afterward, one says to one's self *'That was it?'* "

She was startled at the sepulchral sound with which her

question fell on the banter of the other two, and she saw the shadow of the same surprise flit across Alida's pupils. "I suppose so. One just has to wait."

"Oh, hang waiting!" Ned broke in. "Life's too short for a ghost who can only be enjoyed in retrospect. Can't we do better than that, Mary?"

But it turned out that in the event they were not destined to, for within three months of their conversation with Mrs. Stair they were settled at Lyng, and the life they had yearned for, to the point of planning it in advance in all its daily details, had actually begun for them.

It was to sit, in the thick December dusk, by just such a wide-hooded fireplace, under just such black oak rafters, with the sense that beyond the mullioned panes the downs were darkened to a deeper solitude: it was for the ultimate indulgence of such sensations that Mary Boyne, abruptly exiled from New York by her husband's business, had endured for nearly fourteen years the soul-deadening ugliness of a Middle Western town, and that Boyne had ground on doggedly at his engineering till, with a suddenness that still made her blink, the prodigious windfall of the Blue Star Mine had put them at a stroke in possession of life and the leisure to taste it. They had never for a moment meant their new state to be one of idleness; but they meant to give themselves only to harmonious activities. She had her vision of painting and gardening (against a background of grey walls), he dreamed of the production of his long-planned book on the "Economic Basis of Culture"; and with such absorbing work ahead no existence could be too sequestered: they could not get far enough from the world, or plunge deep enough into the past.

Dorsetshire had attracted them from the first by an air of remoteness out of all proportion to its geographical position. But to the Boynes it was one of the ever-recurring wonders of the whole incredibly compressed island—a nest of counties, as they put it—that for the production of its effects so little of a given quality went so far: that so few miles made a distance, and so short a distance a difference.

"It's that," Ned had once enthusiastically explained, "that gives such depth to their effects, such relief to their contrasts. They've been able to lay the butter so thick on every delicious mouthful."

The butter had certainly been laid on thick at Lyng: the old house hidden under a shoulder of the downs had almost all the finer marks of commerce with a protracted past. The mere fact that it was neither large nor exceptional made it, to the Boynes, abound the more completely in its special charm—the charm of having been for centuries a deep dim reservoir of life. The life had probably not been of the most vivid order: for long periods, no doubt, it had fallen as noiselessly into the past as the quiet drizzle of autumn fell, hour after hour, into the fish pond between the yews; but these backwaters of existence sometimes breed, in their sluggish depths, strange acuities of emotion, and Mary Boyne had felt from the first the mysterious stir of intenser memories.

The feeling had never been stronger than on this particular afternoon when, waiting in the library for the lamps to come, she rose from her seat and stood among the shadows of the hearth. Her husband had gone off, after luncheon, for one of his long tramps on the downs. She had noticed of late that he preferred to go alone; and, in the tried security of their personal relations, had been driven to conclude that his book was bothering him, and that he needed the afternoons to turn over in solitude the problems left from the morning's work. Certainly the book was not going as smoothly as she had thought it would, and there were lines of perplexity between his eyes such as had never been there in his engineering days. He had often, then, looked fagged to the verge of illness, but the native demon of worry had never branded his brow. Yet the few pages he had so far read to her—the introduction, and a summary of the opening chapter—showed a firm hold on his subject, and an increasing confidence in his powers.

The fact threw her into deeper perplexity, since, now that he had done with business and its disturbing contingencies, the one other possible source of anxiety was eliminated. Unless it were his health, then? But physically he had gained since they had come to Dorsetshire, grown robuster, ruddier and fresher eyed. It was only within the last week that she had felt in him the undefinable change which made her restless in his absence, and as tongue-tied in his presence as though it were *she* who had a secret to keep from him!

The thought that there *was* a secret somewhere between them struck her with a sudden rap of wonder, and she looked about her down the long room.

"Can it be the house?" she mused.

The room itself might have been full of secrets. They seemed to be piling themselves up, as evening fell, like the layers and layers of velvet shadow dropping from the low ceiling, the rows of books, the smoke-blurred sculpture of the hearth.

"Why, of course—the house is haunted!" she reflected.

The ghost—Alida's imperceptible ghost—after figuring largely in the banter of their first month or two at Lyng, had been gradually left aside as too ineffectual for imaginative use. Mary had, indeed, as became the tenant of a haunted house, made the customary inquiries among her rural neighbors, but, beyond a vague "They dü say so, Ma'am," the villagers had nothing to impart. The elusive specter had apparently never had sufficient identity for a legend to crystallize about it, and after a time the Boynes had set the matter down to their profit-and-loss account, agreeing that Lyng was one of the few houses good enough in itself to dispense with supernatural enhancements.

"And I suppose, poor ineffectual demon, that's why it beats its beautiful wings in vain in the void," Mary had laughingly concluded.

"Or, rather," Ned answered in the same strain, "why, amid so much that's ghostly, it can never affirm its separate existence as *the* ghost." And thereupon their invisible housemate had finally dropped out of their references, which were numerous enough to make them soon unaware of the loss.

Now, as she stood on the hearth, the subject of their earlier curiosity revived in her with a new sense of its meaning—a sense gradually acquired through daily contact with the scene of the lurking mystery. It was the house itself, of course, that possessed the ghost-seeing faculty, that communed visually but secretly with its own past; if one could only get into close enough communion with the house, one might surprise its secret, and acquire the ghost sight on one's own account. Perhaps, in his long hours in this very room, where she never trespassed till the afternoon, her husband *had* acquired it already, and was silently carrying about the weight of whatever it had revealed to him. Mary was too well versed in the code of the spectral world not to know that one could not talk about the ghosts one saw: to do so was almost as great a breach of taste as to name a lady in a club. But this explanation did not really satisfy her. "What, after all, except for the fun of the shudder," she reflected, "would he really care for any of their old ghosts?" And thence she was thrown back once more on the fundamental dilemma: the fact that one's greater or less susceptibility to spectral influences had no particular bearing on the case, since, when one *did* see a ghost at Lyng, one did not know it.

"Not till long afterward," Alida Stair had said. Well, supposing Ned *had* seen one when they first came, and had known only within the last week what had happened to him? More and more under the spell of the hour, she threw back her thoughts to the early days of their tenancy, but at first only to recall a lively confusion of unpacking, settling, arranging of books, and calling to each other from remote corners of the house as, treasure after treasure, it revealed itself to them. It was in this particular connection that she presently recalled a certain soft afternoon of the previous October, when, passing from the first rapturous flurry of exploration to a detailed inspection of the old house, she had pressed (like a novel heroine) a panel that opened on a flight of corkscrew stairs leading to a flat ledge of the roof—the roof which, from below, seemed to slope away on all sides too abruptly for any but practiced feet to scale.

The view from this hidden coign was enchanting, and she had flown down to snatch Ned from his papers and give him the freedom of her discovery. She remembered still how, standing at her side, he had passed his arm about her while their gaze flew to the long tossed horizon line of the downs, and then dropped contentedly back to trace the arabesque of yew hedges about the fish pond, and the shadow of the cedar on the lawn.

"And now the other way," he had said, turning her about within his arm; and closely pressed to him, she had absorbed, like some long satisfying draught, the picture of the grey-walled court, the squat lions on the gates, and the lime avenue reaching up to the highroad under the downs.

It was just then, while they gazed and held each other, that she had felt his arm relax, and heard a sharp "Hullo!" that made her turn to glance at him.

Distinctly, yes, she now recalled that she had seen, as she glanced, a shadow of anxiety, of perplexity, rather, fall across his face; and, following his eyes, had beheld the figure of a man—a man in loose greyish clothes, as it appeared to her—who was sauntering down the lime avenue to the court with the doubtful gait of a stranger who seeks his way. Her shortsighted eyes had given her but a blurred impression of slightness and greyishness, with something foreign, or at least unlocal, in the cut of the figure or its dress; but her husband had apparently seen more—seen enough to make him push past her with a hasty "Wait!" and dash down the stairs without pausing to give her a hand.

A slight tendency to dizziness obliged her, after a provisional clutch at the chimney against which they had been leaning, to follow him first more cautiously; and when she had reached the landing she paused again, for a less definite reason, leaning over the banister to strain her eyes through the silence of the brown sun-flecked depths. She lingered there till, somewhere in those depths, she heard the closing of a door; then, mechanically impelled, she went down the shallow flights of steps till she reached the lower hall.

The front door stood open on the sunlight of the court, and hall and court were empty. The library door was open, too, and after listening in vain for any sound of voices within, she crossed the threshold, and found her husband alone, vaguely fingering the papers on his desk.

He looked up, as if surprised at her entrance, but the shadow of anxiety had passed from his face, leaving it even, as she fancied, a little brighter and clearer than usual.

"What was it? Who was it?" she asked.

"Who?" he repeated, with the surprise still all on his side.

"The man we saw coming toward the house."

He seemed to reflect. "The man? Why, I thought I saw Peters; I dashed after him to say a word about the stable drains, but he had disappeared before I could get down."

"Disappeared? But he seemed to be walking so slowly when we saw him."

Boyne shrugged his shoulders. "So I thought; but he must have got up steam in the interval. What do you say to our trying a scramble up Meldon Steep before sunset?"

That was all. At the time the occurrence had been less than nothing, had, indeed, been immediately obliterated by the magic of their first vision from Meldon Steep, a height which they had dreamed of climbing ever since they had first seen its bare spine rising above the roof of Lyng. Doubtless it was the mere fact of the other incident's having occurred on the very day of their ascent to Meldon that had kept it stored away in the fold of memory from which it now emerged; for in itself it had no mark of the portentous. At the moment there could have been nothing more natural than that Ned should dash himself from the roof in the pursuit of dilatory tradesmen. It was the period when they were always on the watch for one or the other of the specialists employed about the place; always lying in wait for them, and rushing out at them with questions, reproaches or reminders. And certainly in the distance the grey figure had looked like Peters.

Yet now, as she reviewed the scene, she felt her husband's explanation of it to have been invalidated by the look of anxiety on his face. Why had the familiar appearance of Peters made him anxious? Why, above all, if it was of such prime necessity to confer with him on the subject of the stable drains, had the failure to find him produced such a look of relief? Mary could not say that any one of these questions had occurred to her at the time, yet, from the promptness with which they now marshalled themselves at her summons, she had a sense that they must all along have been there, waiting their hour.

✣ II ✣

WEARY with her thoughts, she moved to the window. The library was now quite dark, and she was surprised to see how much faint light the outer world still held.

As she peered out into it across the court, a figure shaped itself far down the perspective of bare limes: it looked a mere blot of deeper grey in the greyness, and for an instant, as it moved toward her, her heart thumped to the thought "It's the ghost!"

She had time, in that long instant, to feel suddenly that the man of whom, two months earlier, she had had a distant vision from the roof, was now, at his predestined hour, about to reveal himself as *not* having been Peters; and her spirit sank under the impending fear of the disclosure. But almost with the next tick of the clock the figure, gaining substance and character, showed itself even to her weak sight as her husband's; and she turned to meet him, as he entered, with the confession of her folly.

"It's really too absurd," she laughed out, "but I never *can* remember!"

"Remember what?" Boyne questioned as they drew together.

"That when one sees the Lyng ghost one never knows it."

Her hand was on his sleeve, and he kept it there, but with no response in his gesture or in the lines of his preoccupied face.

"Did you think you'd seen it?" he asked, after an appreciable interval.

"Why, I actually took *you* for it, my dear, in my mad determination to spot it!"

"Me—just now?" His arm dropped away, and he turned from her with a faint echo of her laugh. "Really, dearest, you'd better give it up, if that's the best you can do."

"Oh, yes, I give it up. Have *you?*" she asked, turning round on him abruptly.

The parlormaid had entered with letters and a lamp, and the light struck up into Boyne's face as he bent above the tray she presented.

"Have *you?*" Mary perversely insisted, when the servant had disappeared on her errand of illumination.

"Have I what?" he rejoined absently, the light bringing out the sharp stamp of worry between his brows as he turned over the letters.

"Given up trying to see the ghost." Her heart beat a little at the experiment she was making.

Her husband, laying his letters aside, moved away into the shadow of the hearth.

"I never tried," he said, tearing open the wrapper of a newspaper.

"Well, of course," Mary persisted, "the exasperating thing is that there's no use trying, since one can't be sure till so long afterward."

He was unfolding the paper as if he had hardly heard her; but after a pause, during which the sheets rustled spasmodically between his hands, he looked up to ask, "Have you any idea *how long*?"

Mary had sunk into a low chair beside the fireplace. From her seat she glanced over, startled, at her husband's profile, which was projected against the circle of lamplight.

"No; none. Have *you*?" she retorted, repeating her former phrase with an added stress of intention.

Boyne crumpled the paper into a bunch, and then, inconsequently, turned back with it toward the lamp.

"Lord, no! I only meant," he exclaimed, with a faint tinge of impatience, "is there any legend, any tradition, as to that?"

"Not that I know of," she answered; but the impulse to add "What makes you ask?" was checked by the reappearance of the parlormaid, with tea and a second lamp.

With the dispersal of shadows, and the repetition of the daily domestic office, Mary Boyne felt herself less oppressed by that sense of something mutely imminent which had darkened her afternoon. For a few moments she gave herself to the details of her task, and when she looked up from it she was struck to the point of bewilderment by the change in her husband's face. He had seated himself near the farther lamp, and was absorbed in the perusal of his letters; but was it something he had found in them, or merely the shifting of her own point of view, that had restored his features to their normal aspect? The longer she looked the more definitely the change affirmed itself. The lines of tension had vanished, and such traces of fatigue as lingered were of the kind easily attributable to steady mental effort.

He glanced up, as if drawn by her gaze, and met her eyes with a smile.

"I'm dying for my tea, you know; and here's a letter for you," he said.

She took the letter he held out in exchange for the cup she proffered him, and, returning to her seat, broke the seal with the languid gesture of the reader whose interests are all enclosed in the circle of one cherished presence.

Her next conscious motion was that of starting to her feet, the letter falling to them as she rose, while she held out to her husband a newspaper clipping.

"Ned! What's this? What does it mean?"

He had risen at the same instant, almost as if hearing her cry before she uttered it; and for a perceptible space of time he and she studied each other, like adversaries watching for an advantage, across the space between her chair and his desk.

"What's what? You fairly made me jump!" Boyne said at length, moving toward her with a sudden half-exasperated laugh. The shadow of apprehension was on his face again, not now a look of fixed foreboding, but a shifting vigilance of lips and eyes that gave her the sense of his feeling himself invisibly surrounded.

Her hand shook so that she could hardly give him the clipping.

"This article—from the *Waukesha Sentinel*—that a man named Elwell has brought suit against you—that there was something wrong about the Blue Star Mine. I can't understand more than half."

They continued to face each other as she spoke, and to her astonishment she saw that her words had the almost immediate effect of dissipating the strained watchfulness of his look.

"Oh, *that*!" He glanced down the printed slip, and then folded it with the gesture of one who handles something harmless and familiar. "What's the matter with you this afternoon, Mary? I thought you'd got bad news."

She stood before him with her undefinable terror subsiding slowly under the reassurance of his tone.

"You knew about this, then—it's all right?"

"Certainly I knew about it; and it's all right."

"But what *is* it? I don't understand. What does this man accuse you of?"

"Pretty nearly every crime in the calendar." Boyne had tossed the clipping down, and thrown himself into an armchair near the fire. "Do you want to hear the story? It's not particularly interesting—just a squabble over interests in the Blue Star."

"But who is this Elwell? I don't know the name."

"Oh, he's a fellow I put into it—gave him a hand up. I told you all about him at the time."

"I dare say. I must have forgotten." Vainly she strained back among her memories. "But if you helped him, why does he make this return?"

"Probably some shyster lawyer got hold of him and talked him over. It's all rather technical and complicated. I thought that kind of thing bored you."

His wife felt a sting of compunction. Theoretically, she deprecated the American wife's detachment from her husband's professional interests, but in practice she had always found it difficult to fix her attention on Boyne's report of the transactions in which his varied interests involved him. Besides, she had felt during their years of exile, that, in a community where the amenities of living could be obtained only at the cost of efforts as arduous as her husband's professional labors, such brief leisure as he and she could command should be used as an escape from immediate preoccupations, a flight to the life they always dreamed of living. Once or twice, now that this new life had actually drawn its magic circle about them, she had asked herself if she had done right; but hitherto such conjectures had been no more than the retrospective excursions of an active fancy. Now, for the first time, it startled her a little to find how little she knew of the material foundation on which her happiness was built.

She glanced at her husband, and was again reassured by the composure of his face; yet she felt the need of more definite grounds for her reassurance.

"But doesn't this suit worry you? Why have you never spoken to me about it?"

He answered both questions at once. "I didn't speak of it at first because it *did* worry me—annoyed me, rather. But it's all ancient history now. Your correspondent must have got hold of a back number of the *Sentinel*."

She felt a quick thrill of relief. "You mean it's over? He's lost his case?"

There was a just perceptible delay in Boyne's reply. "The suit's been withdrawn—that's all."

But she persisted, as if to exonerate herself from the inward charge of being too easily put off. "Withdrawn it because he saw he had no chance?"

"Oh, he had no chance," Boyne answered.

She was still struggling with a dimly felt perplexity at the back of her thoughts.

"How long ago was it withdrawn?"

He paused, as if with a slight return to his former uncertainty. "I've just had the news now; but I've been expecting it."

"Just now—in one of your letters?"

"Yes; in one of my letters."

She made no answer, and was aware only, after a short interval of waiting, that he had risen, and, strolling across the room, had placed himself on the sofa at her side. She felt him, as he did so, pass an arm about her, she felt his hand seek hers and clasp it, and turning slowly, drawn by the warmth of his cheek, she met his smiling eyes.

"It's all right—it's all right?" she questioned, through the flood of her dissolving doubts; and "I give you my word it was never righter!" he laughed back at her, holding her close.

✤ III ✤

ONE of the strange things she was afterward to recall out of all the next day's strangeness was the sudden and complete recovery of her sense of security.

It was in the air when she woke in her low-ceilinged, dusky room; it went with her downstairs to the breakfast table, flashed out at her from the fire, and reduplicated itself from the flanks of the urn and the sturdy flutings of the Georgian teapot. It was as if in some roundabout way, all her diffused fears of the previous day, with their moment of sharp concentration about the newspaper article—as if this dim questioning of the future, and startled return upon the past, had between them liquidated the arrears of some haunting moral obligation. If she had indeed been careless of her husband's affairs, it was, her new state seemed to prove, because her faith in him instinctively justified such carelessness; and his right to her faith had now affirmed itself in the very face of menace and suspicion. She had never seen him more untroubled, more naturally and unconsciously himself, than after the cross-examination to which she had subjected him: it was almost as if he had been aware of her doubts, and had wanted the air cleared as much as she did.

It was as clear, thank heaven, as the bright outer light that surprised her almost with a touch of summer when she issued from the house for her daily round of the gardens. She had left Boyne at his desk, indulging herself, as she passed the library door, by a last peep at his quiet face, where he bent, pipe in mouth, above his papers; and now she had her own morning's task to perform. The task involved, on such charmed winter days, almost as much happy loitering about the different quarters of her domain as if spring were already at work there. There were such endless possibilities still before her, such opportunities to bring out the latent graces of the old place, without a single irreverent touch of alteration, that the winter was all too short to plan what spring and autumn executed. And her recovered sense of safety gave, on this particular morning, a peculiar zest to her progress through the sweet still place. She went first to the kitchen garden, where the espaliered pear trees drew complicated patterns on the walls, and pigeons were fluttering and preening about the silvery-slated roof of their cot. There was something wrong about the piping of the hothouse, and she was expecting an authority from Dorchester, who was to drive out between rains and make a diagnosis of the boiler. But when she dipped into the damp heat of the greenhouses, among the spiced scents and waxy pinks and reds of old-fashioned exotics—even the flora of Lyng was in the note!—she learned that the great man had not arrived, and, the day being too rare to waste in an artificial atmosphere, she came out again and paced along the springy turf of the bowling green to the gardens behind the house. At their farther end rose a grass terrace, looking across the fish pond and yew hedges to the long house front with its twisted chimney stacks and blue roof angles all drenched in the pale gold moisture of the air.

Seen thus, across the level tracery of the gardens, it sent her, from open windows and hospitably smoking chimneys, the look of some warm human presence, of a mind slowly ripened on a sunny wall of experience. She had never before had such a sense of her intimacy with it, such a conviction that its secrets were all beneficent, kept, as they said to children, "for one's good," such a trust in its power to gather up her life and Ned's into the harmonious pattern of the long long story it sat there weaving in the sun.

She heard steps behind her, and turned, expecting to see the gardener accompanied by the engineer from Dorchester. But only one figure was in sight, that of a youngish slightly built man, who, for reasons she could not on the spot have given, did not remotely resemble her notion of an authority on hothouse boilers. The newcomer, on seeing her, lifted his hat, and paused with the air of a gentleman—perhaps a traveler—who wishes to make it known that his intrusion is involuntary. Lyng occasionally attracted the more cultivated traveler, and Mary half expected to see the stranger dissemble a camera, or justify his presence by producing it. But he made no gesture of any sort, and after a moment she asked, in a tone responding to the courteous hesitation of his attitude: "Is there anyone you wish to see?"

"I came to see Mr. Boyne," he answered. His intonation, rather than his accent, was faintly American, and Mary, at the note, looked at him more closely. The brim of his soft felt hat cast a shade on his face, which, thus obscured, wore to her shortsighted gaze a look of seriousness, as of a person arriving on business, and civilly but firmly aware of his rights.

Past experience had made her equally sensible to such claims; but she was jealous of her husband's morning hours, and doubtful of his having given anyone the right to intrude on them.

"Have you an appointment with my husband?" she asked.

The visitor hesitated, as if unprepared for the question.

"I think he expects me," he replied.

It was Mary's turn to hesitate. "You see this is his time for work: he never sees anyone in the morning."

He looked at her a moment without answering; then, as if accepting her decision, he began to move away. As he turned, Mary saw him pause and glance up at the peaceful house front. Something in his air suggested weariness and disappointment, the dejection of the traveler who has come from far off and whose hours are limited by the timetable. It occurred to her that if this were the case her refusal might have made his errand vain, and a sense of compunction caused her to hasten after him.

"May I ask if you have come a long way?"

He gave her the same grave look. "Yes—I have come a long way."

"Then, if you'll go to the house, no doubt my husband will see you now. You'll find him in the library."

She did not know why she had added the last phrase, except from a vague impulse to atone for her previous inhospitality. The visitor seemed about to express his thanks, but her attention was distracted by the approach of the gardener with a companion who bore all the marks of being the expert from Dorchester.

"This way," she said, waving the stranger to the house; and an instant later she had forgotten him in the absorption of her meeting with the boiler maker.

The encounter led to such far-reaching results that the engineer ended by finding it expedient to ignore his train, and Mary was beguiled into spending the remainder of the morning in absorbed confabulation among the flower pots. When the colloquy ended, she was surprised to find that it was nearly luncheon time, and she half expected, as she hurried back to the house, to see her husband coming out to meet her. But she found no one in the court but an undergardener raking the gravel, and the hall, when she entered it, was so silent that she guessed Boyne to be still at work.

Not wishing to disturb him, she turned into the drawing room, and there, at her writing table, lost herself in renewed calculations of the outlay to which the morning's conference had pledged her. The fact that she could permit herself such follies had not yet lost its novelty; and somehow, in contrast to the vague fears of the previous days, it now seemed an element of her recovered security, of the sense that, as Ned had said, things in general had never been "righter."

She was still luxuriating in a lavish play of figures when the parlormaid, from the threshold, roused her with an inquiry as to the expediency of serving luncheon. It was one of their jokes that Trimmle announced luncheon as if she were divulging a state secret, and Mary, intent upon her papers, merely murmured an absent-minded assent.

She felt Trimmle wavering doubtfully on the threshold, as if in rebuke of such unconsidered assent; then her retreating steps sounded down the passage, and Mary, pushing away her papers, crossed the hall and went to the library door. It was still closed, and she wavered in her turn, disliking to disturb her husband, yet anxious that he should not exceed his usual measure of work. As she stood there, balancing her impulses, Trimmle returned with the announcement of luncheon, and Mary, thus impelled, opened the library door.

Boyne was not at his desk, and she peered about her, expecting to discover him before the bookshelves, somewhere down the length of the room; but her call brought no response, and gradually it became clear to her that he was not there.

She turned back to the parlormaid.

"Mr. Boyne must be upstairs. Please tell him that luncheon is ready."

Trimmle appeared to hesitate between the obvious duty of obedience and an equally obvious conviction of the foolishness of the injunction laid on her. The struggle resulted in her saying: "If you please, Madam, Mr. Boyne's not upstairs."

"Not in his room? Are you sure?"

"I'm sure, Madam."

Mary consulted the clock. "Where is he, then?"

"He's gone out," Trimmle announced, with the superior air of one who has respectfully waited for the question that a well-ordered mind would have put first.

Mary's conjecture had been right, then. Boyne must have gone to the gardens to meet her, and since she had missed him, it was clear that he had taken the shorter way by the south door, instead of going round to the court. She crossed the hall to the French window opening directly on the yew garden, but the parlormaid, after another moment of inner conflict, decided to bring out: "Please, Madam, Mr. Boyne didn't go that way."

Mary turned back. "Where *did* he go? And when?"

"He went out of the front door, up the drive, Madam." It was a matter of principle with Trimmle never to answer more than one question at a time.

"Up the drive? At this hour?" Mary went to the door herself, and glanced across the court through the tunnel of bare limes. But its perspective was as empty as when she had scanned it on entering.

"Did Mr. Boyne leave no message?"

Trimmle seemed to surrender herself to a last struggle with the forces of chaos.

"No, Madam. He just went out with the gentleman."

"The gentleman? What gentleman?" Mary wheeled about, as if to front this new factor.

"The gentleman who called, Madam," said Trimmle resignedly.

"When did a gentleman call? Do explain yourself, Trimmle!"

Only the fact that Mary was very hungry, and that she wanted to consult her husband about the greenhouses, would have caused her to lay so unusual an injunction on her attendant; and even now she was detached enough to note in Trimmle's eye the dawning defiance of the respectful subordinate who has been pressed too hard.

"I couldn't exactly say the hour, Madam, because I didn't let the gentleman in," she replied, with an air of discreetly ignoring the irregularity of her mistress's course.

"You didn't let him in?"

"No, Madam. When the bell rang I was dressing, and Agnes—"

"Go and ask Agnes, then," said Mary.

Trimmle still wore her look of patient magnanimity. "Agnes would not know, Madam, for she had unfortunately burnt her hand in trimming the wick of the new lamp from town"—Trimmle, as Mary was aware, had always been opposed to the new lamp—"and so Mrs. Dockett sent the kitchenmaid instead."

Mary looked again at the clock. "It's after two! Go and ask the kitchenmaid if Mr. Boyne left any word."

She went into luncheon without waiting, and Trimmle presently brought her there the kitchenmaid's statement that the gentleman had called about eleven o'clock, and that Mr. Boyne had gone out with him without leaving any message. The kitchenmaid did not even know the caller's name, for he had written it on a slip of paper, which he had folded and handed to her, with the injunction to deliver it at once to Mr. Boyne.

Mary finished her luncheon, still wondering, and when it was over, and Trimmle had brought the coffee to the drawing room, her wonder had deepened to a first faint tinge of disquietude. It was unlike Boyne to absent himself without explanation at so unwonted an hour and the difficulty of identifying the visitor whose summons he had apparently obeyed made his disappearance the more unaccountable. Mary Boyne's experience as the wife of a busy engineer, subject to sudden calls and compelled to keep irregular hours, had trained her to the philosophic acceptance of surprises; but since Boyne's withdrawal from business he had adopted a Benedictine regularity of life. As if to make up for the dispersed and agitated years, with their "stand-up" lunches, and dinners rattled down to the joltings of the dining cars, he cultivated the last refinements of punctuality and monotony, discouraging his wife's fancy for the unexpected, and declaring that to a delicate taste there were infinite gradations of pleasure in the recurrences of habit.

Still, since no life can completely defend itself from the unforeseen, it was evident that all Boyne's precautions would sooner or later prove unavailable, and Mary concluded that he had cut short a tiresome visit by walking with his caller to the station, or at least accompanying him for part of the way.

This conclusion relieved her from further preoccupation, and she went out herself to take up her conference with the gardener. Thence she walked to the village post office, a mile or so away; and when she turned toward home the early twilight was setting in.

She had taken a footpath across the downs, and as Boyne, meanwhile, had probably returned from the station by the highroad, there was little likelihood of their meeting. She felt sure, however, of his having reached the house before her; so sure that, when she entered it herself, without even pausing to inquire of Trimmle, she made directly for the library. But the library was still empty, and with an unwonted exactness of visual memory she observed that the papers on her husband's desk lay precisely as they had lain when she had gone in to call him to luncheon.

Then of a sudden she was seized by a vague dread of the unknown. She had closed the door behind her on entering, and as she stood alone in the long silent room, her dread seemed to take shape and sound, to be there breathing and lurking among the shadows. Her shortsighted eyes strained through them, half-discerning an actual presence, something aloof, that watched and knew; and in the recoil from that intangible presence she threw herself on the bell rope and gave it a sharp pull.

The sharp summons brought Trimmle in precipitately with a lamp, and Mary breathed again at this sobering reappearance of the usual.

"You may bring tea if Mr. Boyne is in," she said, to justify her ring.

"Very well, Madam. But Mr. Boyne is not in," said Trimmle, putting down the lamp.

"Not in? You mean he's come back and gone out again?"

"No, Madam. He's never been back."

The dread stirred again, and Mary knew that now it had her fast.

"Not since he went out with—the gentleman?"

"Not since he went out with the gentleman."

"But who *was* the gentleman?" Mary insisted, with the shrill note of someone trying to be heard through a confusion of noises.

"That I couldn't say, Madam." Trimmle, standing there by the lamp, seemed suddenly to grow less round and rosy, as though eclipsed by the same creeping shade of apprehension.

"But the kitchenmaid knows—wasn't it the kitchenmaid who let him in?"

"She doesn't know either, Madam, for he wrote his name on a folded paper."

Mary, through her agitation, was aware that they were both designating the unknown visitor by a vague pronoun, instead of the conventional formula which, till then, had kept their allusions within the bounds of conformity. And at the same moment her mind caught at the suggestion of the folded paper.

"But he must have a name! Where's the paper?"

She moved to the desk, and began to turn over the documents that littered it. The first that caught her eye was an unfinished letter in her husband's hand, with his pen lying across it, as though dropped there at a sudden summons.

"My dear Parvis"—who was Parvis?—"I have just received your letter announcing Elwell's death, and while I suppose there is now no further risk of trouble, it might be safer—"

She tossed the sheet aside, and continued her search; but no folded paper was discoverable among the letters and pages of manuscript which had been swept together in a heap, as if by a hurried or a startled gesture.

"But the kitchenmaid *saw* him. Send her here," she commanded, wondering at her dullness in not thinking sooner of so simple a solution.

Trimmle vanished in a flash, as if thankful to be out of the room, and when she reappeared, conducting the agitated underling, Mary had regained her self-possession, and had her questions ready.

The gentleman was a stranger, yes—that she understood. But what had he said? And, above all, what had he looked like? The first question was easily enough answered, for the disconcerting reason that he had said so little—had merely asked for Mr. Boyne, and, scribbling something on a bit of paper, had requested that it should at once be carried in to him.

"Then you don't know what he wrote? You're not sure it *was* his name?"

The kitchenmaid was not sure, but supposed it was, since he had written it in answer to her inquiry as to whom she should announce.

"And when you carried the paper in to Mr. Boyne, what did he say?"

The kitchenmaid did not think that Mr. Boyne had said anything, but she could not be sure, for just as she had handed him the paper and he was opening it, she had become aware that the visitor had followed her into the library, and she had slipped out, leaving the two gentlemen together.

"But then, if you left them in the library, how do you know that they went out of the house?"

This question plunged the witness into a momentary inarticulateness, from which she was rescued by Trimmle, who, by means of ingenious circumlocutions, elicited the statement that before she could cross the hall to the back passage she had heard the two gentlemen behind her, and had seen them go out of the front door together.

"Then, if you saw the strange gentleman twice, you must be able to tell me what he looked like."

But with this final challenge to her powers of expression it became clear that the limit of the kitchenmaid's endurance had been reached. The obligation of going to the front door to "show in" a visitor was in itself so subversive of the fundamental order of things that it had thrown her faculties into hopeless disarray, and she could only stammer out, after various panting efforts: "His hat, mum, was different-like, as you might say—"

"Different? How different?" Mary flashed out, her own mind, in the same instant, leaping back to an image left on it that morning, and then lost under layers of subsequent impressions.

"His hat had a wide brim, you mean, and his face was pale—a youngish face?" Mary pressed her, with a white-lipped intensity of interrogation. But if the kitchenmaid found any adequate answer to this challenge, it was swept away for her listener down the rushing current of her own convictions. The stranger—the stranger in the garden! Why had Mary not thought of him before? She needed no one now to tell her that it was he who had called for her husband and gone away with him. But who was he, and why had Boyne obeyed him?

✣ IV ✣

It leaped out at her suddenly, like a grin out of the dark, that they had often called England so little—"such a confoundedly hard place to get lost in."

A confoundedly hard place to get lost in! That had been her husband's phrase. And now, with the whole machinery of official investigation sweeping its flashlights from shore to shore, and across the dividing straits; now, with Boyne's name blazing from the walls of every town and village, his portrait (how that wrung her!) hawked up and down the country like the image of a hunted criminal; now the little compact populous island, so policed, surveyed and administered, revealed itself as a Sphinxlike guardian of abysmal mysteries, staring back into his wife's anguished eyes as if with the wicked joy of knowing something they would never know!

In the fortnight since Boyne's disappearance there had been no word of him, no trace of his movements. Even the usual misleading reports that raise expectancy in tortured bosoms had been few and fleeting. No one but the kitchenmaid had seen Boyne leave the house, and no one else had seen "the gentleman" who accompanied him. All inquiries in the neighborhood failed to elicit the memory of a stranger's presence that day in the neighborhood of Lyng. And no one had met Edward Boyne, either alone or in company, in any of the neighboring villages, or on the road across the downs, or at either of the local railway stations. The sunny English noon had swallowed him as completely as if he had gone out into Cimmerian night.

Mary, while every official means of investigation was working at its highest pressure, had ransacked her husband's papers for any trace of antecedent complications, of entanglements or obligations unknown to her, that might throw a ray into the darkness. But if any such had existed in the background of Boyne's life, they had vanished like the slip of paper on which the visitor had written his name. There remained no possible thread of guidance except—if it were indeed an exception—the letter which Boyne had apparently been in the act of writing when he received his mysterious summons. That letter, read and reread by his wife, and submitted by her to the police, yielded little enough to feed conjecture.

"I have just heard of Elwell's death, and while I suppose there is now no further risk of trouble, it might be safer—" That was all. The "risk of trouble" was easily explained by the newspaper clipping which had apprised Mary of the suit brought against her husband by one of his associates in the Blue Star enterprise. The only new information conveyed by the letter was the fact of its showing Boyne, when he wrote it, to be still apprehensive of the results of the suit, though he had told his wife that it had been withdrawn, and though the letter itself proved that the plaintiff was dead. It took several days of cabling to fix the identity of the "Parvis" to whom the fragment was addressed, but even after these inquiries had shown him to be a Waukesha lawyer, no new facts concerning the Elwell suit were elicited. He appeared to have had no direct concern in it, but to have been conversant with the facts merely as an acquaintance, and possible intermediary; and he declared himself unable to guess with what object Boyne intended to seek his assistance.

This negative information, sole fruit of the first fortnight's search, was not increased by a jot during the slow weeks that followed. Mary knew that the investigations were still being carried on, but she had a vague sense of their gradually slackening, as the actual march of time seemed to slacken. It was as though the days, flying horror-struck from the shrouded image of the one inscrutable day, gained assurance as the distance lengthened, till at last they fell back in their normal gait. And so with the human imaginations at work on the dark event. No doubt it occupied them still, but week by week and hour by hour it grew less absorbing, took up less space, was slowly but inevitably crowded out of the foreground of consciousness by the new problems perpetually bubbling up from the cloudy caldron of human experience.

Even Mary Boyne's consciousness gradually felt the same lowering of velocity. It still swayed with the incessant oscillations of conjecture; but they were slower, more rhythmical in their beat. There were even moments of weariness when, like the victim of some poison which leaves the brain clear, but holds the body motionless, she saw herself domesticated with the Horror, accepting its perpetual presence as one of the fixed conditions of life.

These moments lengthened into hours and days, till she passed into a phase of stolid acquiescence. She watched the routine of daily life with the incurious eye of a savage on whom the meaningless processes of civilization make but the faintest impression. She had come to regard herself as part of the routine, a spoke of the wheel, revolving with its motion; she felt almost like the furniture of the room in which she sat, an insensate object to be dusted and pushed about with the chairs and tables. And this deepening apathy held her fast at Lyng, in spite of the entreaties of friends and the usual medical recommendation of "change." Her friends supposed that her refusal to move was inspired by the belief that her husband would one day return to the spot from which he had vanished, and a beautiful legend grew up about this imaginary state of waiting. But in reality she had no such belief: the depths of anguish enclosing her were no longer lighted by flashes of hope. She was sure that Boyne would never come back, that he had gone out of her sight as completely as if Death itself had waited that day on the threshold. She had even renounced, one by one, the various theories as to his disappearance which had been advanced by the press, the police, and her own agonized imagination. In sheer lassitude her mind turned from these alternatives of horror, and sank back into the blank fact that he was gone.

No, she would never know what had become of him—no one would ever know. But the house *knew*; the library in which she spent her long lonely evenings knew. For it was here that the last scene had been enacted, here that the stranger had come, and spoken the word which had caused Boyne to rise and follow him. The floor she trod had felt his tread; the books on the shelves had seen his face; and there were moments when the intense consciousness of the old dusky walls seemed about to break out into some audible revelation of their secret. But the revelation never came, and she knew it would never come. Lyng was not one of the garrulous old houses that betray the secrets entrusted to them. Its very legend proved that it had always been the mute accomplice, the incorruptible custodian, of the mysteries it had surprised. And Mary Boyne, sitting face to face with its silence, felt the futility of seeking to break it by any human means.

✣ V ✣

"I DON'T say it *wasn't* straight, and yet I don't say it *was* straight. It was business."

Mary, at the words, lifted her head with a start, and looked intently at the speaker.

When, half an hour before, a card with "Mr. Parvis" on it had been brought up to her, she had been immediately aware that the name had been a part of her consciousness ever since she had read it at the head of Boyne's unfinished letter. In the library she had found awaiting her a small sallow man with a bald head and gold eyeglasses, and it sent a tremor through her to know that this was the person to whom her husband's last known thought had been directed.

Parvis, civilly, but without vain preamble—in the manner of a man who has his watch in his hand—had set forth the object of his visit. He had "run over" to England on business, and finding himself in the neighborhood of Dorchester, had not wished to leave it without paying his respects to Mrs. Boyne; and without asking her, if the occasion offered, what she meant to do about Bob Elwell's family.

The words touched the spring of some obscure dread in Mary's bosom. Did her visitor, after all, know what Boyne had meant by his unfinished phrase? She asked for an elucidation of his question, and noticed at once that he seemed surprised at her continued ignorance of the subject. Was it possible that she really knew as little as she said?

"I know nothing—you must tell me," she faltered out; and her visitor thereupon proceeded to unfold his story. It threw, even to her confused perceptions, and imperfectly initiated vision, a lurid-glare on the whole hazy episode of the Blue Star Mine. Her husband had made his money in that brilliant speculation at the cost of "getting ahead" of someone less alert to seize the chance; and the victim of his ingenuity was young Robert Elwell, who had "put him on" to the Blue Star scheme.

Parvis, at Mary's first cry, had thrown her a sobering glance through his impartial glasses.

"Bob Elwell wasn't smart enough, that's all; if he had been, he might have turned round and served Boyne the same way. It's the kind of thing that happens everyday in business. I guess it's what the scientists call the survival of the fittest—see?" said Mr. Parvis, evidently pleased with the aptness of his analogy.

Mary felt a physical shrinking from the next question she tried to frame: it was as though the words on her lips had a taste that nauseated her.

"But then—you accuse my husband of doing something dishonorable?"

Mr. Parvis surveyed the question dispassionately. "Oh, no, I don't. I don't even say it wasn't straight." He glanced up and down the long lines of books, as if one of them might have supplied him with the definition he sought. "I don't say it *wasn't* straight, and yet I don't say it *was* straight. It was business." After all, no definition in his category could be more comprehensive than that.

Mary sat staring at him with a look of terror. He seemed to her like the indifferent emissary of some evil power.

"But Mr. Elwell's lawyers apparently did not take your view, since I suppose the suit was withdrawn by their advice."

"Oh, yes; they knew he hadn't a leg to stand on, technically. It was when they advised him to withdraw the suit that he got desperate. You see, he'd borrowed most of the money he lost in the Blue Star, and he was up a tree. That's why he shot himself when they told him he had no show."

The horror was sweeping over Mary in great deafening waves.

"He shot himself? He killed himself because of *that*?"

"Well, he didn't kill himself, exactly. He dragged on two months before he died." Parvis emitted the statement as unemotionally as a gramophone grinding out its record.

"You mean that he tried to kill himself, and failed? And tried again?"

"Oh, he didn't have to *try* again," said Parvis grimly.

They sat opposite each other in silence, he swinging his eyeglasses thoughtfully about his finger, she, motionless, her arms stretched along her knees in an attitude of rigid tension.

"But if you knew all this," she began at length, hardly able to force her voice above a whisper, "how is it that when I wrote you at the time of my husband's disappearance you said you didn't understand his letter?"

Parvis received this without perceptible embarrassment: "Why, I didn't understand it—strictly speaking. And it wasn't the time to talk about it, if I had. The Elwell business was settled when the suit was withdrawn. Nothing I could have told you would have helped you to find your husband."

Mary continued to scrutinize him. "Then why are you telling me now?"

Still Parvis did not hesitate. "Well, to begin with, I supposed you knew more than you appear to—I mean about the circumstances of Elwell's death. And then people are talking of it now; the whole matter's been raked up again. And I thought if you didn't know you ought to."

She remained silent, and he continued: "You see, it's only come out lately what a bad state Elwell's affairs were in. His wife's a proud woman, and she fought on as long as she could, going out to work, and taking sewing at home when she got too sick—something with the heart, I believe. But she had his mother to look after, and the children, and she broke down under it, and finally had to ask for help. That called attention to the case, and the papers took it up, and a subscription was started. Everybody out there liked Bob Elwell, and most of the prominent names in the place are down on the list, and people began to wonder why—"

Parvis broke off to fumble in an inner pocket. "Here," he continued, "here's an account of the whole thing from the *Sentinel*—a little sensational, of course. But I guess you'd better look it over."

He held out a newspaper to Mary, who unfolded it slowly, remembering, as she did so, the evening when, in that same room, the perusal of a clipping from the *Sentinel* had first shaken the depths of her security.

As she opened the paper, her eyes, shrinking from the glaring headlines, "Widow of Boyne's Victim Forced to Appeal for Aid," ran down the column of text to two portraits inserted in it. The first was her husband's, taken from a photograph made the year they had come to England. It was the picture of him that she liked best, the one that stood on the writing table upstairs in her bedroom. As the eyes in the photograph met hers, she felt it would be impossible to read what was said of him, and closed her lids with the sharpness of the pain.

"I thought if you felt disposed to put your name down—" she heard Parvis continue.

She opened her eyes with an effort, and they fell on the other portrait. It was that of a youngish man, slightly built, with features somewhat blurred by the shadow of a projecting hat brim. Where had she seen that outline before? She stared at it confusedly, her heart hammering in her ears. Then she gave a cry.

"This is the man—the man who came for my husband!"

She heard Parvis start to his feet, and was dimly aware that she had slipped backward into the corner of the sofa, and that he was bending above her in alarm. She straightened herself, and reached out for the paper, which she had dropped.

"It's the man! I should know him anywhere!" she persisted in a voice that sounded to her own ears like a scream.

Parvis's answer seemed to come to her from far off, down endless fog-muffled windings.

"Mrs. Boyne, you're not very well. Shall I call somebody? Shall I get a glass of water?"

"No, no, no!" She threw herself toward him, her hand

frantically clutching the newspaper. "I tell you, it's the man! I *know* him! He spoke to me in the garden!"

Parvis took the journal from her, directing his glasses to the portrait. "It can't be, Mrs. Boyne. It's Robert Elwell."

"Robert Elwell?" Her white stare seemed to travel into space. "Then it was Robert Elwell who came for him."

"Came for Boyne? The day he went away from here?" Parvis's voice dropped as hers rose. He bent over, laying a fraternal hand on her, as if to coax her gently back into her seat. "Why, Elwell was dead! Don't you remember?"

Mary sat with her eyes fixed on the picture, unconscious of what he was saying.

"Don't you remember Boyne's unfinished letter to me—the one you found on his desk that day? It was written just after he'd heard of Elwell's death." She noticed an odd shake in Parvis's unemotional voice. "Surely you remember!" he urged her.

Yes, she remembered: that was the profoundest horror of it. Elwell had died the day before her husband's disappearance; and this was Elwell's portrait; and it was the portrait of the man who had spoken to her in the garden. She lifted her head and looked slowly about the library. The library could have borne witness that it was also the portrait of the man who had come in that day to call Boyne from his unfinished letter. Through the misty surgings of her brain she heard the faint boom of half-forgotten words—words spoken by Alida Stair on the lawn at Pangbourne before Boyne and his wife had ever seen the house at Lyng, or had imagined that they might one day live there.

"This was the man who spoke to me," she repeated.

She looked again at Parvis. He was trying to conceal his disturbance under what he probably imagined to be an expression of indulgent commiseration; but the edges of his lips were blue. "He thinks me mad; but I'm not mad," she reflected; and suddenly there flashed upon her a way of justifying her strange affirmation.

She sat quiet, controlling the quiver of her lips, and waiting till she could trust her voice; then she said, looking straight at Parvis: "Will you answer me one question, please? When was it that Robert Elwell tried to kill himself?"

"When—when?" Parvis stammered.

"Yes; the date. Please try to remember."

She saw that he was growing still more afraid of her. "I have a reason," she insisted.

"Yes, yes. Only I can't remember. About two months before, I should say."

"I want the date," she repeated.

Parvis picked up the newspaper. "We might see here," he said, still humoring her. He ran his eyes down the page. "Here it is. Last October—the—"

She caught the words from him. "The 20th, wasn't it?" With a sharp look at her, he verified. "Yes, the 20th. Then you *did* know?"

"I know now." Her gaze continued to travel past him. "Sunday, the 20th—that was the day he came first."

Parvis's voice was almost inaudible. "Came *here* first?"

"Yes."

"You saw him twice, then?"

"Yes, twice." She just breathed it at him. "He came first on the 20th of October. I remember the date because it was the day we went up Meldon Steep for the first time." She felt a faint gasp of inward laughter at the thought that but for that she might have forgotten.

Parvis continued to scrutinize her, as if trying to intercept her gaze.

"We saw him from the roof," she went on. "He came down the lime avenue toward the house. He was dressed just as he is in that picture. My husband saw him first. He was frightened, and ran down ahead of me; but there was no one there. He had vanished."

"Elwell had vanished?" Parvis faltered.

"Yes." Their two whispers seemed to grope for each other. "I couldn't think what had happened. I see now. He *tried* to come then; but he wasn't dead enough—he couldn't reach us. He had to wait for two months to die; and then he came back again—and Ned went with him."

She nodded at Parvis with the look of triumph of a child who has worked out a difficult puzzle. But suddenly she lifted her hands with a desperate gesture, pressing them to her temples.

"Oh, my God! I sent him to Ned—I told him where to go! I sent him to this room!" she screamed.

She felt the walls of books rush toward her, like inward falling ruins; and she heard Parvis, a long way off, through the ruins, crying to her, and struggling to get at her. But she was numb to his touch, she did not know what he was saying. Through the tumult she heard but one clear note, the voice of Alida Stair, speaking on the lawn at Pangbourne.

"You won't know till afterward," it said. "You won't know till long, long afterward."

Xingu

MRS. BALLINGER is one of the ladies who pursue Culture in bands, as though it were dangerous to meet alone. To this end she had founded the Lunch Club, an association composed of herself and several other indomitable huntresses of erudition. The Lunch Club, after three or four winters of lunching and debate, had acquired such local distinction that the entertainment of distinguished strangers became one of its accepted functions; in recognition of which it duly extended to the celebrated Osric Dane, on the day of her arrival in Hillbridge, an invitation to be present at the next meeting.

The club was to meet at Mrs. Ballinger's. The other members, behind her back, were of one voice in deploring her unwillingness to cede her rights in favor of Mrs. Plinth, whose house made a more impressive setting for the entertainment of celebrities; while, as Mrs. Leveret observed, there was always the picture gallery to fall back on.

Mrs. Plinth made no secret of sharing this view. She had always regarded it as one of her obligations to entertain the Lunch Club's distinguished guests. Mrs. Plinth was almost as proud of her obligations as she was of her picture gallery; she was in fact fond of implying that the one possession implied the other, and that only a woman of her wealth could afford to live up to a standard as high as that which she had set herself. An all-round sense of duty, roughly adaptable to various ends, was, in her opinion, all that Providence exacted of the more humbly stationed; but the power which had predestined Mrs. Plinth to keep a footman clearly intended her to maintain an equally specialized staff of responsibilities. It was the more to be regretted that Mrs. Ballinger, whose obligations to society were bounded by the narrow scope of two parlormaids, should have been so tenacious of the right to entertain Osric Dane.

The question of that lady's reception had for a month past profoundly moved the members of the Lunch Club. It was not that they felt themselves unequal to the task, but that their sense of the opportunity plunged them into the agreeable uncertainty of the lady who weighs the alternatives of a well-stocked wardrobe. If such subsidiary members as Mrs. Leveret were fluttered by the thought of exchanging ideas with the author of *The Wings of Death*, no forebodings disturbed the conscious adequacy of Mrs. Plinth, Mrs. Ballinger and Miss Van Vluyck. *The Wings of Death* had, in fact, at Miss Van Vluyck's suggestion, been chosen as the subject of discussion at the last club meeting, and each member had thus been enabled to express her own opinion or to appropriate whatever sounded well in the comments of the others.

Mrs. Roby alone had abstained from profiting by the opportunity but it was now openly recognized that, as a member of the Lunch Club, Mrs. Roby was a failure. "It all comes," as Miss Van Vluyck put it, "of accepting a woman on a man's estimation." Mrs. Roby, returning to Hillbridge from a prolonged sojourn in exotic lands—the other ladies no longer took the trouble to remember where—had been heralded by the distinguished biologist, Professor Foreland, as the most agreeable woman he had ever met; and the members of the Lunch Club, impressed by an encomium that carried the weight of a diploma, and rashly assuming that the Professor's social sympathies would follow the line of his professional bent, had seized the chance of annexing a biological member. Their disillusionment was complete. At Miss Van Vluyck's first offhand mention of the pterodactyl Mrs. Roby had confusedly murmured: "I know so little about meters—" and after that painful betrayal of incompetence she had prudently withdrawn from further participation in the mental gymnastics of the club.

"I suppose she flattered him," Miss Van Vluyck summed up—"or else it's the way she does her hair."

The dimensions of Miss Van Vluyck's dining room having restricted the membership of the club to six, the nonconductiveness of one member was a serious obstacle to the exchange of ideas, and some wonder had already been expressed that Mrs. Roby should care to live, as it were, on the intellectual bounty of the others. This feeling was increased by the discovery that she had not yet read *The Wings of Death*. She owned to having heard the name of Osric Dane; but that—incredible as it appeared—was the extent of her acquaintance with the celebrated novelist. The ladies could not conceal their surprise; but Mrs. Ballinger, whose pride in the club made her wish to put even Mrs. Roby in the best possible light, gently insinuated that, though she had not had time to acquaint herself with *The Wings of Death*, she must at least be familiar with its equally remarkable predecessor, *The Supreme Instant*.

Mrs. Roby wrinkled her sunny brows in a conscientious effort of memory, as a result of which she recalled that, oh, yes, she *had* seen the book at her brother's, when she was staying with him in Brazil, and had even carried it off to read one day on a boating party; but they had all got to shying things at each other in the boat, and the book had gone overboard, so she had never had the chance—

The picture evoked by this anecdote did not increase Mrs. Roby's credit with the club, and there was a painful pause, which was broken by Mrs. Plinth's remarking: "I can understand that, with all your other pursuits, you should not find much time for reading; but I should have thought you might at least have *got up The Wings of Death* before Osric Dane's arrival."

Mrs. Roby took this rebuke good-humoredly. She had meant, she owned, to glance through the book; but she had been so absorbed in a novel of Trollope's that—

"No one reads Trollope now," Mrs. Ballinger interrupted.

Mrs. Roby looked pained. "I'm only just beginning," she confessed.

"And does he interest you?" Mrs. Plinth inquired.

"He amuses me."

"Amusement," said Mrs. Plinth, "is hardly what I look for in my choice of books."

"Oh, certainly, *The Wings of Death* is not amusing," ventured Mrs. Leveret, whose manner of putting forth an opinion was like that of an obliging salesman with a variety of other styles to submit if his first selection does not suit.

"Was it *meant* to be?" inquired Mrs. Plinth, who was fond of asking questions that she permitted no one but herself to answer. "Assuredly not."

"Assuredly not—that is what I was going to say," assented Mrs. Leveret, hastily rolling up her opinion and reaching for another. "It was meant to—to elevate."

Miss Van Vluyck adjusted her spectacles as though they were the black cap of condemnation. "I hardly see," she interposed, "how a book steeped in the bitterest pessimism can be said to elevate, however much it may instruct."

"I meant, of course, to instruct," said Mrs. Leveret, flurried by the unexpected distinction between two terms which she had supposed to be synonymous. Mrs. Leveret's enjoyment of the Lunch Club was frequently marred by such surprises; and not knowing her own value to the other ladies as a mirror for their mental complacency she was sometimes troubled by a doubt of her worthiness to join in their debates. It was only the fact of having a dull sister who thought her clever that saved her from a sense of hopeless inferiority.

"Do they get married in the end?" Mrs. Roby interposed.

"They—who?" the Lunch Club collectively exclaimed.

"Why, the girl and man. It's a novel, isn't it? I always think that's the one thing that matters. If they're parted it spoils my dinner."

Mrs. Plinth and Mrs. Ballinger exchanged scandalized glances, and the latter said: "I should hardly advise you to read *The Wings of Death* in that spirit. For my part, when there are so many books one *has* to read, I wonder how any one can find time for those that are merely amusing."

"The beautiful part of it," Laura Glyde murmured, "is surely just this—that no one can tell *how The Wings of Death* ends. Osric Dane, overcome by the awful significance of her own meaning, has mercifully veiled it—perhaps even from herself—as Apelles, in representing the sacrifice of Iphigenia, veiled the face of Agamemnon."

"What's that? It is poetry?" whispered Mrs. Leveret to Mrs. Plinth, who, disdaining a definite reply, said coldly: "You should look it up. I always make it a point to look things up." Her tone added—"Though I might easily have it done for me by the footman."

"I was about to say," Miss Van Vluyck resumed, "that it must always be a question whether a book *can* instruct unless it elevates."

"Oh—" murmured Mrs. Leveret, now feeling herself hopelessly astray.

"I don't know," said Mrs. Ballinger, scenting in Miss Van Vluyck's tone a tendency to depreciate the coveted distinction of entertaining Osric Dane; "I don't know that such a question can seriously be raised as to a book which has attracted more attention among thoughtful people than any novel since *Robert Elsmere*."

"Oh, but don't you see," exclaimed Laura Glyde, "that it's just the dark hopelessness of it all—the wonderful tone scheme of black on black—that makes it such an artistic achievement? It reminded me when I read it of Prince Rupert's *manière noire* . . . the book is etched, not painted, yet one feels the color values so intensely. . . ."

"Who is *he*?" Mrs. Leveret whispered to her neighbor. "Someone she's met abroad?"

"The wonderful part of the book," Mrs. Ballinger conceded, "is that it may be looked at from so many points of view. I hear that as a study of determinism Professor Lupton ranks it with *The Data of Ethics*."

"I'm told that Osric Dane spent ten years in preparatory studies before beginning to write it," said Mrs. Plinth. "She looks up everything—verifies everything. It has always been my principle, as you know. Nothing would induce me, now, to put aside a book before I'd finished it, just because I can buy as many more as I want."

"And what do *you* think of *The Wings of Death*?" Mrs. Roby abruptly asked her.

It was the kind of question that might be termed out of order, and the ladies glanced at each other as though disclaiming any share in such a breach of discipline. They all knew there was nothing Mrs. Plinth so much disliked as being asked her opinion of a book. Books were written to read; if one read them what more could be expected? To be questioned in detail regarding the contents of a volume seemed to her as great an outrage as being searched for smuggled laces at the Custom House. The club had always respected this idiosyncrasy of Mrs. Plinth's. Such opinions as she had were imposing and substantial: her mind, like her house, was furnished with monumental "pieces" that were not meant to be disarranged; and it was one of the unwritten rules of the Lunch Club that, within her own province, each member's habits of thought should be respected. The meeting therefore closed with an increased sense, on the part of the other ladies, of Mrs. Roby's hopeless unfitness to be one of them.

✣ II ✣

MRS. LEVERET, on the eventful day, arrived early at Mrs. Ballinger's, her volume of *Appropriate Allusions* in her pocket.

It always flustered Mrs. Leveret to be late at the Lunch Club: she liked to collect her thoughts and gather a hint, as the others assembled, of the turn the conversation was likely to take. Today, however, she felt herself completely at a loss; and even the familiar contact of *Appropriate Allusions*, which stuck into her as she sat down, failed to give her any reassurance. It was an admirable little volume, compiled to meet all the social emergencies; so that, whether on the occasion of Anniversaries, joyful or melancholy (as the classification ran), of Banquets, social or municipal, or of Baptisms, Church of England or sectarian, its student need never be at a loss for a pertinent reference. Mrs. Leveret, though she had for years devoutly conned its pages, valued it, however, rather for its moral support than for its practical services; for though in the privacy of her own room she commanded an army of quotations, these invariably deserted her at the critical moment, and the only phrase she retained—*Canst thou draw out leviathan with a hook?*—was one she had never yet found occasion to apply.

Today she felt that even the complete mastery of the

volume would hardly have insured her self-possession; for she thought it probable that, even if she *did*, in some miraculous way, remember an Allusion, it would be only to find that Osric Dane used a different volume (Mrs. Leveret was convinced that literary people always carried them), and would consequently not recognize her quotations.

Mrs. Leveret's sense of being adrift was intensified by the appearance of Mrs. Ballinger's drawing room. To a careless eye its aspect was unchanged; but those acquainted with Mrs. Ballinger's way of arranging her books would instantly have detected the marks of recent perturbation. Mrs. Ballinger's province, as a member of the Lunch Club, was the Book of the Day. On that, whatever it was, from a novel to a treatise on experimental psychology, she was confidently, authoritatively "up." What became of last year's books, or last week's even; what she did with the "subjects" she had previously professed with equal authority; no one had ever yet discovered. Her mind was an hotel where facts came and went like transient lodgers, without leaving their address behind, and frequently without paying for their board. It was Mrs. Ballinger's boast that she was "abreast with the Thought of the Day," and her pride that this advanced position should be expressed by the books on her table. These volumes, frequently renewed, and almost always damp from the press, bore names generally unfamiliar to Mrs. Leveret, and giving her, as she furtively scanned them, a disheartening glimpse of new fields of knowledge to be breathlessly traversed in Mrs. Ballinger's wake. But today a number of maturer-looking volumes were adroitly mingled with the *primeurs* of the press—Karl Marx jostled Professor Bergson, and the *Confessions of St. Augustine* lay beside the last work on "Mendelism"; so that even to Mrs. Leveret's fluttered perceptions it was clear that Mrs. Ballinger didn't in the least know what Osric Dane was likely to talk about, and had taken measures to be prepared for anything. Mrs. Leveret felt like a passenger on an ocean steamer who is told that there is no immediate danger, but that she had better put on her lifebelt.

It was a relief to be roused from these forebodings by Miss Van Vluyck's arrival.

"Well, my dear," the newcomer briskly asked her hostess, "what subjects are we to discuss today?"

Mrs. Ballinger was furtively replacing a volume of Wordsworth by a copy of Verlaine. "I hardly know," she said, somewhat nervously. "Perhaps we had better leave that to circumstances."

"Circumstances?" said Miss Van Vluyck drily. "That means, I suppose, that Laura Glyde will take the floor as usual, and we shall be deluged with literature."

Philanthropy and statistics were Miss Van Vluyck's province, and she resented any tendency to divert their guest's attention from these topics.

Mrs. Plinth at this moment appeared.

"Literature?" she protested in a tone of remonstrance. "But this is perfectly unexpected. I understood we were to talk of Osric Dane's novel."

Mrs. Ballinger winced at the discrimination, but let it pass. "We can hardly make that our chief subject—at least not *too* intentionally," she suggested. "Of course we can let our talk *drift* in that direction; but we ought to have some other topic as an introduction, and that is what I wanted to consult you about. The fact is, we know so little of Osric Dane's taste and interests that it is difficult to make any special preparation."

"It may be difficult," said Mrs. Plinth with decision, "but it is necessary. I know what that happy-go-lucky principle leads to. As I told one of my nieces the other day, there are certain emergencies for which a lady should always be prepared. It's in shocking taste to wear colors when one pays a visit of condolence, or a last year's dress when there are reports that one's husband is on the wrong side of the market; and so it is with conversation. All I ask is that I should know beforehand what is to be talked about; then I feel sure of being able to say the proper thing."

"I quite agree with you," Mrs. Ballinger assented; "but—"

And at that instant, heralded by the fluttered parlormaid, Osric Dane appeared upon the threshold.

Mrs. Leveret told her sister afterward that she had known at a glance what was coming. She saw that Osric Dane was not going to meet them halfway. That distinguished personage had indeed entered with an air of compulsion not calculated to promote the easy exercise of hospitality. She looked as though she were about to be photographed for a new edition of her books.

The desire to propitiate a divinity is generally in inverse ratio to its responsiveness, and the sense of discouragement produced by Osric Dane's entrance visibly increased the Lunch Club's eagerness to please her. Any lingering idea that she might consider herself under an obligation to her entertainers was at once dispelled by her manner: as Mrs. Leveret said afterward to her sister, she had a way of looking at you that made you feel as if there was something wrong with your hat. This evidence of greatness produced such an immediate impression on the ladies that a shudder of awe ran through them when Mrs. Roby, as their hostess led the great personage into the dining room, turned back to whisper to the others: "What a brute she is!"

The hour about the table did not tend to revise this verdict. It was passed by Osric Dane in the silent deglutition of Mrs. Ballinger's menu, and by the members of the club in the emission of tentative platitudes which their guest seemed to swallow as perfunctorily as the successive courses of the luncheon.

Mrs. Ballinger's reluctance to fix a topic had thrown the club into a mental disarray which increased with the return to the drawing room, where the actual business of discussion was to open. Each lady waited for the other to speak; and there was a general shock of disappointment when their hostess opened the conversation by the painfully commonplace inquiry: "Is this your first visit to Hillbridge?"

Even Mrs. Leveret was conscious that this was a bad beginning; and a vague impulse of deprecation made Miss Glyde interject: "It is a very small place indeed."

Mrs. Plinth bristled. "We have a great many representative people," she said, in the tone of one who speaks for her order.

Osric Dane turned to her. "What do they represent?" she asked.

Mrs. Plinth's constitutional dislike to being questioned was intensified by her sense of unpreparedness; and her reproachful glance passed the question on to Mrs. Ballinger.

"Why," said the lady, glancing in turn at the other members, "as a community I hope it is not too much to say that we stand for culture."

"For art—" Miss Glyde interjected.

"For art and literature," Mrs. Ballinger amended.

"And for sociology, I trust," snapped Miss Van Vluyck.

"We have a standard," said Mrs. Plinth, feeling herself suddenly secure on the vast expanse of a generalization; and Mrs. Leveret, thinking there must be room for more than one on so broad a statement, took courage to murmur: "Oh, certainly; we have a standard."

"The object of our little club," Mrs. Ballinger continued, "is to concentrate the highest tendencies of Hillbridge—to centralize and focus its intellectual effort."

This was felt to be so happy that the ladies drew an almost audible breath of relief.

"We aspire," the President went on, "to be in touch with whatever is highest in art, literature and ethics."

Osric Dane again turned to her. "What ethics?" she asked.

A tremor of apprehension encircled the room. None of the ladies required any preparation to pronounce on a question of morals; but when they were called ethics it was different. The club, when fresh from the *Encyclopedia Britannica*, the *Reader's Handbook* or Smith's *Classical Dictionary*, could deal confidently with any subject; but when taken unawares it had been known to define agnosticism as a heresy of the Early Church and Professor Froude as a distinguished histologist; and such minor members as Mrs. Leveret still secretly regarded ethics as something vaguely pagan.

Even to Mrs. Ballinger, Osric Dane's question was unsettling, and there was a general sense of gratitude when Laura Glyde leaned forward to say, with her most sympathetic accent: "You must excuse us, Mrs. Dane, for not being able, just at present, to talk of anything but *The Wings of Death*."

"Yes," said Miss Van Vluyck, with a sudden resolve to

carry the war into the enemy's camp. "We are so anxious to know the exact purpose you had in mind in writing your wonderful book."

"You will find," Mrs. Plinth interposed, "that we are not superficial readers."

"We are eager to hear from you," Miss Van Vluyck continued, "if the pessimistic tendency of the book is an expression of your own convictions or—"

"Or merely," Miss Glyde thrust in, "a somber background brushed in to throw your figures into more vivid relief. *Are* you not primarily plastic?"

"*I* have always maintained," Mrs. Ballinger interposed, "that you represent the purely objective method—"

Osric Dane helped herself critically to coffee. "How do you define objective?" she then inquired.

There was a flurried pause before Laura Glyde intensely murmured: "In reading *you* we don't define, we feel."

Osric Dane smiled. "The cerebellum," she remarked, "is not infrequently the seat of the literary emotions." And she took a second lump of sugar.

The sting that this remark was vaguely felt to conceal was almost neutralized by the satisfaction of being addressed in such technical language.

"Ah, the cerebellum," said Mrs. Van Vluyck complacently. "The club took a course in psychology last winter."

"Which psychology?" asked Osric Dane.

There was an agonizing pause, during which each member of the club secretly deplored the distressing inefficiency of the others. Only Mrs. Roby went on placidly sipping her chartreuse. At last Mrs. Ballinger said, with an attempt at a high tone: "Well, really, you know, it was last year that we took psychology, and this winter we have been so absorbed in—"

She broke off, nervously trying to recall some of the club's discussions; but her faculties seemed to be paralyzed by the petrifying stare of Osric Dane. What *had* the club been absorbed in? Mrs. Ballinger, with a vague purpose of gaining time, repeated slowly: "We've been so intensely absorbed in— "

Mrs. Roby put down her liqueur glass and drew near the group with a smile.

"In Xingu?" she gently prompted.

A thrill ran through the other members. They exchanged confused glances, and then, with one accord, turned a gaze of mingled relief and interrogation on their rescuer. The expression of each denoted a different phase of the same emotion. Mrs. Plinth was the first to compose her features to an air of reassurance: after a moment's hasty adjustment her look almost implied that it was she who had given the word to Mrs. Ballinger.

"Xingu, of course!" exclaimed the latter with her accustomed promptness, while Miss Van Vluyck and Laura Glyde seemed to be plumbing the depths of memory, and Mrs. Leveret, feeling apprehensively for *Appropriate Allusions*, was somehow reassured by the uncomfortable pressure of its bulk against her person.

Osric Dane's change of countenance was no less striking than that of her entertainers. She too put down her coffee cup, but with a look of distinct annoyance; she too wore, for a brief moment, what Mrs. Roby afterward described as the look of feeling for something in the back of her head; and before she could dissemble these momentary signs of weakness, Mrs. Roby, turning to her with a deferential smile, had said: "And we've been so hoping that today you would tell us just what you think of it."

Osric Dane received the homage of the smile as a matter of course; but the accompanying question obviously embarrassed her, and it became clear to her observers that she was not quick at shifting her facial scenery. It was as though her countenance had so long been set in an expression of unchallenged superiority that the muscles had stiffened, and refused to obey her orders.

"Xingu—" she said, as if seeking in her turn to gain time.

Mrs. Roby continued to press her. "Knowing how engrossing the subject is, you will understand how it happens that the club has let everything else go to the wall for the moment. Since we took up Xingu I might almost say—were it not for your books—that nothing else seems to us worth remembering."

Osric Dane's stern features were darkened rather than lit up by an uneasy smile. "I am glad to hear that you make one exception," she gave out between narrowed lips.

"Oh, of course," Mrs. Roby said prettily; "but as you have shown us that—so very naturally!—you don't care to talk of your own things, we really can't let you off from telling us exactly what you think about Xingu; especially," she added, with a still more persuasive smile, "as some people say that one of your last books was saturated with it."

It was an *it*, then—the assurance sped like fire through the parched minds of the other members. In their eagerness to gain the least little clue to Xingu they almost forgot the joy of assisting at the discomfiture of Mrs. Dane.

The latter reddened nervously under her antagonist's challenge. "May I ask," she faltered out, "to which of my books you refer?"

Mrs. Roby did not falter. "That's just what I want you to tell us; because, though I was present, I didn't actually take part."

"Present at what?" Mrs. Dane took her up; and for an instant the trembling members of the Lunch Club thought that the champion Providence had raised up for them had lost a point. But Mrs. Roby explained herself gaily: "At the discussion, of course. And so we're dreadfully anxious to know just how it was that you went into the Xingu."

There was a portentous pause, a silence so big with incalculable dangers that the members with one accord checked the words on their lips, like soldiers dropping their arms to watch a single combat between their leaders. Then Mrs. Dane gave expression to their inmost dread by saying sharply: "Ah—you say *the* Xingu, do you?"

Mrs. Roby smiled undauntedly. "It *is* a shade pedantic, isn't it? Personally, I always drop the article: but I don't know how the other members feel about it."

The other members looked as though they would willingly have dispensed with this appeal to their opinion, and Mrs. Roby, after a bright glance about the group, went on: "They probably think, as I do, that nothing really matters except the thing itself—except Xingu."

No immediate reply seemed to occur to Mrs. Dane, and Mrs. Ballinger gathered courage to say: "Surely everyone must feel that about Xingu."

Mrs. Plinth came to her support with a heavy murmur of assent, and Laura Glyde sighed out emotionally: "I have known cases where it has changed a whole life."

"It has done me worlds of good," Mrs. Leveret interjected, seeming to herself to remember that she had either taken it or read it the winter before.

"Of course," Mrs. Roby admitted, "the difficulty is that one must give up so much time to it. It's very long."

"I can't imagine," said Miss Van Vluyck, "grudging the time given to such a subject."

"And deep in places," Mrs. Roby pursued; (so then it was a book!) "And it isn't easy to skip."

"I never skip," said Mrs. Plinth dogmatically.

"Ah, it's dangerous to, in Xingu. Even at the start there are places where one can't. One must just wade through."

"I should hardly call it *wading*," said Mrs. Ballinger sarcastically.

Mrs. Roby sent her a look of interest. "Ah—you always found it went swimmingly?"

Mrs. Ballinger hesitated. "Of course there are difficult passages," she conceded.

"Yes; some are not at all clear—even," Mrs. Roby added, "if one is familiar with the original."

"As I suppose you are?" Osric Dane interposed, suddenly fixing her with a look of challenge.

Mrs. Roby met it by a deprecating gesture. "Oh, it's really not difficult up to a certain point; though some of the branches are very little known, and it's almost impossible to get at the source."

"Have you ever tried?" Mrs. Plinth inquired, still distrustful of Mrs. Roby's thoroughness.

Mrs. Roby was silent for a moment; then she replied with lowered lids: "No—but a friend of mine did; a very brilliant man; and he told me it was best for women—not to. . . ."

A shudder ran around the room. Mrs. Leveret coughed so that the parlormaid, who was handing the cigarettes, should not hear; Miss Van Vluyck's face took on a nauseated expression, and Mrs. Plinth looked as if she were passing someone she did not care to bow to. But the most remarkable result of Mrs. Roby's words was the effect they produced on the Lunch Club's distinguished guest. Osric Dane's impassive features suddenly softened to an expression of the warmest human sympathy, and edging her chair toward Mrs. Roby's she asked: "Did he really? And—did you find he was right?"

Mrs. Ballinger, in whom annoyance at Mrs. Roby's unwonted assumption of prominence was beginning to displace gratitude for the aid she had rendered, could not consent to her being allowed, by such dubious means, to monopolize the attention of their guest. If Osric Dane had not enough self-respect to resent Mrs. Roby's flippancy, at least the Lunch Club would do so in the person of its President.

Mrs. Ballinger laid her hand on Mrs. Roby's arm. "We must not forget," she said with a frigid amiability, "that absorbing as Xingu is to *us*, it may be less interesting to—"

"Oh, no, on the contrary, I assure you," Osric Dane intervened.

"—to others," Mrs. Ballinger finished firmly; "and we must not allow our little meeting to end without persuading Mrs. Dane to say a few words to us on a subject which, today, is much more present in all our thoughts. I refer, of course, to *The Wings of Death*."

The other members, animated by various degrees of the same sentiment, and encouraged by the humanized mien of their redoubtable guest, repeated after Mrs. Ballinger: "Oh, yes, you really *must* talk to us a little about your book."

Osric Dane's expression became as bored, though not as haughty, as when her work had been previously mentioned. But before she could respond to Mrs. Ballinger's request, Mrs. Roby had risen from her seat, and was pulling down her veil over her frivolous nose.

"I'm so sorry," she said, advancing toward her hostess with out-stretched hand, "but before Mrs. Dane begins I think I'd better run away. Unluckily, as you know, I haven't read her books, so I should be at a terrible disadvantage among you all, and besides, I've an engagement to play bridge."

If Mrs. Roby had simply pleaded her ignorance of Osric Dane's works as a reason for withdrawing, the Lunch Club, in view of her recent prowess, might have approved such evidence of discretion; but to couple this excuse with the brazen announcement that she was foregoing the privilege for the purpose of joining a bridge party was only one more instance of her deplorable lack of discrimination.

The ladies were disposed, however, to feel that her departure— now that she had performed the sole service she was ever likely to render them—would probably make for greater order and dignity in the impending discussion, besides relieving them of the sense of self-distrust which her presence always mysteriously produced. Mrs. Ballinger therefore restricted herself to a formal murmur of regret, and the other members were just grouping themselves comfortably about Osric Dane when the latter, to their dismay, started up from the sofa on which she had been seated.

"Oh wait—do wait, and I'll go with you!" she called out to Mrs. Roby; and, seizing the hands of the disconcerted members, she administered a series of farewell pressures with the mechanical haste of a railway conductor punching tickets.

"I'm so sorry—I'd quite forgotten—" she flung back at them from the threshold; and as she joined Mrs. Roby, who had turned in surprise at her appeal, the other ladies had the mortification of hearing her say, in a voice which she did not take the pains to lower: "If you'll let me walk a little way with you, I should so like to ask you a few more questions about Xingu. . . ."

❄ III ❄

THE incident had been so rapid that the door closed on the departing pair before the other members had time to understand what was happening. Then a sense of the indignity put upon them by Osric Dane's unceremonious desertion began to contend with the confused feeling that they had been cheated out of their due without exactly knowing how or why.

There was a silence, during which Mrs. Ballinger, with a perfunctory hand, rearranged the skillfully grouped literature at which her distinguished guest had not so much as glanced; then Miss Van Vluyck tartly pronounced: "Well, I can't say that I consider Osric Dane's departure a great loss."

This confession crystallized the resentment of the other members, and Mrs. Leveret exclaimed: "I do believe she came on purpose to be nasty!"

It was Mrs. Plinth's private opinion that Osric Dane's attitude toward the Lunch Club might have been very different had it welcomed her in the majestic setting of the Plinth drawing rooms; but not liking to reflect on the inadequacy of Mrs. Ballinger's establishment she sought a roundabout satisfaction in deprecating her lack of foresight.

"I said from the first that we ought to have had a subject ready. It's what always happens when you're unprepared. Now if we'd only got up Xingu—"

The slowness of Mrs. Plinth's mental processes was always allowed for by the club; but this instance of it was too much for Mrs. Ballinger's equanimity.

"Xingu!" she scoffed. "Why, it was the fact of our knowing so much more about it than she did—unprepared though we were—that made Osric Dane so furious. I should have thought that was plain enough to everybody!"

This retort impressed even Mrs. Plinth, and Laura Glyde, moved by an impulse of generosity, said: "Yes, we really ought to be grateful to Mrs. Roby for introducing the topic. It may have made Osric Dane furious, but at least it made her civil."

"I am glad we were able to show her," added Miss Van Vluyck, "that a broad and up-to-date culture is not confined to the great intellectual centers."

This increased the satisfaction of the other members, and they began to forget their wrath against Osric Dane in the pleasure of having contributed to her discomfiture.

Miss Van Vluyck thoughtfully rubbed her spectacles. "What

surprised me most," she continued, "was that Fanny Roby should be so up on Xingu."

This remark threw a slight chill on the company, but Mrs. Ballinger said with an air of indulgent irony: "Mrs. Roby always has the knack of making a little go a long way; still, we certainly owe her a debt for happening to remember that she'd heard of Xingu." And this was felt by the other members to be a graceful way of canceling once and for all the club's obligation to Mrs. Roby.

Even Mrs. Leveret took courage to speed a timid shaft of irony. "I fancy Osric Dane hardly expected to take a lesson in Xingu at Hillbridge!"

Mrs. Ballinger smiled. "When she asked me what we represented— do you remember?—I wish I'd simply said we represented Xingu!"

All the ladies laughed appreciatively at this sally, except Mrs. Plinth, who said, after a moment's deliberation: "I'm not sure it would have been wise to do so."

Mrs. Ballinger, who was already beginning to feel as if she had launched at Osric Dane the retort which had just occurred to her, turned ironically on Mrs. Plinth. "May I ask why?" she inquired.

Mrs. Plinth looked grave. "Surely," she said, "I understood from Mrs. Roby herself that the subject was one it was as well not to go into too deeply?"

Miss Van Vluyck rejoined with precision: "I think that applied only to an investigation of the origin of the—of the—"; and suddenly she found that her usually accurate memory had failed her. "It's a part of the subject I never studied myself," she concluded.

"Nor I," said Mrs. Ballinger.

Laura Glyde bent toward them with widened eyes. "And yet it seems—doesn't it—the part that is fullest of an esoteric fascination?"

"I don't know on what you base that," said Miss Van Vluyck argumentatively.

"Well, didn't you notice how intensely interested Osric Dane became as soon as she heard what the brilliant foreigner—he *was* a foreigner, wasn't he—had told Mrs.

Roby about the origin—the origin of the rite—or whatever you call it?"

Mrs. Plinth looked disapproving, and Mrs. Ballinger visibly wavered. Then she said: "It may not be desirable to touch on the—on that part of the subject in general conversation; but, from the importance it evidently has to a woman of Osric Dane's distinction, I feel as if we ought not to be afraid to discuss it among ourselves—without gloves—though with closed doors, if necessary."

"I'm quite of your opinion," Miss Van Vluyck came briskly to her support; "on condition, that is, that all grossness of language is avoided."

"Oh, I'm sure we shall understand without that," Mrs. Leveret tittered; and Laura Glyde added significantly: "I fancy we can read between the lines," while Mrs. Ballinger rose to assure herself that the doors were really closed.

Mrs. Plinth had not yet given her adhesion. "I hardly see," she began, "what benefit is to be derived from investigating such peculiar customs—"

But Mrs. Ballinger's patience had reached the extreme limit of tension. "This at least," she returned; "that we shall not be placed again in the humiliating position of finding ourselves less up on our own subjects than Fanny Roby!"

Even to Mrs. Plinth this argument was conclusive. She peered furtively about the room and lowered her commanding tones to ask: "Have you got a copy?"

"A—a copy?" stammered Mrs. Ballinger. She was aware that the other members were looking at her expectantly, and that this answer was inadequate, so she supported it by asking another question. "A copy of what?"

Her companions bent their expectant gaze on Mrs. Plinth, who, in turn, appeared less sure of herself than usual. "Why, of—of—the book," she explained.

"What book?" snapped Miss Van Vluyck, almost as sharply as Osric Dane.

Mrs. Ballinger looked at Laura Glyde, whose eyes were interrogatively fixed on Mrs. Leveret. The fact of being deferred to was so new to the latter that it filled her with an insane temerity. "Why, Xingu, of course!" she exclaimed.

A profound silence followed this challenge to the resources of Mrs. Ballinger's library, and the latter, after glancing nervously toward the Books of the Day, returned with dignity: "It's not a thing one cares to leave about."

"I should think *not!*" exclaimed Mrs. Plinth.

"It *is* a book, then?" said Miss Van Vluyck.

This again threw the company into disarray, and Mrs. Ballinger, with an impatient sigh, rejoined: "Why—there *is* a book—naturally. . . ."

"Then why did Miss Glyde call it a religion?"

Laura Glyde started up. "A religion? I never—"

"Yes, you did," Miss Van Vluyck insisted; "you spoke of rites; and Mrs. Plinth said it was a custom."

Miss Glyde was evidently making a desperate effort to recall her statement; but accuracy of detail was not her strongest point. At length she began in a deep murmur: "Surely they use to do something of the kind at the Eleusinian mysteries—"

"Oh—" said Miss Van Vluyck, on the verge of disapproval; and Mrs. Plinth protested: "I understood there was to be no indelicacy!"

Mrs. Ballinger could not control her irritation. "Really, it is too bad that we should not be able to talk the matter over quietly among ourselves. Personally, I think that if one goes into Xingu at all—"

"Oh, so do I!" cried Miss Glyde.

"And I don't see how one can avoid doing so, if one wishes to keep up with the Thought of the Day—"

Mrs. Leveret uttered an exclamation of relief. "There—that's it!" she interposed.

"What's it?" the President took her up.

"Why—it's a—a Thought: I mean a philosophy."

This seemed to bring a certain relief to Mrs. Ballinger and Laura Glyde, but Miss Van Vluyck said: "Excuse me if I tell you that you're all mistaken. Xingu happens to be a language."

"A language!" the Lunch Club cried.

"Certainly. Don't you remember Fanny Roby's saying that there were several branches, and that some were hard to trace? What could that apply to but dialects?"

Mrs. Ballinger could no longer restrain a contemptuous laugh. "Really, if the Lunch Club has reached such a pass that it has to go to Fanny Roby for instruction on a subject like Xingu, it had almost better cease to exist!"

"It's really her fault for not being clearer," Laura Glyde put in.

"Oh, clearness and Fanny Roby!" Mrs. Ballinger shrugged. "I dare say we shall find she was mistaken on almost every point."

"Why not look it up?" said Mrs. Plinth.

As a rule this recurrent suggestion of Mrs. Plinth's was ignored in the heat of discussion, and only resorted to afterward in the privacy of each member's home. But on the present occasion the desire to ascribe their own confusion of thought to the vague and contradictory nature of Mrs. Roby's statements caused the members of the Lunch Club to utter a collective demand for a book of reference.

At this point the production of her treasured volume gave Mrs. Leveret, for a moment, the unusual experience of occupying the center front; but she was not able to hold it long, for *Appropriate Allusions* contained no mention of Xingu.

"Oh, that's not the kind of thing we want!" exclaimed Miss Van Vluyck. She cast a disparaging glance over Mrs. Ballinger's assortment of literature, and added impatiently: "Haven't you any useful books?"

"Of course I have," replied Mrs. Ballinger indignantly; "I keep them in my husband's dressing room."

From this region, after some difficulty and delay, the parlormaid produced the W-Z volume of an *Encyclopedia* and, in deference to the fact that the demand for it had come from Miss Van Vluyck, laid the ponderous tome before her.

There was a moment of painful suspense while Miss Van Vluyck rubbed her spectacles, adjusted them, and turned to Z; and a murmur of surprise when she said: "It isn't here."

"I suppose," said Mrs. Plinth, "it's not fit to be put in a book of reference."

"Oh, nonsense!" exclaimed Mrs. Ballinger. "Try X."

Miss Van Vluyck turned back through the volume, peering short-sightedly up and down the pages, till she came to a stop and remained motionless, like a dog on a point.

"Well, have you found it?" Mrs. Ballinger inquired after a considerable delay.

"Yes. I've found it," said Miss Van Vluyck in a queer voice.

Mrs. Plinth hastily interposed: "I beg you won't read it aloud if there's anything offensive."

Miss Van Vluyck, without answering, continued her silent scrutiny.

"Well, what *is* it?" exclaimed Laura Glyde excitedly.

"*Do* tell us!" urged Mrs. Leveret, feeling that she would have something awful to tell her sister.

Miss Van Vluyck pushed the volume aside and turned slowly toward the expectant group.

"It's a river."

"A *river*?"

"Yes: in Brazil. Isn't that where she's been living?"

"Who? Fanny Roby? Oh, but you must be mistaken. You've been reading the wrong thing," Mrs. Ballinger exclaimed, leaning over her to seize the volume.

"It's the only Xingu in the *Encyclopedia*; and she *has* been living in Brazil," Miss Van Vluyck persisted.

"Yes: her brother has a consulship there," Mrs. Leveret interposed.

"But it's too ridiculous! I—we—why we *all* remember studying Xingu last year—or the year before last," Mrs. Ballinger stammered.

"I thought I did when *you* said so," Laura Glyde avowed.

"*I* said so?" cried Ballinger.

"Yes. You said it had crowded everything else out of your mind."

"Well *you* said it had changed your whole life!"

"For that matter Miss Van Vluyck said she had never grudged the time she'd given it."

Mrs. Plinth interposed: "I made it clear that I knew nothing whatever of the original."

Mrs. Ballinger broke off the dispute with a groan. "Oh, what does it all matter if she's been making fools of us? I believe Miss Van Vluyck's right—she was talking of the river all the while!"

"How could she? It's too preposterous," Miss Glyde exclaimed.

"Listen." Miss Van Vluyck had repossessed herself of the Encyclopedia, and restored her spectacles to a nose reddened by excitement. " 'The Xingu, one of the principal rivers of Brazil, rises on the plateau of Mato Grosso, and flows in a northerly direction for a length of no less than one-thousand one-hundred eighteen miles, entering the Amazon near the mouth of the latter river. The upper course of the Xingu is auriferous and fed by numerous branches. Its source was first discovered in 1884 by the German explorer von den Steinen, after a difficult and dangerous expedition through a region inhabited by tribes still in the Stone Age of culture.' "

The ladies received this communication in a state of stupefied silence from which Mrs. Leveret was the first to rally. "She certainly *did* speak of its having branches."

The word seemed to snap the last thread of their incredulity. "And of its great length," gasped Mrs. Ballinger.

"She said it was awfully deep, and you couldn't skip—you just had to wade through," Miss Glyde added.

The idea worked its way more slowly through Mrs. Plinth's compact resistances. "How could there by anything improper about a river?" she inquired.

"Improper?"

"Why, what she said about the source—that it was corrupt?"

"Not corrupt, but hard to get at," Laura Glyde corrected. "Someone who'd been there had told her so. I dare say it was the explorer himself—doesn't it say the expedition was dangerous?"

" 'Difficult and dangerous,' " read Miss Van Vluyck.

Mrs. Ballinger pressed her hands to her throbbing temples. "There's nothing she said that wouldn't apply to a river—to this river!" She swung about excitedly to the other members. "Why, do you remember her telling us that she hadn't read *The Supreme Instant* because she'd taken it on a boating party while she was staying with her brother, and someone had 'shied' it overboard—'shied' of course was her own expression."

The ladies breathlessly signified that the expression had not escaped them.

"Well—and then didn't she tell Osric Dane that one of her books was simply saturated with Xingu? Of course it was, if one of Mrs. Roby's rowdy friends had thrown it into the river!"

This surprising reconstruction of the scene in which they had just participated left the members of the Lunch Club inarticulate. At length, Mrs. Plinth, after visibly laboring with the problem, said in a heavy tone: "Osric Dane was taken in too."

Mrs. Leveret took courage at this. "Perhaps that's what Mrs. Roby did it for. She said Osric Dane was a brute, and she may have wanted to give her a lesson."

Miss Van Vluyck frowned. "It was hardly worthwhile to do it at our expense."

"At least," said Miss Glyde with a touch of bitterness, "she succeeded in interesting her, which was more than we did."

"What chance had we?" rejoined Mrs. Ballinger. "Mrs. Roby monopolized her from the first. And *that*, I've no doubt, was her purpose—to give Osric Dane a false impression of her own standing in the club. She would hesitate at nothing to attract attention: we all know how she took in poor Professor Foreland."

"She actually makes him give bridge teas every Thursday," Mrs. Leveret piped up.

Laura Glyde struck her hands together. "Why, this is Thursday, and it's *there* she's gone, of course; and taken Osric with her!"

"And they're shrieking over us at this moment," said Mrs. Ballinger between her teeth.

This possibility seemed too preposterous to be admitted. "She would hardly dare," said Miss Van Vluyck, "confess the imposture to Osric Dane."

"I'm not so sure: I thought I saw her make a sign as she left. If she hadn't made a sign, why should Osric Dane have rushed out after her?"

"Well, you know, we'd all been telling her how wonderful Xingu was, and she said she wanted to find out more about it," Mrs. Leveret said, with a tardy impulse of justice to the absent.

This reminder, far from mitigating the wrath of the other members, gave it a stronger impetus.

"Yes—and that's exactly what they're both laughing over now," said Laura Glyde ironically.

Mrs. Plinth stood up and gathered her expensive furs about her monumental form. "I have no wish to criticize," she said; "but unless the Lunch Club can protect its members against the recurrence of such—such unbecoming scenes, I for one—"

"Oh, so do I!" agreed Miss Glyde, rising also.

Miss Van Vluyck closed the Encyclopedia and proceeded to button herself into her jacket. "My time is really too valuable—" she began.

"I fancy we are all of one mind," said Mrs. Ballinger, looking searchingly at Mrs. Leveret, who looked at the others.

"I always deprecate anything like a scandal—" Mrs. Plinth continued.

"She has been the cause of one today!" exclaimed Miss Clyde.

Mrs. Leveret moaned: "I don't see how she *could!*" and Miss Van Vluyck said, picking up her notebook: "Some women stop at nothing."

"—But if," Mrs. Plinth took up her argument impressively, "anything of the kind had happened in *my* house" (it never would have, her tone implied), "I should have felt that I owed it to myself either to ask for Mrs. Roby's resignation—or to offer mine."

"Oh, Mrs. Plinth—" gasped the Lunch Club.

"Fortunately for me," Mrs. Plinth continued with an awful magnanimity, "the matter was taken out of my hands by our President's decision that the right to entertain distinguished guests was a privilege vested in her office; and I think the other members will agree that, as she was alone in this opinion, she ought to be alone in deciding on the best way of effacing its—its really deplorable consequences."

A deep silence followed this outbreak of Mrs. Plinth's long-stored resentment.

"I don't see why *I* should be expected to ask her to resign—" Mrs. Ballinger at length began; but Laura Glyde turned back to remind her: "You know she made you say that you'd got on swimmingly in Xingu."

An ill-timed giggle escaped from Mrs. Leveret, and Mrs. Ballinger energetically continued "—But you needn't think for a moment that I'm afraid to!"

The door of the drawing room closed on the retreating backs of the Lunch Club, and the President of that distinguished association, seating herself at her writing table, and pushing away a copy of *The Wings of Death* to make room for her elbow, drew forth a sheet of the club's notepaper, on which she began to write: "My dear Mrs. Roby—"

Autres Temps . . .

MRS. LIDCOTE, as the huge menacing mass of New York defined itself far off across the waters, shrank back into her corner of the deck and sat listening with a kind of unreasoning terror to the steady onward drive of the screws.

She had set out on the voyage quietly enough—in what she called her "reasonable" mood—but the week at sea had given her too much time to think of things and had left her too long alone with the past.

When she was alone, it was always the past that occupied her. She couldn't get away from it, and she didn't any longer care to. During her long years of exile she had made her terms with it, had learned to accept the fact that it would always be there, huge, obstructing, encumbering, bigger and more dominant than anything the future could ever conjure up. And, at any rate, she was sure of it, she understood it, knew how to reckon with it; she had learned to screen and manage and protect it as one does an afflicted member of one's family.

There had never been any danger of her being allowed to forget the past. It looked out at her from the face of every acquaintance, it appeared suddenly in the eyes of strangers when a word enlightened them: "Yes, *the* Mrs. Lidcote, don't you know?" It had sprung at her the first day out, when, across the dining room, from the captain's table, she had seen Mrs. Lorin Boulger's revolving eyeglass pause and the eye behind it grow as blank as a dropped blind. The next day, of course, the captain had asked: "You know your ambassadress, Mrs. Boulger?" and she had replied that, No, she seldom left Florence, and hadn't been to Rome for more than a day since the Boulgers had been sent to Italy. She was so used to these phrases that it cost her no effort to repeat them. And the captain had promptly changed the subject.

No, she didn't, as a rule, mind the past, because she was used to it and understood it. It was a great concrete fact in her path that she had to walk around every time she moved in any direction. But now, in the light of the unhappy event that had summoned her from Italy,—the sudden unanticipated news of her daughter's divorce from Horace Pursh and remarriage with Wilbour Barkley—the past, her own poor miserable past, stared up at her with eyes of accusation, became, to her disordered fancy, like the afflicted relative suddenly breaking away from nurses and keepers and publicly parading the horror and misery she had, all the long years, so patiently screened and secluded.

Yes, there it had stood before her through the agitated weeks since the news had come—during her interminable journey from India, where Leila's letter had overtaken her, and the feverish halt in her apartment in Florence, where she had had to stop and gather up her possessions for a fresh start—there it had stood grinning at her with a new balefulness which seemed to say: "Oh, but you've got to look at me *now*, because I'm not only your past but Leila's present."

Certainly it was a master stroke of those arch-ironists of the shears and spindle to duplicate her own story in her daughter's. Mrs. Lidcote had always somewhat grimly fancied that, having so signally failed to be of use to Leila in other ways, she would at least serve her as a warning. She had even abstained from defending herself, from making the best of her case, had stoically refused to plead extenuating circumstances, lest Leila's impulsive sympathy should lead to deductions that might react disastrously on her own life. And now that very thing had happened, and Mrs. Lidcote could hear the whole of New York saying with one voice: "Yes, Leila's done just what her mother did. With such an example what could you expect?"

Yet if she had been an example, poor woman, she had been an awful one; she had been, she would have supposed, of more use as a deterrent than a hundred blameless mothers as incentives. For how could anyone who had seen anything of her life in the last eighteen years have had the courage to repeat so disastrous an experiment?

Well, logic in such cases didn't count, example didn't count, nothing probably counted but having the same impulses in the blood; and that was the dark inheritance she had bestowed upon her daughter. Leila hadn't consciously copied her; she had simply "taken after" her, had been a projection of her own long-past rebellion.

Mrs. Lidcote had deplored, when she started, that the "Utopia" was a slow steamer, and would take eight full days to bring her to her unhappy daughter; but now, as the moment of reunion approached, she would willingly have turned the boat about and fled back to the high seas. It was not only because she felt so unprepared to face what New York had in store for her, but because she needed more time to dispose of what the "Utopia" had already given her. The past was bad enough, but the present and future were worse, because they were less comprehensible, and because, as she grew older, surprises and inconsequences troubled her more than the worst certainties.

There was Mrs. Boulger, for instance. In the light, or rather the darkness, of new developments, it might really be that Mrs. Boulger had not meant to cut her, but had simply failed to recognize her. Mrs. Lidcote had arrived at this hypothesis simply by listening to the conversation of the persons sitting next to her on deck—two lively young women with the latest Paris hats on their heads and the latest New York ideas in them. These ladies, as to whom it would have been impossible for a person with Mrs. Lidcote's old-fashioned categories to determine whether they were married or unmarried, "nice" or "horrid," or any one or other of the definite things which young women, in her youth and her society, were conveniently assumed to be, had revealed a familiarity with the world of New York that, again according to Mrs. Lidcote's traditions, should have implied a recognized place in it. But in the present fluid state of manners what did anything imply except what their hats implied—that no one could tell what was coming next?

They seemed, at any rate, to frequent a group of idle and opulent people who executed the same gestures and revolved on the same pivots as Mrs. Lidcote's daughter and her friends: their Coras, Matties and Mabels seemed at any moment likely to reveal familiar patronymics, and once one of the speakers, summing up a discussion of which Mrs. Lidcote had missed the beginning, had affirmed with headlong confidence: "Leila? Oh, *Leila's* all right."

Could it be *her* Leila, the mother had wondered, with a sharp thrill of apprehension? If only they would mention surnames! But their talk leaped elliptically from allusion to allusion, their unfinished sentences dangled over bottomless pits of conjecture, and they gave their bewildered hearer the impression not so much of talking only of their intimates, as of being intimate with everyone alive.

Her old friend Franklin Ide could have told her, perhaps; but here was the last day of the voyage, and she hadn't yet found courage to ask him. Great as had been the joy of discovering his name on the passenger list and seeing his friendly bearded face in the throng against the taffrail at Cherbourg, she had as yet said nothing to him except, when they had met: "Of course I'm going out to Leila."

She had said nothing to Franklin Ide because she had always instinctively shrunk from taking him into her confidence. She was sure he felt sorry for her, sorrier perhaps than anyone had ever felt; but he had always paid her the supreme tribute of not showing it. His attitude allowed her to imagine that compassion was not the basis of his feeling for her, and it was part of her joy in his friendship that it was the one relation seemingly unconditioned by her state, the only one in which she could think and feel and behave like any other woman.

Now, however, as the problem of New York loomed nearer, she began to regret that she had not spoken, had not at least questioned him about the hints she had gathered on the way. He did not know the two ladies next to her, he did not even, as it chanced, know Mrs. Lorin Boulger; but he knew New York, and New York was the sphinx whose riddle she must read or perish.

Almost as the thought passed through her mind his stooping shoulders and grizzled head detached themselves against the blaze of light in the west, and he sauntered down the empty deck and dropped into the chair at her side.

"You're expecting the Barkleys to meet you, I suppose?" he asked.

It was the first time she had heard any one pronounce her daughter's new name, and it occurred to her that her friend, who was shy and inarticulate, had been trying to say it all the way over and had at last shot it out at her only because he felt it must be now or never.

"I don't know. I cabled, of course. But I believe she's at—they're at—*his* place somewhere."

"Oh, Barkley's; yes, near Lenox, isn't it? But she's sure to come to town to meet you."

He said it so easily and naturally that her own constraint was relieved, and suddenly, before she knew what she meant to do, she had burst out: "She may dislike the idea of seeing people."

Ide, whose absent shortsighted gaze had been fixed on the slowly gliding water, turned in his seat to stare at his companion.

"Who? Leila?" he said with an incredulous laugh.

Mrs. Lidcote flushed to her faded hair and grew pale again. "It took *me* a long time—to get used to it," she said.

His look grew gently commiserating. "I think you'll find"—he paused for a word—"that things are different now—altogether easier."

"That's what I've been wondering—ever since we started." She was determined now to speak. She moved nearer, so that their arms touched, and she could drop her voice to a murmur. "You see, it all came on me in a flash. My going off to India and Siam on that long trip kept me away from letters for weeks at a time; and she didn't want to tell me beforehand—oh, I understand *that*, poor child! You know how good she's always been to me; how she's tried to spare me. And she knew, of course, what a state of horror I'd be in. She knew I'd rush off to her at once and try to stop it. So she never gave me a hint of anything, and she even managed to muzzle Susy Suffern—you know Susy is the one of the family who keeps me informed about things at home. I don't yet see how she prevented Susy's telling me; but she did. And her first letter, the one I got up at Bangkok, simply said the thing was over—the divorce, I mean—and that the very next day she'd—well, I suppose there was no use waiting; and *he* seems to have behaved as well as possible, to have wanted to marry her as much as—"

"Who? Barkley?" he helped her out. "I should say so! Why what do you suppose—" He interrupted himself. "He'll be devoted to her, I assure you."

"Oh, of course; I'm sure he will. He's written me—really beautifully. But it's a terrible strain on a man's devotion. I'm not sure that Leila realizes—"

Ide sounded again his little reassuring laugh. "I'm not sure that you realize. *They're* all right."

It was the very phrase that the young lady in the next seat had applied to the unknown "Leila," and its recurrence on Ide's lips flushed Mrs. Lidcote with fresh courage.

"I wish I knew just what you mean. The two young women next to me—the ones with the wonderful hats—have been talking in the same way."

"What? About Leila?"

"About *a* Leila; I fancied it might be mine. And about society in general. All their friends seem to be divorced; some of them seem to announce their engagements before they get their decree. One of them—*her* name was Mabel—as far as I could make out, her husband found out that she meant to divorce him by noticing that she wore a new engagement ring."

"Well, you see Leila did everything 'regularly,' as the French say," Ide rejoined.

"Yes; but are these people in society? The people my neighbors talk about?"

He shrugged his shoulders. "It would take an arbitration commission a good many sittings to define the boundaries of society nowadays. But at any rate they're in New York; and I assure you you're *not*; you're farther and farther from it."

"But I've been back there several times to see Leila." She hesitated and looked away from him. Then she brought out slowly: "And I've never noticed—the least change—in—in my own case— "

"Oh," he sounded deprecatingly, and she trembled with the fear of having gone too far. But the hour was past when such scruples could restrain her. She must know where she was and where Leila was. "Mrs. Boulger still cuts me," she brought out with an embarrassed laugh.

"Are you sure? You've probably cut *her*; if not now, at least in the past. And in a cut if you're not first you're nowhere. That's what keeps up so many quarrels."

The word roused Mrs. Lidcote to a renewed sense of realities. "But the Purshes," she said—"the Purshes are so strong! There are so many of them, and they all back each other up, just as my husband's family did. I know what it means to have a clan against one. They're stronger than any number of separate friends. The Purshes will *never* forgive Leila for leaving Horace. Why, his mother opposed his marrying her because of—of me. She tried to get Leila to promise that she wouldn't see me when they went to Europe on their honeymoon. And now she'll say it was my example."

Her companion, vaguely stroking his beard, mused a moment upon this; then he asked, with seeming irrelevance, "What did Leila say when you wrote that you were coming?"

"She said it wasn't the least necessary, but that I'd better come, because it was the only way to convince me that it wasn't."

"Well, then, that proves she's not afraid of the Purshes."

She breathed a long sigh of remembrance. "Oh, just at first, you know—one never is."

He laid his hand on hers with a gesture of intelligence and pity. "You'll see, you'll see," he said.

A shadow lengthened down the deck before them, and a steward stood there, proffering a Marconigram.

"Oh, now I shall know!" she exclaimed.

She tore the message open, and then let it fall on her knees, dropping her hands on it in silence.

Ide's inquiry roused her: "It's all right?"

"Oh, quite right. Perfectly. She can't come; but she's sending Susy Suffern. She says Susy will explain." After another silence she added, with a sudden gush of bitterness: "As if I needed any explanation!"

She felt Ide's hesitating glance upon her. "She's in the country?"

"Yes. 'Prevented last moment. Longing for you, expecting you. Love from both.' Don't you *see*, the poor darling, that she couldn't face it?"

"No, I don't." He waited. "Do you mean to go to her immediately?"

"It will be too late to catch a train this evening; but I shall take the first tomorrow morning." She considered a moment. "Perhaps it's better. I need a talk with Susy first. She's to meet me at the dock, and I'll take her straight to the hotel with me."

As she developed this plan, she had the sense that Ide was still thoughtfully, even gravely, considering her. When she ceased, he remained silent a moment; then he said almost ceremoniously: "If your talk with Miss Suffern doesn't last too late, may I come and see you when it's over? I shall be dining at my club, and I'll call you up at about ten, if I may. I'm off to Chicago on business tomorrow morning, and it would be a satisfaction to know, before I start, that your cousin's been able to reassure you, as I know she will."

He spoke with a shy deliberateness that, even to Mrs. Lidcote's troubled perceptions, sounded a long-silenced note of feeling. Perhaps the breaking down of the barrier of reticence between them had released unsuspected emotions in both. The tone of his appeal moved her curiously and loosened the tight strain of her fears.

"Oh, yes, come—do come," she said, rising. The huge threat of New York was imminent now, dwarfing, under long reaches of embattled masonry, the great deck she stood on and all the little specks of life it carried. One of them, drifting nearer, took the shape of her maid, followed by luggage-laden stewards, and signing to her that it was time to go below. As they descended to the main deck, the throng swept her against Mrs. Lorin Boulger's shoulder, and she heard the ambassadress call out to someone, over the vexed sea of hats: "So sorry! I should have been delighted, but I've promised to spend Sunday with some friends at Lenox."

❄ II ❄

SUSY SUFFERN'S explanation did not end till after ten o'clock, and she had just gone when Franklin Ide, who, complying with an old New York tradition, had caused himself to be preceded by a long white box of roses, was shown into Mrs. Lidcote's sitting room.

He came forward with his shy half-humorous smile and, taking her hand, looked at her for a moment without speaking.

"It's all right," he then pronounced.

Mrs. Lidcote returned his smile. "It's extraordinary. Everything's changed. Even Susy has changed; and you know the extent to which Susy used to represent the old New York. There's no old New York left, it seems. She talked in the most amazing way. She snaps her fingers at the Purshes. She told me—*me*, that every woman had a right to happiness and that self-expression was the highest duty. She accused me of misunderstanding Leila; she said my point of view was conventional! She was bursting with pride at having been in the secret, and wearing a brooch that Wilbour Barkley'd given her!"

Franklin Ide had seated himself in the armchair she had pushed forward for him under the electric chandelier. He threw back his head and laughed. "What did I tell you?"

"Yes; but I can't believe that Susy's not mistaken. Poor dear, she has the habit of lost causes; and she may feel that, having stuck to me, she can do no less than stick to Leila."

"But she didn't—did she—openly defy the world for you? She didn't snap her fingers at the Lidcotes?"

Mrs. Lidcote shook her head, still smiling. "No. It was enough to defy *my* family. It was doubtful at one time if they would tolerate her seeing me, and she almost had to disinfect herself after each visit. I believe that at first my sister-in-law wouldn't let the girls come down when Susy dined with her."

"Well, isn't your cousin's present attitude the best possible proof that times have changed?"

"Yes, yes; I know." She leaned forward from her sofa-corner, fixing her eyes on his thin kindly face, which gleamed on her indistinctly through her tears. "If it's true, it's—it's dazzling. She says Leila's perfectly happy. It's as if an angel had gone about lifting gravestones, and the buried people walked again, and the living didn't shrink from them."

"That's about it," he assented.

She drew a deep breath, and sat looking away from him down the long perspective of lamp-fringed streets over which her windows hung.

"I can understand how happy you must be," he began at length.

She turned to him impetuously. "Yes, yes; I'm happy. But I'm lonely, too—lonelier than ever. I didn't take up much room in the world before; but now—where is there a corner for me? Oh, since I've begun to confess myself, why shouldn't I go on? Telling you this lifts a gravestone from *me!* You see, before this, Leila needed me. She was unhappy, and I knew it, and though we hardly ever talked of it I felt that, in a way, the thought that I'd been through the same thing, and down to the dregs of it, helped her. And her needing me helped *me*. And when the news of her marriage came my first thought was that now she'd need me more than ever, that she'd have no one but me to turn to. Yes, under all my distress there was a fierce joy in that. It was so new and wonderful to feel again that there was one person who wouldn't be able to get on without me! And now what you and Susy tell me seems to have taken my child from me; and just at first that's all I can feel."

"Of course it's all you feel." He looked at her musingly. "Why didn't Leila come to meet you?"

"That was really my fault. You see, I'd cabled that I was not sure of being able to get off on the "Utopia," and apparently my second cable was delayed, and when she received it she'd already asked some people over Sunday—one or two of her old friends, Susy says. I'm so glad they should have wanted to go to her at once; but naturally I'd rather have been alone with her."

"You still mean to go, then?"

"Oh, I must. Susy wanted to drag me off to Ridgefield with her over Sunday, and Leila sent me word that of course I might go if I wanted to, and that I was not to think of her; but I know how disappointed she would be. Susy said she was afraid I might be upset at her having people to stay, and that, if I minded, she wouldn't urge me to come! But if *they* don't mind, why should I? And of course, if they're willing to go to Leila it must mean—"

"Of course. I'm glad you recognize that," Franklin Ide exclaimed abruptly. He stood up and went over to her, taking her hand with one of his quick gestures. "There's something I want to say to you," he began—

The next morning, in the train, through all the other contending thoughts in Mrs. Lidcote's mind there ran the warm undercurrent of what Franklin Ide had wanted to say to her.

He had wanted, she knew, to say it once before, when, nearly eight years earlier, the hazard of meeting at the end of a rainy autumn in a deserted Swiss hotel had thrown them for a fortnight into unwonted propinquity. They had walked and talked together, borrowed each other's books and newspapers, spent the long chill evenings over the fire in the dim lamplight of her little pitch-pine sitting room; and she had been wonderfully comforted by his presence, and hard frozen places in her had melted, and she had known that she would be desperately sorry when he went. And then, just at the end, in his odd indirect way, he had let her see that it rested with her to have him stay. She could still relive the sleepless night she had given to that discovery. It was preposterous, of course, to think of repaying his devotion by accepting such a sacrifice; but how find reasons to convince him? She could not bear to let him think her less touched, less inclined to him than she was: the generosity of his love deserved that she should repay it with the truth. Yet how let him see what she felt, and yet refuse what he offered? How confess to him what had been on her lips when he made the offer: "I've seen what it did to one man; and there must never, never be another"? The tacit ignoring of her past had been the element in which their friendship lived, and she could not suddenly, to him of all men, begin to talk of herself like a guilty woman in a play. Somehow, in the end, she had managed it, had averted a direct explanation, had made him understand that her life was over, that she existed only for her daughter, and that a more definite word from him would have been almost a breach of delicacy. She was so used to behaving as if her life were over! And, at any rate, he had taken her hint, and she had been able to spare her sensitiveness and his. The next year, when he came to Florence to see her, they met again in the old friendly way; and that till now had continued to be the tenor of their intimacy.

And now, suddenly and unexpectedly, he had brought up the question again, directly this time, and in such a form that she could not evade it: putting the renewal of his plea, after so long an interval, on the ground that, on her own showing, her chief argument against it no longer existed.

"You tell me Leila's happy. If she's happy, she doesn't need you—need you, that is, in the same way as before. You wanted, I know, to be always in reach, always free and available if she should suddenly call you to her or take refuge with you. I understood that—I respected it. I didn't urge my case because I saw it was useless. You couldn't, I understand well enough, have felt free to take such happiness as life with me might give you while she was unhappy, and, as you imagined, with no hope of release. Even then I didn't feel as you did about it; I understood better the trend of things here. But ten years ago the change hadn't really come; and I had no way of convincing you that it was coming. Still, I always fancied that Leila might not think her case was closed, and so I chose to think that ours wasn't either. Let me go on thinking so, at any rate, till you've seen her, and confirmed with your own eyes what Susy Suffern tells you."

❄ III ❄

ALL through what Susy Suffern told and retold her during their four-hours' flight to the hills this plea of Ide's kept coming back to Mrs. Lidcote. She did not yet know what she felt as to its bearing on her own fate, but it was something on which her confused thoughts could stay themselves amid the welter of new impressions, and she was inexpressibly glad that he had said what he had, and said it at that particular moment. It helped her to hold fast to her identity in the rush of strange names and new categories that her cousin's talk poured out on her.

With the progress of the journey Miss Suffern's communications grew more and more amazing. She was like a cicerone preparing the mind of an inexperienced traveler for the marvels about to burst on it.

"You won't know Leila. She's had her pearls reset. Sargent's to paint her. Oh, and I was to tell you that she hopes you won't mind being the least bit squeezed over Sunday. The house was built by Wilbour's father, you know, and it's rather old-fashioned—only ten spare bedrooms. Of course that's small for what they mean to do, and she'll show you the new plans they've had made. Their idea is to keep the present house as a wing. She told me to explain—she's so dreadfully sorry not to be able to give you a sitting room just at first. They're thinking of Egypt for next winter, unless, of course, Wilbour gets his appointment. Oh, didn't she write you about that? Why, he wants Rome, you know—the second secretaryship. Or, rather, he wanted England; but Leila insisted that if they went abroad she must be near you. And of course what she says is law. Oh, they quite hope they'll get it. You see Horace's uncle is in the Cabinet—one of the assistant secretaries—and I believe he has a good deal of pull—"

"Horace's uncle? You mean Wilbour's, I suppose," Mrs. Lidcote interjected, with a gasp of which a fraction was given to Miss Suffern's flippant use of the language.

"Wilbour's? No, I don't. I mean Horace's. There's no bad feeling between them, I assure you. Since Horace's engagement was announced—you didn't know Horace was engaged? Why, he's marrying one of Bishop Thorbury's girls: the red-haired one who wrote the novel that everyone's talking about. *This Flesh of Mine*. They're to be married in the cathedral. Of course Horace *can*, because it was Leila who—but, as I say, there's not the *least* feeling, and Horace wrote himself to his uncle about Wilbour."

Mrs. Lidcote's thoughts fled back to what she had said to Ide the day before on the deck of the "Utopia." "I didn't take up much room before, but now where is there a corner for me?" Where indeed in this crowded, topsy-turvy world, with its headlong changes, and helter-skelter readjustments, its new tolerances and indifferences and accommodations, was there room for a character fashioned by slower sterner processes and a life broken under their inexorable pressure? And then, in a flash, she viewed the chaos from a new angle, and order seemed to move upon the void. If the old processes were changed, her case was changed with them; she, too, was a part of the general readjustment, a tiny fragment of the new pattern worked out in bolder freer harmonies. Since her daughter had no penalty to pay, was not she herself released by the same stroke? The rich arrears of youth and joy were gone; but was there not time enough left to accumulate new stores of happiness? That, of course, was what Franklin Ide had felt and had meant her to feel. He had seen at once what the change in her daughter's situation would make in her view of her own. It was almost—wondrously enough!—as if Leila's folly had been the means of vindicating hers.

Everything else for the moment faded for Mrs. Lidcote in the glow of her daughter's embrace. It was unnatural, it was almost terrifying, to find herself standing on a strange threshold, under an unknown roof, in a big hall full of pictures, flowers, firelight, and hurrying servants, and in this spacious unfamiliar confusion to discover Leila, bareheaded, laughing, authoritative, with a strange young man jovially echoing her welcome and transmitting her orders; but once Mrs. Lidcote had her child on her breast, and her child's "It's all right, you old darling!" in her ears, every other feeling was lost in the deep sense of well-being that only Leila's hug could give.

The sense was still with her, warming her veins and pleasantly fluttering her heart, as she went up to her room after luncheon. A little constrained by the presence of visitors, and not altogether sorry to defer for a few hours the "long talk" with her daughter for which she somehow felt herself tremulously unready, she had withdrawn, on the plea of fatigue, to the bright luxurious bedroom into which Leila had again and again apologized for having been obliged to squeeze her. The room was bigger and finer than any in her small apartment in Florence; but it was not the standard of affluence implied in her daughter's tone about it that chiefly struck her, nor yet the finish and complexity of its appointments. It was the look it shared with the rest of the house, and with the perspective of the gardens beneath its windows, of being part of an "establishment"—of something solid, avowed, founded on sacraments and precedents and principles. There was nothing about the place, or about Leila and Wilbour, that suggested either passion or peril: their relation seemed as comfortable as their furniture and as respectable as their balance at the bank.

This was, in the whole confusing experience, the thing that confused Mrs. Lidcote most, that gave her at once the deepest feeling of security for Leila and the strongest sense of apprehension for herself. Yes, there was something oppressive in the completeness and compactness of Leila's well-being. Ide had been right: her daughter did not need her. Leila, with her first embrace, had unconsciously attested the fact in the same phrase as Ide himself and as the two young women with the hats. "It's all right, you old darling!" she had said: and her mother sat alone, trying to fit herself into the new scheme of things which such a certainty betokened.

Her first distinct feeling was one of irrational resentment. If such a change was to come, why had it not come sooner? Here was she, a woman not yet old, who had paid with the best years of her life for the theft of the happiness that her daughter's contemporaries were taking as their due. There was no sense, no sequence, in it. She had had what she wanted, but she had had to pay too much for it. She had had to pay the last bitterest price of learning that love has a price: that it is worth so much and no more. She had known the anguish of watching the man she loved discover this first, and of reading the discovery in his eyes. It was a part of her history that she had not trusted herself to think of for a long time past: she always took a big turn about that haunted corner. But now, at the sight of the young man downstairs, so openly and jovially Leila's, she was overwhelmed at the senseless waste of her own adventure, and wrung with the irony of perceiving that the success or failure of the deepest human experiences may hang on a matter of chronology.

Then gradually the thought of Ide returned to her. "I chose to think that our case wasn't closed," he had said. She had been deeply touched by that. To everyone else her case had been closed so long! *Finis* was scrawled all over her. But here was one man who had believed and waited, and what if what he believed in and waited for were coming true? If Leila's "all right" should really foreshadow hers?

As yet, of course, it was impossible to tell. She had fancied, indeed, when she entered the drawing room before luncheon, that a too-sudden hush had fallen on the assembled group of Leila's friends, on the slender vociferous young women and the lounging golf-stockinged young men. They had all received her politely, with the kind of petrified politeness that may be either a tribute to age or a protest at laxity; but to them, of course, she must be an old woman because she was Leila's mother, and in a society so dominated by youth the mere presence of maturity was a constraint.

One of the young girls, however, had presently emerged from the group, and, attaching herself to Mrs. Lidcote, had listened to her with a blue gaze of admiration which gave the older woman a sudden happy consciousness of her long-forgotten social graces. It was agreeable to find herself attracting this young Charlotte Wynn, whose mother had been among her closest friends, and in whom something of the soberness and softness of the earlier manners had survived. But the little colloquy, broken up by the announcement of luncheon, could of course result in nothing more definite than this reminiscent emotion.

No, she could not yet tell how her own case was to be fitted into the new order of things; but there were more people—"older people" Leila had put it—arriving by the afternoon train, and that evening at dinner she would doubtless be able to judge. She began to wonder nervously who the newcomers might be. Probably she would be spared the embarrassment of finding old acquaintances among them; but it was odd that her daughter had mentioned no names.

Leila had proposed that, later in the afternoon, Wilbour should take her mother for a drive: she said she wanted them to have a "nice, quiet talk." But Mrs. Lidcote wished her talk with Leila to come first, and had, moreover, at luncheon, caught stray allusions to an impending tennis match in which her son-in-law was engaged. Her fatigue had been a sufficient pretext for declining the drive, and she had begged Leila to think of her as peacefully resting in her room till such time as they could snatch their quiet moment.

"Before tea, then, you duck!" Leila with a last kiss had decided; and presently Mrs. Lidcote, through her open window, had heard the fresh loud voices of her daughter's visitors chiming across the gardens from the tennis court.

❄ IV ❄

LEILA had come and gone, and they had had their talk. It had not lasted as long as Mrs. Lidcote wished, for in the middle of it Leila had been summoned to the telephone to receive an important message from town, and had sent word to her mother that she couldn't come back just then, as one of the young ladies had been called away unexpectedly and arrangements had to be made for her departure. But the mother and daughter had had almost an hour together, and Mrs. Lidcote was happy. She had never seen Leila so tender, so solicitous. The only thing that troubled her was the very excess of this solicitude, the exaggerated expression of her daughter's annoyance that their first moments together should have been marred by the presence of strangers.

"Not strangers to me, darling, since they're friends of yours," her mother had assured her.

"Yes; but I know your feeling, you queer wild mother. I know how you've always hated people." (*Hated people!* Had Leila forgotten why?) "And that's why I told Susy that if you preferred to go with her to Ridgefield on Sunday I should perfectly understand, and patiently wait for our good hug. But you didn't really mind them at luncheon, did you, dearest?"

Mrs. Lidcote, at that, had suddenly thrown a startled look at her daughter. "I don't mind things of that kind any longer," she had simply answered.

"But that doesn't console me for having exposed you to the bother of it, for having let you come here when I ought to have *ordered* you off to Ridgefield with Susy. If Susy hadn't been stupid she'd have made you go there with her. I hate to think of you up here all alone."

Again Mrs. Lidcote tried to read something more than a rather obtuse devotion in her daughter's radiant gaze. "I'm glad to have had a rest this afternoon, dear; and later—"

"Oh, yes, later, when all this fuss is over, we'll more than make up for it, shan't we, you precious darling?" And at this point Leila had been summoned to the telephone, leaving Mrs. Lidcote to her conjectures.

These were still floating before her in cloudy uncertainty when Miss Suffern tapped at the door.

"You've come to take me down to tea? I'd forgotten how late it was," Mrs. Lidcote exclaimed.

Miss Suffern, a plump peering little woman, with prim hair and a conciliatory smile, nervously adjusted the pendent bugles of her elaborate black dress. Miss Suffern was always in mourning, and always commemorating the demise of distant relatives by wearing the discarded wardrobe of their next of kin. "It isn't *exactly* mourning," she would say; "but it's the only stitch of black poor Julia had—and of course George was only my mother's step-cousin."

As she came forward Mrs. Lidcote found herself humorously wondering whether she were mourning Horace Pursh's divorce in one of his mother's old black satins.

"Oh, *did* you mean to go down for tea?" Susy Suffern peered at her, a little fluttered. "Leila sent me up to keep you company. She thought it would be cozier for you to stay here. She was afraid you were feeling rather tired."

"I was; but I've had the whole afternoon to rest in. And this wonderful sofa to help me."

"Leila told me to tell you that she'd rush up for a minute

before dinner, after everybody had arrived; but the train is always dreadfully late. She's in despair at not giving you a sitting room; she wanted to know if I thought you really minded."

"Of course I don't mind. It's not like Leila to think I should." Mrs. Lidcote drew aside to make way for the housemaid, who appeared in the doorway bearing a table spread with a bewildering variety of tea cakes.

"Leila saw to it herself," Miss Suffern murmured as the door closed. "Her one idea is that you should feel happy here."

It struck Mrs. Lidcote as one more mark of the subverted state of things that her daughter's solicitude should find expression in the multiplicity of sandwiches and the piping hotness of muffins; but then everything that had happened since her arrival seemed to increase her confusion.

The note of a motor horn down the drive gave another turn to her thoughts. "Are those the new arrivals already?" she asked.

"Oh, dear, no; they won't be here till after seven." Miss Suffern craned her head from the window to catch a glimpse of the motor. "It must be Charlotte leaving."

"Was it the little Wynn girl who was called away in a hurry? I hope it's not on account of illness."

"Oh, no; I believe there was some mistake about dates. Her mother telephoned her that she was expected at the Stepleys, at Fishkill, and she had to be rushed over to Albany to catch a train."

Mrs. Lidcote meditated. "I'm sorry. She's a charming young thing. I hoped I should have another talk with her this evening after dinner."

"Yes; it's too bad." Miss Suffern's gaze grew vague. "You *do* look tired, you know," she continued, seating herself at the tea table and preparing to dispense its delicacies. "You must go straight back to your sofa and let me wait on you. The excitement has told on you more than you think, and you mustn't fight against it any longer. Just stay quietly up here and let yourself go. You'll have Leila to yourself on Monday."

Mrs. Lidcote received the teacup which her cousin

proffered, but showed no other disposition to obey her injunctions. For a moment she stirred her tea in silence; then she asked: "Is it your idea that I should stay quietly up here till Monday?"

Miss Suffern set down her cup with a gesture so sudden that it endangered an adjacent plate of scones. When she had assured herself of the safety of the scones she looked up with a fluttered laugh. "Perhaps, dear, by tomorrow you'll be feeling differently. The air here, you know—"

"Yes, I know." Mrs. Lidcote bent forward to help herself to a scone. "Who's arriving this evening?" she asked.

Miss Suffern frowned and peered. "You know my wretched head for names. Leila told me—but there are so many—"

"So many? She didn't tell me she expected a big party."

"Oh, not big: but rather outside of her little group. And of course, as it's the first time, she's a little excited at having the older set."

"The older set? Our contemporaries, you mean?"

"Why—yes." Miss Suffern paused as if to gather herself up for a leap. "The Ashton Gileses," she brought out.

"The Ashton Gileses? Really? I shall be glad to see Mary Giles again. It must be eighteen years," said Mrs. Lidcote steadily.

"Yes," Miss Suffern gasped, precipitately refilling her cup.

"The Ashton Gileses; and who else?"

"Well, the Sam Fresbies. But the most important person, of course, is Mrs. Lorin Boulger."

"Mrs. Boulger? Leila didn't tell me she was coming."

"Didn't she? I suppose she forgot everything when she saw you. But the party was got up for Mrs. Boulger. You see, it's very important that she should—well, take a fancy to Leila and Wilbour; his being appointed to Rome virtually depends on it. And you know Leila insists on Rome in order to be near you. So she asked Mary Giles, who's intimate with the Boulgers, if the visit couldn't possibly be arranged; and Mary's cable caught Mrs. Boulger at Cherbourg. She's to be only a fortnight in America; and getting her to come directly here was rather a triumph."

"Yes; I see it was," said Mrs. Lidcote.

"You know, she's rather—rather fussy; and Mary was a little doubtful if—"

"If she would, on account of Leila?" Mrs. Lidcote murmured.

"Well, yes. In her official position. But luckily she's a friend of the Barkleys. And finding the Gileses and Fresbies here will make it all right. The times have changed!" Susy Suffern indulgently summed up.

Mrs. Lidcote smiled. "Yes; a few years ago it would have seemed improbable that I should ever again be dining with Mary Giles and Harriet Fresbie and Mrs. Lorin Boulger."

Miss Suffern did not at the moment seem disposed to enlarge upon this theme; and after an interval of silence Mrs. Lidcote suddenly resumed: "Do they know I'm here, by the way?"

The effect of her question was to produce in Miss Suffern an exaggerated access of peering and frowning. She twitched the tea things about, fingered her bugles, and, looking at the clock, exclaimed amazedly: "Mercy! Is it seven already?"

"Not that it can make any difference, I suppose," Mrs. Lidcote continued. "But did Leila tell them I was coming?"

Miss Suffern looked at her with pain. "Why, you don't suppose, dearest, that Leila would do anything—"

Mrs. Lidcote went on: "For, of course, it's of the first importance, as you say, that Mrs. Lorin Boulger should be favorably impressed, in order that Wilbour may have the best possible chance of getting Rome."

"I *told* Leila you'd feel that, dear. You see, it's actually on *your* account—so that they may get a post near you—that Leila invited Mrs. Boulger."

"Yes, I see that." Mrs. Lidcote, abruptly rising from her seat, turned her eyes to the clock. "But, as you say, it's getting late. Oughtn't we to dress for dinner?"

Miss Suffern, at the suggestion, stood up also, an agitated hand among her bugles. "I do wish I could persuade you to stay up here this evening. I'm sure Leila'd be happier if you would. Really, you're much too tired to come down."

"What nonsense, Susy!" Mrs. Lidcote spoke with a sudden sharpness, her hand stretched to the bell. "When do we dine? At half-past eight? Then I must really send you packing. At my age it takes time to dress."

Miss Suffern, thus projected toward the threshold, lingered there to repeat: "Leila'll never forgive herself if you make an effort you're not up to." But Mrs. Lidcote smiled on her without answering, and the icy light-wave propelled her through the door.

❄ V ❄

MRS. LIDCOTE, though she had made the gesture of ringing for her maid, had not done so.

When the door closed, she continued to stand motionless in the middle of her soft spacious room. The fire which had been kindled at twilight danced on the brightness of silver and mirrors and sober gilding; and the sofa toward which she had been urged by Miss Suffern heaped up its cushions in inviting proximity to a table laden with new books and papers. She could not recall having ever been more luxuriously housed, or having ever had so strange a sense of being out alone, under the night, in a wind-beaten plain. She sat down by the fire and thought.

A knock on the door made her lift her head, and she saw her daughter on the threshold. The intricate ordering of Leila's fair hair and the flying folds of her dressing gown showed that she had interrupted her dressing to hasten to her mother; but once in the room she paused a moment, smiling uncertainly, as though she had forgotten the object of her haste.

Mrs. Lidcote rose to her feet. "Time to dress, dearest? Don't scold! I shan't be late."

"To dress?" Leila stood before her with a puzzled look. "Why, I thought, dear—I mean, I hoped you'd decided just to stay here quietly and rest."

Her mother smiled. "But I've been resting all the afternoon!"

"Yes, but—you know you *do* look tired. And when Susy told me just now that you meant to make the effort—"

"You came to stop me?"

"I came to tell you that you needn't feel in the least obliged—"

"Of course. I understand that."

There was a pause during which Leila, vaguely averting herself from her mother's scrutiny, drifted toward the dressing table and began to disturb the symmetry of the brushes and bottles laid out on it. "Do your visitors know that I'm here?" Mrs. Lidcote suddenly went on.

"Do they—of course—why, naturally," Leila rejoined, absorbed in trying to turn the stopper of a salts bottle.

"Then won't they think it odd if I don't appear?"

"Oh, not in the least, dearest. I assure you they'll *all* understand.' Leila laid down the bottle and turned back to her mother, her face alight with reassurance.

Mrs. Lidcote stood motionless, her head erect, her smiling eyes on her daughter's. "Will they think it odd if I *do?*"

Leila stopped short, her lips half parted to reply. As she paused, the color stole over her bare neck, swept up to her throat, and burst into flame in her cheeks. Thence it sent its devastating crimson up to her very temples, to the lobes of her ears, to the edges of her eyelids, beating all over her in fiery waves, as if fanned by some imperceptible wind.

Mrs. Lidcote silently watched the conflagration; then she turned away her eyes with a slight laugh. "I only meant that I was afraid it might upset the arrangement of your dinner table if I didn't come down. If you can assure me that it won't, I believe I'll take you at your word and go back to this irresistible sofa." She paused, as if waiting for her daughter to speak; then she held out her arms. "Run off and dress, dearest; and don't have me on your mind." She clasped Leila close, pressing a long kiss on the last afterglow of her subsiding blush. "I do feel the least bit overdone, and if it won't inconvenience you to have me drop out of things, I believe I'll basely take to my bed and stay there till your party scatters. And now run off, or you'll be late; and make my excuses to them all."

❄ VI ❄

THE Barkleys' visitors had dispersed, and Mrs. Lidcote, completely restored by her two days' rest, found herself, on the following Monday, alone with her children and Miss Suffern.

There was a note of jubilation in the air, for the party had "gone off" so extraordinarily well, and so completely, as it appeared, to the satisfaction of Mrs. Lorin Boulger, that Wilbour's early appointment to Rome was almost to be counted on. So certain did this seem that the prospect of a prompt reunion mitigated the distress with which Leila learned of her mother's decision to return almost immediately to Italy. No one understood this decision; it seemed to Leila absolutely unintelligible that Mrs. Lidcote should not stay on with them till their own fate was fixed, and Wilbour echoed her astonishment.

"Why shouldn't you, as Leila says, wait here till we can all pack up and go together?"

Mrs. Lidcote smiled her gratitude with her refusal. "After all, it's not yet sure that you'll be packing up."

"Oh, you ought to have seen Wilbour with Mrs. Boulger," Leila triumphed.

"No, you ought to have seen Leila with her," Leila's husband exulted.

Miss Suffern enthusiastically appended: "I *do* think inviting Harriet Fresbie was a stroke of genius!"

"Oh, we'll be with you soon," Leila laughed. "So soon that it's really foolish to separate."

But Mrs. Lidcote held out with the quiet firmness which her daughter knew it was useless to oppose. After her long months in India, it was really imperative, she declared, that she should get back to Florence and see what was happening to her little place there; and she had been so comfortable on the "Utopia" that she had a fancy to return by the same ship. There was nothing for it, therefore, but to acquiesce in her decision and keep her with them till the afternoon before the day of the "Utopia's" sailing. This arrangement fitted in with certain projects which, during her two days' seclusion, Mrs. Lidcote had silently matured. It had become to her of the first importance to get away as soon as she could, and the little place in Florence, which held her past in every fold of its curtains and between every page of its books, seemed now to her the one spot where that past would be endurable to look upon.

She was not unhappy during the intervening days. The sight of Leila's well-being, the sense of Leila's tenderness, were, after all, what she had come for; and of these she had had full measure. Leila had never been happier or more tender; and the contemplation of her bliss, and the enjoyment of her affection, were an absorbing occupation for her mother. But they were also a sharp strain on certain overtightened chords, and Mrs. Lidcote, when at last she found herself alone in the New York hotel to which she had returned the night before embarking, had the feeling that she had just escaped with her life from the clutch of a giant hand.

She had refused to let her daughter come to town with her; she had even rejected Susy Suffern's company. She wanted no viaticum but that of her own thoughts; and she let these come to her without shrinking from them as she sat in the same high-hung sitting room in which, just a week before, she and Franklin Ide had had their memorable talk.

She had promised her friend to let him hear from her, but she had not kept her promise. She knew that he had probably come back from Chicago, and that if he learned of her sudden decision to return to Italy it would be impossible for her not to see him before sailing; and as she wished above all things not to see him she had kept silent, intending to send him a letter from the steamer.

There was no reason why she should wait till then to write it. The actual moment was more favorable, and the task, though not agreeable, would at least bridge over an hour of her lonely evening. She went up to the writing table, drew out a sheet of paper and began to write his name. And as she did so, the door opened and he came in.

The words she met him with were the last she could have imagined herself saying when they had parted. "How in the world did you know that I was here?"

He caught her meaning in a flash. "You didn't want me to, then?" He stood looking at her. "I suppose I ought to have taken your silence as meaning that. But I happened to meet Mrs. Wynn, who is stopping here, and she asked me to dine with her and Charlotte, and Charlotte's young man. They told me they'd seen you arriving this afternoon, and I couldn't help coming up."

There was a pause between them, which Mrs. Lidcote at last surprisingly broke with the exclamation: "Ah, she *did* recognize me then!"

"Recognize you?" He stared. "Why—"

"Oh, I saw she did, though she never moved an eyelid. I saw it by Charlotte's blush. The child has the prettiest blush. I saw that her mother wouldn't let her speak to me."

Ide put down his hat with an impatient laugh. "Hasn't Leila cured you of your delusions?"

She looked at him intently. "Then you don't think Margaret Wynn meant to cut me?"

"I think your ideas are absurd."

She paused for a perceptible moment without taking this up; then she said, at a tangent: "I'm sailing tomorrow early. I meant to write to you—there's the letter I'd begun."

Ide followed her gesture, and then turned his eyes back to her face. "You didn't mean to see me, then, or even to let me know that you were going till you'd left?"

"I felt it would be easier to explain to you in a letter—"

"What in God's name is there to explain?" She made no reply, and he pressed on: "It can't be that you're worried about Leila, for Charlotte Wynn told me she'd been there last week, and there was a big party arriving when she left: Fresbies and Gileses, and Mrs. Lorin Boulger—all the board of examiners! If Leila has passed *that*, she's got her degree."

Mrs. Lidcote had dropped down into a corner of the sofa where she had sat during their talk of the week before. "I was stupid," she began abruptly. "I ought to have gone to Ridgefield with Susy. I didn't see till afterward that I was expected to."

"You were expected to?"

"Yes. Oh, it wasn't Leila's fault. She suffered—poor darling; she was distracted. But she'd asked her party before she knew I was arriving."

"Oh, as to that—" Ide drew a deep breath of relief. "I can understand that it must have been a disappointment not to have you to herself just at first. But, after all, you were among old friends or their children: the Gileses and Fresbies—and little Charlotte Wynn." He paused a moment before the last name, and scrutinized her hesitatingly. "Even if they came at the wrong time, you must have been glad to see them all at Leila's."

She gave him back his look with a faint smile. "I didn't see them."

"You didn't see them?"

"No. That is, excepting little Charlotte Wynn. That child is exquisite. We had a talk before luncheon the day I arrived. But when her mother found out that I was staying in the house she telephoned her to leave immediately, and so I didn't see her again."

The color rushed to Ide's sallow face. "I don't know where you get such ideas!"

She pursued, as if she had not heard him: "Oh, and I saw Mary Giles for a minute too. Susy Suffern brought her up to my room the last evening, after dinner, when all the others were at bridge. She meant it kindly—but it wasn't much use."

"But what were you doing in your room in the evening after dinner?"

"Why, you see, when I found out my mistake in coming,—how embarrassing it was for Leila, I mean—I simply told her I was very tired, and preferred to stay upstairs till the party was over."

Ide, with a groan, struck his hand against the arm of his chair. "I wonder how much of all this you simply imagined!"

"I didn't imagine the fact of Harriet Fresbie's not even asking if she might see me when she knew I was in the house. Nor of Mary Giles's getting Susy, at the eleventh hour, to smuggle her up to my room when the others wouldn't know where she'd gone; nor poor Leila's ghastly fear lest Mrs. Lorin Boulger, for whom the party was given, should guess I was in the house, and prevent her husband's giving Wilbour the second secretaryship because she'd been obliged to spend a night under the same roof with his mother-in-law!"

Ide continued to drum on his chair arm with exasperated fingers. "You don't *know* that any of the acts you describe are due to the causes you suppose."

Mrs. Lidcote paused before replying, as if honestly trying to measure the weight of this argument. Then she said in a low tone: "I know that Leila was in an agony lest I should come down to dinner the first night. And it was for me she was afraid, not for herself. Leila is never afraid for herself."

"But the conclusions you draw are simply preposterous. There are narrow-minded women everywhere, but the women who were at Leila's knew perfectly well that their going there would give her a sort of social sanction, and if they were willing that she should have it, why on earth should they want to withhold it from you?"

"That's what I told myself a week ago, in this very room, after my first talk with Susy Suffern." She lifted a misty smile to his anxious eyes. "That's why I listened to what you said to me the same evening, and why your arguments half-convinced me, and made me think that what had been possible for Leila might not be impossible for me. If the new dispensation had come, why not for me as well as for the others? I can't tell you the flight my imagination took!"

Franklin Ide rose from his seat and crossed the room to a chair near her sofa-corner. "All I cared about was that it seemed—for the moment—to be carrying you toward me," he said.

"I cared about that, too. That's why I meant to go away without seeing you." They gave each other grave look for look. "Because, you see, I was mistaken," she went on. "We were both mistaken. You say it's preposterous that the women who didn't object to accepting Leila's hospitality should have objected to meeting me under her roof. And so it is; but I begin to understand why. It's simply that society is much too busy to revise its own judgments. Probably no one in the house with me stopped to consider that my case and Leila's were identical. They only remembered that I'd done something which, at the time I did it, was condemned by society. My case had been passed on and classified: I'm the woman who has been cut for nearly twenty years. The older people have half-forgotten why, and the younger ones have never really known: it's simply become a tradition to cut me. And traditions that have lost their meaning are the hardest of all to destroy."

Ide sat motionless while she spoke. As she ended, he stood up with a short laugh and walked across the room to the window. Outside, the immense black prospect of New York, strung with its myriad lines of light, stretched away into the smoky edges of the night. He showed it to her with a gesture.

"What do you suppose such words as you've been using—'society,' 'tradition,' and the rest—mean to all the life out there?"

She came and stood by him in the window. "Less than nothing, of course. But you and I are not out there. We're shut up in a little tight round of habit and association, just as we're shut up in this room. Remember, I thought I'd got out of it once; but what really happened was that the other people went out, and left me in the same little room. The only difference was that I was there alone. Oh, I've made it habitable now, I'm used to it; but I've lost any illusions I may have had as to an angel's opening door."

Ide again laughed impatiently. "Well, if the door won't open, why not let another prisoner in? At least it would be less of a solitude—"

She turned from the dark window back into the vividly lighted room.

"It would be more of a prison. You forget that I know all about that. We're all imprisoned, of course—all of us middling people, who don't carry our freedom in our brains. But we've accommodated ourselves to our different cells, and if we're moved suddenly into the new ones we're likely to find a stone wall where we thought there was thin air, and to knock ourselves senseless against it. I saw a man do that once."

Ide, leaning with folded arms against the window frame, watched her in silence as she moved restlessly about the room, gathering together some scattered books and tossing a handful of torn letters into the paper basket. When she ceased, he rejoined: "All you say is based on preconceived theories. Why didn't you put them to the test by coming down to meet your old friends? Don't you see the inference they would naturally draw from your hiding yourself when they arrived? It looked as though you were afraid of them—or as though you hadn't forgiven them. Either way, you put them in the wrong instead of waiting to let them put you in the right. If Leila had buried herself in a desert do you suppose society would have gone to fetch her out? You say you were afraid for Leila and that she was afraid for you. Don't you see what all these complications of feeling mean? Simply that you were too nervous at the moment to let things happen naturally, just as you're too nervous now to judge them rationally." He paused and turned his eyes to her face. "Don't try to just yet. Give yourself a little more time. Give *me* a little more time. I've always known it would take time."

He moved nearer, and she let him have her hand. With the grave kindness of his face so close above her she felt like a child roused out of frightened dreams and finding a light in the room.

"Perhaps you're right—" she heard herself begin; then something within her clutched her back, and her hand fell away from him.

"I know I'm right: trust me," he urged. "We'll talk of this in Florence soon."

She stood before him, feeling with despair his kindness, his patience and his unreality. Everything he said seemed like a painted gauze let down between herself and the real facts of life; and a sudden desire seized her to tear the gauze into shreds.

She drew back and looked at him with a smile of superficial reassurance. "You *are* right—about not talking any longer now. I'm nervous and tired, and it would do no good. I brood over things too much. As you say, I must try not to shrink from people." She turned away and glanced at the clock. "Why, it's only ten! If I send you off I shall begin to brood again; and if you stay we shall go on talking about the same thing. Why shouldn't we go down and see Margaret Wynn for half an hour?"

She spoke lightly and rapidly, her brilliant eyes on his face. As she watched him, she saw it change, as if her smile had thrown a too vivid light upon it.

"Oh, no—not tonight!" he exclaimed.

"Not tonight? Why, what other night have I, when I'm off

at dawn? Besides, I want to show you at once that I mean to be more sensible—that I'm not going to be afraid of people any more. And I should really like another glimpse of little Charlotte." He stood before her, his hand in his beard, with the gesture he had in moments of perplexity. "Come!" she ordered him gaily, turning to the door.

He followed her and laid his hand on her arm. "Don't you think—hadn't you better let me go first and see? They told me they'd had a tiring day at the dressmaker's. I dare say they have gone to bed."

"But you said they'd a young man of Charlotte's dining with them. Surely he wouldn't have left by ten? At any rate, I'll go down with you and see. It takes so long if one sends a servant first. She put him gently aside, and then paused as a new thought struck her. "Or wait; my maid's in the next room. I'll tell her to go and ask if Margaret will receive me. Yes, that's much the best way."

She turned back and went toward the door that led to her bedroom; but before she could open it she felt Ide's quick touch again.

"I believe—I remember now—Charlotte's young man was suggesting that they should all go out—to a music hall or something of the sort. I'm sure—I'm positively sure that you won't find them."

Her hand dropped from the door, his dropped from her arm, and as they drew back and faced each other she saw the blood rise slowly through his sallow skin, redden his neck and ears, encroach upon the edges of his beard, and settle in dull patches under his kind troubled eyes. She had seen the same blush on another face, and the same impulse of compassion she had then felt made her turn her gaze away again.

A knock on the door broke the silence and a porter put his head into the room.

"It's only just to know how many pieces there'll be to go down to the steamer in the morning."

With the words she felt that the veil of painted gauze was torn in tatters, and that she was moving again among the grim edges of reality.

"Oh, dear," she exclaimed, "I never *can* remember! Wait a minute; I shall have to ask my maid."

She opened her bedroom door and called out: "Annette!"

The Triumph of Night

IT WAS CLEAR that the sleigh from Weymore had not come; and the shivering young traveler from Boston, who had counted on jumping into it when he left the train at Northridge Junction, found himself standing alone on the open platform, exposed to the full assault of nightfall and winter.

The blast that swept him came off New Hampshire snow-fields and ice-hung forests. It seemed to have traversed interminable leagues of frozen silence, filling them with the same cold roar and sharpening its edge against the same bitter black-and-white landscape. Dark, searching and sword-like, it alternately muffled and harried its victim, like a bullfighter now whirling his cloak and now planting his darts. This analogy brought home to the young man the fact that he himself had no cloak, and that the overcoat in which he had faced the relatively temperate air of Boston seemed no thicker than a sheet of paper on the bleak heights of Northridge. George Faxon said to himself that the place was uncommonly well-named. It clung to an exposed ledge over the valley from which the train had lifted him, and the wind combed it with teeth of steel that he seemed actually to hear scraping against the wooden sides of the station. Other building there was none: the village lay far down the road, and thither—since the Weymore sleigh had not come—Faxon saw himself under the necessity of plodding through several feet of snow.

He understood well enough what had happened: his hostess had forgotten that he was coming. Young as Faxon was, this sad lucidity of soul had been acquired as the result of long experience, and he knew that the visitors who can least afford to hire a carriage are almost always those whom their hosts forget to send for. Yet to say that Mrs. Culme had forgotten him was too crude a way of putting it. Similar incidents led him to think that she had probably told her maid to tell the butler to telephone the coachman to tell one of the grooms (if no one else needed him) to drive over to Northridge to fetch the new secretary; but on a night like this, what groom who respected his rights would fail to forget the order?

Faxon's obvious course was to struggle through the drifts to the village, and there rout out a sleigh to convey him to Weymore; but what if, on his arrival at Mrs. Culme's, no one remembered to ask him what this devotion to duty had cost? That, again, was one of the contingencies he had expensively learned to look out for, and the perspicacity so acquired told him it would be cheaper to spend the night at the Northridge inn, and advise Mrs. Culme of his presence there by telephone. He had reached this decision, and was about to entrust his luggage to a vague man with a lantern, when his hopes were raised by the sound of bells.

Two sleighs were just dashing up to the station, and from the foremost there sprang a young man muffled in furs.

"Weymore? No, these are not the Weymore sleighs."

The voice was that of the youth who had jumped to the platform—a voice so agreeable that, in spite of the words, it fell consolingly on Faxon's ears. At the same moment the wandering station lantern, casting a transient light on the speaker, showed his features to be in the pleasantest harmony with his voice. He was very fair and very young—hardly in the twenties, Faxon thought—but this face, though full of a morning freshness, was a trifle too thin and fine-drawn, as though a vivid spirit contended in him with a strain of physical weakness. Faxon was perhaps the quicker to notice such delicacies of balance because his own temperament hung on lightly quivering nerves, which yet, as he believed, would never quite swing him beyond a normal sensibility.

"You expected a sleigh from Weymore?" the newcomer continued, standing beside Faxon like a slender column of fur.

Mrs. Culme's secretary explained his difficulty, and the other brushed it aside with a contemptuous. "Oh, *Mrs. Culme!*" that carried both speakers a long way toward reciprocal understanding.

"But then you must be—" The youth broke off with a smile of interrogation.

"The new secretary? Yes. But apparently there are no notes to be answered this evening." Faxon's laugh deepened the sense of solidarity which had so promptly established itself between the two.

His friend laughed also. "Mrs. Culme," he explained, "was lunching at my uncle's today, and she said you were due this evening. But seven hours is a long time for Mrs. Culme to remember anything."

"Well," said Faxon philosophically, "I suppose that's one of the reasons why she needs a secretary. And I've always the inn at Northridge," he concluded.

"Oh, but you haven't, though! It burned down last week."

"The deuce it did!" said Faxon; but the humor of the situation struck him before its inconvenience. His life, for years past, had been mainly a succession of resigned adaptations, and he had learned, before dealing practically with his embarrassments, to extract from most of them a small tribute of amusement.

"Oh, well, there's sure to be somebody in the place who can put me up."

"No one *you* could put up with. Besides, Northridge is three miles off, and our place—in the opposite direction—is a little nearer." Through the darkness, Faxon saw his friend sketch a gesture of self-introduction. "My name's Frank Rainer, and I'm staying with my uncle at Overdale. I've driven over to meet two friends of his, who are due in a few minutes from New York. If you don't mind waiting till they arrive I'm sure Overdale can do you better than Northridge. We're only down from town for a few days, but the house is always ready for a lot of people."

"But your uncle—?" Faxon could only object, with the odd sense, through his embarrassment, that it would be magically dispelled by his invisible friend's next words.

"Oh, my uncle—you'll see! I answer for *him!* I dare say you've heard of him—John Lavington?"

John Lavington! There was a certain irony in asking if one had heard of John Lavington! Even from a post of observation as obscure as that of Mrs. Culme's secretary the rumor of John Lavington's money, of his pictures, his politics, his charities and his hospitality, was as difficult to escape as the roar of a cataract in a mountain solitude. It might almost have been said that the one place in which one would not have expected to come upon him was in just such a solitude as now surrounded the speakers—at least in this deepest hour of its desertedness. But it was just like Lavington's brilliant ubiquity to put one in the wrong even there.

"Oh, yes, I've heard of your uncle."

"Then you *will* come, won't you? We've only five minutes to wait," young Rainer urged, in the tone that dispels scruples by ignoring them; and Faxon found himself accepting the invitation as simply as it was offered.

A delay in the arrival of the New York train lengthened their five minutes to fifteen; and as they paced the icy platform Faxon began to see why it had seemed the most natural thing in the world to accede to his new acquaintance's suggestion. It was because Frank Rainer was one of the privileged beings who simplify human intercourse by the atmosphere of confidence and good humor they diffuse. He produced this effect, Faxon noted, by the exercise of no gift but his youth, and of no art but his sincerity; and these qualities were revealed in a smile of such sweetness that Faxon felt, as never before, what Nature can achieve when she deigns to match the face with the mind.

He learned that the young man was the ward, and the only nephew, of John Lavington, with whom he had made his home since the death of his mother, the great man's sister. Mr. Lavington, Rainer said, had been "a regular brick" to him—"But then he is to everyone, you know"—and the young fellow's situation seemed in fact to be perfectly in keeping with his person. Apparently the only shade that had ever rested on him was cast by the physical weakness which Faxon had already detected. Young Rainer had been threatened with tuberculosis, and the disease was so far advanced that, according to the highest authorities, banishment to Arizona or New Mexico was inevitable. "But luckily my uncle didn't pack me off, as most people would have done, without getting another opinion. Whose? Oh, an awfully clever chap, a young doctor with a lot of new ideas, who simply laughed at my being sent away, and said I'd do perfectly well in New York if I didn't dine out too much, and if I dashed off occasionally to Northridge for a little fresh air. So it's really my uncle's doing that I'm not in exile—and I feel no end better since the new chap told me I needn't bother." Young Rainer went on to confess that he was extremely fond of dining out, dancing and similar distractions; and Faxon, listening to him, was inclined to think that the physician who had refused to cut him off altogether from those pleasures was probably a better psychologist than his seniors.

"All the same you ought to be careful, you know." The sense of elder-brotherly concern that forced the words from Faxon made him, as he spoke, slip his arm through Frank Rainer's.

The latter met the movement with a responsive pressure. "Oh, I *am*: awfully, awfully. And then my uncle has such an eye on me!"

"But if your uncle has such an eye on you, what does he say to your swallowing knives out here in this Siberian wild?"

Rainer raised his fur collar with a careless gesture. "It's not that that does it—the cold's good for me."

"And it's not the dinners and dancers? What is it, then?" Faxon good-humoredly insisted; to which his companion answered with a laugh: "Well, my uncle says it's being bored; and I rather think he's right!"

His laugh ended in a spasm of coughing and a struggle for breath that made Faxon, still holding his arm, guide him hastily into the shelter of the fireless waiting room.

Young Rainer had dropped down on the bench against the wall and pulled off one of his fur gloves to grope for a handkerchief. He tossed aside his cap and drew the handkerchief across his forehead, which was intensely white and beaded with moisture, though his face retained a healthy glow. But Faxon's gaze remained fastened to the hand he had uncovered: it was so long, so colorless, so wasted, so much older than the brow he passed it over.

"It's queer—a healthy face but dying hands," the secretary mused: he somehow wished young Rainer had kept on his glove.

The whistle of the express drew the young men to their feet, and the next moment two heavily-furred gentlemen had descended to the platform and were breasting the rigor of the night. Frank Rainer introduced them as Mr. Grisben and Mr. Balch, and Faxon, while their luggage was being lifted into the second sleigh, discerned them, by the roving lantern gleam, to be an elderly grey-headed pair, of the average prosperous business cut.

They saluted their host's nephew with friendly familiarity, and Mr. Grisben, who seemed the spokesman of the two, ended his greeting with a genial—"and many many more of them, dear boy!" which suggested to Faxon that their arrival coincided with an anniversary. But he could not press the inquiry, for the seat allotted him was at the coachman's side, while Frank Rainer joined his uncle's guests inside the sleigh.

A swift flight (behind such horses as one could be sure of John Lavington's having) brought them to tall gateposts, an illuminated lodge, and an avenue on which the snow had been leveled to the smoothness of marble. At the end of the avenue the long house loomed up, its principal bulk dark, but one wing sending out a ray of welcome; and the next moment Faxon was receiving a violent impression of warmth and light, of hothouse plants, hurrying servants, a vast spectacular oak hall like a stage setting, and, in its unreal middle distance, a small figure, correctly dressed, conventionally featured, and utterly unlike his rather florid conception of the great John Lavington.

The surprise of the contrast remained with him through his hurried dressing in the large luxurious bedroom to which he had been shown. "I don't see where he comes in," was the only way he could put it, so difficult was it to fit the exuberance of Lavington's public personality into his host's contracted frame and manner. Mr. Lavington, to whom

Faxon's case had been rapidly explained by young Rainer, had welcomed him with a sort of dry and stilted cordiality that exactly matched his narrow face, his stiff hand, and the whiff of scent on his evening handkerchief. "Make yourself at home—at home!" he had repeated, in a tone that suggested, on his own part, a complete inability to perform the feat he urged on his visitor. "Any friend of Frank's . . . delighted . . . make yourself thoroughly at home!"

❄ II ❄

In spite of the balmy temperature and complicated conveniences of Faxon's bedroom, the injunction was not easy to obey. It was wonderful luck to have found a night's shelter under the opulent roof of Overdale, and he tasted the physical satisfaction to the full. But the place, for all its ingenuities of comfort, was oddly cold and unwelcoming. He couldn't have said why, and could only suppose that Mr. Lavington's intense personality—intensely negative, but intense all the same—must, in some occult way, have penetrated every corner of his dwelling. Perhaps, though, it was merely that Faxon himself was tired and hungry, more deeply chilled than he had known till he came in from the cold, and unutterably sick of all strange houses, and of the prospect of perpetually treading other people's stairs.

"I hope you're not famished?" Rainer's slim figure was in the doorway. "My uncle has a little business to attend to with Mr. Grisben, and we don't dine for half an hour. Shall I fetch you, or can you find your way down? Come straight to the dining room—the second door on the left of the long gallery."

He disappeared, leaving a ray of warmth behind him, and Faxon, relieved, lit a cigarette and sat down by the fire.

Looking about with less haste, he was struck by a detail that had escaped him. The room was full of flowers—a mere "bachelor's room," in the wing of a house opened only for a few days, in the dead middle of a New Hampshire winter! Flowers were everywhere, not in senseless profusion, but placed with the same conscious art that he had remarked in the grouping of the blossoming shrubs in the hall. A vase of arums stood on the writing table, a cluster of strange-hued carnations on the stand at his elbow, and from bowls of glass and porcelain clumps of freesia bulbs diffused their melting fragrance. The fact implied acres of glass—but that was the least interesting part of it. The flowers themselves, their quality, selection and arrangement, attested on someone's part—and on whose but John Lavington's?—a solicitous and a sensitive passion for that particular form of beauty. Well, it simply made the man, as he had appeared to Faxon, all the harder to understand!

The half hour elapsed, and Faxon, rejoicing at the prospect of food, set out to make his way to the dining room. He had not noticed the direction he had followed in going to his room, and was puzzled, when he left it, to find that two staircases, of apparently equal importance, invited him. He chose the one to his right, and reached, at its foot, a long gallery such as Rainer had described. The gallery was empty, the doors down its length were closed; but Rainer had said: "The second to the left," and Faxon, after pausing for some chance enlightenment which did not come, laid his hand on the second knob to the left.

The room he entered was square, with dusky picture-hung walls. In its center, about a table lit by veiled lamps, he fancied Mr. Lavington and his guests to be already seated at dinner; then he perceived that the table was covered not with viands but with papers, and that he had blundered into what seemed to be his host's study. As he paused Frank Rainer looked up.

"Oh, here's Mr. Faxon. Why not ask him—?"

Mr. Lavington, from the end of the table, reflected his nephew's smile in a glance of impartial benevolence.

"Certainly. Come in, Mr. Faxon. If you won't think it a liberty—"

Mr. Grisben, who sat opposite his host, turned his head toward the door. "Of course Mr. Faxon's an American citizen?"

Frank Rainer laughed. "That's all right! . . . Oh, no, not one of your pin-pointed pens, Uncle Jack! Haven't you got a quill somewhere?"

Mr. Balch, spoke slowly and as if reluctantly, in a muffled

voice of which there seemed to be very little left, raised his hand to say: "One moment: you acknowledge this to be—?"

"My last will and testament?" Rainer's laugh redoubled. "Well, I won't answer for the 'last.' It's the first, anyway."

"It's a mere formula," Mr. Balch explained.

"Well, here goes." Rainer dipped his quill in the inkstand his uncle had pushed in his direction, and dashed a gallant signature across the document.

Faxon, understanding what was expected of him, and conjecturing that the young man was signing his will on the attainment of his majority, had placed himself behind Mr. Grisben, and stood awaiting his turn to affix his name to the instrument. Rainer, having signed, was about to push the paper across the table to Mr. Balch; but the latter, again raising his hand, said in his sad imprisoned voice: "The seal—?"

"Oh, does there have to be a seal?"

Faxon, looking over Mr. Grisben at John Lavington, saw a faint frown between his impassive eyes. "Really, Frank!" He seemed, Faxon thought, slightly irritated by his nephew's frivolity.

"Who's got a seal?" Frank Rainer continued, glancing about the table. "There doesn't seem to be one here."

Mr. Grisben interposed. "A wafer will do. Lavington, you have a wafer?"

Mr. Lavington had recovered his serenity. "There must be some in one of the drawers. But I'm ashamed to say I don't know where my secretary keeps these things. He ought to have seen to it that a wafer was sent with the document."

"Oh, hang it—" Frank Rainer pushed the paper aside: "It's the hand of God—and I'm as hungry as a wolf. Let's dine first, Uncle Jack."

"I think I've a seal upstairs," said Faxon.

Mr. Lavington sent him a barely perceptible smile. "So sorry to give you the trouble—"

"Oh, I say, don't send him after it now. Let's wait till after dinner!"

Mr. Lavington continued to smile on his guest, and the latter, as if under the faint coercion of the smile, turned from the room and ran upstairs. Having taken the seal from his writing case he came down again, and once more opened the door of the study. No one was speaking when he entered—they were evidently awaiting his return with the mute impatience of hunger, and he put the seal in Rainer's reach, and stood watching while Mr. Grisben struck a match and held it to one of the candles flanking the inkstand. As the wax descended on the paper Faxon remarked again the strange emaciation, the premature physical weariness, of the hand that held it: he wondered if Mr. Lavington had ever noticed his nephew's hand, and if it were not poignantly visible to him now.

With this thought in mind, Faxon raised his eyes to look at Mr. Lavington. The great man's gaze rested on Frank Rainer with an expression of untroubled benevolence; and at the same instant Faxon's attention was attracted by the presence in the room of another person, who must have joined the group while he was upstairs searching for the seal. The newcomer was a man of about Mr. Lavington's age and figure, who stood just behind his chair, and who, at the moment when Faxon first saw him, was gazing at young Rainer with an equal intensity of attention. The likeness between the two men—perhaps increased by the fact that the hooded lamps on the table left the figure behind the chair in shadow—struck Faxon the more because of the contrast in their expression. John Lavington, during his nephew's clumsy attempt to drop the wax and apply the seal, continued to fasten on him a look of half-amused affection; while the man behind the chair, so oddly reduplicating the lines of his features and figure, turned on the boy a face of pale hostility.

The impression was so startling that Faxon forgot what was going on about him. He was just dimly aware of young Rainer's exclaiming: "Your turn, Mr. Grisben!" of Mr. Grisben's protesting: "No—no; Mr. Faxon first," and of the pen's being thereupon transferred to his own hand. He received it with a deadly sense of being unable to move, or even to understand what was expected of him, till he became conscious of Mr. Grisben's paternally pointing out the precise spot on which he was to leave his autograph. The effort to fix his attention and steady his hand prolonged the process of signing, and when he stood up—a strange weight of fatigue on all his limbs—the figure behind Mr. Lavington's chair was gone.

Faxon felt an immediate sense of relief. It was puzzling that the man's exit should have been so rapid and noiseless, but the door behind Mr. Lavington was screened by a tapestry hanging, and Faxon concluded that the unknown looker-on had merely had to raise it to pass out. At any rate he was gone, and with his withdrawal the strange weight was lifted. Young Rainer was lighting a cigarette, Mr. Balch inscribing his name at the foot of the document, Mr. Lavington—his eyes no longer on his nephew—examining a strange white-winged orchid in the vase at his elbow. Everything suddenly seemed to have grown natural and simple again, and Faxon found himself responding with a smile to the affable gesture with which his host declared: "And now, Mr. Faxon, we'll dine."

❄ III ❄

"I WONDER how I blundered into the wrong room just now; I thought you told me to take the second door to the left," Faxon said to Frank Rainer as they followed the older men down the gallery.

"So I did; but I probably forgot to tell you which staircase to take. Coming from your bedroom, I ought to have said the fourth door to the right. It's a puzzling house, because my uncle keeps adding to it from year to year. He built this room last summer for his modern pictures."

Young Rainer, pausing to open another door, touched an electric button which sent a circle of light about the walls of a long room hung with canvases of the French Impressionist school.

Faxon advanced, attracted by a shimmering Monet, but Rainer laid a hand on his arm.

"He bought that last week. But come along—I'll show you all this after dinner. Or *he* will, rather—he loves it."

"Does he really love things?"

Rainer stared, clearly perplexed at the question. "Rather!

Flowers and pictures especially! Haven't you noticed the flowers? I suppose you think his manner's cold; it seems so at first; but he's really awfully keen about things."

Faxon looked quickly at the speaker. "Has your uncle a brother?"

"Brother? No—never had. He and my mother were the only ones."

"Or any relation who—who looks like him? Who might be mistaken for him?"

"Not that I ever heard of. Does he remind you of someone?"

"Yes."

"That's queer. We'll ask him if he's got a double. Come on!"

But another picture had arrested Faxon, and some minutes elapsed before he and his young host reached the dining room. It was a large room, with the same conventionally handsome furniture and delicately grouped flowers; and Faxon's first glance showed him that only three men were seated about the dining table. The man who had stood behind Mr. Lavington's chair was not present, and no seat awaited him.

When the young men entered, Mr. Grisben was speaking, and his host, who faced the door, sat looking down at his untouched soup plate and turning the spoon about in his small dry hand.

"It's pretty late to call them rumors—they were devilish close to facts when we left town this morning," Mr. Grisben was saying, with an unexpected incisiveness of tone.

Mr. Lavington laid down his spoon and smiled interrogatively. "Oh, facts—what *are* facts? Just the way a thing happens to look at a given minute. . . ."

"You haven't heard anything from town?" Mr. Grisben persisted.

"Not a syllable. So you see. . . . Balch, a little more of that *petite marmite*. Mr. Faxon . . . between Frank and Mr. Grisben, please."

The dinner progressed through a series of complicated courses, ceremoniously dispensed by a prelatical butler attended by three tall footmen, and it was evident that Mr.

Lavington took a certain satisfaction in the pageant. That, Faxon reflected, was probably the joint in his armor—that and the flowers. He had changed the subject—not abruptly but firmly—when the young men entered, but Faxon perceived that it still possessed the thoughts of the two elderly visitors, and Mr. Balch presently observed, in a voice that seemed to come from the last survivor down a mine shaft: "If it *does* come, it will be the biggest crash since '93."

Mr. Lavington looked bored but polite. "Wall Street can stand crashes better than it could then. It's got a robuster constitution."

"Yes; but—"

"Speaking of constitutions," Mr. Grisben intervened: "Frank, are you taking care of yourself?"

A flush rose to young Rainer's cheeks.

"Why, of course! Isn't that what I'm here for?"

"You're here about three days in the month, aren't you? And the rest of the time it's crowded restaurants and hot ballrooms in town. I thought you were to be shipped off to New Mexico?"

"Oh, I've got a new man who says that's rot."

"Well, you don't look as if your new man were right," said Mr. Grisben bluntly.

Faxon saw the lad's color fade, and the rings of shadow deepen under his gay eyes. At the same moment his uncle turned to him with a renewed intensity of attention. There was such solicitude in Mr. Lavington's gaze that it seemed almost to fling a shield between his nephew and Mr. Grisben's tactless scrutiny.

"We think Frank's a good deal better," he began; "this new doctor—"

The butler, coming up, bent to whisper a word in his ear, and the communication caused a sudden change in Mr. Lavington's expression. His face was naturally so colorless that it seemed not so much to pale as to fade, to dwindle and recede into something blurred and blotted out. He half rose, sat down again and sent a rigid smile about the table.

"Will you excuse me? The telephone. Peters, go on with the dinner." With small precise steps he walked out of the door which one of the footmen had thrown open.

A momentary silence fell on the group; then Mr. Grisben once more addressed himself to Rainer. "You ought to have gone, my boy; you ought to have gone."

The anxious look returned to the youth's eyes. "My uncle doesn't think so, really."

"You're not a baby, to be always governed by your uncle's opinion. You came of age today, didn't you? Your uncle spoils you . . . that's the matter. . . ."

The thrust evidently went home, for Rainer laughed and looked down with a slight accession of color.

"But the doctor—"

"Use your common sense, Frank! You had to try twenty doctors to find one to tell you what you wanted to be told."

A look of apprehension overshadowed Rainer's gaiety. "Oh, come—I say! . . . What would *you* do?" he stammered.

"Pack up and jump on the first train." Mr. Grisben leaned forward and laid his hand kindly on the young man's arm. "Look here: my nephew Jim Grisben is out there ranching on a big scale. He'll take you in and be glad to have you. You say your new doctor thinks it won't do you any good; but he doesn't pretend to say it will do you harm, does he? Well, then—give it a trial. It'll take you out of hot theaters and night restaurants, anyhow. . . . And all the rest of it. . . . Eh, Balch?"

"Go!" said Mr. Balch hollowly. "Go *at once*," he added, as if a closer look at the youth's face had impressed on him the need of backing up his friend.

Young Rainer had turned ashy pale. He tried to stiffen his mouth into a smile. "Do I look as bad as all that?"

Mr. Grisben was helping himself to terrapin. "You look like the day after an earthquake," he said.

The terrapin had encircled the table, and been deliberately enjoyed by Mr. Lavington's three visitors (Rainer, Faxon noticed, left his plate untouched) before the door was thrown open to readmit their host.

Mr. Lavington advanced with an air of recovered composure. He seated himself, picked up his napkin and consulted the gold-monogrammed menu. "No, don't bring back the filet. . . . Some terrapin; yes. . . ." He looked affably about the table. "Sorry to have deserted you, but the storm has played the deuce with the wires, and I had to wait a long time before I could get a good connection. It must be blowing up a blizzard."

"Uncle Jack," young Rainer broke out, "Mr. Grisben's been lecturing me."

Mr. Lavington was helping himself to terrapin. "Ah—what about?"

"He thinks I ought to have given New Mexico a show."

"I want him to go straight out to my nephew at Santa Paz and stay there till his next birthday." Mr. Lavington signed to the butler to hand the terrapin to Mr. Grisben, who, as he took a second helping, addressed himself again to Rainer. "Jim's in New York now, and going back the day after tomorrow in Olyphant's private car. I'll ask Olyphant to squeeze you in if you'll go. And when you've been out there a week or two, in the saddle all day and sleeping nine hours a night, I suspect you won't think much of the doctor who prescribed New York."

Faxon spoke up, he knew not why. "I was out there once: it's a splendid life. I saw a fellow—oh, a really *bad* case—who'd been simply made over by it."

"It *does* sound jolly," Rainer laughed, a sudden eagerness in his tone.

His uncle looked at him gently. "Perhaps Grisben's right. It's an opportunity—"

Faxon glanced up with a start: the figure dimly perceived in the study was now more visibly and tangibly planted behind Mr. Lavington's chair.

"That's right, Frank: you see your uncle approves. And the trip out there with Olyphant isn't a thing to be missed. So drop a few dozen dinners and be at the Grand Central the day after tomorrow at five."

Mr. Grisben's pleasant grey eye sought corroboration of his host, and Faxon, in a cold anguish of suspense, continued to watch him as he turned his glance on Mr. Lavington. One could not look at Lavington without seeing the presence at his back, and it was clear that, the next minute, some change in Mr. Grisben's expression must give his watcher a clue.

But Mr. Grisben's expression did not change: the gaze he

fixed on his host remained unperturbed, and the clue he gave was the startling one of not seeming to see the other figure.

Faxon's first impulse was to look away, to look anywhere else, to resort again to the champagne glass the watchful butler had already brimmed; but some fatal attraction, at war in him with an overwhelming physical resistance, held his eyes upon the spot they feared.

The figure was still standing, more distinctly, and therefore more resemblingly, at Mr. Lavington's back; and while the latter continued to gaze affectionately at his nephew, his counterpart, as before, fixed young Rainer with eyes of deadly menace.

Faxon, with what felt like an actual wrench of the muscles, dragged his own eyes from the sight to scan the other countenances about the table; but not one revealed the least consciousness of what he saw, and a sense of mortal isolation sank upon him.

"It's worth considering, certainly—" he heard Mr. Lavington continue; and as Rainer's face lit up, the face behind his uncle's chair seemed to gather into its look all the fierce weariness of old unsatisfied hates. That was the thing that, as the minute labored by, Faxon was becoming most conscious of. The Watcher behind the chair was no longer merely malevolent: he had grown suddenly, unutterably tired. His hatred seemed to well up out of the very depths of balked effort and thwarted hopes, and the fact made him more pitiable, and yet more dire.

Faxon's look reverted to Mr. Lavington, as if to surprise in him a corresponding change. At first none was visible: his pinched smile was screwed to his blank face like a gaslight to a whitewashed wall. Then the fixity of the smile became ominous: Faxon saw that its wearer was afraid to let it go. It was evident that Mr. Lavington was unutterably tired too, and the discovery sent a colder current through Faxon's veins. Looking down at his untouched plate, he caught the soliciting twinkle of the champagne glass; but the sight of the wine turned him sick.

"Well, we'll go into the details presently," he heard Mr. Lavington say, still on the question of his nephew's future.

"Let's have a cigar first. No—not here, Peters." He turned his smile on Faxon. "When we've had coffee I want to show you my pictures."

"Oh, by the way, Uncle Jack—Mr. Faxon wants to know if you've got a double?"

"A double?" Mr. Lavington, still smiling, continued to address himself to his guest. "Not that I know of. Have you seen one, Mr. Faxon?"

Faxon thought: "My God if I look up now they'll *both* be looking at me!" To avoid raising his eyes he made as though to lift the glass to his lips; but his hand sank inert, and he looked up. Mr. Lavington's glance was politely bent on him, but with a loosening of the strain about his heart he saw that the figure behind the chair kept its gaze on Rainer.

"Do you think you've seen my double, Mr. Faxon?"

Would the other face turn if he said yes? Faxon felt a dryness in his throat. "No," he answered.

"Ah? It's possible I've a dozen. I believe I'm extremely usual-looking," Mr. Lavington went on conversationally; and still the other face watched Rainer.

"It was . . . a mistake . . . a confusion of memory. . . ." Faxon heard himself stammer. Mr. Lavington pushed back his chair, and as he did so Mr. Grisben suddenly leaned forward.

"Lavington! What have we been thinking of? We haven't drunk Frank's health!"

Mr. Lavington reseated himself. "My dear boy! . . . Peters, another bottle. . . ." He turned to his nephew. "After such a sin of omission I don't presume to propose the toast myself . . . but Frank knows. . . . Go ahead, Grisben!"

The boy shone on his uncle. "No, no. Uncle Jack! Mr. Grisben won't mind. Nobody but *you*—today!"

The butler was replenishing the glass. He filled Mr. Lavington's last, and Mr. Lavington put out his small hand to raise it. . . . As he did so, Faxon looked away.

"Well, then—All the good I've wished you in all the past years. . . . I put it into the prayer that the coming ones may be healthy and happy and many . . . and *many*, dear boy!"

Faxon saw the hands about him reach out for their glasses. Automatically, he reached for his. His eyes were still on the table, and he repeated to himself with a trembling vehemence: "I won't look up! I won't. . . . I won't. . . ."

His fingers clasped the glass and raised it to the level of his lips. He saw the other hands making the same motion. He heard Mr. Grisben's genial "Hear! Hear!" and Mr. Balch's hollow echo. He said to himself, as the rim of the glass touched his lips: "I won't look up! I swear I won't—" and he looked.

The glass was so full that it required an extraordinary effort to hold it there, brimming and suspended, during the awful interval before he could trust his hand to lower it again, untouched, to the table. It was this merciful preoccupation which saved him, kept him from crying out, from losing his hold, from slipping down into the bottomless blackness that gaped for him. As long as the problem of the glass engaged him he felt able to keep his seat, manage his muscles, fit unnoticeably into the group; but as the glass touched the table his last link with safety snapped. He stood up and dashed out of the room.

❄ IV ❄

IN the gallery, the instinct of self-preservation helped him to turn back and sign to young Rainer not to follow. He stammered out something about a touch of dizziness, and joining them presently; and the boy nodded sympathetically and drew back.

At the foot of the stairs Faxon ran against a servant. "I should like to telephone to Weymore," he said with dry lips.

"Sorry, sir; wires all down. We've been trying the last hour to get New York again for Mr. Lavington."

Faxon shot on to his room, burst into it, and bolted the door. The lamplight lay on furniture, flowers, books; in the ashes a log still glimmered. He dropped down on the sofa and hid his face. The room was profoundly silent, the whole house was still: nothing about him gave a hint of what was going on, darkly and dumbly, in the room he had flown from, and with the covering of his eyes oblivion and reassurance seemed to fall on him. But they fell for a moment only; then his lids opened again to the monstrous vision. There it was, stamped on his pupils, a part of him forever, an indelible horror burnt into his body and brain. But why into his—just his? Why had he alone been chosen to see what he had seen? What business was it of *his* in God's name? Any one of the other, thus enlightened, might have exposed the horror and defeated it; but *he*, the one weaponless and defenseless spectator, the one whom none of the others would believe or understand if he attempted to reveal what he knew—*he* alone had been singled out as the victim of this dreadful initiation!

Suddenly he sat up, listening: he had heard a step on the stairs. Someone, no doubt, was coming to see how he was—to urge him, if he felt better, to go down and join the smokers. Cautiously he opened his door; yes, it was young Rainer's step. Faxon looked down the passage, remembered the other stairway and darted to it. All he wanted was to get out of the house. Not another instant would he breathe its abominable air! What business was it of *his*, in God's name?

He reached the opposite end of the lower gallery, and beyond it saw the hall by which he had entered. It was empty, and on a long table he recognized his coat and cap. He got into his coat, unbolted the door, and plunged into the purifying night.

The darkness was deep, and the cold so intense that for an instant it stopped his breathing. Then he perceived that only a thin snow was falling, and resolutely he set his face for flight. The trees along the avenue marked his way as he hastened with long strides over the beaten snow. Gradually, while he walked, the tumult in his brain subsided. The impulse to fly still drove him forward, but he began to feel that he was flying from a terror of his own creating, and that the most urgent reason for escape was the need of hiding his state, of shunning other eyes till he should regain his balance.

He had spent the long hours in the train in fruitless broodings on a discouraging situation, and he remembered how his bitterness had turned to exasperation when he found that the Weymore sleigh was not awaiting him. It was absurd, of course; but, though he had joked with Rainer over Mrs. Culme's forgetfulness, to confess it had cost a pang.

That was what his rootless life had brought him to: for lack of a personal stake in things his sensibility was at the mercy of such trifles. . . . Yes; that, and the cold and fatigue, the absence of hope and the haunting sense of starved aptitudes, all these had brought him to the perilous verge over which, once or twice before, his terrified brain had hung.

Why else, in the name of any imaginable logic, human or devilish, should he, a stranger, be singled out for this experience? What could it mean to him, how was he related to it, what bearing had it on his case? . . . Unless, indeed, it was just because he was a stranger—a stranger everywhere—because he had no personal life, no warm screen of private egotisms to shield him from exposure, that he had developed this abnormal sensitiveness to the vicissitudes of others. The thought pulled him up with a shudder. No! Such a fate was too abominable; all that was strong and sound in him rejected it. A thousand times better regard himself as ill, disorganized, deluded, than as the predestined victim of such warnings!

He reached the gates and paused before the darkened lodge. The wind had risen and was sweeping the snow into his face. The cold had him in its grasp again, and he stood uncertain. Should he put his sanity to the test and go back? He turned and looked down the dark drive to the house. A single ray shone through the trees, evoking a picture of the lights, the flowers, the faces grouped about that fatal room. He turned and plunged out into the road. . . .

He remembered that, about a mile from Overdale, the coachman had pointed the road to Northridge; and he began to walk in that direction. Once in the road he had the gale in his face, and the wet snow on his moustache and eyelashes instantly hardened to ice. The same ice seemed to be driving a million blades into his throat and lungs, but he pushed on, the vision of the warm room pursuing him.

The snow in the road was deep and uneven. He stumbled across ruts and sank into drifts, and the wind drove against him like a granite cliff. Now and then he stopped, gasping, as if an invisible hand had tightened an iron band about his body; then he started again, stiffening himself against the stealthy penetration of the cold. The snow continued to descend out of a pall of inscrutable darkness, and once or twice he paused, fearing he had missed the road to Northridge; but, seeing no sign of a turn, he ploughed on.

At last, feeling sure that he had walked for more than a mile, he halted and looked back. The act of turning brought immediate relief, first because it put his back to the wind, and then because, far down the road, it showed him the gleam of a lantern. A sleigh was coming—a sleigh that might perhaps give him a lift to the village! Fortified by the hope, he began to walk back toward the light. It came forward very slowly, with unaccountable zigzags and waverings; and even when he was within a few yards of it he could catch no sound of sleigh bells. Then it paused and became stationary by the roadside, as though carried by a pedestrian who had stopped, exhausted by the cold. The thought made Faxon hasten on, and a moment later he was stooping over a motionless figure huddled against the snowbank. The lantern had dropped from its bearer's hand, and Faxon, fearfully raising it, threw its light into the face of Frank Rainer.

"Rainer! What on earth are you doing here?"

The boy smiled back through his pallor. "What are *you*, I'd like to know?" he retorted; and, scrambling to his feet with a clutch on Faxon's arm, he added gaily: "Well, I've run you down!"

Faxon stood confounded, his heart sinking. The lad's face was grey.

"What madness—" he began.

"Yes, it *is*. What on earth did you do it for?"

"I? Do what? . . . Why I. . . . I was just taking a walk. . . . I often walk at night. . . ."

Frank Rainer burst into a laugh. "On such nights? Then you hadn't bolted?"

"Bolted?"

"Because I'd done something to offend you? My uncle thought you had."

Faxon grasped his arm. "Did your uncle send you after me?"

"Well, he gave me an awful rowing for not going up to your room with you when you said you were ill. And when we found you'd gone we were frightened—and he was awfully upset—so I said I'd catch you. . . . You're *not* ill, are you?"

"Ill? No. Never better." Faxon picked up the lantern. "Come; let's go back. It was awfully hot in that dining room."

"Yes; I hoped it was only that."

They trudged on in silence for a few minutes; then Faxon questioned: "You're not too done up?"

"Oh, no. It's a lot easier with the wind behind us."

"All right. Don't talk any more."

They pushed ahead, walking, in spite of the light that guided them, more slowly than Faxon had walked alone into the gale. The fact of his companion's stumbling against a drift gave Faxon a pretext for saying: "Take hold of my arm," and Rainer obeying, gasped out: "I'm blown!"

"So am I. Who wouldn't be?"

"What a dance you led me! If it hadn't been for one of the servants happening to see you—"

"Yes; all right. And now, won't you kindly shut up?"

Rainer laughed and hung on him. "Oh, the cold doesn't hurt me. . . ."

For the first few minutes after Rainer had overtaken him, anxiety for the lad had been Faxon's only thought. But as each laboring step carried them nearer to the spot he had been fleeing, the reasons for his flight grew more ominous and more insistent. No, he was not ill, he was not distraught and deluded—he was the instrument singled out to warn and save; and here he was, irresistibly driven, dragging the victim back to his doom!

The intensity of the conviction had almost checked his steps. But what could he do or say? At all costs he must get Rainer out of the cold, into the house and into his bed. After that he would act.

The snowfall was thickening, and as they reached a stretch of the road between open fields the wind took them at an angle, lashing their faces with barbed thongs. Rainer stopped to take breath, and Faxon felt the heavier pressure of his arm.

"When we get to the lodge, can't we telephone to the stable for a sleigh?"

"If they're not all asleep at the lodge."

"Oh, I'll manage. Don't talk!" Faxon ordered; and they plodded on. . . .

At length the lantern ray showed ruts that curved away from the road under tree darkness.

Faxon's spirits rose. "There's the gate! We'll be there in five minutes."

As he spoke he caught, above the boundary hedge, the gleam of a light at the farther end of the dark avenue. It was the same light that had shone on the scene of which every detail was burnt into his brain; and he felt again its overpowering reality. No—he couldn't let the boy go back!

They were at the lodge at last, and Faxon was hammering on the door. He said to himself: "I'll get him inside first, and make them give him a hot drink. Then I'll see—I'll find an argument. . . ."

There was no answer to his knocking, and after an interval Rainer said: "Look here—we'd better go on."

"No!"

"I can, perfectly—"

"You shan't go to the house, I say!" Faxon redoubled his blows, and at length steps sounded on the stairs. Rainer was leaning against the lintel, and as the door opened the light from the hall flashed on his pale face and fixed eyes. Faxon caught him by the arm and drew him in.

"It was cold out there," he sighed; and then, abruptly, as if invisible shears at a single stroke had cut every muscle in his body, he swerved, drooped on Faxon's arm, and seemed to sink into nothing at his feet.

The lodgekeeper and Faxon bent over him, and somehow, between them, lifted him into the kitchen and laid him on a sofa by the stove.

The lodgekeeper, stammering: "I'll ring up the house," dashed out of the room. But Faxon heard the words without heeding them: omens mattered nothing now, beside this woe fulfilled. He knelt down to undo the fur collar about Rainer's throat, and as he did so he felt a warm moisture on his hands. He held them up, and they were red. . . .

❄ V ❄

THE palms threaded their endless line along the yellow river. The little steamer lay at the wharf, and George Faxon, sitting in the verandah of the wooden hotel, idly watched the coolies carrying the freight across the gangplank.

He had been looking as such scenes for two months. Nearly five had elapsed since he had descended from the train at Northridge and strained his eyes for the sleigh that was to take him to Weymore: Weymore, which he was never to behold! . . . Part of the interval—the first part—was still a great grey blur. Even now he could not be quite sure how he had got back to Boston, reached the house of a cousin, and been thence transferred to a quiet room looking out on snow under bare trees. He looked out a long time at the same scene, and finally one day a man he had known at Harvard came to see him and invited him to go out on a business trip to the Malay Peninsula.

"You've had a bad shake-up, and it'll do you no end of good to get away from things."

When the doctor came the next day it turned out that he knew of the plan and approved it. "You ought to be quiet for a year. Just loaf and look at the landscape," he advised.

Faxon felt the first faint stirrings of curiosity.

"What's been the matter with me, anyway?"

"Well, overwork, I suppose. You must have been bottling up for a bad breakdown before you started for New Hampshire last December. And the shock of that poor boy's death did the rest."

Ah, yes—Rainer had died. He remembered. . . .

He started for the East, and gradually, by imperceptible degrees, life crept back into his weary bones and leaden brain. His friend was patient and considerate, and they traveled slowly and talked little. At first Faxon had felt a great shrinking from whatever touched on familiar things. He seldom looked at a newspaper and he never opened a letter without a contraction of the heart. It was not that he had any special cause for apprehension, but merely that a great trail of darkness lay on everything. He had looked too deep down into the abyss. . . . But little by little health and energy returned to him, and with them the common promptings of curiosity. He was beginning to wonder how the world was going, and when, presently, the hotelkeeper told him there were no letters for him in the steamer's mailbag, he felt a distinct sense of disappointment. His friend had gone into the jungle on a long excursion, and he was lonely, unoccupied and wholesomely bored. He got up and strolled into the stuffy reading room.

There he found a game of dominoes, a mutilated picture puzzle, some copies of *Zion's Herald* and a pile of New York and London newspapers.

He began to glance through the papers, and was disappointed to find that they were less recent than he had hoped. Evidently the last numbers had been carried off by luckier travelers. He continued to turn them over, picking out the American ones first. These, as it happened, were the oldest: they dated back to December and January. To Faxon, however, they had all the flavor of novelty, since they covered the precise period during which he had virtually ceased to exist. It had never before occurred to him to wonder what had happened in the world during that interval of obliteration; but now he felt a sudden desire to know.

To prolong the pleasure, he began by sorting the papers chronologically, and as he found and spread out the earliest number, the date at the top of the page entered into his consciousness like a key slipping into a lock. It was the seventeenth of December: the date of the day after his arrival at Northridge. He glanced at the first page and read in blazing characters: "Reported Failure of Opal Cement Company. Lavington's name involved. Gigantic Exposure of Corruption Shakes Wall Street to Its Foundations."

He read on, and when he had finished the first paper he turned to the next. There was a gap of three days, but the Opal Cement "Investigation" still held the center of the stage. From its complex revelations of greed and ruin his eye wandered to the death notices, and he read: "Rainer. Suddenly, at Northridge, New Hampshire, Francis John, only son of the late . . ."

His eyes clouded, and he dropped the newspaper and sat for a long time with his face in his hands. When he looked up again he noticed that his gesture had pushed the other papers from the table and scattered them at his feet. The uppermost lay spread out before him, and heavily his eyes began their search again. "John Lavington comes forward with plan for reconstructing company. Offers to put in ten millions of his own—The proposal under consideration by the District Attorney."

Ten millions . . . ten millions of his own. But if John Lavington was ruined? . . . Faxon stood up with a cry. That was it, then—that was what the warning meant! And if he had not fled from it, dashed wildly away from it into the night, he might have broken the spell of iniquity, the powers of darkness might not have prevailed! He caught up the pile of newspapers and began to glance through each in turn for the headline: "Wills Admitted to Probate." In the last of all he found the paragraph he sought, and it stared up at him as if with Rainer's dying eyes.

That—*that* was what he had done! The powers of pity had singled him out to warn and save, and he had closed his ears to their call, and washed his hands of it, and fled. Washed his hands of it! That was the word. It caught him back to the dreadful moment in the lodge when, raising himself up from Rainer's side, he had looked at his hands and seen that they were red. . . .

SOURCES

"The Fullness of Life," uncollected, 1893.

"The Muse's Tragedy," "A Journey," "The Pelican," and "Souls Belated" are from *The Greater Inclination*, 1899.

"Copy" is from *Crucial Instances*, 1901.

"The Descent of Man," "The Mission of Jane," "The Other Two," "The Dilettante," "Expiation," and "The Lady's Maid's Bell" are from *The Descent of Man*, 1904.

"The Last Asset" is from *The Hermit and the Wild Woman*, 1908.

"His Father's Son," "The Legend," "The Eyes," and "Afterward" are from *Tales of Men and Ghosts*, 1910.

"Xingu," "Autres Temps . . . ," and "The Triumph of Night" are from *Xingu*, 1916.

SELECTED BIBLIOGRAPHY

WORKS BY EDITH WHARTON

The Decoration of Houses, 1897 Study
The Greater Inclination, 1899 Stories
The Touchstone, 1900 Novella
Crucial Instances, 1901 Stories
The Valley of Decision, 1902 Novel
Italian Villas and Their Gardens, 1904 Travel
The Descent of Man, 1904 Stories
The House of Mirth, 1905 Novel
Madame de Treymes, 1907 Novella
The Fruit of the Tree, 1907 Novel
A Motor-Flight Through France, 1908 Travel
The Hermit and the Wild Woman, and Other Stories, 1908 Stories
Artemis to Actaeon, and Other Verse, 1908 Poems
Tales of Men and Ghosts, 1910 Stories
Ethan Frome, 1911 Novel
The Custom of the Country, 1913 Novel
Xingu and Other Stories, 1916 Stories
Summer, 1917 Novel
The Age of Innocence, 1920 Novel
In Morocco, 1920 Travel
Old New York, 1924 Novel Series
  False Dawn
  The Old Maid
  The Spark
  New Year's Day
The Writing of Fiction, 1925 Study
The Children, 1928 Novel
Hudson River Bracketed, 1929 Novel

The Gods Arrive, 1932 Novel
A Backward Glance, 1934 Autobiography
The Buccaneers, 1938 Unfinished Novel

BIOGRAPHY AND CRITICISM

Ammons, Elizabeth. *Edith Wharton's Argument with America*. Athens, Georgia: University of Georgia Press, 1980.

Auchincloss, Louis. *Edith Wharton*. University of Minnesota Pamphlets on American Writers, 12. Minneapolis: Univ. of Minnesota Press, 1961.

——. *Edith Wharton: A Woman of Her Time*. New York: Viking, 1971.

Bell, Millicent. *Edith Wharton and Henry James: The Story of Their Friendship*. New York: Braziller, 1965.

Brooks, Van Wyck. *The Confident Years: 1885–1915*. New York: Dutton, 1952.

Fryer, Judith. *Felicitous Space: The Imaginative Structures of Edith Wharton and Willa Cather*. Chapel Hill, N.C.: University of North Carolina Press, 1986.

Howe, Irving, ed. *Edith Wharton: A Collection of Critical Essays*. Englewood Cliffs, N.J.: Prentice-Hall, 1962.

Kazin, Alfred. *On Native Grounds*. New York: Harcourt, Brace, 1942.

Lewis, R. W. B. *Edith Wharton: A Biography*. New York: Harper and Row, 1975.

Lewis, R. W. B., ed., *The Collected Short Stories of Edith Wharton*, Vols. I and II. New York: Charles Scribner's Sons, 1968.

Lewis, R. W. B. and Nancy. *The Letters of Edith Wharton*. New York: Charles Scribner's Sons, 1988.

Lindberg, Gary H. *Edith Wharton and the Novel of Manners*. Charlottesville: Univ. Press of Virginia, 1975.

Lubbock, Percy. *Portrait of Edith Wharton*. New York: D. Appleton-Century, 1947.

McDowell, Margaret B. *Edith Wharton*. Twayne's United States Authors Series, 265. New York: Twayne, 1976.

Nevius, Blake. *Edith Wharton: A Study of Her Fiction*. Berkeley: Univ. of California Press, 1953.

Poirier, Richard. *A World Elsewhere: The Place of Style In American Literature*. New York: Oxford Univ. Press, 1966.

Wolff, Cynthia Griffin. *A Feast of Words: The Triumph of Edith Wharton*. New York: Oxford Univ. Press, 1977.

READ MORE IN PENGUIN

BY THE SAME AUTHOR

The Age of Innocence

Into the world of propriety which composed the rigid code of Old New York society returns the Countess Olenska, separated from her European husband and bearing with her an independence and impulsive awareness of life which stirs the educated sensitivity of Newland Archer, engaged to be married to May Welland, 'that terrifying product of the social system he belonged to and believed in, the young girl who knew nothing and expected everything'.

The Custom of the Country

Mr and Mrs Spragg are hoping to forge an entré into society and arrange a suitably ambitious match for their only daughter. As she unfolds the story of Undine Spragg, from New York to Europe, Edith Wharton affords us a detailed glimpse of what might be called the interior décor of upper-class America and its *nouveau riche* fringes.

The House of Mirth

First published in 1905, when it profoundly shocked society, *The House of Mirth* is a novel of manners that helped to carve out for the author an area of social fiction into which not even Henry James could trespass. 'A passionate social prophet', wrote Edmund Wilson, 'is precisely what Edith Wharton became. At her strongest and most characteristic, she is a brilliant example of the writer who relieves an emotional strain by denouncing his (*sic*) generation.'